T0064289

THE

MONSOON CLOUDS

THE

MONSOON CLOUDS

Bharat Kumar Regmi

PARTRIDGE
A Penguin Random House Company

To order additional copies of this book, contact
Partridge India
000 800 10062 62
orders.india@partridgepublishing.com

www.partridgepublishing.com/india

Contents

The Little Foothills

Pasang

Far Beyond the Hamlet

Mandakini

Back to the Hamlet

Acknowledgement

My eldest daughter, Rajani, greatly supported me in the whole process of preparing this manuscript. I am really thankful to her. To my friends, John and Kerry, too, without whose help it would not have been possible to complete it. Likewise, I extend my sincere acknowledgement to Dr Hari Sharma, Mr Lok Bahadur Paudel Chhetri, and Mr Sushil K Lamsal for their invaluable suggestions. I feel lucky to have encouragement from my wife, Shanti, and daughters, Roshani and Roji.

The Little Foothills

One

The still summer day was hot and humid. The first monsoon rains, after falling heavily for a week, had paused to begin again.

He wiped his forehead with the back of his right hand and threw his dark-brown eyes around.

It was a common country setting. To the north, a mountain stretched from east to west, looking south. A tall ash tree stood in the middle of the brow of the mountain and an old chestnut tree stooped at the eastern extremity with its gnarled branches. In between the trees – the ash and chestnut – the ridge was dotted with rough-surfaced stones. This was the burial place for the Gurungs. To the west from the ash tree, the ridge was rugged.

The southern part of this mountain fell away gently: at first a grassy slope; after that, an irregular line of rhododendron flowers; then, below the rhododendrons, a blend of scattered houses and different species of trees, above all the chestnut and *chilaune*; further below, finely cut terraces, rice and millet fields among the fodder trees dispersed throughout. Down these terraced fields lay a small flat stretch of land sticking out from the mountain. It was on this flat land that a tiny hamlet of three houses, Narrow Flatland, nestled next to a sharply etched terraced landscape with sporadic clusters of trees around. The land then developed into twin foothills which ran parallel to the south. The foothills, starkly barren in the beginning, plunged down becoming green with sisal plants and old-looking bonsai-like shrubs. Below this, a few houses scattered amidst the terraced fields. Further down, there was a dark wood, or more appropriately speaking, a dense forest with tall straight leafy chestnut and *chilaune* trees. Finally, at the bottom, a river ran west. The two little streams, which originated up in the mountain and rushed down, merged into this river. Across the river, the geography practically repeated; another mountain began with a dense forest.

At the southern end of the western foothill, just before it plunged down, there was a huge rugged structure of immense cliffs in parts of which wild bushes had grown and on the rocky ledges of which vultures had made their homes. Hundreds of bats would come out from numerous caves formed in this rugged structure and would dart about in the evening sky, frightening the children who walked near here in the evening.

Beyond the purlieus, far away, the views of mountains, terraced fields, woods, sprinkled houses, predominantly roofed with thatch and a very few with tin, now glinting in the afternoon sun, extended in all directions except in the north where the mountain itself had blocked any other views.

It was an ordinary setting, not much different than in any other parts of the Mahabharata Range in Nepal.

The barrenness of the twin foothills – sprinkled only with wormwood clumps and patchily covered with varied types of short grasses – looked uncommon in the larger green landscape. On the western side of the eastern foothill, the slope had smoothed at the bottom and had become a small meadow, where, amid the unusual barrenness, a knotted *chilaune* oddly stood. Little down the meadow, the tiny stream burbled.

A few cows were already in the meadow. A few others were lumbering down the slope. Goats were still busy scampering about the slope and the sides of the stream, cropping the monsoon grasses.

The sun was descending over the contours of the western mountains; the shadow had crossed the flint underneath the knotted *chilaune*. It was this flint on which his grandmother, with her seamed and slack face, would sit the whole day looking at grazing cows and goats. Sitting here, she would stare at the rows of the mountains stretched to the horizon or just into the empty space as if recalling her past, the past apparently full of joys and sorrows, full of struggle and happiness, and full of events. And once the shadow would cross the flint, she would remind him that it was time to take the cattle back to the shed.

His whole childhood, the formative years, had passed in the nearness of the old woman.

Now she was not alive. She had breathed her last two weeks ago. The thirteen-day mourning period had just ended. Death had come to her all of a sudden. She was fine until the morning. She had come to the foothills with them to graze the cattle in the afternoon and, as always, had gone to sleep early in the evening. However, the next day, she was found dead in her bed. No pains. No long-drawn-out bedridden posture. She was a religious woman, so she did not have to wait long to die. It was said so.

It still felt her voice was echoing, blended with the soft gurgles of the stream, "Ashok, Grandson, the shadow has crossed the flint. It's time to go. Gather the cows and goats."

He ruffled up the strands of his hair, fallen towards the forehead, picked up his stick and book, and walked down towards the meadow.

Just below the meadow, Bikram and Hari, stripped to their waist, were splashing in a small pond which they had built the day before. Both were his cousins – Bikram from his father's elder brother whom he would call Uncle and Hari from his father's younger brother whom he would call Little Uncle; in fact, both of them, Uncle and Little Uncle, were known to all in the hamlet and the surrounding villages with these names. Both the cousins were of the same age. They were still in their teens. Bikram was a bit fat and dark, like his brother Gopal. Hari had taken after his brother Dinesh, slender and olive-coloured. Gopal had gone to Dubai, whereas Dinesh had opted for Malaysia.

He called, "Bikram, Hari, gather the cattle. The shadow is already a foot away from the flint."

"All right, Dai," saying together, they came out of the pond, put on their shirts, picked up their sticks, and dispersed, whistling, in opposite directions, while Ashok threw both the stick and book on the ground and sat beneath the knotted *chilaune*, looking at them whistling and walking on the slope.

Ashok had already passed his mid-twenties. Yet he was still in the hamlet, pursuing a little farming and grazing cattle. Not only Gopal and Dinesh, but also nearly all the youth in the surrounding villages – Gurunggaun up in the mountain, Magargaun to the west, and Khadkagaun to the east – had left for India, the Gulf countries, or Malaysia. A few who had more money or who could borrow from their relatives had gone to Korea, Japan, or some other countries. Gopal had been sending money home; his mother, Kaushalya – whom he addressed as Aama – had said this during an evening meal, stitching leaf plates sitting beside the hearth, almost a week ago. He had brusquely responded that he did not wish to leave his country solely for money.

But deep inside, he was worried if he could rear his family staying in the country. The vain attempts of finding a job, which he had begun immediately after he completed his Bachelor's, had tired him. He had run from pillar to post in the cities. He had knocked the door of many offices. He had appeared for more than a dozen exams to get a job, but never got it, and the reason for this he did not know. He did not have the start-up capital for a business and did not possess the knack or the astuteness required for it. With his college qualifications in hand, he thought it below his dignity to live the life of a peasant: working in the fields and grazing the cattle. Aama did not like it too, yet she did not tell him directly to go abroad. Life, always difficult, was becoming even more difficult.

The train of thought was interrupted by a soft touch on his arm. He turned around. A little black kid was trying to nibble the edge of the sleeve of his shirt as though it was grass or a wormwood plant. He took the kid in his lap. His cousins were now in the meadow, counting the cattle. Satisfied with the count, they drove the herd towards the brow of the foothill, the eastern one. Picking up the book and the stick, he followed them, the kid still in his lap. A few crows and mynah birds perched on the backs of lumbering cows and pecked at the flies and ticks. The chubby kids skipped about their mothers.

"Dai, let's bring our cattle here tomorrow also," Hari proposed, thrashing a stubbornly slow bull. The bull walked a few fast steps but to slow down soon.

"No, not tomorrow. Don't you remember what Grandmother would say?" Ashok said.

"Dai, please," Hari pleaded.

This stretch of grazing was the boys' most favourite one. The fields lay at least half a mile away here. Putting out the cattle to the vacant slope, they could play in the meadow and on the bank of the stream. Grandmother would often insist on grazing at other places – on the border of the fields and woods and on the bank of another stream, the one to the east of the eastern foothill, where the succulent grass would grow thick and fast. The animals at those places, however, needed extra attention to be stopped from cropping the grain plants and fodder seedlings. So, for most of the time, the children had to stand attentively with sticks to tame them. Ashok also, from his inside, preferred these foothills than those places, the bank of the other stream or the border of the fields and woods, where he could not even open his books, to borrow which he would have to travel all the way down to the small library in the bazaar, a two-hour fast walk from the hamlet. Here, in these foothills, putting out the cows and goats to the slope, he could finish many chapters. Yet it was difficult for him to exhibit his childlike desire, at least to his cousins who were younger than him.

"We'll see," he said reluctantly.

The herd reached the brow, which offered a broader prospect of the surroundings.

There was a narrow path going along the brow. This path linked Narrow Flatland to another village to the south. A trail, narrower even the narrow path, dusty and scattered with dung, solely built by animals' hooves, descended to the other side of the foothill. This trail also led to Narrow Flatland, using a different route, a longer one. This was meant mainly for the animals in order to prevent them from cropping at the fields, which they could do walking along the narrow path that went along the brow. At the bottom of the eastern side of the foothill, the other stream, the one to the east, smoothly snaked down among the fields decorated with maize plants ready to harvest.

The herd followed the descending trail without lashes; they were acquainted with the trail and the time for return.

"Look!" Hari shouted, looking up.

A kestrel was dancing straight above them, poising and flapping its wings.

"Yesterday also it was dancing here at this time," Bikram said. "*Naacha, naacha baudai, chilla khaja diunla.* Dance, dance, o, kestrel. I'll give you ghee rice."

A *kakakul* swooped down and perched on a branch of a tall *chilaune* in the nearby wood and cried a thirsty cry. Grandmother would say that it drank only the rainwater deposited in the knotholes of the trees.

"You know, Hari, Grandmother and I saw a *kakakul* killing a big snake a few days ago before she died. It must be this one. Aha, their fighting was so exciting to look at. This much long snake was slithering down the slope. Right there," Bikram said, stretching both his arms wide and then showing a place beneath the *chilaune*.

"Suddenly, the *kakakul* swooped down from the sky, spread its talons, caught the snake, and flew high up. So fast! Its claws were so pointed! The snake fought back and fell on the ground. But the *kakakul* dived down again and grabbed hold of the snake around the neck and flew again. The snake was still fighting. We were so afraid it would fall down on us. The *kakakul* took the snake near that sisal plant," he added.

The afternoon sun shone brightly in the western sky. But a threatening thick black monsoon cloud was scudding in from the south-east firmly and determinedly.

"Bikram, let's come here this evening to play," Hari suggested.

"If my mother doesn't ask me to fetch water," Bikram said, trying to balance his stick in a vertical position on the tip of his first finger. "One, two, three, four . . ."

The stick fell.

"Look at the cows," Ashok said, pointing the cows lumbering down the slope, now vanishing beyond a curve.

The cousins scuttled down, while he took his own speed. The trail smelt of dust and dung. The grass verge had become dusty. In the dung-dropped places the grass had clumped and looked tussocky; the animals never cropped those clumps until the dung was entirely washed away.

After descending to the middle of the foothill, the trail led to the left and passed two other smooth bends and, merging with an uphill path coming from Khadkagaun, branched off to the left, steeply upwards. A little down, where the trail had merged with the path, there was a spring, flowing all year round. The fresh water that sprang out of the ground would feel warm in winter. It was the only source of fresh drinking water for the hamlet, and for Gurunggaun when the well, the one beneath the bamboo grove there, would go dry during winter and spring. In those seasons, in the mornings and evenings, when the women from Gurunggaun came to the spring, it would become crowded and would offer a perfect venue for gossiping. Uncle never failed to come here to have his bath and to perform the daily religious rituals before the eastern sky became pink.

There was another well a little up in the wood, but that would run dry in winter and would become filthy with flooded water and fallen leaves in summer. The water in that well would look clear only during the autumnal months.

The cattle drank from a muddy pond – dug solely for this purpose just down the spring. This stretch of the slope was full of nettle bushes below the spring and fern bushes above it. The wormwood clumps were scattered all over the slope, up and down. A few thistle plants stood still succulent around the pond, whereas in other parts, in drier parts, they had grown old weeks before. Using his stick, Bikram broke off a tender thistle stem, skinned and ate half of it, giving the rest to Hari. In fact, it was this skinned thistle stem which they would eat to satisfy their hunger and thirst whenever they were out on hot days.

An old prickly plant of *timur*, near the spring, had seeded small green seeds. Had his grandmother been alive, she would have certainly set out to pluck the young nettle leaves and fern fronds for the vegetables for the evening meal and the *timur* seeds for chutney, he thought as he sat on a flat stone just above the spring.

"I wish Grandmother would have lived for few more years," Bikram said.

Ashok wished the same.

The long, loud sound of the conch during her funeral procession to the Kali River felt echoing. The memories associated with the old woman were still overwhelming.

To him, during his childhood, she would have been a vast repository of knowledge. She knew so many things. She knew how Brahma split the lotus flower, his seat, into three parts and created the heaven, the skies, and the earth and then grasses, flowers, trees, plants, insects, birds, fishes, animals, and finally humans. She knew how the sun god travelled in a golden chariot pulled by seven horses. She even knew the name of those horses, so difficult for him to remember – Gayatri, Brahati, Jagati, Tristup, and so on – and knew the *yojana*, the distance covered by the sun god in a moment and in a day. She knew how sixty thousand saintly persons – Valikhilyas, each the size of a thumb – sat in front of the sun god, offering prayer to him, how *Gandharvas* sang in front of him, and *Apsaras* danced before the chariot. She knew how and why the *Rahu* gobbled up the sun and moon and caused eclipses. It was from her that he learnt to recognise the evening star, the Pole Star, and Orion. It was from her that he learnt to make a wish after seeing a shooting star.

She knew how to calculate time by the shadows – the shadows of the mountains and foothills and of the banyan and *peepal* trees, just a few hundred feet north of the hamlet. She knew which plants or flowers or weeds could cure what diseases. She knew which mushrooms to eat and which not to. The only thing she did not know was her own birthday; not only the day and the month, she did not even know the year or the nearby years. And it was because her mother could not tell her that. Her mother knew not more than that she was born two years after her elder sister was born, and no one was sure when her elder sister was born.

During his initial days in school, when he was taught that the earth was round and revolved around the sun, that the moon revolved around the earth, that the world was created by some other forces, not by Brahma, it had taken so long to convince himself that his grandmother could be wrong. With the passage of time, his knowledge went beyond her, yet he always held her and her simplicity in high regard. As he sat on the flat stone looking at the cattle drinking water, he remembered how satisfied she would become to see the cattle fully fed and slaked.

After their thirst slaked, the herd ambled up the uphill path on both sides of which lay the grassy meadows where the cattle were to be pastured on rainy days. The meadows soon ran out into a wood fringed by a series of bamboo bushes. This north-facing wood – the damp bed of which was covered with thick fern bushes – was inundated by chestnut and *chilaune* trees. In here, jackals and foxes hid sometimes, making the children afraid and curious. At night, this wood was believed to be haunted by Ban Jhankri, a tall ghost in his white dress riding on a white horse, and his short wife, Banaki. The male ghost was said to do no harm to the humans. But his wife, Banaki, spared no one, Grandmother would caution them. At the foot of a tall *chilaune* tree, amidst the fern bushes, his grandfather and Dhami Uncle had made a shrine for Ban Jhankri and his wife. A black baby goat and rice pudding would be offered to them every year.

A narrow fern-covered trail ran down to the filthy well.

The path they were following went up through the wood for a short while and, branching off left, continued in the form of stone steps, a tight slatted timber wall on its left and a gapped hedgerow on the right; the goats could easily enter the fields through the gaps. The hedge plants varied: predominantly the poinsettia, cactus, *sajiwan*, and *asuro*.

After corralling his cow, Mali, with white patches around the neck and under the belly, in the cowshed, he took out an armful of forage piled on the side of the shed and gave it to Seti, a buffalo, hitched to a post on the east side of the shed. She had been letting out her bellows after sensing their arrival sometime before they reached the hamlet. He enclosed the goats in the pen on another side of the shed, next to which was a *dhiki*. The suckling chubby calf was left loose.

In front of the shed, around the compost heap – the pile of dung and compost materials deposited over many months – the creepers, sown by Grandmother and his wife, Sushmita, had begun to climb over the trellis of the bamboo and *chilaune* branches, which were staked in their original shapes, the branches and the twigs uncut. These branches in their original shape, at present spreading about and looking somewhat straggly, would offer support to the rambling creepers and hanging gourds and beans once they grew. In winter, the manure would be carried to the fields, and the stakes would be removed and used as firewood. New branches would then be staked into the ground for the following year.

The creepers needed the second round of weeding, he thought as he walked to the courtyard.

His two-storey house was round, roofed with slates, and walled with mud and stone: the walls coated, in strata, with white, red, and black soil. Fresh maize cobs, yet to be shucked, were heaped on the narrow veranda in the middle of which lay a *janto*. Fine carvings on the frame of the low wooden door in the middle of the facade and a wooden window built low in the wall just to the left of the door spoke of the skill of the persons, the joiners and carpenters, who had carved the woodwork of the house. Two other small rooms, built on both sides of the house, at the opposite ends of the veranda, could be seen only from the front of the house. In the second storey, there were three little wooden windows, all in the facade and all in black colour. On the outer wall, a few strips ran down longitudinally suggesting the leaks in the roof.

He sat in the *mandir* at the west corner of the yard.

The *tulasi math*, built at the end of the yard near the *mandir*, was clean and smeared with mud and dung. Aama had planted a tiny *tulasi* plant on it. Harishayani Ekadashi was not far away.

A small patch of land, cropped with beans, eggplants, tomatoes, and other annuals, lay in front of the yard. At a corner of the patch, cotton plants and trumpet flowers had grown to a rich green. A few banana plants and saplings with sturdy stems and broad leaves suggested the richness of the soil. He had cut off all old torn leaves and had staked the banana plants which had produced drooping thick bunches, which he hoped, would be ripe by the great festival of Dashain.

Past this patch of land, to the slight left, were Uncle's house and *mandir* and his vegetable plot. From a slight right began the narrow path and ran through the millet fields. This was the path that went along the brow of the little foothill (from where the dusty and dung-scattered trail branched off and descended down the eastern slope of the foothill) and led to the hamlet to the south. The beginning, some 200 feet, of this path had hedgerows on both sides, dominated by the poinsettia and *sajiwan*. Prakash, Gopal's son, was blowing bubbles into the sap of *sajiwan*.

Little Uncle's house was a few hundred feet away towards the east.

After sitting for a while in the *mandir*, he went inside the house to find something to eat, hoping Sushmita had some time to prepare the food. The narrow inside, bisected by a low mud wall with a gap in the middle, allowing an entrance from one part to the other, was dark. The light coming through the low wooden door and window was faint. It took a few moments for him to adjust his eyes.

The ceiling, the rafters, the timbers, and the supporting columns were smeared with a thick black oily layer of years of stain. There were a few small round holes on the inside walls, coated in yellowish grey. In the first section of the bisected inside, a few *gagris, ghaitos, amkhoras,* and *karuwas* and also two or three cauldrons – tarnished with a thick layer of smoke stain – lay on the damp floor. Things of daily necessity were scattered messily on the top of the partition wall. At the far end, on the opposite of the door, a mud bedstead was built against the wall, which could be used both for sitting during the day and for sleeping at night.

The other section of the inside, the kitchen section, was even darker. In the middle of this section lay a hearth, an open clay hearth, still warm with ashes and a smouldering log on it. An old-looking tarnished kettle was on the side of the hearth. Next to the kettle were lying a pair of tongs and an old *dhungro*. From here, a small door gave on to a dark room, the way to the attic.

A tabby cat, so far purring beside the hearth, miaowed. It was Grandmother's cat, Soori. After her death, she had taken to staying at his house.

After failing to find anything to eat, he poured some whey from a wooden *theki* into an *amkhora* and quenched his thirst and walked to the field through the alley between the house and the shed. Soori followed him in a gentle gait, swaying her tail.

Two

The clouds were spreading all over, but a patch of the western sky was still open from where the late afternoon rays slanted into the hamlet. The air was filled with a sweet, damp smell of freshly cut maize stalks and the monsoon grasses. The stalks which had stood in the field, Big Plot, until a few hours ago, were cut down and gathered into stacks. Only a few last rows were left. Worn out, Kaushalya threw the sickle on the ground and perched on the berm of the field, wiping her sweat-smudged face with her calloused hands. Her green *choli* was worn at the elbows and had frayed at the end of both sleeves. The cotton sari and *patuki* looked old.

Madhu and Sarita, her granddaughters – Ashok's daughters – were trying to catch dragonflies, which darted, hovered, and then darted again from one to another maize stump.

"Be careful. Don't play in the field. You'll fall down," she cautioned them. She was worried the pointed stumps would pierce their young skin. On many occasions, their little feet had entangled in rambling pumpkin tendrils and weeds. Madhu had already got two shallow cuts on her legs on which Kaushalya had applied the weed paste, a local remedy learnt from her mother-in-law.

Tired of their efforts, the girls came and sat by her on the berm, their curious eyes still following the dragonflies. Madhu, now five years old, bore a strong resemblance to Ashok in features. Sarita, a year younger than her sister, had taken after her mother in looks and after her grandmother in colour: slightly dark. The still developing complexion at least presaged this much.

Sushmita was uprooting the millet seedlings at the far end of the plot.

Kaushalya sat looking at her Big Plot, the biggest field in the hamlet. It had been their share when the ancestral property was apportioned among the three brothers before the death of her husband. Besides this, they had a few acres of millet fields, a little pasturage, and two little woodlands. But it was this field on which they could depend for their living. She had spent much of her life and labour in it. There was not a single inch of it left untrodden by her feet. After the death of her husband, it was this field that helped her to survive. Every monsoon when it was planted with green rice plants, she felt at peace; every autumn when the rice plants swayed in the autumnal breeze, she got a deep satisfaction; when she saw the mound of golden rice during the harvesting season, she got something to smile at, faintly though; and in spring, the succulent maize stalks pleased her. Even when the monsoon was not good, she never gave up. By the sweat of her brow, she achieved from her Big Plot what other peasants could not get from their fields.

She had not reached even her fifties, but she looked older than sixty. Her hair had gone grey. Her eyes were sunk. Two of her front teeth, which once spoke of her beauty and because of which Ashok's father was attracted to her, years back, had been lost. She had stopped laughing. In fact, the laughs had been very rare throughout her life. Ashok was five at the time of the death of his father. Devaki, her daughter, at that time was still suckling. In after years, twenty years or so, she always lived a life of struggle. A young widowed woman in a constricted society, the lone responsibility of taking care of two small children, their education, marriage, and the earning of a living from a small farming: life had been difficult throughout the years. Happiness came to her very rarely in its true sense.

Once it had come, when Ashok had passed his Bachelor's with high marks. The highest in the whole area, they had said. The villagers would often talk about his smartness. After hearing those nice words, her eyes would shine with pride. She, however, did not understand why he, despite his smartness and her blessing, could not find any jobs. After a few years, when he stopped travelling to the cities to find a job and engaged himself in the farming, she forgot about his schooldays, his smartness, and the job.

Her happiness then came next along with the first pregnancy of Sushmita. She was sure of having a grandson, but after Sushmita mothered two daughters within a year of each other, her gloom deepened even more. Would she never see a grandson? Looking at Sushmita at the far end, she wished it would be a boy this time.

Her mother-in-law was the only one in the world with whom she could share her grief. After Ashok's grandfather died, the two women – both widowed – had found unique reasons for their intimacy. Sitting around the hearth or on the veranda, weeding in the vegetable plot or in the orchard, or perching on the berm of the field, they would chat for hours. Soori would listen to them patiently and would sway her tail in confirmation as if understanding the human language. After her mother-in-law left the world, Kaushalya had again been thrown into an utter sadness. She had further aged.

She took out a *chillim* and a packet of *kakkad* from the pocket of her *choli*, then filled the *chillim,* lit it, and began to inhale, coughing. She was hurrying to finish it before Ashok would appear in the field. He did not like her smoking.

"Grandma, I'm tired", Madhu said, "and also hungry."

"What are you tired of? You haven't done anything," she said.

"Oh, Grandma, you forgot I piled the maize stalks? So many." Her little forehead frowned.

"Those two stalks and you're tired and hungry? This girl! Let me finish cutting. Then we'll go home. Why's your daddy late today? He should have come by now. Go. Catch the dragonflies. But in the orchard, not in the field."

She emptied the *chillim* and put it in the pocket of her *choli* and looked at the granddaughters walking towards the orchard, which was between the house and Big Plot.

The orchard possessed a few fruit trees – one each of pear, plum, peach, and lime – all planted by her husband soon after their marriage. On the western side of the orchard, just below the berm, stood two *khanyu* trees. These fodder trees were no more than saplings at the time she first came to the hamlet after her marriage. With the passage of years, they grew and thrived. In season, when she did not have enough time to go to the millet fields across the stream, they gave fodder. They gave Ashok's grandfather, when he was alive, the fibrous thread to knit *namlo* and *damlo*. In summer, the children would often cluster around them to eat the fruits, which ripened in plenty around the lower part of the trunk, including on and under the ground. Four years back, she had asked Ashok to cut down their limbs, hoping the branches would come again. But they did not come; rather both the trees began to die. The trunks became hollowed inside. They looked old. Untimely old, like her. The nestlings of mynah birds could be heard chirping inside the knotholes of these trees in spring.

"Aama, why do you suffer yourself by working this much? You never listen to me," Ashok said as soon as he stepped into the field. He picked up the sickle and began to strike off the maize stalks. "Go home and rest. I'll finish it. Don't do the dishes and don't make the fire. Sushmita and I'll be there in a moment."

"What will I get just by sitting? Little work doesn't do harm."

"Now you say little work and cough the whole night."

She left, followed by her granddaughters. They loved their grandma more than their parents.

Ashok cut off the last standing stalk and, throwing it on the pile, plucked a peach from a hanging branch. It was a late-season peach variety, yet to ripen. He wiped off its velvety hairy skin on his shirt and, crunching it, walked towards Sushmita. The earth in the field, which was wet because of the recent rains, squelched under his feet when he walked.

"Why are you eating the unripe peach?" Sushmita said. "Didn't you see the roasted maize in the kitchen?"

"No, I didn't. Sushmita, go home and set the fire. Don't let Aama do it. She won't stop coughing," Ashok said as he sat on the berm, looking at her face and growing stomach.

"It's she herself. Who has asked her to work? It's not me," she said, binding the millet seedlings into bunches. "I hope this much will be enough for at least three days. Aama says we're sowing millet from tomorrow."

"If it doesn't rain. I hate to dig in the rain amidst those nasty maize leaves."

"You can't say that. If it doesn't rain in the monsoon, when will it rain?" she said, gazing at him. Her eyes were shaped as the petal of the lotus.

"And don't stay here for too long just gazing at nothing. I can't milk Seti today. My hands hurt because of uprooting these seedlings," she said, looking at her palms, and then walked towards the house.

Her long wavy chestnut-brown hair, tied back in a band, cascaded down to her waist. With her delicate complexion, she was strikingly beautiful, matchless not only in the hamlet but also in the nearby villages. Each and every part of her body spoke of unmistakable beauty even after the birth of two children.

Ashok recalled the memories of the early days of their marriage as he uprooted the pumpkin tendrils and weeds. It was six years ago when Uncle (who had arranged the marriage) had taken him to her village, a four-hour walk and a two-hour ride on a sweat-and-vomit-smelling old bus. No sooner had his eyes been set on her than he was completely smitten by the beauty she possessed. As her eyes dropped on the ground and her lips curled into a faint smile, he had then and there nodded his head in yes to the marriage. After the marriage, the closer he became to her, the more besotted he got. To him, she was the most beautiful woman he had ever seen. At times, when the other men threw their covetous eyes towards her, he would think he made a mistake by choosing such a beautiful woman as his wife. He would be filled with unbearable anger and jealousy on such occasions. Years after the marriage and after mothering two children, her charm had not diminished at all. These days, with the third baby in her womb, her beauty radiated even more strongly coupled with a kind of delicacy. Perhaps it had been the reason that he was hesitating to leave the hamlet, even after all his friends had left.

The sun dipped below the horizon. The lines of the clouds towards the west became hued in variegated colours – red, purple, orange, and gold. The flocks of the crows and mynah birds, after their voyage, returned and perched on the spreading branches of the tall trees – each one of banyan and *peepal* in the *chautari* and a *simal* tree a little down, past Big Plot.

He walked to the house.

"The streams are swollen, but I don't know when we'll sow rice in Big Plot," Kaushalya murmured from her seat beside the hearth.

She was stitching the plates out of the chestnut leaves. This time in the evening for her was for stitching the leaf plates or spinning wick out of the cotton bales sitting on a straw mat beside the hearth always at the same place. If in a good mood, she would tell her granddaughters the stories: *once upon a time . . .* or *the Tales of Tota and Maina* or *Sisir and Basanta*. In the dim light of the paraffin lamp, her eyes would glisten from the two hollows.

"The seedlings are also half a foot tall," Sushmita said, stoking up the fire with more firewood and blowing it with the *dhungro*. A thick smoke rose from the hearth and spread around. The firewood was much too damp to burn. She poured some paraffin into the hearth. The fire flared.

"Don't finish the paraffin, Sushmita. Not much is left. I don't think we're going to the bazaar any time soon. We should have dried the firewood today. The sun was strong," Kaushalya said.

"Grandma, I'm not going to eat the roasted maize. I need rice," Madhu declared from the mud-bedstead, their favourite place to play in the evening. The two sisters were tossing and turning in the smelly old bedding, having their own chats.

"We can't afford rice every day, Madhu. Don't be so stubborn. Look at your sister. She's younger than you, yet she never quarrels over the food," Sushmita said, roasting maize kernels in a *karahi*.

"*Mummyyy*, I have got a bellyache."

"You see, how clever this girl is! Her belly suddenly aches," Sushmita said.

Kaushalya went to the attic and brought two handfuls of rice, just for the girls (and for her own if there was left some). In the attic, in the pit, the rice was not more than two *muris*. The festive season was underway. The rice harvesting season was still four months away. But it was difficult for the baby teeth of her granddaughters to chew the roasted maize. Her own teeth were too weak to chew such tough kernels. The half-crushed grains would get into the gaps of her decaying teeth, giving dull pains for hours. They would stick so stubbornly that nothing could take them out.

"This buffalo! She's giving the same amount of milk as she would give two months ago. And milking is so easy," Ashok said as he entered the kitchen with a bucketful of fresh milk, still foamy.

Soori appeared, miaowing.

"How quickly this cat can smell!" he said, putting the milk in a *kunde*. He then scooped a ladleful of milk and poured it on the floor beside the hearth.

Soori lapped it and, licking her nose, whiskers, and paws, slunk away into another room, the dark one leading to the attic.

"I don't know where to find the ploughmen and yokes of oxen. Last year we had already sown Big Plot by this time," Kaushalya said again. "You shouldn't have quarrelled with Uncle."

"It wasn't my wish to quarrel. But he was shouting at you as if you let Seti loose knowingly. How could I tolerate?" he said, sitting on a round *pirka* beside her.

"Yet you should have kept quiet. After all, he's your uncle. He's the one who has always helped us in need." Sushmita agreed with Kaushalya. She always supported her mother-in-law when it came to little differences between the mother and son.

Inside, he too thought he had made a mistake by presenting himself rudely in front of Uncle, who had been helping them throughout the years as an anchor, a custodian of his family, after his father died. Until the year before, it was Uncle to whom he would request for the ploughman and oxen. Uncle had two yokes of oxen and a regular ploughman. His fields were on the sides of the streams and had already been sown, soon after the first rains.

This year also he was about to talk with Uncle to fix the dates for *ropain*. In the meantime, however, something unwanted happened. About ten days ago, their buffalo, Seti, broke loose in the middle of the night and trampled Uncle's vegetable plot, cropping the young leaves. The damage was more by trampling than by cropping. By dawn, when they were aware of her absence in the shed, her hooves had already left indentations all over the plot and the nearby fields. Uncle had told them off furiously for not hitching Seti properly. Not only he, but also Auntie had presented herself rudely. Kaushalya did not say anything; she just cried silently, cursing Seti and her fate as to why Seti did not trample on her own fields. But Ashok could not tolerate the situation. He became involved in an aggressive quarrel. From that day on, the conversation between the two families came to an end. Kaushalya could not dare to speak to them and could not even say sorry because of the embarrassment. Ashok could not bury his ego.

Now, as he did not know where to find the ploughmen and oxen (all were busy in their own fields), he realised he should have kept quiet.

He began to chew maize; his temple moved up and down and in and out. With fresh whey he had churned out that very morning, the maize tasted delicious.

In this season of early monsoon, the harvesting season for maize, maize was their breakfast, lunch, snacks, and dinner. An alternative to maize was maize itself. The only difference was that sometimes it came as boiled and sometimes as roasted; if it came in the morning in the form of *dhindo*, in the afternoon it came as bread. There was no question of likes and dislikes. The preference of the tongue had no value.

The next three days, the monsoon turned out to be a blessing with rain during the night and sunshine during the day, giving the peasants enough time to work the whole day and to sleep in peace at night. Ashok and his family busied themselves planting the millet seedlings. The edges of the maize leaves were sharp and hairy enough to cause rashes on the bare parts of their bodies. The mud was soggy. Still, it was far easier to dig on the dry days than to dig on the rainy days among the grown-up maize plants. Throughout these three days, Sushmita plucked out the maize leaves, cut down the maize plants which were too close to the others, weeded the field for Ashok to dig, planted the yams and beans, or joined her mother-in-law to sow the seedlings. The children spent their time playing in the piles of maize leaves, amusing themselves with tiny red ladybirds with black spots or chewing at maize stems, the taste of which, to an extent, gave them the taste of sugarcane or telling each other the stories which they had heard from Grandma and remembered only half or so.

However, as soon as they finished the millet planting, *ropain* in Big Plot came as a real worry.

Time had matured. The plot had been sown by the end of June last year. This year the monsoon started a little late, only at the end of June. The much-awaited Asar Pandhra, the auspicious day for *ropain*, had already passed, but Big Plot was yet to be sown. If they did not sow the seedlings within a week or so, they would become pale, reducing the production by half during the harvest. Where would they get the ploughman? Whom to ask? He wished they also had a yoke of oxen and a regular ploughman.

The shaft of anxiety became clearer in their faces with the passing of each day.

On several occasions, Ashok tried to talk to Uncle. However, each time his steps were stopped by an irrepressible sense of ego. Rather, on occasions, he thought it better to plough himself if he found a yoke of oxen, which he hesitatingly shared with his mother, who, in turn, with her brimming eyes, declared that if she saw her son, a *Brahman putra*, ploughing, she would die then and there. In her irritating tone, Sushmita complained to him why he was determined to cause tears in his mother's eyes.

Within another two or three days, once it became clear that there was no other way of finding the ploughman and the yoke of oxen, he could not wait any longer, for *ropain* in Big Plot was far more important than his pride. He stepped into Uncle's yard.

Uncle and Auntie were sitting around the hearth. In a corner of the room was Pooja with her son Prakash. Bikram was probably in the shed, busy feeding the cattle.

"Sit," Auntie said brusquely.

He touched their feet and sat beside the hearth, confused how to start.

It was again Auntie who said, "Ashok, I had never expected to hear those words from you. After all, I cared for you not different than Gopal." This opened the way for the conversation.

"Auntie, I'm here to say sorry to both of you. You aren't different than my mother. Truly speaking, after the death of my father, Uncle is like my own father. I don't have any disrespect for you. Don't take seriously what I said that day. Don't keep me away from your blessing, without which, my life would be difficult," Ashok said.

"I had forgiven you long ago. I was thinking to ask you to have *ropain* in Big Plot. It's getting late," Uncle said, easing his problem.

Ashok wondered what a nice person Uncle was. He solved his problem so readily, so fast. Did he forget everything that was bothering him until now? Why did he take that event so seriously? Why did he not talk to him earlier? Why did he not come to see him the same day or the day after and say sorry? After all, he was his uncle, many years older than him. He felt guiltier as Auntie scooped a glassful of milk and gave it to him.

"When are you ready?" Uncle asked.

"Whenever you say, Uncle. With the millet sowed, we have nothing to do. It feels so awkward to live idle in this season."

"I'll ask Padam to find another ploughman for the day after tomorrow."

"OK, Uncle. We'll arrange accordingly. Has Gopal sent any letters?"

"Yes, I got one last week. He says he has got a new job with a good salary."

"I wish I also could have gone. But with an aging mother and a pregnant wife and the two children at home, I'm simply afraid to leave."

"I'm sure Sushmita will have a son this time," Auntie said, blowing the fire.

"Didi will surely have a son. Her stomach is so big," Pooja added.

"I don't see any difference whether it's a son or a daughter. The only thing I'm worried about is how to feed these many mouths," Ashok said.

"How can you say that? God will take care of them," Auntie said.

Ashok walked to his house, light-hearted.

A fresh aroma of trumpet flowers was in the cool monsoon air. Fireflies were shining in the dark. The whole sky was blocked by the monsoon clouds.

Three

The monsoon had given a new life to everything on the mountain slope. The wind smelt of summer aroma. Trees, shrubs, and grasses all around looked greener. The fresh water coming out of the numerous summer springs swirled down here and there before finding their destiny in the little streams on the two sides of the hamlet.

Across the streams, the peasants were seen busy channelling water to their fields, digging and hoeing, furrowing and harrowing, and sowing fresh green rice seedlings in the watery fields. The air was full of the soft gurgles of the running water, the occasional caws of the crows, the chats of peasants, the hum and hiss of ploughmen, and of the *asare geet*. The peasants were in the festive mood of *ropain*. It was the busiest time of the year, the time of harvesting the maize and sowing the rice and millet, the time of eating a *mana* and producing a *muri*. The southern slope of the mountain was humming with the monsoon life.

After two consecutive days of labour – waking up before dawn, walking to the stream with a *sekhu* on his back and a spade in his hand, rebuilding the washed-away dam with the sod and stones so difficult to find on the flooded banks, channelling water to the field, uprooting the remaining maize stumps and pumpkin tendrils, digging the corners and adding mud to the berms, or smoothing the field – Ashok stood under the banyan in the *chautari*, bidding goodbye to Padam and his friend, the other ploughman.

In Big Plot, the sowers were still sowing the last remaining patch.

The sky looked patched with thinly scattered clouds, which scudded around forming themselves into changing shapes: now similar to trees, now to animals, now again to birds. The setting sun had given colours to the western sky – yellowish, reddish, pinkish, difficult to ascertain. The birds were flying back to the trees in flocks. A pair of squirrels was not yet tired of playing up and down in the aerial roots of the banyan, a few of which had become entangled with the bamboo thicket just below the *chautari*.

The whole view – the darkening hued western sky, the terraced fields, the fading figures of the peasants and oxen returning home, the rows of mountains up to the horizons, now progressively obscuring, and Big Plot sown with green rice seedlings, planted in lines, in a sequential unison – appeared like a big canvas, a big canvas with a splendid piece of art in its middle, a muddy background and green rice plant motif sketched by human hands.

Tired yet pleased, he sat on a flat stone in the *chautari*. This *chautari* was built by his grandfather or great grandfather. The immense boughs of the trees, extending high and wide against the sky, suggested it was several years old. And the wide stones laid on it? They must have been carried from the river at the foot of the mountain. Such big flat stones did not exist in the hamlet or in the foothills or on the sides of the little streams. Throughout the years, since as long as he could remember, these tall trees had been offering a shady bower for the villagers who came here, especially during the dry, hot days.

His grandfather, before he died, would come here practically every day in spring. Smoking *kakkad*, he would weave baskets from slivered bamboo or would knit *namlo* or *damlo* from the threads of the *khanyu* branches or from the fibres of the nettle and sisal plants, which grew wild all around. Sometimes, he would bring his leather-covered old *Mahabharata* and *Ramayana* and, wearing thick glasses, would turn the worm-eaten pages with his fragile middle finger and would read aloud. After his death, Ashok's grandmother would often come to this place and perch on the same stone where her husband would sit. At least once a month, she would uproot the weeds, which pushed out through the gaps of the stones.

It was on these lateral branches of the banyan along which he, with Gopal and Dinesh, would walk in his early teens: so scary even to recall. It was this place where they, once they crossed the playful years and found it awkward to play in the little foothills with younger brothers, would come every afternoon. They would spend hours, talking or playing *bagh chal*. The deep lines carved on a wide stone were still there. The playing and talking stopped after both the cousins went abroad. Yet he continued to come and sit here, looking around and reading his books or imagining himself working abroad.

The twilight darkened; frogs croaked; fireflies shone here and there; and cicadas grew to utter deep resonant sounds. The birds in the trees became silent. The squirrels disappeared into their drey in the bamboo grove. He walked towards his home, the tableau of the big canvas in his mind.

At home, around the hearth, his mother was telling stories to the children. Sushmita was preparing food.

That night he slept a full length of sleep, for Big Plot was sown.

That year the monsoon in that part of the country took a good course throughout the season. The radio, the National Panasonic, the only one in the hamlet, always hung on the wall of Uncle's house, would often broadcast the news about the rain-wrought havoc in other parts of the country. But it turned out to be good in his part of the land. Enough rain for the crops yet no floods, no landslides. He still remembered how, a year before, Little Uncle had quarrelled with a peasant from Khadkagaun over the issue of the turn of the scarce water to flood the field. The quarrel had turned into a violent fight resulting in a deep gash on the forehead of the peasant. Little Uncle had hit the peasant on the forehead with the back of a spade. The matter, like many others, eventually came to Uncle and was settled after Little Uncle paid a fine. But, this year, nature blessed them with the lushness of water, yet no floods and no landslides.

The rice plants in the fields grew steadily – each day becoming greener, sturdier, and taller. The maize harvest was safely gathered in before crows could damage the cobs, which had come, at least in two in each plant, as many as four in some. The monkeys, which would often come to the hamlet before the harvest, were not on the scene. The millet fields became green with healthy plants and rich heads, the wide leaves of yam in between and different types of beans on the edge. Around the manure heap in front of the shed, the annuals grew rich with the gourds and pods hanging down from the stakes and trellis. A few varieties of gourds rambled over the shed, fruiting lushly. The monsoon was good.

Ashok remained busy in the fields. Occasionally, he would take the cattle to the little foothills to graze, and he himself would sit under the old *chilaune*, reading novels or folk stories or simply looking at the surroundings. Every evening when it did not rain, he went to the *chautari* and spent his time until the sun set. Yet all the time, the question still remained. The question of survival, rearing his growing family! It would niggle his mind and would eat at his brain constantly as woodworms would eat the wood of his old house.

The monsoon was not a blessing every year. There were no other source of income except for the selling of ghee in autumn, which would be hardly enough to buy a few clothes and groceries. Furthermore, what if Seti and Mali would not calve next year? It was simply impossible to earn a living from his little farm.

In addition, he owed a couple of thousand to Uncle, which was increasing every month. While good in every other sense, Uncle was notorious for charging high interest. Fortunately, he was his uncle and charging him only twenty per cent a year. Otherwise, it would be thirty to fifty, depending on his swinging mood.

He must go abroad, he would think while sitting on the flat stone under the banyan.

Kaushalya was too worried about the upcoming baby. "Hey Prabhu! Please give me a grandson this time," she would mumble many times a day, sometimes so loudly that her mumblings could take the form of clearly understandable voice. He would not say anything. Sushmita would pray to the gods and goddesses silently and nervously.

And they heard her. She gave birth to a son, Rabindra, the name given by Narayan, a young pundit, smart and talkative, who had just returned to his village after the completion of his studies in India and who was known as Pundit Ji or simply Pundit, without *Ji* (while calling him in his absence) throughout the villages. It was just before Dashain when she mothered Rabindra. Ashok sat in the *chautari*, anxious to hear the news and to know Sushmita give birth without any problems. Four years ago, when Sarita was born, the afterbirth had not come out on time. His cousins and he had to carry her, turn by turn, to the health centre in the bazaar where the so-called doctor had almost refused to open the door saying the office hours were already over. Sushmita was moaning with pain throughout.

He wished the episode would not repeat this time. Auntie was consoling Sushmita as a doula because there was not a single trained midwife in the surroundings.

Anxious, he sat on the flat stone with his pounding heart, walked purposelessly, plucked the leaves from the grass verge and squeezed them with his palms and fingers, picked up stones and threw them into the bamboo grove, then went up to the orchard and, after hearing the painful groans coming out through the holes in the back of the house, came back again to the *chautari* and stood impatiently. In the late afternoon, no sooner did Auntie call him than he ran towards the house.

Rabindra was born and Sushmita was fine. Kaushalya's dark face was lit with a deep, contented expression. Frequently, she would laugh ear to ear, exposing her toothless gum and say, "He looks like Ashok, *natikuti*, exactly." She was guessing.

To Ashok, the little red face was too immature to picture. His wife's glistening eyes were fixed on him. She had already forgotten the pain. The two girls, unnoticed by anyone, were curiously looking at the newborn baby, their brother. He stretched both his arms out and put them around his daughters, looking at Sushmita and the little boy.

The arrival of Rabindra gave Kaushalya an enormous amount of joy. Her dark face looked brighter. Her laughs came frequently, and the smiles became continuous. She busied herself at home around her grandson. She would prepare food for Sushmita as best as she could, unlike during the birth of her granddaughters. She would wash her old saris and would cut them into pieces for the nappy for her grandson. She would clean his soiled clothes and sometimes would even wash her daughter-in-law's clothes, so unusual in a traditional society. Sunning in the yard, she would massage her grandson with mustard oil. She would not get tired of talking about him with those who approached her yard.

Sitting beside him on the straw mat in the yard, she would look around with her old glistening eyes. For the first time after many years, since she had lost her husband, the surroundings became so beautiful to her. After many years, she noticed the flocks of parrots flying from the south, roaring over the yard and settling in the millet fields. After such a long time, she gazed high into the sky to watch the flocks of *karyangkurungs* flying south. She was amazed why those birds would make a round just over the mountain with a Kali Temple on its top. It must be the divine power of Goddess Kali, she would conclude. After many years, she looked narrowly at *sayapatri* and *makhamali* flowers around. The autumn fascinated her.

That year luck truly smiled on her; her joy was added to by the rich harvest. During the day of *dain*, sitting on one side of the threshing floor, the farmyard, she looked at the mound of golden grains. It already looked as big as it was last year, and there were still nearly half of the stalks yet to be threshed. It was long back – before the death of her husband – that Big Plot had given such a rich produce. After that she had hardly experienced such kindness of the season. The last year's was the worst one. The rice stock did not last even for six months. It had given out before the monsoon.

Ashok and Padam were threshing. Little Uncle was undoing the bundles of stalks on the hayrick and pitching them in the farmyard. Children were flailing around the yard, flinging themselves onto the hay and driving the oxen round. A red ox was tethered to a chestnut post founded in the middle, then the others, roped one after another in a straight line with a long jute string, each of their steps crushing the stalks.

"This year, the monsoon truly blessed us. After so many years the harvest is this good. Long before this Big Plot had given, I think, twelve *muris,*" Uncle said, stroking his chin.

"It was twelve and half *muris*. I still remember," Kaushalya corrected.

"This time, it'll be more than that. Last year, the mound was this big and it was seven *muris*. We still have half to thresh. I'm sure it won't be less than fourteen," Padam said while he threw a threshed bale towards the oxen.

"Last year, ours was fifteen *muris*. This year, it was more than twenty-five," Uncle said proudly. He was the richest in the hamlet and the surrounding villages.

If it would be fourteen *muris*, even after selling a quarter of it, the remaining would see the whole year out, Kaushalya thought. The millet field also had given a lot this year, and the maize was still in a large amount in the attic. She was filled with joy.

Ashok, however, had not the same amount of ecstasy. He continued threshing, his attention intermittently on chats going on in the yard and on the letter received from Gopal a few days back. The letter was not long. It was just a couple of sentences as if he had written in a hurry, yet it had left a strong effect. "Dai, why don't you come to Dubai? You can make fifteen thousand a month without much difficulty . . . . I'll find a job for you . . . ." Gopal had written. To people like him, living out in the sticks, fifteen thousand a month was a large amount. Even during the richest harvest from the hard labour of three people continuously for five to six months he could never make more than ten thousand. Here, Gopal was talking about fifteen thousand a month!

He paused for a while. There was a pain at his back from the continuous threshing. He wiped the sweat on his face and looked at his palms still full of calluses grown by beating the millet the week before.

Next to him, Padam was threshing. He wore an old blue shirt, the topmost button broken and undone and the collar and armpits torn, showing the signs of age, like his own hair and face. With each strike, his collarbone moved up and down, and a sound came from his mouth *hm . . . hm . . . hm . . .* rhythmically.

During Ashok's childhood, Padam was a young, sturdy lad. After his father died, he had begun to work for Uncle to pay the loan accumulated for years, increasing unreasonably. Quite often early in the morning, Uncle would call him loudly, turning his face towards Padam's house up in the mountain, "He . . . Padam, Padam Bahaduuur, Padme . . . hey . . . Padmeee . . . ." Padam would respond, "Coming," sometimes from his house and sometimes from the way. He would appear in the hamlet with his whistles. The whole day he would plough the fields, would chop the firewood, would carry the heavy loads (of salt, sugar, manure, or groceries) from the bazaar, or would do whatever he was asked to do. In the evening, he would walk up to the mountain again, whistling or playing the leaf so melodiously.

On a few occasions, chiefly during the festive seasons, he would not listen or pretend not to listen to Uncle. On such occasions, Ashok and Gopal would have to go to his house to call him. They would find him lying on the veranda, his wife scolding him for spending the whole night in the *rodhi ghar* singing with other women. Scolding him, she would put forage in a wooden trough for a mother pig and the farrow. The short, quick grunts of those little piglets, their rooting the ground with little flat snouts, competing for the forage and, in that competition, the fall of the smallest piglet, the runt of the litter, in the trough would be so fine-looking a scene. A few roosters and hens and pullets would always roam around the yard and the terraces under the orange trees scratching the earth. After staying a few more minutes watching those views curiously, they would walk down to the hamlet to report it to Uncle, upon which he would grow frowns on his forehead.

Padam was charming. Humorous too. So Ashok and Gopal would love to visit his house whenever they went up to the mountain either to offer sacrifice to a little stone-made shrine of Bhanger under the old chestnut or to have the wonderful view of the Himalayas in the far north. On occasions, they would go to the forest on the northern face of the mountain, which was a complete wilderness, full of wild bushes and varieties of trees, including rhododendrons, wild raspberries, barberries, and, deeper inside, the cinnamon trees, and, finally, firebush plants that flamed bright red in season. The whole day they would roam in the forest, plucking flowers and wild berries, depending on the season, digging the cinnamon roots, and chasing rabbits and partridges and pheasants, which were plentiful on that side of the mountain. In the afternoon, on their return, they would visit Padam's house to slake their thirst. They would find him doing things – shaping the chestnut or *chilaune* wood into a plough or a yoke, sharpening sickles against a round whetstone fixed at the western end of the yard, making forage for the pigs or putting manure around the orange trees, or just sitting on the veranda under the dilapidated thatch roof talking to his wife while tightening the leather strips around his *madal* or playing his flute, which he played truly well. It was on one of those occasions, sitting on the veranda, looking at their hamlet below, for the first time in their life, they had, upon Padam's humorous encouragement, tasted *chhang* and the pig meat, religiously prohibited to their caste; Ashok still remembered.

Now it had been years. Ashok had become twenty-six. Padam crossed into the forties. He grew wrinkles. He begat three sons and a daughter. His head, because of carrying heavy loads, went bald. The agility slowed down, yet he continued to come to the hamlet upon Uncle's call; he continued to work the whole day as though his life was created to work for Uncle. In the evening, he walked up to the mountain wearily, scratching his head and pulling long on his *kakkad*. But he no longer whistled, nor did he play the leaf. His youthful exuberance had exhausted.

Ashok looked at him threshing bales, his collarbones moving up and down.

From the rick, Little Uncle was saying, "Farming is so difficult. I think I would have better gone to Malaysia along with my son."

Unlike Uncle, Little Uncle, the youngest in his generation, was frank. He would speak whatever he thought. In his twenties, he used to be a popular guy. He would dress smartly; he would comb his hair neatly; he would talk to ladies giving admiring glances and throwing romantic winks without hesitation. During Dashain and Tihar, he could swing the *ping*, the *pirke* one, swiftly, and he could spend many nights in the *rodhi ghar*, singing with his melodious voice. He was famous among the women. After his marriage to Little Auntie, who actually had eloped with him, impressed by his qualities, he was threatened to be disinherited by his father. He was allowed to stay at home only because of his mother (for whom Little Uncle was the dearest son). It had taken months for the old man to forget that his youngest daughter-in-law was the eloped one.

"You always talk nonsense. Who gives a job to such a useless guy?" Uncle said. He was much older than Little Uncle. He never enjoyed light comments.

"No, Dai. I'm sure I can find something, at least better than this unpredictable farming. Dinesh was telling me that there're many older than us working in Malaysia," he said, throwing a bale of hay in the yard. He would address Uncle as *Dai*.

Uncle continued threshing.

Little Uncle was telling the truth, Ashok agreed. The farming was unpredictable, solely depending on nature, which appeared in unexpected forms: floods, slides, droughts, hailstorms, and many other unwanted forms. One year it would be good, but another year, it would be worse, compelling him to take some more money from Uncle to buy rice and other necessities, at least for the festivals.

This year, he had thought to pay a little, at least the interest, with the money they had made by selling ghee, but the money was spent for buying a few clothes for the family and in the rituals associated with the birth of Rabindra and for the treatment of Sarita who burnt her right hand after putting it on a hot griddle when Sushmita had gone to the attic, leaving the griddle over the fire and Sarita on its side. She put her hand on it, curiously or for whatever reason, and burnt it, terribly. Poor Sarita suffered for two months. The scar was still there, despite the fact that Kaushalya had been regularly applying into it the traditional medicines – arnica and the sap of poinsettia – which she had learnt from her mother-in-law. The loan remained unpaid, upon which Uncle had got slightly irritated, and Ashok had tried to convince him that he would pay, at least some, after selling the grain.

The limited sources of income never matched the ever-growing expense.

"Kaushalya, I'm thirsty," Uncle said. "Can you bring water?"

"Me too," Little Uncle echoed.

"Aama, stay here. I'll bring. Uncle, shall I bring whey? I churned it the last evening. I hope it hasn't gone off," Ashok said.

"Add some water to it," Uncle advised.

Ashok walked to the house.

On the veranda, he found Rabindra sleeping in a cradle; the nostrils of his tiny nose were flaring rhythmically each time he breathed. His little lips were curled and moving as if he was suckling his mother's breast even in his sleep. For a moment, the father kept looking at the son, then rocked the cradle slowly.

"Let him sleep. Why are you disturbing him?" Inside, Sushmita was busy preparing food in the dark kitchen.

"The kitchen smells *sooo* good today. How many items have you prepared, my dear Sushmita?" he said, taking some potato pickles from a *dekchi* and putting it in his mouth.

"How does it taste?" Sushmita asked, stirring the rice, which had got a yellowish colour and shiny texture because of the ghee and turmeric added to it.

"As tasty as your lips, hot and spicy." Clicking his tongue, Ashok said in a humorous tone, which was so rare from his mouth. Whenever he tried to be humorous, it sounded not much real.

"You're the father of three children. Joking doesn't suit you," Sushmita said. She picked a little rice from the *dekchi* and pressed it to ensure if it was cooked.

"I'm still young and handsome, you know, Sushmita? The rice mound is so big," he said as he shook the *theki* and poured whey into a steel jug. "It's fresh."

"If we work hard, Big Plot gives us a lot," Sushmita said, putting the *dekchi* out of the hearth.

"It's not because of we, it's because of the good monsoon. You remember the last year's harvest? Didn't we work hard?"

"Whatever. Could you please send Aama? The food is ready. I can't take all at a time."

Ashok walked back to the field with the jug and steel glasses.

Padam was threshing the last bale. Uncle was winnowing, and Little Uncle was unhitching the oxen from the post. The oxen, tired and dizzied by the long round trudge, staggered about flicking flies away with their dung-smeared tails before sitting on the ground, crushing the rice stumps. The children were still flinging onto the hay.

"Mummy, I'm hungry," Madhu said. "Is it ghee rice, Mummy?" Playing so far, she, followed by all other children, ran towards Sushmita as soon as she appeared with a basket on her back.

"Let your uncles eat first. They have been working for the whole day and you're hungry? Can't you wait for a while?" Kaushalya shouted, cradling Rabindra in her arms. He had woken up.

Poor Madhu felt embarrassed for being shouted at in front of the others. Grandma had changed a lot after Rabindra was born. These days Grandma's voices towards her and her sister were mixed with occasional shouts, which would not be the case before their brother was born. She had very little time for them; the stories had become less frequent; and this year, she did not even take them to the woods to search chestnut and to the millet fields to pluck the ripe guava. It was difficult to understand for her little mind why Grandma changed so much after her brother was born. She wished she too was born as a boy. She looked at her father, who stretched his hand towards her and gave a gentle stroke, which felt warm and dear to her.

"No, no. Sushmita, give the children first. We'll eat after storing the rice in the attic," Uncle said, winnowing.

With the whole mound of the rice winnowed and the last sack filled, Kaushalya's face brightened more.

"Fifteen *muris*," she said as Uncle filled the last sack. She was counting from the beginning. "I knew my grandson came to this house as a *lachchhin*."

The sacks were carried to the attic. The soft hay, crushed by the hooves of the oxen, was once again baled in big round shapes, and put in the rick built on the vacant side of the orchard, close to the cowshed. Kaushalya was sure the hay would see the whole year out or would be enough at least until the monsoon, if used economically.

Towards the late afternoon, after both the uncles and Padam left, after Kaushalya walked to the house with Rabindra in her arms and the children went to the other end of the field, Ashok perched on the berm and, looking at the dilapidated roof of the shed, said, "Sushmita, it's getting very difficult to run the family. I need to do something. Perhaps go abroad."

The roof, under the extended pear branches, had become much thinner. Madhu and Sarita must have been pulling thatches from that part, which was not more than a few feet above the field berm, to use as tinder to get the fire started during the wet days. In fact, the whole roof, especially around the ridge where the dried leaves and tendrils of the creepers still existed, was damaged and looked rotten, demanding the new thatches. In the lower edges, the supporting poles under the roof were exposed. *Could it be fixed with chestnut leaves to last at least for a year?* He wondered. He had not thought about the new roof: yet another expense.

Sushmita stared at him to assess if he really meant what he said. It was the first time that he had said those words, which she did not expect to hear from him. At least at present. The children were too small. Her mother-in-law was getting older and weaker.

"How can you say that? How can you leave us alone?" she asked.

"You're not the only alone in the area. Many others are going abroad, leaving their wives and children behind."

"Our situation is different. The children are small. Aama is ageing. I can't handle it," she said and began to sweep the farmyard to gather the scattered rice grains.

The empty farmyard looked vacant. A few days back, Ashok and Uncle had plucked out the rice stumps, and Sushmita and Pooja had smeared the earth with red soil and fresh dung. Small mounds of black mud and uprooted stumps lay on the side of the farmyard. Beyond the farmyard, stumps were on the ground. Some still fresh, sprouting again. He knew that within a few days, the stumps would be crushed by the children and the cattle. The few remaining would sprout later. Then, at the very start of spring, Padam would come and plough the field. All remnants of stumps would vanish. The rice plants would lose their existence wholly.

Without responding to Sushmita, he walked towards the other end of the field, crushing the stumps. The earth in the field was soft, little spongy. In places near the berm of the field, mud holes had been formed, apparently by rats. A few panicles were carried to the holes. Fortunately, the rats had not done much damage. Perhaps they had just begun. Soori was walking from this hole to that, anticipating a pleasant feast. The children, including a few from Gurunggaun, were playing leapfrog and *dandi biyo*. For coming two months or so, until it would be tilled, Big Plot would serve as a playground for the children, not only from the hamlet but also from the villages around, for it was the biggest field.

Four

In the hedgerows, poinsettias came out in vermilion red petals and wide green leaves. The winter came and matured gradually. Other hedge plants either died back or remained with old leaves. Poinsettias, however, enduring the wintry weather, blossomed fully. Reigning over the hedgerows, they continued to flower until midwinter or even later.

Mountain ebonies blossomed into white and pink flowers. Bougainvillea flowers dominated the scene up in Gurunggaun.

Towards the end of January, Padam came and ploughed Big Plot, furrowing deep and unravelling clods of earth. Ashok and Sushmita smashed the clods with mallets the hafts of which were rough and knotted causing calluses to grow all over the palm. They backpacked the manure to the field and sprinkled it. The field was ploughed once again before the maize seeds were sown. Within a week, the maize sprouted and began to grow. New green shoots, tiny but each with a dormant capacity of growing a full plant, came up.

The spring came along. Narrow Flatland turned into spring colours. Foliage became dense in the banyan and *peepal*. The old leaves became pale and brown and came off, being taken over by the new ones. Birds became busy feeding on the red flowers of the *simal* tree before the flowers exhausted, and the tree spewed fibre-like silky cotton into the air.

The fruit trees in the orchard blossomed with white and pink flowers. Mulberry trees bore little hairy green berries, which soon became purple and black. Wild raspberries and barberries flowered and fruited, inviting birds as well as children. The rhododendrons in the village up in the mountain came into exquisite blooms. Cuckoos were heard. Not long after the parent birds were seen carrying small twigs in their beaks in order to build nests in the tree branches or in bushes, their nestlings chirped the first chirrups deeper inside the greenery.

Peasants were hopeful of yet another good season. So far the maize had been growing well presaging a rich harvest. *If it rained a couple of times, it would be enough for the maize*, they often said, gazing at the sky. And so was saying Uncle, who, nowadays, would sit in the *chautari* under the banyan shade, weaving or knitting: his skilled hands criss-crossing and interweaving the bamboo splits or the sisal or nettle fibres. His fame as a basket or twine weaver spread far and wide. In winter and spring, whenever he was free, he would sit in the bower of the trees and would set about either weaving or knitting.

"The maize plants look so succulent," he had said to Ashok while splitting a bamboo can just two days back, on Baisakh first, the first day of the first month of yet another year of Bikram Sambat.

"Yes, Uncle. I hope the weather would bless us this year too," Ashok had responded. The maize plants in Big Plot were already two feet tall, demanding the second round of digging, which he was planning to do as soon as possible after collecting the firewood for the upcoming rainy season.

But the next day, the weather turned foul and broke furiously. Before noon, a few patches of cotton-shaped clouds were gathering up in the sky. Ashok and Sushmita were in the wood: Ashok in a *chilaune* tree, cutting away the branches, and Sushmita trimming the branches underneath the tree. A little away, in his lot of the wood, Uncle was observing the scions of the fodder trees which he had grafted in the early spring and covered with soil and dung to replant them in summer. Padam was chopping the *chilaune* branches.

"Sushmita, isn't it enough? Let me climb down. It'll rain hard today. The clouds are so thick," Ashok said, throwing the sickle on the ground.

"It's enough. We have more than the last year's. We can collect some more before the monsoon starts," she said, plucking the yellow raspberries from a nearby bush. "The girls die for these berries."

He sat, trying to play a leaf.

"You're too old to play the leaf. You're the father of three children, but you behave as if you're unmarried. Pile the wood."

"You know, Sushmita? I got married too early. My contemporaries are still enjoying their unmarried life."

"Who asked you to get married so early? It wasn't me."

"It was you. Why did you look that much beautiful that time?"

"And now?"

"Even today you're the most beautiful to me."

"You? Nobody can talk to you," she said, looking at him and then into the sky. "The rain is coming on. I had put the clothes out in the sun. I forgot to tell Aama to take them in."

"Let's sit here for a while. It's so peaceful."

She sat by him and, putting some spit on her left heel with the index finger, tried to locate the exact spot of the tiny chestnut spines which had pierced through the unevenly worn-away side of her rubber flip-flop.

"Let me see it," he said and took her foot in his lap. There were small dots in the arch of the foot. "I'll remove them when we're at home."

"It's prickling," Sushmita said as she began to collect the dried twigs.

It was a pleasant afternoon. Sitting there and listening to the cooing of doves felt peaceful. Staying or roaming in the woods had always been a preferred moment for him. Sitting under trees in the striped light or walking among bushes under the forest canopy while listening to varieties of forest sounds always gave him peace, made him free, momentarily though, from the stark realities of life, which were progressively turning out to be starker day by day. In his childhood, as he would walk through those fern-grown trails in the wood, the wood would whisper bizarre sounds and would offer the mixed smell of trees, bushes, grasses, and damp soil. Walking in the dappled shafts of light rustling the fallen leaves and removing the gossamer criss-crossed amongst bushes and tree trunks would give him a feeling that he himself was a character of Grandmother's fairy tales, he remembered nostalgically.

Up in the sky, the clouds became fluffier and spread wider, gradually covering the whole sky. Crows had returned to the tall trees. They might have already sensed the coming danger. Perhaps Uncle and Padam had already left. There was no sound of chopping on that side.

"Let's go. It's getting late. Don't be romantic," Sushmita said, putting the *namlo* on her head and trying to stand up with the pile of wood on her back. "Pull me up."

Giving his hand to her, he asked with his soft, caring voice, "Is it heavy?"

"No, it's fine. And it's not far," she replied.

He knew it was heavy, although she did not say so. In fact, she never complained while carrying those heavy loads. He looked at the darkening sky before he carried his pile.

Before they passed the wood, the clouds set in releasing hailstones, round and big. The house was not far, but the path, the stone steps, was steep. The rain had made it slippery. Sushmita was walking ahead with her bare feet. Both straps of her flip-flops, which she had joined by burning them, had broken again. At a point, her feet slipped, and she fell down. The tightly bound pile she was carrying tumbled down a few steps. Fortunately, she did not come by an injury, but her body and clothes were covered with mud. The berries spilled over the muddy ground. Frustrated, with a grimace of pain on her face, she tried to carry the pile again. The hailstones were hitting hard against her head and body.

"No, Sushmita. Leave it. I'll take care of it," Ashok shouted. "Go home."

"Sushmita, come. Come along. We'll take it when the rain halts," Kaushalya appeared, calling them. "Come. Quickly." The umbrella she was holding had collapsed and turned inside out.

Sushmita followed Kaushalya. Cursing the hailstones and his poverty-struck life, Ashok walked with his heavy feet, the pile of wood on his back and the hailstones hitting him hard. He put the pile in the corner of the shed and went back to bring the other.

After an hour of hailstorm, the rain set in and continued with intermittent gusts of wind. By the time the gusts and the spattering died down, it had been too late to go to the fields to assess the damage. So they went to the bed.

"The damage must be huge," he said, embracing Sushmita tightly.

"Grandmother would say the hailstones work as manure for the plants," she whispered. She was aroused by the sensual touch and warm breath on her neck.

"Only if any leaves are left." He continued running his hand around her soft body.

She came closer to him, whispering, "Don't make noise. The children will awake."

He pressed his hands against her bosoms, gasping.

The next day the sky cleared with deep-blue colour; the rising sun looked big and bright. But the destruction was complete. Only a few maize plants had been left with tattered leaves. Not only the maize, but all other trees and plants had suffered the ferocity of nature. The destruction could be seen everywhere – in the orchard, in the *chautari*, in the vegetable plot, in the hedgerows, and in the woods. All green leaves had come away from the tree and scattered on the ground. The trees and bushes carried no more fruits. The spring looked to have been undone, to have turned into the late autumn or early winter, to have taken the reverse path. Sitting on the berm, Ashok looked at his field, which he was planning to dig and now looked vacant.

"What shall we do?" he asked.

"I hope it'll come again," Sushmita said, touching a small pile of the hailstones in a ditch between the cowshed and the field which always remained damp, free from the reach of the sun. Nearby, a baby mynah was lying dead surrounded by ants.

"Poor bird!" she added.

"You hope. I don't hope," he said.

"Why do you think always negatively? Believe in god."

"Your god never cares about the poor."

Just below Big Plot, standing in his field, Little Uncle was saying, "Look, everything is destroyed. That's why I hate this farming. If these hailstones ought to have fallen, they should have fallen a few weeks back. At least, we could sow the maize again. Now we neither have the maize plants nor do we have enough time to sow them."

With her upset face, Little Auntie was clicking her tongue, "*Ch . . . ch . . . ch . . . . hare.* What are we going to eat? What to feed the cattle?"

In the yard, amidst the rubble gathered by the wind and rain, he saw the remnants of bird shells. The nest under the eaves had disappeared. The parent swallows were chirping, looking at the line of the nest on the wall.

A few more days passed by. Ashok had said he did not hope, but somewhere inside, he had a glimmer of hope that the maize plants would come again. And they did come back, except for a few which had been completely destroyed. After a brief pause, the spring reappeared. Grasses sprouted green. Leaves grew to cover bushes and trees giving hope to the peasants.

"You see? What had I said? They're back again," Sushmita said, showing the tiny plants.

"But I don't think they'll bear the cobs," Ashok said.

"Why do you say so?" Sushmita looked at him a bit irritatingly. She sat on the berm and touched a damaged shoot gently. "It may take two weeks longer, but I'm sure the plants would produce good cobs."

"OK, my queen, I agree with you. Are you happy now?"

"I don't know why your voice sounds angry every time you speak these days. Can't you speak nicely?" Sushmita walked to the house with a shaft of disappointment on her face.

With a feeling of slight guilt over his own words, he stood on the berm, listening to the receding footsteps of his wife in the yard. Why was his behaviour becoming more and more irritating? Why was his mind so much occupied by the thoughts of Dubai? He tried to concentrate himself on a pair of mynah birds which had again set about making the nest in the knothole of the *khanyu* tree near the orchard.

Ashok and Sushmita did the digging and weeding in Big Plot, hoping for a good harvest.

But again, the second part of the spring also turned to be unfriendly to the peasants. Days became hotter and drier. After the hailstones, clouds ceased to appear in the sky. Two weeks, three weeks, then a month, the sky remained calm, bright, and hot. Soil dried out. *Kakakuls* cried loud to the heavens for rain. Both the streams went dry. Drinking water became scarce even in the all-weather spring below the hamlet. With the well gone dry in Gurunggaun, there would be a long queue of pitchers and buckets, and it would take almost half an hour to fill up one. The green grass in the berm of the fields wrinkled and died. Sushmita and Pooja had to roam along the streams and in the woods to find a basketful of grass. Some days they had to travel all the way up to the other side of the mountain for a half a basket of grass.

The hot sun soon shrivelled the maize plants. The leaves looked somewhat alive in the morning. However, by noon they shrivelled and became like spikes. They could not grow, could not develop brace roots, and could not bear the cobs. Those very few which were born were poorly filled.

There was no water even to sow the rice seeds. Ashok struggled hard to water a small patch of his field on the side of the stream, carrying water in a bucket from a puddle, and to sow the seeds. He covered the sown patch with the wormwoods, but soon, the birds uncovered the bed and ate the seeds. Different types of ants could be seen making holes and heaps and marching around through the tiny paths designed by the tiny creatures themselves.

In the meantime, before June, Seti dried up. It had been four months after she had conceived. Now, because of the lack of the green fodder, she stopped giving milk. Mali had stopped long back, depriving the girls of the milk. This time, it was Rabindra's turn to be deprived. He was still suckling at his mother's breast, and after the *annaprashan*, he was being fed the solids as well. But he was largely dependent on Seti's milk for the last few days. As she dried up, they had to buy milk from his Little Uncle, whose buffalo was still giving milk and who had no children at home.

Desperate for milk was Soori too. She had mothered three kittens: one black, two tabbies, similar to her. She could be seen carrying those kittens in her teeth from place to place in order to save them from their father, a fat black cat from Gurunggaun, which would often visit the hamlet. She would sit on the side of the hearth, miaowing in expectation of the milk, which no longer poured on the hollowed spot on the floor beside the hearth.

Life went on, becoming even more miserable. Gopal had sent one more letter, full of tempting words: the illuminated city, the cars, the buildings, the well-developed infrastructure, and the regularly paid salary. He had sent the letter to Uncle together with a parcel, wrapped with glossy papers, containing gifts to his family, including a watch with a yellow chain for Uncle, saris for Auntie and Pooja, soft and silky, Sushmita had said. For Prakash, there were colourful shirts printed with tall palm trees and the blue sky. Prakash would walk around the hamlet, wearing those new clothes while his daughters would follow him in their faded blue frocks.

Why was he staying in the hamlet? Why would he not go to Dubai from where Gopal was sending so many gifts? Were his family going to live in such a dearth forever? Would his children never get new clothes? The evening the parcel had arrived, Ashok asked himself while he sat on the dried grass on the brow of the little foothill, looking at the mountains. He even did not read the book, which he had borrowed from a friend. He sat just thinking. As the pale red sun went below the horizon, he stood and walked to the hamlet.

At home, Madhu was crying. Sushmita had smacked her for losing her exercise book, soft-covered and thin with lines of mountains printed on it, which she had bought a week before at a small stationer's in the bazaar. Fussing about her forgetfulness, Kaushalya was trying to locate her mislaid bunch of keys, which would be the usual case.

He took his daughter into his arms, wiped her tears, and said, "Don't cry, my little daughter. I'll buy a new one."

"You're the one spoiling the children," Sushmita said, frying *gundruk*, the only vegetable available in the attic. The long drought had not allowed the pumpkin tendrils and pigweeds to grow in the field which would have been the seasonal vegetables. The beans and potatoes were for the festivals. The rotten *gundruk* had a familiar taste and smell. For him, it was the best vegetable combined with *dhindo*.

It was later in the evening, after they went to the bed in the tiny room which was far too small for them and Rabindra, Ashok again said, after Rabindra fell asleep, "I think I have to go abroad. The family can't run this way. I need to do something."

"Let's do something in the hamlet . . .," Sushmita said, yawning. "I mean in our own country. There's no guarantee of finding a good job abroad."

Sushmita was aware of the scarcity they were faced with. But she did not have any big ambition in her life. She could live a poor life. What she simply wanted was peace and happiness in the faces of all family, but, for quite a long time, she had been reading frequent sadness or irritation on her husband's face even for a small family matter. She knew that it was because of the scarcity and the burden of responsibility. The trend of going abroad had been increasing rapidly. Many of her friends' husbands had left the villages. Yet she wanted her husband to stay in the hamlet.

"What can we do in the hamlet? You know this farming! We don't have money to do business. Jobs don't seem to have been created for people like us," he said.

In fact, a couple of weeks ago, borrowing money from Uncle, he had once again travelled to Kathmandu, slinging an old rucksack on his shoulder, inside which were an extra pair of clothes and his certificates, which had worn out because of being folded and unfolded many times. After humiliatingly presenting himself in front of the reception of different private offices and seeing the people in long queues, the expectant faces, in front of the public offices, he had returned with a firm resolve that from now on he would not spend even a rupee and would not waste a single minute in search of a job in Nepal.

"We'll talk tomorrow . . . . Let's sleep now . . . ."

Sushmita yawned once more, then turned to the other side, and soon began to breathe rhythmically.

The woodworms were cutting the trusses continuously. They had been busy cutting those trusses for many years, since as long as he remembered. The sound would become louder at night, mainly at quiet night, giving him a continuous sense of insecurity that the whole roof would come down. Once, during his childhood, Devaki, his sister, had posed a question to him, so simple a question yet so logical. "Dai, can these insects eat up the trusses? Will this roof fall down?"

"I don't think these tiny insects can eat up these solid trusses. They're trying to eat, but they can't. They don't have strong teeth," he had answered, trying to assure her. But he himself was not assured. Soon after, without letting his sister know, he had tried to ferret out the hidden insects in the trusses under the roof. Upon his failure, he had left the room with the fear that the roof would fall down and crush him. Those insects and their progeny, generation to generation, hidden behind the trusses under the roof, continued to cut down through the years, making a mild noise and always niggling him. Luckily, the trusses had survived so far, but he was worried they would come down one day. After all they were made of wood, perishable.

Aama was coughing from inside. These days, her coughs had become more frequent. She was ailing much quicker than she was aging. He should have taken her to Kathmandu to see a good doctor after the doctor in Pokhara had advised. She had declined, saying it would cost a lot, and he had not pressed her.

Sushmita's and Rabindra's breathing became steadier: Rabindra's short and quick and Sushmita's long and deep. *How quickly they could get off to sleep*, he wondered. He turned over. The small round hole on the wall was giving on to a narrow view of the moonlit outside. An owl was hooting in the wood, making the night sombre.

Five

The first pre-monsoon rains came only after the middle of June, the first droplets of which were absorbed by the dried soils before they fell on the earth. For it had already been late, Ashok and Sushmita at once started their work in the fields. The seeding of the rice and millet; the harvesting of maize, drastically poor due to the long drought; the cutting of the berms and corners of the fields, and the clearing of the irrigation channels; and, once the monsoon began, the planting of rice and millet occupied much of their time. The rain came hard at first. Big Plot suffered falls on the northern side – not more than two or three feet below the berm of which was Little Uncle's field – losing a few more feet and once again worrying them that Big Plot, with these falls every year, would become narrower and narrower and ultimately would disappear altogether or would not retain the fame of being the biggest in the hamlet. Little Uncle would dig the corners of his field deep every time, making the slope easy to slide. Later, he would incorporate the fallen part in his own, little by little, every year. Ashok suspected it was a deliberate attempt. Little squabbles would erupt between them on the issue. Ultimately, Ashok would be blamed for not having the respect and regard for the elderly.

As they would do with the slides every year, they carried stones from the bank of the stream, brought wormwood clumps and the sod and tried their best to repair the slides. The fallen part of the field, however, did not return to the original shape. Like every other time.

The rain, which came heavily at first, ended before the usual time. Towards the beginning of August, it let up gradually, and before mid-August, it drew to a virtual close. The fields, which would normally remain mossy throughout summer and autumn, became dry and cracked before September.

With a poor harvest of maize, the attic went empty, and they had to buy the grains from the bazaar. Ashok brought a sack of rice, the cheapest one, some of the grains crushed, rotten and smelly, the eating of which required swallowing without chewing in order to avoid stones, no matter how painfully Sushmita would try to remove all those tiny stones, which resembled the rice grains in size, shape, and colour.

Once again the festive season came, bringing joy as well as the sense of burden to Ashok and Sushmita. On the one hand, the season, brisk and balmy, gave them relief from hard labour. The festivals, falling one after another, offered the opportunity of being with relatives and having fun and sharing joys and sorrows. The villages filled with the sweet fragrance of rice and millet flowers. Very early in the morning, putting the fried maize kernels, in their *patukis*, the women walked through the dewy grass to carry *geru* and *kamero*. The houses were painted; the paths were repaired; Kali Temple, up in the mountain, was decorated; and in each village around, the *pirke ping* was set. The *rodhi song* and *malsiri* became frequent in Gurunggaun and Magargaun. The *sayapatri* and *makhamali* flowers flowered all around.

Devaki came before Dashain with her two daughters, as almost of the same age as Madhu and Sarita. The hamlet filled with more than half a dozen children of the same age group, who, free from worries, walked around the hamlet, the little foothills and the woods playing their little games. They took to ferreting out chestnuts hidden under the leaves and the weeds. They took to plucking the guavas, both ripe and unripe, which grew aplenty in the millet fields. They would cry out loud at the flocks of green parrots passing over the hamlet and at the *karyangkurungs* flying high in the sky. In the evenings, they would cluster in the yard to play.

They would ask riddles and would tell folk stories. Seeing them talking and playing, free from anxiety, was amusing for Ashok too.

But on the other hand, the festivals also brought the sense of burden to him, just like to the majority of the villagers, adding an additional burden of debt. With Sorha Shraddha gone by, Dashain approached. The rice which he had bought immediately after the monsoon was already consumed; the attic was empty again. No grains, no sugar, no oil, and no other groceries. His children were still roaming in the old dresses whereas the others had already got the new ones.

So one day, after the morning chores, he went to Uncle's yard with his heavy feet to ask for the loan.

A few others were already in the yard for Dashain-loan. Sitting on the veranda, Uncle was making entries and getting thumbprints of debtors on a ledger. For larger amounts, whether given at a time or accumulated over the months and years, he would not forget to prepare a *kapali tamsuk*, securing normally a piece of land or gold as a mortgage. For smaller amounts, thumbprints on the ledger were enough. Ashok perched on a cane basket, put on the yard with its bottom turned up, waiting for the others to leave.

And after the last peasant left the yard, he received Uncle's piercing look. Uncle had a different look when it was about money: a look, very different than the one he exposed at other normal times, somewhat stern look of a lender. On such occasions, he would behave in the same way to everyone, no matter who the person was. He had already sensed Ashok was there for the money. So he looked at him with his piercing eyes, knitting his brows.

Turning the pages of the ledger, he said, "Look, Ashok, it has already been more than fifty thousand rupees. I don't know how you're going to pay. You're my nephew. I can't ask you for a bond. But I'm beginning to worry."

A bit humiliated, a bit embarrassed, Ashok sat sipping at the tea Auntie had just given to him. He had very few words to speak on such occasions, except repeating the same weak phrases – *Uncle, I'll pay soon.* But when and how, he himself did not know.

In a low tone, he said, "Uncle, I know I owe you a lot. But I'll pay it soon. I'm thinking of going to Dubai to work."

"How much do you need?" Uncle asked.

"Dashain is just a week away. Tihar will come soon. The children's clothes are torn. There're no sugar, salt, oil, and paraffin at home. Devaki is here. I hope three thousand rupees would do."

Uncle went in, brought a thick wad of hundred rupee notes, and counted with care. Then he gave Ashok twenty-five notes, saying, "I can give you only this much. And listen to me. Something needs to be done now."

"Yes, Uncle." Ashok put the notes in his pocket.

He was not sure what Uncle meant by *something needs to be done.* Was he supporting his idea of going to Dubai? Or did he want anything as a bond for the loan? Perhaps Big Plot? Once Kaushalya had told him that, during the partition, Uncle was desperate to get Big Plot in his share. It was his grandmother, who, considering the fragile health of Ashok's father, had given the right of first choice to him which his grandfather could not decline. So was he interested in getting Big Plot by other means? No, Uncle could not be mean; he tried to convince himself and walked to his house with heavy feet and a firm resolve that he would soon leave the country for work.

In the yard, the children were playing *yati, yati pani, gangai rani.* Sitting in the *mandir*, Kaushalya was trying hard to thread a tiny thread through a needle, saying, "My old eyes just can't see the narrow eye of this needle." She was perhaps trying to patch her torn blouse with pieces of her old sari. Little oddments of sari were scattered around. Next to her, Devaki was massaging Rabindra with warm oil. Rabindra, now a year old, tickled with the warm oil massage, was giggling at a piece of oddments, which he was gripping under the tight grip of his little hand. The giggles, the baby sounds, yet to make any senses, and in that giggling the exposition of his milk teeth made Kaushalya and Devaki giggle themselves. Sushmita was sieving the maize flour on the veranda.

Sitting beside her, Ashok said, "I have decided to go abroad."

She paused sieving and looked at him, without any particular emotion on her face. She was aware that he had gone to Uncle's house to request him for the money. Each time he begged money from Uncle, the whole day he would look humiliated. If Uncle refused to give him the money, the degree of humiliation would be much higher.

"Did he refuse to give?" she asked.

"No. He gave. But how long are we going to get from him? It's more than fifty thousand and growing ever larger."

Sushmita did not speak. Nowadays, whenever the matter came, she would not object. From the dearth which was getting worse with the passage of each month, each season, and each year; from the ailing health of her mother-in-law which required adequate care and medicines; and from his tense face, it had dawned on her that something ought to be done. There was nothing much in the hamlet they could do to get out of poverty. She had come at the situation differently, in a more realistic way. She was not alone in the villages. There were many others whose husbands had left the country. If he would go abroad for a few years to work, they could work off the loan or even could buy some fields and life would become more settled, she would think these days.

Devaki returned to her home the day after Tihar. The faint marks of colourful rows of *tika* she had put on her brother's forehead were still there, the garlands of *sayapatri* and *makhamali* flowers were still afresh, the lines of oil she had poured across the threshold still existed there, but she left making him feel sad. After her marriage, every time she came to the hamlet, it amused him and his family, and each time she left, it saddened all of them, his mother specially. Every time she would look at her daughter until she would disappear in the bend across the stream.

Thus, the festive season passed by in the hamlet. The green parrots flew back south. The autumn drew on. The days began to draw in. The rice plants were gathered in. The millet fields became bare, left only with the sprinkled yam leaves, yet to be dug out. The leaves in the trees aged and became pale and brown. The poinsettias reigned over the hedgerows along the narrow path.

Ashok sent a letter to Gopal, requesting to find a job for him.

In Kathmandu, after standing for hours in a long queue and giving someone much more money than he should have been charged, he managed to get a passport. He met the agent Gopal had recommended, who, with all his politeness and outward appearance, tried to give an impression that he was a genuine agent, not like the others who would disappear after receiving the money.

Choosing an agent was a risky step. The money could be just gobbled. The passport could be lost. Sometimes, after stepping on the soil of a strange country, they would have to stay for months without work or would have to engage in hard labour instead of the job promised to them, risking their very survival. He had been told this through the letters from Gopal. He had heard from many others in the villages, on the bus during his travel to Kathmandu, or in the hotels around the bus station where he would meet many others, either looking for an agent or already cheated by them.

So while choosing the agent, he could not take any risks. He just followed what Gopal had asked him. He expressed his wish of going abroad for work. The agent asked him to present at least seventy thousand rupees initially. The rest could be given at a later date.

"But my cousin had said the money could be given once the visa comes," Ashok said.

"That's why I'm asking seventy thousand. Otherwise, I would have asked for the whole amount, one lakh thirty thousand."

"One lakh thirty thousand? But Gopal had said it would not cost more than one lakh."

"That was three years ago. Look, Dai, Dubai is far better than other cities. It's safe. The salary is good. Don't lose the chance. Many others are wishing to go."

Ashok did not speak; he just looked at the agent. The amount was not small for him. How was he to arrange so much money? Would Uncle give it to him? Would his mother and wife agree to sell a few *tolas* of gold jewellery they had hidden inside an old wooden trunk in the attic so dear to them? Could he take a loan from other people or banks? Would they give it to him? He thought about different options. And what about if, after paying the amount, he could not get a visa? He dreaded as he thought. Swallowing hard, he stood silent looking at the agent talking over the phone. A few others, much younger than him, all hurrying to go abroad, increasingly crowded the narrow room.

"I'll find money and come back, sir," Ashok said and stepped out, humiliated by his own word *sir* to a person who might have not even completed his Bachelor's.

"Don't be too late. Vacancies are limited. There're lots of people looking for this job." The agent's voice receded as he walked out. A public bus passed by blowing a plume of smoke, nearly hitting him. Kathmandu was increasingly becoming crowded. Each time he visited, he found the city more crowded with people, vehicles, and houses. The rice paddies were being changed into concrete structures. The city was sprawling in every direction up to the base of the mountains, unplanned and haphazard. The beauty of the city was steadily decaying.

Why not call Gopal? He thought as he walked along. Maybe he could help him. After all, it was he who was encouraging Ashok towards this direction and was suggesting he should opt for abroad for work. Gopal was younger than him. Nor did he go to college, yet he was earning money. Sometimes (or most of the time) Ashok would think he made a mistake by having a degree with no technical knowledge. Why did he spend so much money for the useless certificate? Actually, a big part of the loan to Uncle was due to his studies, the books, innumerable trips to Kathmandu, and the cost of lodging. It would be far better if he had studied the subjects which would give him a job in the country. Or rather he would have abstained from any higher education. The theoretical knowledge he possessed and the certificates he carried had nothing to do with farming. Nor did it have anything of value for the line of work he was going to do, the labour job, the agent had said. The thoughts were crowding in his mind as he waited at an Internet cafe for his turn to make a call to Gopal.

"Dai, I don't have at the moment. I have just sent all my savings to my brother-in-law. If it's after six or seven months, I can help you some. Why don't you talk to my father? He can help you with the money," Gopal said over the phone. But he did not know how difficult his father was when it came to lending money to someone.

Ashok returned to the hamlet.

Six

The knot of the bamboo stem exploded in the hearth, frightening Rabindra who had dozed in the lap of his mother, sucking at her breast. Frightened was Soori too, which was purring on the side of the hearth. Both the girls, Madhu and Sarita, laughed at this sudden explosion, which scared their brother and the tabby together.

"Why are you putting the bamboo stems in without splitting?" Sushmita pulled the stem out. Putting the ashes deposited in the hearth aside, she fed the fire with dried maize stalks. The fire blazed – dwarfing the flickering faint light coming out of the paraffin lamp on the wall and brightening their faces as well as the dark glossy rafters and trusses and the bronze and steel utensils – then faded away, as quickly as it had blazed, demanding more stalks.

Kaushalya, who was sleeping in the mud bedstead in the other section of the inside, said, in her weak voice, "Sushmita, why are you finishing fire . . . w. . . o . . . o . . . d?" Before she completed her words, the cough broke.

The evening had worn on. Outside, it was raining. The unseasonal rains had started before he came from Kathmandu. And since it had been raining and raining continuously, often with waves of cold wind.

The temperature on the mountain slope never went below zero. It never snowed. Winter hardly lasted more than two months. It seldom felt wintry, especially in those years when it did not rain. During the sunny days, the temperature would rise above twenty degrees as soon as the sun came out. Yet during the rainy days, the cold could be a matter of concern for the peasants who did not have warm clothes, such as a sweater, coat, shawl, or blanket.

The family had clustered around the hearth taking their evening meal – millet bread and tomato chutney, a typical meal during wintry evenings – and keeping warm by the fire. Madhu had stopped fussing over the food. Both the girls, still far from teenagers, had got the sense of the responsibility, of the realisation that they were not children any longer. The perpetual scarcity, Grandma's ailing health, combined with coughs, sometimes unremitting, and the tension on the faces of their parents had made them think more maturely than their real age. Their childhood had been prematurely snatched away.

"Madhu, it's time for bed," Ashok said, walking to the other section of the inside.

He put his hand over the forehead of his mother. It was hot. The fever had not come down even with the double dose of paracetamol, which he had bought months back and put in a hole in the wall. Perhaps the date had expired. The label on the packet was not legible; it had faded.

Kaushalya had developed a mild fever the day after Ashok went to Kathmandu. It was getting worse with the passage of every day, Sushmita had said before he stepped into the slippery yard. At first, she had thought it might be a cold or flu and the temperature would come down, but it did not. By the time he came back from Kathmandu, she had been in bed for a week. With her old eyes sunken, the parched lips pressed in, the wrinkled cheeks hollowed, and grey hair in disarray, she looked pitiable. Uncle, as usual, had done whatever he could do. He had prepared all those medicines he had known: the paste and liquid from the bark of the trees and the leaves of the weeds, Sushmita had said. And after his medicines did not work, he himself had gone to Magargaun to call Dhami Uncle.

Dhami Uncle came in his peculiar dress – a white *kachhad*, a grey *bhoto*, and a brown waistcoat. He wore a red turban. A shabby old bag hung loosely on his shoulder. He came with his nut-brown freckled face, sunken cheeks, the square chin, and the bulbous nose. Sitting next to

Kaushalya, he looked at her eyes carefully, felt the nerves in her wrist, and slowly moved *akshata* in a bronze plate. He divided them into parts – two of the grains in each part – and mixed them and separated again, his eyes closed and his mouth whispering mantras; he repeated the process many times.

Ashok did not have much faith in superstition, but deep inside him, who was bred with years of superstitious cultures, he had not enough courage to discard the social beliefs, particularly in such difficult situations. He could not ignore what Dhami Uncle was doing and saying.

Dhami Uncle finally opened his eyes. Making his tone as serious as possible, he declared, "Dai, Kaushalya Bhauju has come under the shadow of a ghost, a very powerful *murkatta*, the headless. It wants sacrifice of a black or red kid in the new moon. Today, I offer some ghee, barley, and black sesame, and vow the sacrifice will be offered in the new moon. But we need to sacrifice either a black or red kid in the new moon within two months."

Then, he asked Sushmita to prepare a burning piece of wood, some barley and black sesame, pure ghee, wick strings, thread, a chestnut leaf, and a jug of pure water.

"Are you sure it's the *murkatta* that's troubling her?" Uncle sought more assurances.

"Yes, Dai. Every time I spelled, I saw the same *murkatta*," he confirmed, touching his sunken cheek with his right index finger.

With the burning firewood thrown in the wood, where the *murkatta* was believed to haunt even during the daytime, he left the yard, saying, "Dai, I have asked the *murkatta* to leave her. There's no need to worry. You can continue with your medicine. But you mustn't forget about the sacrifice in the new moon. Otherwise, it'll give trouble to all the villagers."

He left the yard, but despite his assurance, the fever did not come down. The coughs became more frequent.

Now it had been two weeks since she became bedridden.

"Aama, eat some *jaulo*," Ashok said, pressing her calloused feet, contrastingly cold. She had taken less than half a bowl of *jaulo* at noon, then had not taken anything except for the bitter liquid medicine prepared by Uncle.

"Don't worry about me. It seems it's time for me to go. Last night, in my dream, your father was calling me, asking me to hurry up." She was trying hard to control her cough.

"Don't say so, Aama. You'll be all right." Sushmita sat on the mat on the floor, her eyes filled with tears.

Except for a few squabbles on petty matters, Kaushalya and Sushmita had lived a life of mutual understanding. They had regard for each other. As soon as Sushmita came into the house as a daughter-in-law, their relationship had developed as a mother and daughter rather than a mother-in-law and daughter-in-law, which were often inharmonious in the prevailing social structure. After the death of Ashok's grandmother, their relations had become even deeper. What she could not tell Ashok, she could tell Sushmita easily. After two or three days of her present sickness, after it was known that it was not merely a cold or flu, Sushmita had made her bed on the floor beside the mud bedstead. She would sleep there or would just doze, waking up many times to check if Kaushalya was all right, to see if her quilt was in position, or if she needed hot water. Tears rolled down her cheeks. She could not see the pathetic situation of her mother-in-law or in a true sense her mother.

"Why don't you take her to the hospital? I don't think Dhami Uncle can cure," she said, wiping her tears.

Kaushalya opened her mouth to say something, but before she uttered her words, a strong fit of coughing seized her throat.

"I'll talk to Uncle tomorrow. Let her rest."

Spreading the quilt over his mother, he went to his room.

Outside, the drizzling was continuing. The wind was chilly, but a patch of the northern sky had cleared, and the stars were twinkling there. Getting into the bed, he burrowed himself under the old quilt that would require not less than an hour to make him warm, especially his feet. The woodworms, like every night, were busy cutting the trusses.

The next day the sky opened brilliantly. The sunshine fell on the hamlet. Birds flew freely in the sky twittering their tweets. Soori came out and padded across the orchard and into Big Plot, scaring the feeding doves. Seti welcomed the sunshine with her short grunts while Mali mooed in an amusing tone.

But Kaushalya breathed her last.

From the very start of the day, a crow had been crowing as if heralding an unpleasant event. Sushmita threw stones at it many times, but each time, it came back and perched somewhere and cawed his ominous crows, looking at the yard. Asking Sushmita to move Aama into the *mandir*, in the warm sunshine, for which she had been wishing for days, Ashok went to the field across the stream to bring fodder for the cattle. They had been fed solely on hay for days.

Clambering was difficult. The mossy bark of the mountain ebony had become slippery with the rain. He got somehow up to the first knot. Then suddenly, loud screams echoed through. The screams were followed by different voices, mixed voices of his uncles and aunties, a kind of hullabaloo, as if an unwanted incident had come about. He climbed down, scratching his legs and ran to the hamlet. In the yard, the little hamlet had gathered. Aama lay on a mat near the *tulasi math*, dead.

The yard was filled with crying and sobbing. Uncle was calling to Padam and the others in Gurunggaun up in the mountain to come down to the hamlet. Little Uncle was pouring *tulasi-water* in her mouth. The crow was still crowing, looking evilly at the yard.

Kaushalya was staring at nothing. Her grey hair strayed around her forehead and temples, her mouth was open and her lips slightly curved, as if wanting to smile or to say something. Ashok could not contain himself.

"Aama!" a loud voice came from his mouth and echoed across the hamlet. He threw himself over her chest and sobbed his heart out like a child, uncontrollably. He had lost her, his mother, forever. Once more, he had become an orphan. What an unlucky son he was; he could not even give her a spoonful of water before she died.

Mourners soon gathered in the yard. The conch was blown. Her dead body, wrapped in a yellow shroud and decorated with flowers and sandalwood, was tied to a green bamboo bier. The religious rituals began. He abandoned himself to the feelings of helplessness, a burden of guilt that his mother died without receiving proper medicines, that if treated well she could have survived a few more years. He followed the funeral procession to the Kali River, sometimes giving his shoulders to the bier and at times just touching it, his head shaved, his soul continuously eaten up by the burden of guilt and regret.

On the bank of the Kali, before giving a flame to the fire, he looked at his mother's face for the final time in his life. The firewood in the pyre, doused in paraffin, quickly burnt. The earthly life of his mother came to an end. Uncle asked him to collect a little remnant of the ashes in a bronze urn. The rest of the ashes were swept away into the Kali, whose ripples absorbed them quickly.

"It's the same place where your father was cremated," Uncle said, looking at the ripples hazed in the yellow rays of the setting sun. Ashok tried to bring back the faded picture of his father in his mind. Aama had said to him that in her dream she was calling him. He wished they could meet again.

The sun set behind the mountains.

The next day, Pundit Ji appeared in the yard with his deep sigh and, after drinking a glassful of milk and gulping a few bananas, set about making the *rekhi* on the altar. A *havan* was dug out. He took out his books – old-looking, sepia-coloured, bound with leather strips, handed over to him by his father before his death. Throughout the ceremony, Ashok did whatever he was asked to do with his sincere wish that Aama could get *moksha* or would reincarnate to live a happy life, not like the one she had just lived.

Desperate to see Kaushalya again, Soori walked around miaowing low, deep miaows for a few days and disappeared. No one knew where she went. Seti and Mali kept crying long and loud for days.

Seven

Ashok struck the branch hard with a recently sharpened sickle, cutting it off at the first strike. Thick milky sap exuded and dripped down from the cut. It was the last *khanyu* tree remaining in his field. Now it too went leafless. He looked around. His part of the millet fields looked bare, only covered with the remnants of dried-out maize and millet stumps, brown weeds, black sprinkles of manure which they had sprinkled throughout the day, and a few leafless *khanyu* trees and mountain ebonies. The winter was not even half over. However, the fodder trees had already been exhausted, leaving him no options for the remaining months, but to buy from Uncle or to let Sushmita wander miles from the hamlet with an empty basket on her back in search of grass.

Below, on the ground, Sushmita was piling the fodder branches. A little down, on the bank of the stream where the stream had turned into cascades and below each cascade the water stood in the little puddles, Madhu was plucking the fresh sprigs of mint, grown plentifully on the sides of the stream. In one of those puddles, Sarita was scooping her hands in amusing efforts to catch tiny fish, which mostly ended in a handful of murky water and sometimes in other water insects, but never in fish. Rabindra was amusingly looking at her, his shorts soaked and soiled and darned at the back.

Ashok threw the sickle on the ground and clambered down.

"You're not going to stay for more than five years. Let me tell you. And you'll come every year or at least once in two years on leave," Sushmita said, looking straight deep into his eyes.

"Why don't you trust me? I have told you many times. As soon as I pay Uncle and save some more, I won't stay a single day," he said.

It had been more than a year since Kaushalya died. One-year rituals had been performed; he had taken off the white clothes and put on the usual ones. The situation, however, had not improved. On the contrary, it had been steadily deteriorating. The debt had reached nearly eighty thousand, and there was no sign in sight that it would come down as long as he stayed in the hamlet, pursuing farming. His efforts of diversifying into ginger farming in the millet fields had gone in vain. Following many other peasants, he had branched out into this farming, much touted as a cash crop. He toiled tirelessly for months for this new crop, hoping to get cash right away after the harvest. Giving due response to their sweat, the sturdy shoots came up. They grew fast and developed into green leaves, spreading a kind of spicy fragrance in the air, unique to them. The roots spread wide and thick under the soil. The produce was much more than they had anticipated. But unfortunately, the price of ginger went down sharply the reasons for which he did not know. He was told that the demand was low. Apart from this, the same year, one of the sole two businessmen in the bazaar who bought ginger from the peasants had moved elsewhere. The remaining merchant did not have enough space to store the surfeit. The peasants crowded in front of his shutters, carrying baskets and sacks filled with ginger. The price went down every day. Once he had to return home with the ginger he had taken to sell. The ginger rotted. Again, without experience, just following the others, he tried to dry the remaining ginger through traditional methods, drying it in smoke. In this effort, he decayed it; the merchant in the bazaar refused to buy.

"Can't we try the winter vegetables in our Big Plot? I'm sure the vegetables will make more money than the maize. A few peasants in my birthplace have started vegetable farming instead of grains. They're making good money," she tried to persuade him with yet another idea.

"They have plenty of water even during winter. You know how scarce the water becomes in our village at that time? Both the streams dry up. Are you going to carry water from the spring to water the vegetables? You know the market. What happened to our ginger?" he said and turned to her. "Look, I'm not the only one leaving the hamlet. You know nearly all the men of my age have gone abroad. They're sending money to their families. How can we live in this cash-strapped situation?"

"Dinesh hasn't sent even a penny. His wife told me," she said still with a faint hope.

"I know him very well. He spends money on girls and alcohol. Otherwise, he could have sent some. Gopal has already sent five lakh in these three years," he said, "and both Bikram and Hari have got jobs. Uncle told me."

"Have you talked to him about money?" she asked, continuing to gaze him straight.

"I need one lakh fifty thousand for my visa, ticket, and other costs. Devaki has promised fifty thousand. I have asked Gopal for fifty thousand without letting Uncle know. The rest, I hope he'll give me."

"I'm afraid of staying alone. Can't we start anything new here in the hamlet with that money?"

"You aren't a child. What's there to be afraid of? And starting here something? Who will give me the loan if I say I'm going to plant potato or tomato or eggplant or whatever here in the hamlet?"

"Nobody can argue with you. Do as you wish." Her forehead frowned slightly. She tied the pile of the fodder with the *namlo*. The irritation further radiated her beauty. Beauty was also exhibited through the upper part of her white bosom that was unconsciously exposed in her attempt of tying the pile. He looked at her, at her exposed bosom, until she caught his eyes looking at the private part of her body. Adjusting her blouse, she called the children, "Madhu, come. It's time to go."

She carried the bundle and walked, followed by him and the children.

His mind strayed to thinking about a place: far away, somewhere in the world, a large illuminated city, wide roads, big buildings, new cars, good work, and salaries in foreign currency as Gopal had mentioned in his letter. Even in the night, during his sleep, the fantastic images continuously came to his mind. Like other nights, the familiar, soothing sound of the *madal* and *rodhi song* from Gurunggaun reached his ears smoothly, and his wife breathed warmly beside him, yet the sleep was miles away from him. He tossed and turned, thinking.

Soon after, he was working on his Uncle for the loan he needed for his venture. It was a cool spring day. The maize plants had sprouted in the fields. The tailorbirds were busy gathering twigs to sew nests inside the green bushes; the squirrels had come out of their drey and set out running up and down the bamboo canes; and the cuckoos were cooing melodiously, perching on the tree branches. Uncle, sitting in the *chautari*, was weaving a basket.

Ashok had been trying to talk to him for days, but he had not found an appropriate moment for talking about the big amount which he sometimes was afraid Uncle would not give him. So, as he saw him, weaving a basket with all his calmness, he went to the *chautari*. Touching Uncle's feet, he sat on a stone next to him and for a while talked about this and that matter and finally worked around to what he wanted to ask, "Uncle, it's becoming difficult for me to run the family. You know the cost is growing, and there's no income. Due to the uncertainty of the monsoon, we can't rely on farming. Last year, I tried with ginger, but it went in vain. I have decided to go abroad for a few years."

"Yes. The monsoon has become unpredictable. Sometimes there's too much rain and sometimes no rain. The farming is getting worse each and every year. It wouldn't be the case in our time. And it's not easy to find men to work in the fields. I couldn't sow the millet fields. They're barren.

I'm getting older. With the boys outside of the country, it has become very difficult to continue farming," Uncle said.

He paused weaving and lit a cigarette – Yak, his favourite brand. He looked in a relaxed and talking mood. He added, "Can Sushmita handle all these things alone? I mean the farming, the cattle, and the children? Can you find work abroad? It was easy for Gopal to find work, but Bikram had to wait months to find one."

"Gopal has written to me that he would find work for me. I have discussed with Sushmita. At first, she was somewhat worried, but now she's convinced. She's aware of the reality. I know after my leaving it'll be difficult for her to handle all these things. But you and Auntie are here to support her. The only problem, Uncle, is money. Devaki has promised fifty thousand. If you give me fifty thousand, the problem could be resolved."

Uncle did not speak; he just took two or three continuous puffs at his cigarette, hollowing his cheeks and looking into the distance, almost feigning indifference to what Ashok said. The waft of smoke came out of his mouth and nose and spread into the air.

A pair of barbet birds came, flying from across the stream. Hiding in a tree, they set in uttering a series of sad melodious cries, intermittently. A pale leaf fell from the *peepal* tree and rested in Ashok's lap. He took it and looked at both sides. A few lines were scribbled on its front. Those were scribbled by the birds, using their beaks, Grandmother would often say. Chewing on its pointed tip for a while, he threw it and added, "Uncle, I promise I'll pay all your debt with my first salaries. I have also told Sushmita that I'll work hard to work off your loan at the earliest."

Uncle still did not speak but continued smoking until the cigarette smouldered wholly and stubbed out the remaining stump against a stone. The worries about the possibilities of his request being spurned unsettled Ashok. The whole idea of going abroad depended on the availability of money, for which he had got only two options, either to borrow from Uncle or to sell the ancestral jewellery.

After a long silence, Uncle said, "Let me see." He started weaving again.

The same evening, he went to Uncle's house for more requests. Beside the hearth, Uncle and Auntie were shucking the maize. Pooja was stitching leaf plates, sitting in her usual place, just below the ladder.

Ashok sat beside them and saying, "How good these cobs look? But difficult to shell," he himself set about shucking. His palm was swollen by shelling the maize the previous day.

"This is the last lot for the seeds. But insects have already attacked them. I'm so vexed at these insects. They leave nothing in the attic. Rice, maize, millet, beans, whatever they find, they just spoil," Auntie said. "I'm afraid if we put this maize for some more days in the attic, we won't have them even for seed."

"Uncle, did you think about my request this afternoon?" Ashok asked Uncle reluctantly.

"What request?" Auntie was curious to know. Uncle did not share much about financial matters to Auntie. Nor did he tolerate interventions from her.

"Why do you need to know? It's the matter between us," Uncle said, slightly irritatingly. "Look, Ashok, I don't say I don't have money. But isn't it too much what you're asking? How and when are you going to pay? You know what the interest rate is? If the other people have borrowed, I wouldn't have given them a penny less than a monthly five per cent. You're my son. Still you know how hard it has become for Gopal to earn this money, if you give three per cent a month, I'll consider. But we need to make a *kapali tamsuk*. This is a large amount. I can't take risks," Uncle said.

"I promise to pay as soon as possible, Uncle. I hope it won't take more than a year. I'll work hard. Uncle, I'm now assured. I'll leave for Kathmandu tomorrow to meet the agent. I met him last year. Hope, he's still there. I'll also call Gopal and will be back in less than a week," Ashok said. He was not in a position to bargain over the interest rate.

"Be sure you won't give the agent a single penny until the visa is in your hand. After taking money, they just disappear. They're very clever. I lost fifty thousand when Bikram went to Malaysia. I wanted to report to the police about the fraud, but some others told me that I would be losing more money in the process and would never get back what I lost. All have created a nexus. I met the agent many times, but he always had excuses. These fellows are not trustworthy at all. Never give them any money before you get a visa."

"I won't. I know them. I'll talk to Sushmita and prepare for tomorrow. I'll leave now," Ashok said and left.

The next morning, he left for Kathmandu with a Chinese camouflage bag on his back, the children still in bed and Sushmita throwing her worried eyes on his leaving. Throughout his way, he was thinking about his upcoming travel to Dubai: the thoughts sometimes amusing him with the possibility of working in a good company and at times worrying and scaring with the possibility of ending up in an alien land. His thoughts continued throughout the travel on a crowded public bus with dishevelled seats along the highway on the side of rushing rivers on the banks of which, on grassy meadows, he could see the children grazing their cattle, reminding him of the little foothills.

Pasang

One

As I saw Pradip, Pradip Tuladhar, at the airport, waving his right hand at me, I felt relaxed. The nervousness of the first flight, the edginess of the first time going abroad, the anxiety of the destiny not yet guaranteed and of leaving Sushmita and the children behind all on their own, which had overawed my thoughts throughout the journey, lessened to a great extent as I saw him at the airport. The first experience of flying in the air, high in the sky above the mountains, should have been exciting or even romantic. For a person like me who had grown up in a remote village – a place where simply looking at a plane from the ground would be a matter of curiosity and flying on board would have been considered as a fantasy or a kind of luxury, not easily available – the flight of slightly more than an hour with amazing views of the contours of the Himalayas and of vastly stretched plateau should have been enjoyable. But I could not enjoy at all. Throughout the flight and long hours I had spent at the airport in Kathmandu among strangers, the anxiety, the rawness of an air journey, made me nervous. It scared me so much that at times I felt as if going back to my own little world, Narrow Flatland. So as I saw Pradip, my boss, there, at the receiving area of the airport, I felt relaxed. Anchored.

He was the same Pradip Tuladhar – an athletic figure with medium height, neatly combed jet-black hair, as if dyed the same morning – whom I had met, a few weeks back, in a restaurant in Kathmandu where I was waiting for the agent who had promised me to arrange a visa for Dubai. My first meeting with him there in the restaurant had been unexpected, a bit surprising.

At a table of the restaurant, I was waiting for the agent. Pradip came in and sat a few tables down from mine. He was dressed in a charming manner: livid jeans and jacket and blue canvas shoes, which offered a casual yet an impressive effect. A pair of black goggles matched his athletic body. He undid the cellophane of a packet of cigarettes, the Marlboro Light, took out a stick, and lit it in a unique way, between his thumb and first finger.

He started the conversation.

"Bhai, where're you from?"

"From a village near Pokhara," I said a bit hesitatingly.

"What do you do here in Kathmandu?" he asked again, pulling long on his Marlboro.

"I'm not staying here. I came today," I responded.

The openness he showed in our first conversation, his style, and his way of holding the cigarette were appealing. I liked the way he talked and the way he laughed, exposing his gapped teeth and a little bit of his upper gum. During the short conversation, I told him the whole of my story, the reason for being there in the restaurant. As he told me that he had got a restaurant in Lhasa, Tibet, and was looking for a smart guy with working knowledge of English to work at the reception or as a barman, I was at once tempted to go to Lhasa. I wondered if I could work in his restaurant in Lhasa, rather than going to Dubai, where the job was not guaranteed yet. As we went on chatting, he proposed why not I would go to Lhasa to work in his restaurant. As if he had read my mind. He promised me a salary, which was not bad. The airfare to Lhasa was to be borne by him. More than that, I was not supposed to pay him any money. I could save the money, that one lakh fifty thousand rupees, which I was asked to pay to the agent for the travel to Dubai, the money for which I had to mortgage Big Plot or had to sell the jewellery of my wife. It was an offer to which it was not wise to say no. Besides, talking to him was so intimate that, then and there, I made my mind to go to Lhasa to work in his restaurant. Afterwards, he handled everything: the visa, the ticket, and the work permit.

It was thus, I flew to Lhasa, whereas Sushmita and Uncle time and again had asked me to go to Dubai. They did not appreciate the idea of working in Lhasa.

Now, to my satisfaction, he was at the airport with the same smile, with the same friendly look. I greeted him, "Namaste, Pradip Dai."

Taking out a white *khada* out of his pocket and putting it around my neck, he said, "Welcome to Tibet. It's a Tibetan tradition to welcome the guest with a *khada*."

I had seen some passengers at the airport in Kathmandu getting it from their relatives. Now I myself was getting it, a *khada*, soft and white.

"Ashok, he's Pasang La. My friend."

The name was not new to me. I had heard the similar name several times, but this suffix *La* was new. Was it his surname? *Maybe*, I thought and greeted him, "Namaste."

Pasang had a brawny body with a tawny pock-marked face, black hair, and light green eyes. He looked calm. His facial expression, always looking slightly smiling, offered a kind of deep-inherited happiness, a kind of perpetual contentedness.

"*Tashi delek, Aashok La*," Pasang said, adding an additional *a* to my name and negating my conjecture that the suffix *La* would connote his surname. What was that *La*, I wanted to ask yet kept quiet.

Outside, we were welcomed by a bright day. I saw a little valley amidst the barren and brown mountains. Above, the cerulean sky stretched miles and miles in all directions. I had never seen such a blue sky.

Pasang drove on towards a little town nestled below a mountain spur, the town of a few traditional Tibetan houses: mud-walled, flat earthen roof with rocks at the end, colourful doors and windows, the prayer flags in different colours, and whitewashed exteriors. Heavy door panels hung at the doors. There were a few concrete houses. A few shanty shops too.

The town looked ancient, similar to the valley itself. So was the runway of the airport. The white plane on which I had flown was still on the runway with blue stripes and with the Chinese flag and the words *AIR CHINA* (and a few Chinese characters, possibly its Chinese translation) written on it. Still. Blending in with the quietness.

We left the little town and drove on a bent asphalt road which ran parallel above a river, which, with wide sandy banks on both sides, wound away between the mountains towards the east. It must be the same river that I had seen from the plane, the name of which I was told as the Yarlung Tsangpo in Tibetan, the Brahmaputra in Nepalese – the only river named after a male in Hindu culture. The sole signs of greenery – the willows, trimmed and now budded with new twigs, on the sides of the road, and the wheat and barley plants, freshly sprouted, in the terraced fields, down the road – soon exhausted, then resumed the barrenness and brownness again.

With his hand on the steering wheel and his eyes slanted at the asphalt road, Pasang was driving as calmly as the mountains around. Pradip was silent in the front seat. I was cautioned not to speak much, a precaution to avoid altitude sickness. Pradip had already told me in Kathmandu that some people might develop altitude sickness in Tibet, at that high altitude. And it was the main reason why my wife had not appreciated the idea of working in Tibet.

I did not have nausea or a headache, the early symptoms of acute altitude sickness. There was, however, something new, something unusual in my brain, a kind of emptiness or thoughtlessness. The hollow constant sound, which I had experienced while flying, was now in my ears like a drone. Perhaps I had developed mild symptoms of altitude sickness. Pasang gave me a pill and a bottle of water and asked me to relax. He told me, in his uniquely pronounced Nepalese, that the body could take two weeks or so to adapt to the altitude problem. At least I had not developed the acute symptoms.

His father was originally from Nepal, married to a Tibetan, Pasang told me as we drove on. He was a half-Tibetan, half-Nepalese. What I was impressed about was his way of speaking Nepalese: something amusing or funny, making the listeners confused with his odd pronunciation, his words sometimes giving a different meaning than what he intended to express.

After driving about thirty minutes, we reached a small place of three or four traditional houses and two shacks, small grocery, or tea shacks, on the left side of the road below a steep slope. There, on the walls of those houses, I saw one more addition, which I had not noticed in the township near the airport: the cowpat pasted for drying. I assumed it must be cow dung. Not unlike in the Terai, the southern Nepal. Pasang pulled the Toyota Land Cruiser off the road and got out saying, "*Aashok*," as if he was saying to himself.

The place was hardly more than those houses. A few yaks were grazing on the slope: full of brown cliffs, blending with the browns of the mountains and the scattered little scrub, also without particular colours to be distinct from the brownness. Below the asphalt road, the slope sharply fell down to the river. A fountain had originated somewhere amidst the cliffs and gurgled down and merged into the river.

We sat on a bench in front of a shack. I could see a few Tibetan people, both men and women. The men were wearing *chupa*, a long robe with wide sleeves caught up at the waist by a girdle and a hat. The women were in long-sleeved shirts and close-fitting robes with decorated aprons. A few children crowded around and looked at us curiously. What I could see in those Tibetans was a kind of satisfaction, a kind of innocence or truth being reflected from their faces, a similitude of the calmness and peace on Pasang's face, similar to the quiet surroundings.

Inside the shop, in front of which we sat on a bench, was a girl whose age was difficult to guess. Pasang told her something in Tibetan. In response, she smiled and gave us three bowls of tea, the butter tea and *tsampa*. Pasang engaged himself in talking with that young lady while Pradip walked across the road, holding the cigarette with his thumb and first finger, puffing out wisps of smoke. His wrinkled forehead, somewhat-sunken cheeks, and greying moustache, despite his jet-black hair and athletic body, indicated he was not less than fifty.

The shadow of the mountain, on whose slope we were, gradually descended: first over the cliffs, scrub and the grazing yaks, then on the little houses, us, the asphalt road, and eventually on and across the river. By the time we left, the sun was far in the west.

The mountain shadow, grazing yaks, and the cliffs called up memories of the childhood in the little foothills: memories of the little streams, the grazing of the cattle, those naive games, the shadow crossing the flint, and Grandmother's call to collect the cattle. The faded memories appeared in the emptiness of my brain. Those bygone years, the past time! Here I was in the present. As if I was in a dream, hard to believe. I was amazed at being in a new place – the open sky in its true blueness, the Yarlung Tsangpo, the mountains, the cliffs, the little houses, the shacks, the butter tea and *tsampa*, the serenity and the solitude: a new chapter in my life.

The road and the river went along, almost parallel, but soon, the river became two – one, the Yarlung Tsangpo, continuing upstream towards the west, and the other, the Lhasa River, (I was told the name by Pasang) meandering up to the slight north, which we followed for our drive with the repetition of the same views: the dominating brownness offered by the mountains, the cerulean sky, infrequent settlements on the side of the road and before and after those settlements a few pollarded poplar and willow trees – young, many of them in the form of mere seedlings and saplings – and again the barrenness, a few feet down snaking bluish green river over which waterfowl stretched their wings.

At a point, through a narrow gap – a mountain spur, possibly cut for the purpose of the road – we entered yet another valley, bigger. Pasang pulled in the Land Cruiser on the edge of the road. On the left of the road, an image of Buddha was carved on a cliff. A colourful big image and below the image a few bonsai trees, perhaps pine or fir (for me, it was difficult to recognise conifer trees as they did not grow in my hamlet, and I had seldom seen them before), a miniature structure of a red temple, artistically created with a gilded roof, a white shrine for burning incense, hanging *khadas* and prayer flags offered a picturesque view. On the opposite side of the road, there was a ditch running parallel with the road. Beyond that, a flat grassy land, dotted with mounds – difficult to ascertain if they were made for some purposes or they were created naturally or, more possibly, they were remnants of soil excavated during the cutting of the spur and the construction of the highway – and beyond, the Lhasa River. Across the river there was a small flat land beneath a barren mountain.

"Lhasa," Pradip said.

The afternoon rays slanting from behind were telling us that we were at the western point of the valley. From there, in the east, the whole of the valley could be seen surrounded by the barren and brown mountains from all sides, but with the green vegetation in it, like an oasis amongst the deserted mountains.

I was standing there on the side of the asphalt road, a little away on one side the Lhasa River, and on the other side was the colourful image of Buddha carved on the cliff and eight miles away, according to Pasang, the magnificent view of the city and the Potala Palace. The majesty, the sanctity, and the beauty being revealed from the city and the palace were inexplicable, ancient, and mysterious.

"Are you still sleeping, Ashok? It's already nine," Pradip was calling me.

"Just woke up, Dai," I responded, unlatching the door.

"Did you sleep well?" he asked.

"I think so," I said. In fact, I did not know if I had a good sleep. I slept the full length of time, but the sleep came in brief snatches, with bizarre and formless dreams.

He was in a white-striped blue tracksuit, fitted well to his athletic body.

"It's difficult to have a sound sleep in high altitude for the first few days," he said. "And what about your headache?"

I had complained about the mild headache, which I had developed before going to bed the previous night.

"No." I shook my head. I did not have the headache, although a slight sense of emptiness was still there.

"I can say you aren't much affected by the altitude. I was a bit worried. Bidur suffered for nearly half a month. In Tibet, altitude becomes a serious problem for many newcomers. Freshen up yourself. Let's have *tsampa*. Afterwards, I'll take you for *kora*. I'll be waiting for you in the living room."

"What's that? I mean the *kora*."

"A religious activity. Or truly speaking, a part of daily life here in Tibet. Circling around the monasteries, temples, or any other sacred places. Clockwise. It's one of the most sacred activities among the Tibetans."

"Oh, it must be fascinating," I said.

The sun had already come up high. Through the old wooden window I could see a patch of the blue sky. What I could see through the window were also a few Tibetan houses and narrow alleys. I was informed that the name of the locality was Barkhor, the oldest locality in the city, purely Tibetan, unchanged for centuries. Pradip had told me that the previous evening, when we had entered a narrow street, full of people, rickshaws, small groceries, and butcheries.

A mild cool breeze entered the room. The blue curtains billowed. The room, which must have remained closed for days, smelt of butter, juniper, and maybe other Tibetan herbs in addition to the dampness of the room itself.

Pradip and his wife Bayang were waiting for me in the living room. They did not have any children, he had said to me during our first meeting in Kathmandu.

"Namaste," I greeted Bayang.

"*Tashi delek*. Did you sleep well?" she too expressed her concern about my sleep.

"Yes! I had so many dreams. But I don't remember any of them," I responded.

Both of them laughed.

Bayang, with her tall figure, ebony and wavy hair, and light green eyes, had a pleasant personality. Slightly taller than Pradip, she was dressed in a yellow long-sleeved shirt and a brown close-fitting robe with a striped apron.

A sweet smell wafted up from the incense sticks, permeating the air. The previous day, on my first arrival, I had not seen the room properly. Now, in relative freshness, I was quite taken with the room, with the settings of the room decorated in all its finery. It was a medium-sized room with walls on three sides and a narrow wooden door on the remaining one. In the middle, there were a cream sofa and two low tables elaborately carved with dragon and bamboo motifs. The two cabinets with paintings stood side by side against the wall on one side of the room. On the opposite wall, there were hanging wall carpets and *thangkas*. A few wooden chairs were positioned just beneath the paintings. On the other wall, the third one, I saw a television and a few bowls – bronze, copper, and wooden. There were sets of chopsticks and knives with silver rings kept on the shelves of an open cabinet. Next to the cabinet, a bronze bowl and a butter churn were on the floor, which was fully covered with a blue carpet, minutely painted.

I sat on the sofa alongside Pradip.

"How old are you?" he asked and lit a cigarette.

"Twenty-nine."

"You're much younger than me. Did you ever work in Nepal? I mean in a restaurant or a hotel."

"No, Dai. You know, I didn't find a job."

"Oh, yes. You had told me in Kathmandu. How old are your children?"

"The eldest daughter is eight. The middle one, also a daughter, is seven. The youngest is turning three."

"Is she also a daughter?" Bayang asked. She was pouring butter tea in our bowls.

"No. He's a boy. Otherwise, I would have been in my own village, waiting for one more," I laughed.

"You're in Tibet. It's better to have local foods. You may not like it now. Later, I'm sure you'll adapt to the taste. It'll keep you away from the altitude sickness," he said, kneading *tsampa* and yak butter in a bowl. I did the same, mimicking him.

"Do you eat yak meat?" he asked.

"I haven't eaten so far. Isn't it a cow?"

"Yes, in a way. But it looks different than the normal cow. I can't force you. Later, you'll know yourself how difficult is it to survive in

Tibet without meat," he said, putting *balep* on my plate. "These loaves are filled with vegetables. You can also find them with meat."

I took one of it, which tasted similar to wheat or barley bread, the taste familiar to me.

"Yaks graze at a very high altitude. They can survive days just by licking stones," Bayang said, pouring tea in our bowls, once more.

She could speak Nepalese, better than Pasang. Was she also a Nepalese in origin? Or did she learn the language from him? I did not ask in the first meeting with her.

"When are you bringing your wife? Bring her as soon as possible. Girls are beautiful in Tibet. You'll fall in love," she said, putting more *balep* on the plate, "as he fell in love with me."

She laughed, looking at Pradip.

"There's no chance for me to fall in love with any other woman. I have got a pretty wife, and I love her," I responded.

"I'll see," she said. "How's the taste of *balep*? Take more."

Pradip was lost in the wisps of smoke. From the very first meeting in Kathmandu, I had noticed that whenever he smoked, holding his cigarette with his thumb and first finger; he, otherwise so frank, looked lost in his thoughts. During his puffs, his forehead between his eyebrows would crease and his head would bend a little up.

After a few moments, towards the end of the breakfast, as Bayang left the room, he plunged into the real matter, which I wanted to know as soon as I stepped in Lhasa, but somehow, could not speak about. "You just arrived yesterday. I suggest you to have rest for a few more days, at least two weeks. Then you can start your work. In the meantime, you can go to the restaurant and see what the others do. There're five others working in the restaurant. All local except Bidur. I want to be very clear about things. I don't want any misunderstandings arising between us."

He further said, grinding his cigarette in the ashtray, "Your salary, as I had said in Kathmandu, will be two thousand Chinese Yuan. You can stay here with us for a few days. Then you can stay with Bidur, or I can find a room for you. You need to pay the rent yourself. Bidur is working in the kitchen. Whenever I'm in the restaurant, I look after the reception. Now, since you're here, I want you to take care of it in my absence. Otherwise, you'll work as a waiter. The restaurant is more than busy during the tourist season. I'm glad to know you can speak English. I need a person who can speak English because most of the customers are foreigners."

Speaking candidly, he made it easy for me. I was a bit worried whether he would give me the same amount as he had promised me in Kathmandu. The whole reason of leaving the family and coming to Lhasa – the separation of home and hearth – was solely associated with the money. So, as soon as I stepped in Lhasa, I was anxious to know about the salary, but my newness and shyness had deterred me from asking. When Pradip gave me the information, I felt relieved.

"All right, Dai," I said.

He lit another cigarette and switched on the television.

Xizang TV, the local channel, was broadcasting a melodious song sung by a young Tibetan couple. It was not possible for me to understand the language. It sounded like *so ya rie lo . . . Lhasa rie*. Along with the song, the television offered the changing scenes – of the blue sky, green pastureland, and grazing yaks and sheep, a few of them ruminating, then a serene turquoise lake, a clear river, and pine trees. The melody and the scenic beauty were touching.

"Let's go for *kora*. I'll also show you the restaurant," Pradip said and stood.

"Bayang, we'll come later in the evening. After dinner," he said as we stepped down the stairs.

At the end of the messy courtyard, the mastiff was there, still tethered to a post as I had seen it the last evening. It looked calm, but it scared me as I met its gaze.

"What a frightening dog!" the words came from my mouth without my notice.

"It's very strong and honest. It doesn't harm familiar people," Pradip said.

"Tiger, my boy!" he called the mastiff, which, in response, ran towards Pradip but was impeded by the chain it was tethered with. By its speed, even in those few steps, I was so scared I wanted to be far from it as soon as possible.

Outside, the stone-paved alleyway was full of people and rickshaws laden with varied stuff. The whitewashed houses on sides, those small groceries and floating stands, the unfamiliar sounds and smells, those faces and their speaking of Tibetan: to me, all they were new and amusing.

The alleyway became more crowded and finally led us to a street, a stone-paved street, along which hundreds or even thousands of people were treading in one direction, clockwise. Some were spinning prayer wheels, some counting beads and chanting mantras, and some others moving forward measuring the path with their body.

"Barkhor Street! They perform *kora* in this street from the early morning until the late evening," Pradip said.

The view of an old-looking stone-paved street, lined by whitewashed houses with colourful windows on either sides and slowly trodden in by thousands of people in pursuance of their faith under the blue sky! The shops on the side offered everything – handicrafts, carpets, garments, paintings, pottery, and many other things. Many alleys from different sides were absorbed in the main street as if rivulets were absorbed in a river. We went along the street, pursuing our *kora*, amidst thousands of devotees, until we reached a big yard in front of a gorgeous white temple with gilded and red roof: gilded in the centre and dark-red on the peripheries.

"Jokhang Temple. Do you know it was built by Bhrikuti, a Nepalese princess married to a Tibetan king? Here, they know her as Harit Tara. I'll take you inside later," Pradip said, pointing to the temple.

". . . *Bhrikuti Tara Udaain Uttar China Tibbata* . . . . Bhrikuti Tara, the star, rose in the north, in Tibet, China. Do you remember the poem?" he asked, uttering the excerpt of the poem. "During our schooldays we would read it loud and rhythmically."

"We too," I said. The architectural majesty of the temple was distinct even from the outside.

"It was under her instruction that this temple was constructed. She's said to have played a significant role in expanding Buddhism in Tibet," he said.

Showing a structure in the yard, he added, "And that one Jowo Utra, literally meaning the wooden enclosure. Devotees light butter lamps in there. During Butter Lamp festival, this whole yard lights up."

Standing there, next to him, I took in the surroundings: the blue sky, the wide stone-paved yard, and the two tall pillars in front of the temple, hundreds of pigeons on the ground.

"The restaurant is only a short distance from here. Let's go," Pradip said and walked along the stone-paved yard; I followed him. I was desperate to see my working place as soon as possible.

Two

It was a two-storey building with four colourful windows in the facade. From outside, it looked old; the plaster in places had come away from the walls. But inside, it was elegant: elegantly decorated walls, decorated with *thangkas*; nicely arranged tables with flowered vases and sets of beautiful tableware on each of them; a small reception area on one side of the room and behind the reception bottles and glasses of different shapes arrayed on the glass shelves. Then I saw a pale brown girl with curly hair, emerald eyes, and elegant neck – a beauty, distinct from than I had seen so far – looking outside through the window, and at the farthest end of the room, a bearded white man, practically identical to the old days picture of Ernest Hemingway, sipping at his tea (or coffee) leisurely and reading, with all seriousness, a book *The Old Man and the Sea*, Hemingway's novel; this was the first view of the restaurant I came upon, the first impression I was given about the place where I was supposed to work. The restaurant was on the first floor. On the ground floor was a garment store. I had seen the store before walking upstairs through the spiral cemented stairway. The windows gave on to a view of Jokhang Temple and its wide stone-paved yard.

"Pema, where're the others?" Pradip asked the girl.

"Bidur and Tenzing are in the kitchen. The others haven't arrived yet," she said, looking at me.

"Good morning, sir," she greeted Pradip. Perhaps she was not expecting his early arrival with a new person to her and was not prepared to greet him. She became a little nervous (I supposed). It might be due to that nervousness, she forgot to greet him before she spoke. Now, after realising that she greeted him only after she said something, her nervousness grew even more. Her pale-brown face became red. Before Pradip introduced me to her, she scurried into the kitchen to hide her nervousness.

"Good morning, Dai." A young man and a girl came from inside. Bidur and Tenzing, I guessed. Pema had uttered those names.

"Bidur, this is Ashok about whom I had told you. He can speak English. For a few days, explain to him about the restaurant work. All right?" Pradip said, stressing the word *English*. He had not heard me speaking English as yet, and honestly speaking, I myself was not sure whether I could speak it in a practical sense. I had told him that in Kathmandu based on my limited knowledge of written English. I had very few chances to speak, to converse in English with other people, especially with foreigners, except with my teacher – an American who came to Nepal under the Peace Corps programme – in high school, which was a long time ago. I was not sure whether my pronunciation was comprehensible to foreigners. I should not have exaggerated, should not have blown up about myself. It was soon to be tested in a real sense. What if I could not converse? Pradip lit another cigarette. By the frequency of his smoking, it could be taken that he was a heavy smoker.

"All right, Dai," Bidur responded. Then he said to me, "Namaste, Ashok Dai." He addressed me as *Dai* as he had addressed Pradip. He looked younger than me.

"She's Tenzing," Pradip said, grinding his cigarette in the ashtray.

"*Tashi delek,*" Tenzing said shyly. She had a petite figure, reddish-white face, black wavy hair, light green eyes, and gleaming teeth.

"Namaste," I responded.

Pema was looking from the kitchen door – still curious, shy, and nervous as if wishing to come out but unable to gather enough courage.

"I'll leave now," Pradip said and walked out, leaving me with my workmates.

"Where in Nepal are you from?" I asked him.

"My village is near the border, not far from Khasa."

"How long have you been in this restaurant?"

"For two years."

"Your family?"

"I'm not married yet. My parents are in the village," he replied, smiling.

"Are there many Nepalese here?"

"No . . . not many. There're less than fifty, working here. It's not easy to get a work permit. Many people, even if they come here, can't work because of altitude sickness. I also had a serious problem in initial days. I was thinking of returning home. But later, I adapted to it. Summer is very pleasant here, in this valley, with a lot of greenery and blooming flowers. The level of oxygen goes up. But winter is terrible. You can't even see a single scrap of green vegetation. You feel suffocated. You're lucky. The warm days are around the corner."

He continued, "There're few others. Businessmen. Very rich. I have heard it said their forefathers came here years ago and started the business. Most of them are adapted to local society. Do you want to eat anything? I even forgot whether you ate anything or not."

It was not difficult to surmise that he loved talking. Certainly, for him to find a person from his own country as a workmate had become a matter of delight.

"No, I took a heavy breakfast. I want to make a phone call to my wife. She must be waiting for my call in the public booth in the bazaar. From where can I make the call?"

"There's a public booth near here. Right at the corner, on Yuduo Road. I'll send Pema to show you. You can go to the Potala Palace as well. Just to see from outside. We can go inside later. Inside, there're huge golden statues of lamas," Bidur said, asking Pema to help me. She was craning again out of the window.

"You can speak Tibetan?"

"You'll also learn. Quickly," he laughed. He wore dark-brown colours. He could not be considered as a handsome man, but his dark eyes, a little pouty lips, and gleaming teeth – that exposed fully when he laughed – offered a kind of smartness, friendliness, or even a sort of attraction to the opposite sex, I guessed.

The bearded white man was still reading as I walked out, following Pema, both of us wishing to converse but confused about how to start.

Over the phone, I told Sushmita everything about my travel, my stay, the restaurant, and the salary. I also talked to my daughters. She had been waiting for my phone call. She told me that she saw me in her dreams. In her dreams, both of us were planting vegetables in our Big Plot. The children were watering those plants. She told me that she had not thought she would miss me so much and would feel so lonely in my absence. My eyes were dewy as I came out of the booth. Both Pema and the old woman, working there as an operator or a money collector, looked at me with their sympathetic eyes.

"This is the way to the Potala. Go straight. Turn right at the end of this road. You'll see it. It's just a ten-minute walk from here. If you take another road, the road in front of our restaurant, go straight and turn left, it won't take more than fifteen minutes. Lunch time is about to start. I have to go to the restaurant," Pema said, still with her shy face.

"Thank you, Pema. I'll take the longer one," I said, pronouncing her name for the first time.

We walked together until we came to the restaurant, then she walked up through the spiral stairway. I moved ahead along the street, stealing a glance at her just before she entered the restaurant.

I walked along the street, Duosenge Road, looking at the shops, which lined up on both sides of the street and sold curios, paintings, and trekking gear; looking at the people walking along; or at the rickshaws moving ahead in twisting motions. The street soon ended and merged onto another street, Beijing East Road, which led straight to the Potala; I could see as I turned left.

The Potala stood gorgeously, awe-inspiringly, in the middle of the city. The whole facade of the white structure with the brownish-red part in the middle, which I had seen the previous day from the end of the valley, could be seen in its completeness. The structure was built on a hill. I walked along the paved ground amidst thousands of devotees, the Potala on my right. At the end of the facade, a cave-like restaurant was carved into a giant cliff. On my left, just in front of the restaurant, was a hillock with a small temple-like structure. In between the Potala and the temple-like structure was a gate, an arched structure. The *kora-path* then curved to the right leading behind the Potala. I walked along, spinning the wheels carved with mantras.

After completing a round, I entered a park and sat on a rustic bench beside a small pool under a willow tree. A little away, at the end of the valley towards the north, the brown mountains were nakedly standing. The clear water of the pool was reflecting the images of the overhung branches of the willow and the blue sky. The reflected images were moving along with the rippling of the water. A pair of doves came and rested, ruffling and then cooing, on the grassy ground and summoned up memories of Narrow Flatland and my family. It had just been three days since I left them but with the knowledge that I would not see them for a long time, I desperately longed for them. I felt so as I sat on the rustic bench listening to the pair of doves, cooing.

I got back to the restaurant to find a few tourists taking their lunch. The bearded one was not there. Pema, along with another waitress, was engaged with the customers. At the reception, I saw a slim, handsome lad, who must be Chhawang. Bidur had said Chhawang took care of the reception when Pradip was not in the restaurant.

Bidur was in the kitchen frying something in a pan. He looked smart in his chef's uniform, a white double-breasted jacket and a white toque on his head. His dark-brown colour looked even darker against the white uniform.

"Come, Ashok Dai. This is our life. Every day. Life isn't easy in a restaurant," he said, continuing his frying. "Did you see the Potala?"

"From outside. It looks magnificent."

"Yes, it *does*. There're many monasteries in Tibet. The Tibetans are religious and spiritual," he said. "I stay near the Potala, just behind it."

"Bidur La, chicken tikka. Four portions." Pema came with the order slip and put it on a table. Sliding a brief sideways glance at me, she went out. I was again confused what this *La* meant after the name of Bidur?

"It's a respect, somewhat similar to *Mr* or *sir* in English or *Ji* in our language. They normally use it to address the senior or whom they respect," he said upon my curiosity.

"How much do you get a month?" I was curious to know.

"Tenzing, bring some marinated chicken," he said to Tenzing, who was chopping onion. Turning to me, he added, "Two thousand and five hundred a month. Chinese Yuan. Not more than twenty-five thousand rupees. But in winter, it's only half. You know, tourists rarely come that time."

"Pradip didn't tell me that," I said.

"You'll know," he replied, threading the chicken onto skewers.

His working was fast. Adjusting the oven temperature, roasting the chicken pieces, cutting onions into rings, pouring lemon juice and mixing masala in the rings, arranging the roasted chicken pieces and decorating with mixed onion rings took no more than ten minutes.

I came to the reception. Some customers had already left. A few others were paying their bills. Pradip was at the reception, looking at a ledger and doing calculations. I took a menu and plunged into it. The menu contained different dishes – Tibetan, Nepalese, Indian, and Continental. The drink menu also covered varieties of hard and soft drinks. While looking at the menu, I twice or thrice managed to look at Pema, who was taking orders from the late customers.

After the customers left the restaurant, we took our lunch together. It was during this lunch that I was introduced to Chhawang and Dolma, my workmates. It was also during the lunch that I was given more information, information about the working hours, the tourist season, the holidays, and so on.

"Aren't you tired? I want you to have some rest. You must be careful at this altitude. You can start your work after about a week," Pradip said shortly after the lunch. His worry about my health had not gone away.

"No, Dai. I'm not tired. I want to start right from today," I said. It was not that I was not tired, but I did not want to stay idle. My family and hamlet were coming to my mind awfully, so I wanted to keep myself busy.

"You can start from tomorrow. Today, just watch how others work."

The restaurant became full in the early evening, six o'clock; the clock on the wall was showing. The bearded white man again came there. Ordering a bottle of Lhasa beer, he sat at the same table where he had sat earlier, reading *The Old Man and the Sea.*

I knew I had read that book before, somewhere. Maybe, I had borrowed it from my teacher, or maybe, I had borrowed it from my colleague who was doing his Bachelor's in literature. Probably it was his textbook. I did not remember the story in its entirety, but it was about an old Cuban fisherman and his battle with a giant fish in a faraway sea, about a detailed description of how he was able to bring the fish ashore after almost three days of struggle, and how the fish was eaten by sharks. The story ended with the fisherman dreaming of his youth and of lions on an African beach. It was something like that. After many years, as I saw the book, the blurred memory of the book, the blue sea, and other images associated with that book were brought back. What was also brought back was the seriousness reflected in the image of a bearded face of Hemingway.

I wanted to talk to the man about the book, but I was nervous. Pradip was at the reception and could hear our conversation. What if I was unable to converse with him; I was afraid. Then again, I thought it could be a good chance, a chance to show to Pradip and my workmates that I could converse in English. If I didn't speak how could I know whether my language was comprehensible or not?

Gathering courage, I went to the table and said to him, "Excuse me, sir?" My voice was nervous.

He looked at me with the same seriousness, which almost deterred me to continue further conversation with him.

"Sir, may I see the book?" I somehow asked.

"Sure," he said. I heard his voice, as serious as his face.

As I took the book and looked at the cover page, he asked, "Do you know about this book?"

"I had read it many years ago, but I forgot the story. Perhaps it's about a long battle between an aging fisherman and a giant fish in the sea," I replied, paging through the book.

"You speak English well. Where did you learn?" he asked me.

"In my school. We had an American teacher," I responded; I was being encouraged by his curiosity.

"Why did you come to Lhasa?" he asked.

"To work. I just came yesterday. I'm going to work in this restaurant."

"That's good. I'll be here for a month before going to Mount Kailash and will return after a month. I have finished this book. If you want, you can read it and return later. I'm Mark from the United States," he said.

"Thank you, sir. I'm Ashok," I said humbly.

Pradip and Pema were listening to our conversation. They were watching him giving me the book. Pema was gazing at me and the book in my hand. I felt good and excited. *Were they impressed?*

This very over-excitement, however, led me to a situation of perfect embarrassment that very evening.

There were still a few other customers. Chhawang, Pema, and Dolma were taking orders and serving them. After Mark left, I went to the kitchen to find Tenzing filling a few plates and bowls, probably five, with naan, rice, and chicken curry. Chhawang came in and took three plates, two in his left hand and one in his right and bowls atop the plates.

"I'll help you," I said and followed him, carrying the remaining two plates and bowls in my hands. Mimicking him, I tried to put the plates on the table in front of the customers. It was right at that moment the plate on my left hand slanted. The bronze bowl atop it slipped and fell on the ground with a harsh noise. The chicken curry spilled all over the floor. A few thick yellow oily drips spattered on the customer. The customers looked at me furiously; one of them nearly punched me. He was clenching his right fist.

Pradip came hurriedly. He begged excuses with the customers, "Extremely sorry for this mess. It was just a mistake. He's new in the restaurant."

"Why are you keeping such a bastard in your restaurant? Look, he spoilt all my clothes."

What a mess I created in the very first attempt! I was so embarrassed and afraid that my uttering of *sorry* was barely audible. As I tried to clean the floor, Pradip, with slight anger, said to me, "Leave it."

Pema came with a mop and cleaned it. It felt all eyes were on me. I went by the window table and stood nervous, humiliated, and frustrated.

No sooner had all the customers gone out than I went to Pradip and said, "Sorry, Dai."

"It's all right. I had asked you not to work today. I knew you needed a few more days to acclimatise," he responded. He took my mistake as an effect of the altitude. It was his greatness. He was a very humble person. His behaviour towards his employees was not arrogant at all; rather it was friendly and caring.

Such was my first experience with the waiter job: the mixture of contradictory feelings. Enthusiasm for the work in a new place, in a serene land and embarrassment over my ignorance about my job, despite my education; hope for scraping a living for me and my family and desperation of my compulsion to have left the hamlet; the warmth of my boss and gleam of Pema's emerald eyes and humiliation from the tourist who nearly punched me. Was it the right decision for me to come to Lhasa to work, despite the suggestion of my wife not to come? But what else could I do in the hamlet?

And in the evening, as I followed Pradip to his house through the old alleys, hissing the ancient stories, I was trying to convince myself, to justify my arrival in Lhasa and to be engaged in a job as a waiter. Yet a niggling thought about the disagreement, the gap between my educational background and my new profession and, with that, the strangeness and absurdity of my coming were somehow bothering me throughout the walk through those old alleys. In the courtyard, the mastiff, Tiger, was unhitched, burrowing his head under his belly. At least, I did not have to face his frightening look. Quietly but hastily, I followed Pradip upstairs to his flat.

Three

Pradip had advised me to have a rest for a few days, yet I came to the restaurant every day and stayed the whole day, keeping myself busy in the waiter job. It was difficult for me to stay alone in his house. The walk around Lhasa, the central Lhasa, including *kora* around Jokhang or the Potala, never took more than an hour, which was feasible to do in the morning or after the lunch hour when I had nearly two hours off. During that time, it was possible even to go to the park, the one behind the Potala, to sit under the willow near the pool and see the brown mountains in the north. So I came to the restaurant every day.

And initially, it was not easy to convince me about myself working as a waiter. It took days to overcome the niggling thought about the misalliance between my education and job. It took time for the pain of the mismatch to come off. In initial days, I had to come under many other instances of embarrassment, sometimes spilling the food from the plate on the floor, sometimes giving the meals to those who did not order it or the opposite way, putting too much whisky or adding too much water or ice, using a whisky glass for water and a juice glass for whisky, or many such others. For days, I had to come under embarrassing moments. To my workmates, I, with awkward styles of doing things, looking so immature for the restaurant job, was perhaps a subject of fun or even a subject of jokes. And to my boss? Perhaps he was thinking that he had chosen a wrong person for the job.

Anyway, my life in the restaurant started. It started with animated expressions in all artificial humbleness – *have you booked a table, sir/ madam? Table for how many people, sir? Can I take your order, sir? What would you want to start with?* As a waiter, I was supposed to do many things: setting tables, welcoming customers, taking orders, giving the order slips to Bidur or Tenzing in the kitchen, serving customers, cleaning tables and many such, which were not defined clearly. In addition, I had to work at the reception during the absence of my boss. Seen from outside or taken superficially, it did not require a great deal of theoretical knowledge to clean tables, to hold plates, and to serve meals, yet it needed a great amount of practice, the practical knowledge which I did not possess. The knowledge I had acquired through my study had nothing to do with my new profession, except the broken spoken English. The others in the restaurant were smart. Chhawang could hold three to four plates at a time and could carry the equal number of glasses. But I could not hold even two plates or two glasses. Bidur could make dishes while, at the same time, chopping onion or garlic or ginger or other vegetables, so fast and so nicely. I could not do that. Pema could set the table clothes on all tables in the restaurant within minutes whereas I needed far longer time. And once completed, they did not look nice at all. Pema had to reset them again.

One more thing, physically bothering me, was the utter tiredness at the end of the day. I had not thought working in a restaurant would become so much tiring for a man who had spent so many years living as a peasant, which required hard physical labour. Here I was tired more than in my fields. The long standing postures, the fast short walks inside the restaurant, and the busy moments during lunch and dinner times would make me utterly exhausted at the end of the day. Some nights, while sleeping, I would experience sudden cramps in my legs. The physical exhaustion was added to because of the altitude. I did not develop acute symptoms, but I never felt fresh as I would feel in the hamlet. There was a constant blankness in my brain; there was a continuous sense of lack of energy. There was a continuous feeling of lack of appetite. Bidur was perfectly right when he had said life in the restaurant was not easy.

If it was not always, more than often, the little hamlet and my family came to my mind sharply in initial days in the restaurant. Frequently and deeply, I longed to see them right away, which I knew was not possible to be realised. I had left the hamlet to earn a living, to make money necessary for survival of the family. Coming to Lhasa and working in a restaurant was linked with the future of my children. Despite my longing, it was not wise and possible to return at my will, bare hand. I was supposed to adapt anyhow to the realities, supposed to continue in Lhasa. I was supposed to suppress my will.

So, swallowing all pains, swallowing all pride of being an educated man and of being the eldest person in the restaurant, I started my new profession.

And it was Mark whose company helped me a lot to adapt myself in my initial days amidst those frustrations of a restaurant job. The bearded white man often came to the restaurant almost regularly before he left for Mount Kailash, and when he came there, he came with a book, sometimes books. Staying in the restaurant and studying for hours was his pastime or might be his hobby. Sitting in the restaurant at the same table, having teas or beers, and reading books with the same seriousness and the same solemnity seemed to be part of his life in Lhasa. It fascinated me. The seriousness he had on his face was impressive; I had hardly seen anyone sitting in a place and reading for hours before. From the second day, after he knew my name, he called me by my first name which gave me a kind of intimate feeling. He said he was a professor at a university in the United States and had been, for many years, visiting Tibet at least once a year, but always via Hong Kong or mainland China. He told me that next year he would try to visit via Nepal. It was an opportunity for me to talk to him every day. It helped me to practise my language as well as to overcome my shyness while talking with foreigners. Before he left for

Mount Kailash, he gave me a few books. After a month, he returned and stayed a week in Lhasa. Before leaving, he gave me a few more books.

And it was Pasang who offered me a great mental support in the new environment. From quite early on, he appeared to me as a pleasant personality with strong religious faith. He would come to the restaurant on a regular basis to have butter tea, coffee, or beer or just to spend time. On occasions, he would ask me (when I was free after the dinner time) to join him for the drink while, contrastingly, cautioning not to drink too much. He would ask me about Hinduism, about which I had so little knowledge. During lunch off, he would take me to *kora* around Jokhang or the Potala or would drive me in his Land Cruiser. I enjoyed his company. I enjoyed his simplicity and friendliness, enjoyed, with slight embarrassment, his talking about me and Pema, and his way of talking and pronouncing the words of my language difficultly, sometimes impossible to come across. He, too, was comfortable with my company. I thought so.

And through him, I met two other people whose company too proved to be very helpful to my adaptation to the new environment. Obviously, he, along with Pradip, had many friends and acquaintances, yet there were two – Dorje and Weihong – with whom they used to drink and play mah-jong. All they, of an age older than mine, were close friends. To this group of four, I had given my own name: a *close circle* or just a *circle*. This *circle*, with the occasional addition of a few others, but mainly just the four of them, used to come to the restaurant and stay in a separate room – the way to which was only through the kitchen, unnoticed by the people or customers at the reception – to drink and play cards or mah-jong, until late at night. After finishing the work, I would go to the room and would stay with them. In fact, I had to. I was staying in Pradip's house and had to wait for him. It was in those early days, in that hidden room, I developed relations with them, the members of the *circle*.

Dorje was an interesting man, full of humour. I had met him before I met him in the restaurant. It had come about all of a sudden. On the first or second Sunday, my day off, I was sitting on the rustic bench under the willow in the park.

"Are you from Nepal?" I heard someone speak in my language from behind. I looked around to find a short, barrel-chested beefy man around his fifties looking at me. Pot-bellied, freckled brown face, shaved head under a hat, a wide mouth, and a prominent nose – it was his personality, difficult to forget once you met him.

"I'm asking you. Are you from Nepal?" he asked again in his bellowing voice.

"Yes," I replied, almost panicking with this sudden encounter with a person, who spoke in his bellowing voice.

"Are you working here?"

"Yes, in Pradip's restaurant," I said, trying to adjust myself.

"Oh," he said. "I'm Dorje. I'm doing business here. She's my wife." He pointed towards a woman standing next to him, a beautiful figure yet dwarfed, to an extent dominated, by the unique personality of her husband. After seeing him, it was difficult to stray away the eyes.

"I'm Ashok," I said, greeting both of them.

"See you again," he said and walked away in his unique gait, strutting like a duck, his head upright and chest ahead.

Such was my impression of Dorje, the disposition he gave me during our first encounter. His humorous disposition came to me later; once he came to the restaurant to have dinner and to play cards or when he invited Pradip and Pasang to his house to have lunch and play mah-jong. I went there with Pradip. It was at these lunches and dinners, during these mah-jong and cards, I came to know about his full personality, his interesting physical feature added to by his friendliness and sense of humour, an absorbing personality, capable of drawing the attention of those around him. During the games and meals, whenever he spoke, people paid attention to what he said.

Yet another character in the *circle* was Weihong, a Tibetan beauty, possibly in her late thirties. It was difficult to guess her age, and she never told it. She would remain of the same age for years, so went the stories about her age among her acquaintances. She was gifted with a tall height, like Bayang, black wavy hair, light hazel eyes, shining teeth, and a great deal of sense of humour and articulation: quite an amusing woman to talk to and to be with. She was able to offer comic relief to viewers with her sexual and sensual styles. And her eyes? Sliding, within a minute, to all directions, towards males in particular. Was it her habit? Or did she have an insatiable appetite for male looks? I was not sure, but her attempts of attracting as many of men as possible, irrespective of their age, from the twenties to the sixties, were amazing. Sometimes I wondered if she would be able to continue that type of life in her fifties or sixties. It was not that she fitted into my image of a respectable or dignified woman, the image which had grown in me as a result of upbringing in a traditional constricted Hindu society, but she was friendly, frank and, more than that, sexy. In some ways, to me, she was a typical character, sibylline.

In addition to Tibetan and Chinese, she was well versed in English and Nepalese too. She always dominated the get-togethers and gatherings with her articulate manners until and unless she got drunk. Too much drinking was her problem. Once drunk, she hugged anyone, kissed anyone, and danced with anyone with an earthy sense of humour. Bidur had told me that she was unmarried. She changed her boyfriend very rapidly, almost fortnightly. Jokingly, exposing his white teeth, he had told me that she would approach me soon. Anyway, she was a well-spoken and attractive woman.

Her presence in the restaurant was very frequent, not only confined to dinner and mah-jong, but also extended to other occasions, both during the day as well as late at night. She would call me *Aashok* – my name with double *a*, just like Pasang. I was also invited for those late-night drinks. And while drinking, her manner was often titilating, saucy; frequently, she gave me winks, making me nervous.

Anyway, to my amusement or even a kind of privilege, I was well-accepted in the *circle*, the group of middle-aged people, despite the difference of age and despite the difference in status – all of them were from well-to-do family whereas I myself was a worker in a restaurant. But their friendliness and easiness did not allow me to think in that way.

This nearness with the *circle*, however, along with a slight favour from Pradip, a few but intimate conversations with Mark and getting books from him and reading those books in the leisure time, put me in slight oddness, in a kind of strangeness among my workmates. I was not accepted by them as I should have been. There was created a typical kind of boundary between us, especially between myself and the girls in the restaurant. The girls did not behave with me as they behaved with Bidur and Chhawang. I did not receive their laughs, their intimacy; their regards or respects I received though. They did not open out themselves to me. Dolma seldom talked to me. And Pema? The shyness in her face, which I had seen the first day, was always there. Tenzing was mostly occupied with Bidur. In a way, I was an odd man out among my workmates in the restaurant, older than all of them and behaving differently.

And it was because of this feeling, the feeling of not being accepted by them, I was, in retrospect, drawn to the *circle* more and more. And it was thus my relations from the early days in Lhasa were defined as to have working relations with my workmates and intimate and friendly with the *circle*.

My life began in Lhasa. Gradually, I grew to adjust to my life in the city and to my work in the restaurant.

I stayed another two months or so with Pradip in his house. Every morning, I would have the breakfast – butter tea, *tsampa,* and *balep* – in the finely decorated dining room smelling of the aroma of incense sticks. Every morning, I would walk through the crowded alleys and Barkhor Street, pursuing *kora*; would stand a few minutes at the stone-paved yard in front of Jokhang Temple, before going to the restaurant. I would work throughout the day. In the late evening, I would walk back through the old alleys, worn out. I had got rid of the fear of Tiger, the mastiff. I was not afraid of it anymore.

Afterwards, I shifted to Bidur's place, near the park behind the Potala. It was a two-storey cemented building – not of the Tibetan style – with six compartmented narrow rooms, yet to be painted; it lacked the Tibetan flavour and finish I had seen in other houses. The unpainted doors, the unfinished wooden frames, the cheap-looking glasses in the windows, the unpainted and cracked walls, the unfinished roof with different-sized cemented pillars, and the exposed rusted iron rods from those pillars, as if waiting for more upper extensions, now the idea of extension abruptly given up due to lack of finances or disputes between the owners or any other reasons whatsoever, gave off a sense of oddity in the neighbourhood. Perhaps the building was solely meant for letting out to individual tenants.

I moved to that house. On the lower floor, Jaya and Thakur had occupied one room. Another was rented by two ladies, Bindira and Prabha. All they worked in the same beauty parlour. Yet another room on the lower floor was occupied by Prahlad, a cook in a star hotel. Bidur was on the upper floor. One room on that floor was kept for the household goods. One room was vacant.

I rented that vacant room. The house had the western orientation, and all rear windows, including mine, looked east, offering the view until far away. A narrow bed just beside the window was positioned in such a way, depending on the position of sitting, it was possible to see the backside of the Potala and the park behind it as well as the willow and the pool clearly towards the south. To the north, there was a complete view of mountains. After coming to the room, I would always look at those scenes before I slept.

As Bidur had told me, there were not many Nepalese working in the city. In addition to those who stayed in that house, there were a few others, staying separately, in the place where they worked, with whom we did not have much time to meet. The tourist season had made all of us pretty busy. Bidur had told me that after around the middle of October, once the tourists would start to leave and the things would slow down, we would have more leisure time.

Among those in the house, my friendship developed with Thakur, a man from mid-south part of the country, somewhere near the Bagmati River – Madhesh, as he preferred to say – more intimately than with the others. Slightly younger than me, he had been out of the country for many years.

"You see, Ashok Ji, I left Nepal when I was fourteen. I worked in India for five years and another four years in the Gulf. This is my fourth year in this place. Sometimes I am afraid my whole life will be spent in foreign countries, in search of survival and little money, away from my land and from my daughters," he had said.

He had his wife and two daughters in his village, somewhere on the bank of the Bagmati River. Unlike his roommate, Jaya, from the same village, he was endowed with a great deal of practicality and a good sense of responsibility towards his family whom he had left for years. Soon after I moved to the house, it appeared to me that he was living a simple life, an abstemious life. Although he had not got a degree of formal education, he had read many books. We became close friends. We would go for our *kora* together. Every Sunday we made our meals together, walked together and went to the monasteries, also together. And if Pasang had free time, we had the luxury of riding in his Land Cruiser together.

It was on such drives that I gathered a little knowledge about the geography of the city, the name of the streets, and the sense of direction in the crowded alleys and the name of the rivulets in the valley. It was also during such moments when I went to Drepung and Sera Monastery, talked to lamas and stayed under the calmness of poplar trees, watched the little hares skipping around, and listened to the doves cooing. Through Pasang's driving, I was acquainted with a few miles of highways linking Lhasa with other cities, the highways upstream and downstream the Lhasa River and yet another highway towards the north-west up the Tilung River, a tributary to the Lhasa River. I knew about little cairns, the mini *stupas* erected on the passes, on the riverbanks, near the monasteries or anywhere in holy places by stacking flat stones.

On one occasion, on our way to Sera Monastery or on our return, Pasang pulled in his Land Cruiser on the side of a gravelled road and then showing Thakur and me two big flat stones at the foot of a barren and rocky mountain spur, he asked, "Do you know what those stones are for?"

We shook our head side to side.

He said, "They're our final destinations. Once we Tibetans die, we're brought there and are laid on those stones. Our bodies are cut into pieces way before dawn and are given to *dakinis*: the vultures, the angels from heaven. Then this life is gone, forever. That's our burial place, the sky burial. My father was buried there, and my mother was buried there. One day, I myself will be buried there. Life is so short."

He was calm. Once more he said, "If we all have to die, why do we quarrel and fight? Why do we compete with each other? Why do we behave so selfishly? Why don't we live in peace and love each other?"

Those were his words, elegantly revealing the simple truth. The reality of life and the hollowness of human arrogance were being exposed from those flat stones. I saw, in my imagination, a human body being cut into pieces before the first lights and given to the vultures and those vultures gulping the carrion. I sensed the whole philosophy of Buddha being revealed through simple yet philosophical expression of my Tibetan friend, Pasang. I was moved by the great philosophy of life being expressed so simply, so pragmatically on a sunny day under the blue sky near the sky burial place at the foot of a brown rocky mountain.

As presumed, along with the maturing of summer and with the valley becoming green and greener, like an oasis among the browns, the number of tourists in the city grew steadily. The restaurants, the streets, the alleys, the yards in front of Jokhang and the Potala and the park behind it became crowded with the western and Han faces. The arrivals of tourists made us busy. The restaurant was always overcrowded during the evening. Some days we hardly had time to talk to each other. I had to be entirely engaged at the reception. Pradip's appearance in the restaurant became less. He rarely came, and whenever he came, he did not stay long.

Four months, a third of a year of my stay in the city, passed by with those and similar activities. I accepted myself working in the restaurant to a large extent. I would call my wife every two or three weeks. In the late evenings, after I would return from the restaurant and would sit by the window looking at the park, the willow, the rustic bench, and the pool, I would imagine myself with them. The imagination would become more vivid in the moonlit nights when the water in the pool would gleam and the willow branches would rustle with the cool night breeze.

During occasional conversation, I was informed that things had not changed much since I left. The monsoon was not good this year. The rain came late, but once it came, it came in torrents. Big Plot suffered slides at many places. The children were fine, but there was no milk for them as the hamlet did not have a milking buffalo. Even Uncle did not have one. She often complained there was no cash at all. She was concerned about the upcoming Dashain. Last time, she had borrowed some from Devaki, my sister, for *ropain*, for the festivals and for the children. I promised I would send before or during Dashain.

Whenever I talked to her, my eyes always became wet and possibly hers as well; I could sense that from her voice. I would convince myself that I was not the only one who had left the birthplace, that it was not only me who had a great yearning to return to the country. All working there, away from their birthplace, must have had the same feeling.

Truly, all were longing for their soil and their family. Such feelings would be often expressed during the rare gatherings, on festive occasions, in particular, when we would meet each other. Even people like Jaya, who had been living a freer and unmarried life and would not show much concern about his parents otherwise, would recall his home and family with a greater degree of separation on such gatherings.

One day, spitting on the wall of the room, he said, "Dashain is just round the corner. Diwali and Chhat are not far. But this damned woman neither gives the salary nor gives her words."

Perhaps it was on the day of Shoton festival. All restaurants and beauty parlours were closed for the festival, and all of us living in the house spent the whole day together. Before the sun rose, we walked all the way up to Drepung Monastery to see a big *thangka* carved with a huge image of Buddha exhibited in the monastery, just across the stream among big cliffs. That day the people had gathered there from far and wide to see the *thangka*. Spending the whole day, we came back to the house, played cards, and then prepared dinner together. Bidur had arranged some yoghourt, the speciality of the festival and drinks too. We drank and talked about many things. Thakur looked worried about the late starting of the monsoon. Madhesh was dried out, he told us.

And now Jaya was spitting against his boss, a fat woman, who, according to him, was arrogant and never gave his salary on time. He was drunk, and when he was drunk, in total contrast to his sobriety, which was rarely spoken, carefree, content with his own life, not bothering anyone and not being bothered by anyone, he would become a little arrogant, a little abusive, a little violent, and at times a little sentimental, exhibiting different paradigms of human nature, depending on his moods. He would give frequent digs with his fingers or elbows and would give pats with his palm to the people sitting beside him, to the women in particular, including Bindira and Prabha. I was not sure if there was any sexually abusive intention in those digs and pats, but Bindira and Prabha did not like him much or at least his dastardly deeds after he was drunk. This fact was known to us. So whenever he said something in his drunkenness, we would prefer to keep quiet or change the matter. It was only Thakur who could argue with him.

"Why are you talking so loud? If she gives you your pay, you're going to finish the money before Dashain. Drinking in *nangma*," Thakur said.

"It's my money. I have to get it on time. It's my choice whatever I do with that money."

"It's all because of *you*. I myself haven't received the salary for last three months. She thinks I am doing the same as you are. Last time, she was asking me to give her my wife's bank account. She wants to send the salary to her as if I'm not taking care of my family."

"Oh, my father, my mother, and my country, I miss you all," Jaya filled his glass and gulped wholly at one go. Those words from his mouth at that time sounded a little funny, little ridiculous, yet they revealed his pain, his missing of parents and the birthplace.

So did all of us. Although we were of different cultural or regional backgrounds, our own sets of belief, what was common to us was that we all loved our country, Nepal, the birthplace. Such gatherings were the occasions where we could express ourselves fully.

It was that day I came to know that Jaya was indeed a heavy drinker. I came to know that Bindira had a sweet voice, that Prabha was divorced, and that Prahlad was in love with her. The same day, my suspicion came true that Bidur was in love with Tenzing. In his drunkenness, he told us about that, about how he fell in love with Tenzing and how he now could not think of living without her.

Thus, I spent four months in Lhasa. *Kora* around the Potala, sitting in the park, under the willow, and looking at the mountains had become my daily activities. My engagement with the *circle* was growing. During the day off, they would invite Thakur and me for dinner or drinks.

But my relations with workmates did not change much and kept remaining a bit distanced. I was taken as a serious person, not involved in the lighter side of life, although Pema and Tenzing sometimes displayed a critical expression, a bit satirical, a bit mocking expression, towards me, when I was absorbed with a book, in particular. It was only in late August, after Shoton, during the *linka*, I, for the first time, had the opportunity of mingling with them.

Four

It was early September. We drove on the same road through which I had entered the city for the first time. A little ahead of the carved image of Buddha where Lhasa Valley ended and another long, narrow valley started, we left the highway and turned into a narrow metalled road to our left. Then driving through a narrow bridge, we crossed the Lhasa River and turned left again. There, the road was muddy and rutted. The ruts were filled up with filthy water. After reaching a small patch of a grassy land, nestled in the lap of a brown mountain, the Land Cruisers stopped.

The place looked serene. The first thing I noticed there, before I got off the Land Cruiser or even before it stopped, was a small enclosure – walled by low rustic wood – abutted onto a small barn. A few sheep – rams, ewes, and lambs – grazing so far, flocked together and gazed nervously at the new arrivals. A small girl inside the enclosure, perhaps in her self-amusing job as a shepherd or just playing, looked confused and ran to a thatch-roofed cottage with an extended exterior with new thatches at the rear, from which came out a middle-aged Chinese man and a woman of almost the same age. The cottage was built in the middle of the grassy land; the backside extension must have been recently added to. The presence of the Chinese couple – possibly the landowners or managers or caretakers of the land with their peasant looks, the look roughened by farming and the ultraviolet effect of the Tibetan sun – in that solitary place was unique. Both of them had put the split cane hats on their heads. The couple grinned and said something in Chinese with Bayang. From the limited vocabulary, which I had gathered from little studies during the leisure time in the restaurant, I just understood "*Lee xianseng, ni hao*" meaning, "How are you, Mr Lee?" The little girl, still shy, joined the Lees, holding the hand of the woman. *She must be their daughter*, I guessed.

Pema and the others set forth to take out the things from the Land Cruisers and put them on the grassy land.

"Bayang, I think the place under that willow will be better. The place has both shade and sunlight," Dorje said, pointing to a willow at the end of the land towards the river. "We can also see the river view from there. Set the table there and take out the snacks and tea from the car. Ask Mr Lee for beer. What to take for lunch, we'll decide later. We'll walk around."

"And bring the mah-jong table," Dorje added in his bellowing voice. Dorje and Pradip, apart from their friendship, were also joined with a sort of family relation. Bayang, Pradip's wife, was his distant sister-in-law.

"How can you expect me to do these many things all at once while you enjoy walking?" Bayang said, apparently not happy with so many instructions and Dorje himself wishing to walk around.

But it did not have any effects on Dorje. Without paying attention to her annoyed look, he said, "There're so many of you."

He strolled on the grass along with Pradip and Pasang, smoking. Thakur and I followed them.

Bayang grumbled at having so much work to do and began to set the spot. Bidur and Tenzing looked at me in the same way as Bayang had looked at Dorje, annoyed.

We walked towards the back of the cottage and went to the other side.

The flattened area was not big, yet it looked that every piece of the land, every swath of the earth there, was well taken care of. As we passed the thatched cottage and walked ahead to the opposite side of the enclosure, I saw two small lakes, of similar size and shape, linked by a narrows-like structure, a channel, both the lakes and the narrows-like structure, covered with tall weeds on the sides. Across, we could see a vegetable farm – a small greenhouse farm – covered with white plastic sheets. The two parts of the land were linked by a narrow footbridge. The narrows-like structure had narrowed down under that narrow footbridge. On our side of the narrows-like structure young poplars and willows alternately stood at the gap of ten to twelve feet. The vegetable farm, in spite of its smallness, was done intensely. The land was divided into small allotments, long and narrow, in each of which there were different types of vegetables – tomatoes, potatoes, turnips and cucumbers, all ready to harvest.

"They're hard-working people," Pradip said, obviously indicating the Lees.

Once, about a month back, he had shared with me that the Tibetans normally did not eat vegetables. They preferred meat. Things, however, changed along with the arrival of Han farmers from the mainland, chiefly from Sichuan. Greenhouse farms were set on the riverbanks. Vegetables became popular and easy to get as well. Whenever we went to the market to buy vegetables and other necessities for the restaurant, I could see heaps of vegetables and most of them produced in those greenhouse farms.

At one end of the farm, I saw a tractor with mud-smeared tyres. It must have been the sole thing to dig the wide ruts in the muddy road. Perhaps Mr Lee would go early in the morning to Lhasa to sell his produce and come back through the same muddy way. The regular driving would have made the ruts wide and wider.

We watched the vegetable plots for a while and came back to our side, the side of the cottage, but this time not through the narrow bridge, rather circling the lake.

The yellow and russet leaves were indicating the exhaustion of Lhasa's short autumn. A small stream, the origin of which was somewhere in the mountain, merged into the lake, the one towards the mountain. From there, the water flowed, through the narrows-like structure, to another lake and then, through a tunnel, flowed down and merged into the Lhasa River. The whole system of the rivulet – from the mountain to the lake and to another lake and finally to the river – could be viewed from there. A pair of ducks, followed by little ducklings, so far straying on the ground, waddled to the lake and swam elegantly.

We sat on the ground near the footbridge under a young willow and looked at colourful fish – red and golden – swiftly swimming through the water and the water striders quickly moving on the surface. The land, the nice blend of natural gifts and human ingenuity, spoke of the industriousness of the couple, the commitment to working on the land. The Lees, their farming, their sincerity, and their love for the soil bore, to some extent, a close resemblance to my imaginary picture of Pearl S. Buck's characters – Wang and O-Lan, particularly Wang's love for earth – in her novel *The Good Earth*.

The setting was done. A square mahogany mah-jong table, two other oblong tables and a few steel chairs were set in the tree shade. The snacks, plastic plates, glasses and napkins were put on the tables. A few bottles of beer were kept in the water in a bucket. The carpets were spread out on the ground.

It was my first *linka*. A few days back, soon after the date for the *linka* was fixed, Pema had asked me whether I would attend or not. I had asked them what it was. It was a party; I was supposed to drink and dance, but not to read the book, she had responded teasingly.

"Is nobody hungry? Why doesn't anybody take snacks?" Bayang asked. "Let me begin myself." She took some snacks and sat on the carpet, cross-legged.

"You women have the appetite for food," Dorje said.

"And you men have the appetite for drink and smoke," Bayang responded.

"Pasang, where're the mah-jong tiles?" Dorje opened a bottle and filled the glasses.

"Inside the car. I'll bring them." Pasang brought a box and put near the mah-jong table.

The ladies served the snacks and beer.

"Everyone should drink and dance," Dorje said. "*Sapta.*"

"*Sapta,*" we all said, raising our glasses.

"*Aashok*, you'll also dance today," Pasang said. "With Pema."

"Why with Pema? Why not with me?" Weihong asked.

Everybody laughed. Pema slightly coloured. Perhaps, I did too.

The *linka* soon commenced in its full swing. We all took more sips. The *circle* set for mah-jong. Some others played cards, and some walked around. Thakur and I sat, watching them playing mah-jong. The tiles – minutely carved with the images of bamboo shoots, flowers, Chinese characters and circles – the dice and the shuffling sounds while they slammed the tiles down on the table and the amusement and emotion reflected on the faces of the players was amusing to watch.

Tibetan music played. Dorje refilled his glass, drank at once, and started dancing, leaving the mah-jong. I had not believed that he, with his pot-bellied and barrel-chested figure, could dance so nicely, with such effortless grace and could sing so solemnly with his bellowed voice. Soon he was followed by the others, but it was he who danced in the real sense. The fast up and down and back and forth movements of his feet and hands, his body posture and agility revealed his feel for the dance. Yet another property he possessed to draw the attention of the surrounding people. He danced. He danced single, in couple or in a group according to the demand of the songs. He encouraged all of us to dance. Once, he pulled me towards Pema, held both of our hands and made us dance, but within a minute, I withdrew. He himself danced with her.

The *linka* continued. Towards the afternoon, after the tree shadow could not shadow us any more, we moved into the cottage shed, the newly extended exterior of the cottage, from where we could see the sheep again with their nervous looks gazing at us. Weihong seemed to have got drunk. Drunk were the others as well, but the symptoms of drunkenness looked more obvious in her, on her reddened cheeks, in her narrowing eyes and her movements and voices. She sang many songs, her voice slurred, difficult to come across yet melodious even in that slurredness. At one time, she at once pulled me towards her and, holding my hands, tried to teach me the steps. Going all shy, I tried to free myself. And it was then, myself trying to be free from her and herself trying to hold on me, both of us fell to the ground; she was on top of me and gave me a long kiss, very near my mouth, making me more nervous (and of course tickled due to her warm breath). I was gasping when I stood up.

The celebration went about in full swing.

I was not aware at what time Bidur and Tenzing had disappeared. And Pema too. Still embarrassed (and tickled), I walked to the willow on the edge. They were on the riverbank near the confluence of the Lhasa River and the little tunnel. I walked down to them. Bidur and Tenzing were talking, sitting on the bank. A little away from them, Pema was making a cairn. On the side, there were a few more cairns of different size – a few intact and a few fallen down. Those cairns must have been made by the occasional visitors who came to that little land for the *linka* or for whatever other purposes. For a while, I walked along the bank, upstream, looking at flowing water and the waving ripples. Birds were flying over the river, a few of them swooping down, diving into the water, and again flying up. The transparent water in the river gave off the clear view of the mossy stones. After a brief walk, I came back to the confluence and stood near Pema, who was now making another cairn.

Aware of my presence, she looked at me with her emerald eyes, her body still kneeling over the cairn but her head up exposing her elegant neck. A few streaks of honey-red curly hair from both sides were hanging ahead adding to her beauty.

We had been working together for five months, and during these five months, we had met every day, except on my days off. But I had never been so close to her in such isolation. We had been rarely involved in personal conversation. She was beautiful and attractive. So despite the fact that I was determined to be honest with my wife and was determined not to engage myself with any Tibetan beauties as it had been the case for many other working in the city, at times her beauty would bother me, would make me feeble from inside, to the extent of shaking my determination to spend a morally abstemious life, away from carnal beauty.

A little feeling of romance came to me as I found myself with her on the riverbank, alone. Could I say anything to her, using this splendid occasion of isolation? If so, what to say? Anything romantic? But what?

I picked up a small flat stone from a stack she had gathered for making the cairn. Skipping it across the surface of the river, I asked, "Are you married, Pema?"

The stone hopped three or four times and sank into the river.

"No." I heard and looked at her. She was adding stones to her cairn.

"Do you have a boyfriend?" I asked, picking up another stone.

"Yes, he's in Xigatse, working in a restaurant," she said.

I felt a little bit uncomfortable.

I should have taken the news easily. It was not unnatural for her to have a boyfriend. There should not have been difficulty in taking the reality in. I did not know why, but I felt a kind of uneasiness or even pain after knowing about her boyfriend. Probably it was human nature, a primitive instinct; I felt uncomfortable with this piece of information.

I was consumed by jealousy for her boyfriend who had such a beautiful girl as his girlfriend and whom I had never met before.

I threw the stone with full strength across the river; *splash . . . splash . . . splash*: the stone hopped and reached the other side.

"Yes, I made it," I said, a little louder.

"What?" she asked.

"Nothing," I responded brusquely. I felt relieved to have become brusque with her who had told me that she had a boyfriend.

The gap between the descending sun and the contour of the mountains was narrowing down. On the river, there were reflections of golden rays.

"What about you? Bidur told me that you are married. Is it?" she asked.

"Yes, I have got three children and my wife is beautiful." I gave more information than she wanted with an obvious intention to irritate her, to take revenge for my jealousy of her boyfriend.

"I wasn't asking that," she said with a slight irritation. I became more relieved.

Both of us became silent and stood there, looking at the vanishing sun behind the faraway mountains in the west.

"Ashok Dai, let's go. It's becoming late." Bidur was calling.

Following Pema, I trudged up.

It was a week after the *linka* at the Lees' place.

"Whom and how to ask?" The question, which had been occupying my mind for a couple of days, came almost as a problem as I came out of the public telephone booth. I walked, squinting into the bright sunlight, along Yuduo Road – a wide, strongly built and nicely decorated street, probably the widest in Lhasa, originating from the stone-paved yard of Jokhang and leading to Kangang Road – after calling Sushmita on a Saturday afternoon. The Tibetan sun was bright even in the late afternoon, and I was heading west. There was less than a month for Dashain. I had not yet sent any money to Sushmita, which had made her a little worried or even suspicious of me, of my stay away from home. In our phone conversation, she had expressed her suspicion, implicitly though, that she hoped I still remembered them and that I was not spending much. The money she needed for the festive season was not much. It was twenty thousand rupees or so, and I had saved more than that. In fact, save the first two months when I had to spend money for the initial necessities (clothes, utensils, bedding, and so on), I was saving nearly fifteen thousand rupees a month. I could send her what she needed, but I was planning to send some more, some more to pay to Uncle, which had become, including the interest, more than eighty thousand. Before coming to Lhasa, I had promised him to pay before Dashain. Sushmita had told me that he reminded her of the loan every time she met him.

Strolling along the Yuduo Road, under the blue Tibetan sky, I approached Kangang Road and then walked back. I was more and more absorbed by the same question – how to arrange enough money before Dashain? I could not think about sending only after the festive season or once I had saved enough for the loan. I could not imagine the children roaming about with their gloomy faces and torn-out clothes and barefoot; I could not think of them being deprived of laughter and happiness during the festive season in my absence. Could I send only the amount Sushmita needed, forgetting about the loan? I thought for a while. This idea was not appealing either. How could I forget about the loan and make my wife more embarrassed? How could I not fulfil what I had said to Uncle at the last moment before leaving the hamlet? How could I forget the frowning of his greying brows? I was sure that as soon as Uncle sensed the money arriving at my home, he would not let my wife stay in peace until he got the money. I was aware of his concern for the money. Then how could I arrange the money?

Yuduo Road, in the central Lhasa, was the road for the well-to-do family and high-level officials in Tibet or for the western and Han tourists. On either side of the road, the most sophisticated stores in the city offered their services to the upper class. At the end of the road, I turned left and trudged up the spiral stairway.

Dinner time was about to begin. Bidur and Tenzing were in the kitchen. Chhawang had not arrived yet. Pema and Dolma were setting the tables with their usual indistinct murmuring of Tibetan songs. But their murmuring, which I would enjoy the other days, could not amuse that day. I just went to the reception and sat.

I had saved nearly sixty thousand. I needed equally the same amount. Who would give me that much money? My friends staying at the house were not in a position to give. Bidur himself was planning to go to home for Dashain. Jaya never saved. He always came to us. Thakur, with whom I was expecting, had asked me for some money before I had asked him. It was a week before we went to the *linka*; I had gone to his parlour, during the lunch hour, to have my haircut as well as to request money from him. While trimming hair at my nape, he had asked, "Ashok Ji, my sister-in-law is going to be married soon. They're expecting help from me. Can you lend me some? I asked Bindira and Prabha, but they don't have any."

His face had become darker. No sooner had he finished his than I had said, "What a coincidence? I also wanted to ask you for money."

With this response, both of us had laughed wryly. I did not ask any other Nepalese. There was no use to tap them for the loan, as they were confronted with their own problems, possibly more serious than mine.

I did not ask my Tibetan workmates either. I knew their salaries were given to their parents on the payday. I had seen their parents coming into the restaurant at the end of the month with their weather-beaten faces, seamed by the stack of Tibetan years and hardship, and waiting for Pradip to come and give them money.

And I could not dare ask Pradip.

I sat just behind the reception with no idea of whom to ask. Borrowing money from anyone was always difficult and embarrassing for me. Yet it never left me!

The evening appeared. Chhawang came, turned on the television and the lights, and checked the setting of the tables. With the customers gradually pouring in, I set about filling the glasses with my mind, drifting to my birthplace, the upcoming Dashain, and the loan.

The Xizang TV broadcasted a song, *Chhiring Laso, Chhiring Laso*, the one I had seen Pasang dancing to, with the tapping of his nomad boots in total harmony with the rhythm of the music, either at Dorje's house or at his own.

As I was thinking while listening to the song, Pasang appeared in the restaurant with his usual relaxed and smiling look. Without speaking, he mimicked the song, tapping his fingers on the reception table, which continued until the song gave out. Then he asked me whether Pradip was coming or not that evening.

"I don't know, Pasang La. He didn't tell me anything. Maybe he won't come," I responded. He pulled a chair and sat beside me.

I asked, "Would you like to have some snacks?"

"No, I'll take just a bottle of beer."

I gave him the bottle and glass.

"You don't drink?" he asked, opening the bottle with his teeth. It was his style. He never used the opener. Pasang, whenever he came there for his drinks, wanted me to join him and he would always pay for that. But for me, it would feel awkward to drink a free drink, paid by someone else, in the restaurant where I was working. But it was difficult to avoid his irresistible insistence. I would sit to drink with him, whenever I was free.

"No, Pasang La. I'll join you later. After the guests are gone."

The problem kept consuming me.

After the last guest walked out and the girls set about cleaning the table with their murmuring, I joined Pasang for a drink. Pouring the beer into the glass, I exchanged *sapta* with him and drank the whole glass at once.

Looking at me with little frowns on his forehead, he said, "Are you fine? I sense a marked difference in you. You look sad and pale, and you drink like a drunkard. I never saw you emptying your glass at one go. Tell me what happened to you."

I became a bit hesitant. I knew that Pasang had already read me, that he was aware of some kind of unease inside me, and that any attempt to fake my sadness or to give him a false impression would not satisfy him. Yet, I responded, "Everything is fine."

I poured beer into both the glasses.

"No. Something has happened. You have to tell me. I'm like your brother," he insisted.

I knew he would say so. I told him everything.

"How much do you need?" he asked.

"Around sixty thousand rupees. Six thousand in Chinese Yuan," I responded.

"That little money? You can borrow from me. Why didn't you tell me earlier? You should have told me," he said.

"Really?" I was excited by what he said so easily, but I was still hesitant. "But I can't pay at least five months."

"You can pay whenever you have. Five or ten months, it doesn't matter," his voice came as a great relief to me.

Pasang was rich. The richest in the *circle*, I was told so. I had heard that his business, the business of trekking gear, was running very well. His wife, Chhudun, was a smart businesswoman. It was she who took care of the business and ran as successfully as she ran her house. Their son was studying in the mainland in an expensive university. It was often told among the *circle* that Pasang came into a fortune after he married Chhudun. I had seen them, during *kora* around the Potala, offering generous alms to each and every child lining the stone-paved yard. However, I had not thought he would solve my problem so readily, or he would offer help to me so swiftly. I realised that the degree of any problem, the financial one in particular, would appear with different intensity to different people, according to their capacity. I looked at him with gratitude.

"Pema, can you bring me a case of cigarettes? If the nearby shop is closed, go to the right on Jhinju Road. They open until late," he said to Pema, lighting a cigarette, the last one in his case, and giving money to her.

"When do you need it?" Pasang asked after Pema walked out.

"As soon as possible," I said.

"You can come to my house. Or I'll bring here tomorrow," he said. "*Sapta*, now stop worrying and relax."

"*Sapta*," I said.

Pema came with the packet of cigarettes and joined us.

It was already eleven o'clock when I reached my place. The lights were off in all rooms. All they might have fallen asleep. Before sleeping, as usual, I opened the window; a shaft of moonlight slanted into the room through the window.

Five

After the *linka* at the Lees' place, the *circle* came together less often. A pause was created in get-togethers. Weihong had gone to the mainland to pursue her yearly routine. Dorje became busy with the business. Pradip also, leaving the responsibility of the restaurant upon us for the most of the time, spent his days mostly visiting the monasteries.

One Sunday afternoon, just before Dashain, I was in the room, lying on the bed. I heard a screech, as though a car pulling up in front of our building. From the Land Cruiser, Pasang and Pradip were signalling me to get down.

"Ashok, let's go to Drepung. We'll take you inside the monastery," Pradip said.

"Let me quickly change."

It had already been six months in Lhasa, but I had not got yet the opportunity to see any of the monasteries from inside. I had just heard about the majesty and the tales and mysteries of those monasteries from different persons I met in the city. So the idea of going inside a monastery was exciting.

And it was gorgeous in a true sense. The ancient monastery buildings sprinkled on a sloped patch of the land shadowed by the poplars and willows, below a rugged cliff of a brown mountain on the side of a sharply fallen away stream, spoke for itself the quiddity of its type.

"It used to be the biggest monastery of the world," Pasang said as we entered one of the monastery buildings. I had never seen such huge statues of Buddha in different forms, in different postures, indicating his incarnations in various epochs. A sweet aroma wafted from the burning sandalwood as we walked inside. Fascinated, I followed them bowing my head in front of those statues.

In whole life, I had gathered hardly any knowledge about religion. Even if I knew anything superficially, it was because of reading a few chapters of Mahabharata, Ramayana and a few other epics or because of being told by my grandfather and grandmother and, on occasions, by pundits. And what I got through those sources were more like stories. Many of them must have been purely anecdotal, created by pundits themselves on their experience and knowledge, and exaggerated on their own. I never took religion as religion. Therefore, on matters of religion, I always followed what seniors did, that also for the sake of showing the others. In the case of Buddhism, my knowledge was even more limited, limited to very superficial information about Gautam Buddha's life, a few of Buddhist mantras and the name of Tripitaka. That was all. Yet as I walked inside the monastery following Pradip and Pasang, following them to be on a safe side or to hide the nudity of my knowledge, I was overwhelmed by the colossal statues in different *mudras*, spiritual postures, by the walls adorned with carpets and paintings, by lamas enchanting mantras with a rhythmic solemnity, and by the sutras written in golden letters on ancient-looking brown thick paper and using quills of ancient big birds flying over the serene land (according to my own imagination). I felt I entered a different world, a spiritual world.

The outside environment was equally touching. The ancient structures on the terraced slope, the poplars and willows, the foliage of which were weathering by early signs of winter and the leaves of which had mostly fallen down only with a very few russet and yellow ones left in the branches; on the right of the monastery, while looking down, was the sharply fallen away stream; below a section of the valley; ahead, a stretch of the Lhasa River; across, the brown mountains: the view suggested the uniqueness and the antiquity. A few lamas were studying under the poplars. I just wondered about what Pasang said to me, sitting under a tree. When ten thousand Gelugpa Lamas in their maroon dresses would have wandered inside and outside the monastery; would have studied here and there in the tree shades, enchanted the mantras in rhythmic solemnity; and would have debated on the sutras in the courtyards with their assertive body postures, how marvellous the whole environment would have felt. Imagination itself was more than wonderful!

As we walked over the fallen dried leaves, making the rustling sounds, two hares (or were they rabbits? I never knew the real distinction between them) stood about with their alertness, their ears up as if eavesdropping on the human sound rare to that seclusion and hared away towards the stream. Curious and amused, we followed them and, upon our failure to follow, slaked our thirst with the fresh stream water. From there, we walked along a bridle path among the faintly green, otherwise brown, scrub across the stream, scrunching the pebbles under our feet, until the path gave out and the slope turned into a scree. Then we came back to the stream and sat on a big boulder, enjoying the low gurgle of the stream rushing down.

Later on, in the evening, Thakur complained why I did not tell him about the trip. I should have. His company would definitely have been enjoyable.

Dashain was just a week away.

"Thakur Ji, how did you celebrate Dashain last year?" I asked, looking at the browning grasses – some of them as tall and sharply bladed as in Chitwan, Nepal, in which even elephants and rhinos vanished – as we walked along a long and high wire fence built to protect Lhalu: a wetland in Lhasa, a marshland. Although I had, many a time, passed that part of the city with Pasang in his Land Cruiser, I had not been aware of the vastness and diversity of the wetland in such a precise way. Now, as we walked along the wire fence, before us were the swaths of land textured with variant objects and colours – the water, the weed, the green grasses around the swamp, the browning grasses a bit away from the swamp, and the russet ones farther away.

"How to celebrate your festival in a foreign country? In an alien land? There's nothing to celebrate," he said, his eyes gazed at the farthest patch of the wetland where the tall grasses, just below the bare part of the mountain, looked deep russet, the greenness surely sapped by the hardness of the weather. Past the russet grasses, there stood a few trees, also bare. There were a few houses among those bare trees.

"You know, there aren't many from our country in Lhasa. Most of them are working in restaurants, and they have to work on the day of Dashain also. It's only Pradip, who still celebrates Dashain. All others of Nepalese origin seem to have forgotten it. Last year, we organised a small party in your restaurant. We ate, drank, danced, and played cards. That's all what we did. No *tika*, no *jamara*. But you can talk to Pradip. If he agrees to give the place for the celebration, I'll inform all friends," Thakur added.

"Certainly, I'll request him. I don't think he'll say no. He's such a good man," I responded. "Let's celebrate, in whatever form it may be."

That Sunday, after our *kora*, we had taken a public bus from the nearest stop, the one next to the park, and had come to Lhalu. Walking alongside Lhalu was Thakur's choice. He would often come to this part for a walk or for a view of the marshland, which somehow looked like some part of the riverbank covered with tall bladed grasses near his village, he had shared with me. It was the only place in the valley where he felt relaxed. He was afraid of looking at barren mountains. For a man from Madhesh, who had grown up in the fertile lowlands, who had consumed his childhood among evergreen trees, who had spent early years in an entirely different set-up, a totally contrasting view dominated by enormous mountains without a scrap of greenness must have felt frightening. The reason behind his liking this place was understandable. As we sauntered by along the wire fence, a flock of birds, some kind of waterfowl, flew high above the marshland flapping their white and brown wings and, after making a few rounds in the sky, settled a little away in the marsh. Once, during one of the drives, Pasang had said Lhalu and the Lhasa River would be swarmed by thousands of ruddy shelducks, a type of migratory birds that would come to the valley every year in winter. The flock might be the first fleet of those ruddy shelducks or might be the local species; it was difficult to surmise.

"This is the only place that gives me a kind of freshness and peace. Otherwise, I just get suffocated. Let's sit here for a while," Thakur said, sitting on the ground, slightly mounded and grassy, under a willow. I sat on another mound.

"Don't you like Lhasa?" I asked him while picking up a stone and throwing it in the marshland. A bird flew away from the place where the pebble reached whereas the throwing was purposeless. It was not aimed to scare the bird away.

"Who likes to work abroad? Do you like? But what can we do? I want to settle in the village with my family and want to do a little farming. However, the circumstances always compel me to stay away from them. It seems I'll never have time for my family," he said. His dark face darkened even more.

"My father died when I was in Delhi. Mother died when I was in the Gulf." Adding with a deep sigh, he plucked a blade of a dried grass, chewed on it for a while, and spat. "I couldn't even give them a spoonful of water when they died."

"It's so sad," I said. "By working so many years abroad, you must have saved a lot of money."

"No. How to save? To speak truthfully, I haven't saved any. I had saved a little when I was in the Gulf. But the food, the clothes, the costs of medicine, the festivals, the rituals and customs, the school fees: there're many expenses, and everything has become so expensive. Whatever you save is just for scraping by. And when you're abroad, all your relatives expect from you. You know well."

"Yes, that's right. These days, if you don't have cash, you can't survive," I said. It was difficult to reject what he had just said.

"It seems the whole of my life will be finished up in struggle, the struggle for survival, the endless struggle to get enough to eat and to feed. Happiness always seems to be elusive for people like us. To me, it looks as life is overwhelmed by the problems that appear in a variety of forms. Sometimes it comes as illness and sometimes in the form of droughts and floods on the farms. It always comes, never misses. This year the Bagmati turned the whole field into a desert. My wife was saying the layer of sand is half a foot thick. It may take a few years for the field to get its fertility back."

Fixing his eyes somewhere in the marshland, he had revealed the fate of millions of Nepalese. There was nothing to disagree.

"My wife also told me that the rain came late in the hills. But when it came, came in sheets. She was saying all fertility of the fields vanished away with slides. The paddies and millet plants look pale as though they're sick," I said. "Yet we need to struggle. It's all about life. We need to move on. Happiness lies in accepting the things as they exist."

"They say so, but it's not easy at all to accept the things as they exist. We're not god, not Buddha. We're human beings, full of emotions and expectations. We always expect better. Accepting the things as they exist might be easy for other people, not for me."

My fake philosophy was dwarfed by his strong logic.

"But, Ashok Ji, tell me why did you come to Lhasa? Bidur told me that you have got a college degree. You could have found a good job in Nepal."

"Thakur Ji, you know, things are not that simple. I couldn't find any jobs. I tried a lot but couldn't find. Our education? You know it doesn't give bread. It just produces a spoilt, confused, and incapable group of people. There's a serious flaw in our education system."

"Let's forget about these things. We have come to work in Lhasa. That's all." I stood up, brushing the dirt from my pants.

"If you aren't tired, I'll take you to the riverbank." He also stood.

"Oh, will you? I love to see it."

We walked a little farther along the wire fence and then turned left onto a street, the name of which I did not know. It headed straight towards the Lhasa River. Walking on the street, he told me that many nightclubs, karaoke bars, and massage parlours were newly opened in that part of the city. Many of the Nepalese working in the city, including Jaya and Prahlad, would finish their salaries in those places, Thakur had said.

The street looked lull in the daylight. *It must have thrived at night,* I thought.

"Have you come here at night?" I asked him.

"I came once with Jaya in a karaoke bar. I finished a month's salary for a few bottles of beer and the fake laughs of the girls. The next day, I regretted. I remembered my wife, went to the Lhasa River, and swore I would never do it again. From that day, I have not come here. This place isn't for us. Jaya doesn't listen to me. I told him many times. But he never cared. He finishes his whole earning here," he said. "It's just between us, Ashok Ji. He's a very spoilt man. He drinks a lot, and after getting drunk he can do anything. Last week, he misbehaved with Prabha. She complained to Prahlad. There was almost a fist fight. I somehow managed to calm them down. I asked him to say sorry to her. The matter somehow subsided, but still they don't talk to each other."

"He drinks so much?" I asked.

"He can hit the bottle, however strong it is. We're from the same village. He's unmarried. His parents are very old. I asked him to send money for them, for those aged parents. But he never sends. I don't know what to do with him. He earns more than I do, but he finishes everything just for drinks and girls as if money grows on trees."

Thakur's practical look at life and his family, his simple version of complicated things, his love for his family, and his intimacy with his village was firm. He had a clear analytical perception about many things.

We reached the river and stood about on the shingle bank. Here, the river had narrowed and curved. Towards both ends of the valley, the river looked much wider. At this point, however, the extended belly of the mountain on the other side had pushed the river to the city, and the city, in turn, had adamantly pushed it back to the mountain. The river was forced to narrow itself, tolerating the pushes from both sides.

The Lhasa River, its geography – the curves, twists, and bends – the smooth flow with gentle ripples, the shingle and sandy banks, the glints during the sunrise and sunset, the swiftly swimming fish and water insects, the birds flying over the river, the ducks and geese floating on it and ruffling their feathers, and its colour somehow resembling the sky: it had struck me as being scenic as much as Lhalu, the marshland, had given attraction to Thakur. How would it feel to be on the bank of the river in the full moon night and to see the moonlight gleaming on the water! The thoughts were tempting.

We walked on the riverbank, downstream. A little down, there were a few women and men, the labourers, hammering the stones – a scene similar to any riverbanks in Nepal.

"These pebble stones, I know, would be used for huge constructions – houses, roads, or any other cement constructions – and those who make them painfully would, after such hard work, get a little money to buy bread and butter," Thakur said as we stood about, watching them hammer.

Among them, there was an old man hammering the pebbles with his shaky hand. I could not guess his age precisely. With his old and weak-looking features, his seamed face bathed in sweat, and his fragile hands shaking while hammering, it was not difficult to assume that he was moving towards the end of life. Yet he was hammering the stones with all expectations, with enormous wishes to survive, with loves for his life, revealing the endless struggle of life.

Shagged as we were from the daylong walking, we trudged towards our house. We prepared dinner in his room. Later the others also, once they returned from the work, joined us.

Without the slightest hesitation, Pradip accepted our proposal to celebrate Dashain in his restaurant. And we celebrated. As I was informed by Thakur, with the small Nepalese community in the city and many of them working on that day too, there was not much to celebrate, and as was indicated by him, the celebration took the form of eating, drinking, singing, and dancing. It lacked the cultural flavour I was thinking about. Yet it offered the occasion for mingling and having lighter moments.

The weeks went by. Weihong had not returned yet. So the *circle* was not active yet. Pradip rarely came to the restaurant. I would look after the accounts and all other financial matters associated with the business. I had set a routine for the purpose of reporting to him about the business. I would go by his house twice a week, routinely. He was happy with the flourishing business. During our regular shopping at the farmers' market, he would often tell me that the business this year was the best in his whole life. Bidur was on annual leave. Dorje was busy in his handicraft shop, crowded by tourists even in the last days of the season. During the *kora* around Jokhang, I could see both him and his wife busy selling antiques. He could sell his own sandals as antiques after a few years; the people would often say so behind him. Frequently, I would meet them around the Potala: he himself strutting fast counting the prayer beads and his wife struggling to keep pace with him, her presence behind him dwarfed as always. Pasang continued to come to the restaurant in the evenings to have drinks. His coming there and drinking beer always pleased me.

So in some ways, as the weeks passed by, life seemed to have advanced smoothly, without obvious hassles or difficulties. But this smoothness turned out to be temporary. It was suspended by yet another hiccup, one in the series of hiccups in my life. My wife informed that Seti, our buffalo, which I had bought a few years ago for fifteen thousand rupees and presently would value at more than twenty-five thousand, died during Tihar festival. The death came about suddenly, she told me. On the day before Lakshmi Puja, Seti refused to eat; the following morning she could not stand on her hooves, and she had a terrible swelling in her stomach; and by that afternoon, she died before Sushmita could call the veterinary doctor, I was informed. The information was also about the poor harvest of rice and millet. The produce was reduced by half than last year. It would not even see six months out; I was worried. The smoothness appeared to be fake, or it could not endure in my case too as Thakur had said.

Pasang had again read my face. Upon his question for the reason, I answered him that nothing had happened. I did not want to overburden him with my problems. This time, perhaps, he did not doubt. He just said, "*Aashok*, I think you read too much and think too much. Don't think a lot. Try to enjoy yourself, try to take things easily."

"OK, Pasang La. *Sapta*," I said, trying to smile.

"*Sapta*."

We raised our glasses, looking at the evening crowd in the stone-paved yard in front of Jokhang.

In the late evening, however, while walking to the room, I was worried for the loss, a sudden loss of twenty-five thousand for nothing. The loss had occurred on the day of Lakshmi Puja. Was it indicating a bad omen for the future? It worried me.

Tibet's harsh winter took over the valley and the purlieus with all its strength. The browns of the mountains deepened. The poplars and willows had gone bare of leaves much earlier. The sun was taking the southern course. The raw winds passed through the valley and went south. The ruddy shelducks came in fleets and swarmed around the rivers and on the marshland. Tourists disappeared from the city. Nomads and the people from the countryside came and roamed around the alleys and streets. They stood basking in the sunshine on the stone-paved yards in front of Jokhang and the Potala with their unique nomadic dress and braided hair. Long, sheathed knives hung from their waists. They bore the usual Tibetan look: a kind of easiness and perpetual smile on their weather-roughened faces.

The business slowed down. My workmates had the luxury of abundant time to talk, to play cards and noughts and crosses, or to shuck the sunflower seeds in the restaurant. And for me, time for reading. There would come a few Tibetan customers during dinners, but during lunch times, no one except for a few lads, who would come there to see the girls in the restaurants rather than to eat or drink.

On an occasion, during such leisure, sitting at a table beside the window, I asked Pema, "How does your boyfriend look like?"

She was looking out through the window. Her eyes were fixed on the nomads basking in the afternoon sunshine in the yard. I asked her about her boyfriend in the same way, all of a sudden, as I had asked three months back during the *linka*. My relations with the girls in the restaurant could not become comfortable as if there was a barrier. Was it because of the age difference? Perhaps not. They were friendly with the people much older than me, for example, Dorje and Pasang. Then was it because of my habit, a rarely spoken person, an introvert man, a reserved personality? I did not know, but my relations with them could not become friendly and frank even after months. Including with Pema. Our little conversation on the riverbank during the *linka* did not produce a lasting friendship. Yet there was something in her that always interested me. Was it her beauty? Or was it her careless style, indifferent towards many things? Or indifferent attitude towards myself? Mostly, she was on her own. Whenever she was free, she loved to look out through the window, as I had seen the very first time, the very first day I came to the restaurant. I was attracted to her, in what way I myself was confused though.

"He's very handsome," Pema responded without looking at me.

Maybe it was because of her response or her indifferent attitude or both, I got slightly angry. I wanted to say: *so what*? But holding back anger, I asked in a mild tone, "Why don't you ask him to come here for a few days, or why don't you go to Xigatse to see him?"

As she was about to speak, Pradip and Pasang came in, and she sidled into the kitchen.   "Ashok, let's go for a drive. We'll take you to a new place," Pradip said before I greeted them. "Chhawang can take care of the customers if they come."

It had been fairly long, almost four, maybe five weeks that I had not gone for a drive with them. Driving was Pasang's hobby and to a certain extent Pradip's also. The presence of a third person in the Land Cruiser had added an extra amusement for them. I myself was always pleased to join them.

Unlike previously, this time we did not cross the bridge over the Lhasa River, but rather followed a narrow road that passed the university and ran along the northern side of the river. The road went ahead, passing through a small village with a cluster of few traditional houses. A little ahead, past the village, the flocks of sheep were grazing on the dried scrub. Up, on the slope, we could see a few yaks. The road then wound up leading to a pass, the top of a mountain spur where Pasang pulled in the Land Cruiser on the roadside.

Before us, a little away below, in sight was the complete panoramic view of the valley and the river. The sinuous river emerged from the mountain gap miles away in the east, snaked along the valley with its fascinating glints and disappeared into the mountain gap miles away in the far south-west. The sky looked bluer and closer as if one could touch it. On the other side of the pass, below, was another small valley, separated from Lhasa Valley by the spur on which we were standing. A tiny village, the barren slope smoothly fallen away towards the river and the traffic-less road, only trodden by flocks of sheep and a few young shepherds: the seclusion was so intense that one would not be able to think anything about the outside world. One would feel the whole world confined within the small valley, one's heart would just stick there, in that valley shaded and silhouetted against the afternoon sunlight under the blue sky.

There were little cairns and prayer flags atop the foothill. Both Pradip and Pasang sat on the mounded ground near the cairns facing towards the city and lit their cigarettes. They rarely talked while they had a drive or a walk together. What they had in common was both of them loved smoking and enjoyed the wisps of the smoke.

I gathered a few flat stones from around and set about to make a cairn.

"Who taught you to make the cairn?" Pasang asked, exhaling smoke.

"It was you. Did you forget you told me about it?" I responded, adding stones to the cairn. "And once, I saw Pema making them during the *linka*."

"I think you love Pema. If you love, just tell me. I'll talk to her seriously," Pasang said, grinding his cigarette.

"No, Pasang La. My wife will kill me."

"She's not here. She won't know. *Aashok*, you read too much. Just be like Bidur. Do you know he loves Tenzing?"

"He's unmarried. Free to love whomever he wants."

"Who told you he's unmarried? You say this just because he told you. Nobody has gone to his house. Nobody knows whether he's married or not," Pasang said.

"I don't think one has to lie about his family. Certainly, Bidur isn't that sort." I took the side of my workmate. In fact, I never thought in that way. We had known each other for seven months, but he never mentioned his wife.

"He's married. I have seen him going to public telephone booths every day. I don't think he goes there to call his parents so frequently. It must be his wife. He's a very clever guy."

"Let's go," Pradip said.

"That's why I tell you not to read too much. What do you find in books? Life is in *nangma* and karaoke. Just go there with Pema and enjoy yourself," Pasang said, putting his hand on my shoulder. "OK?"

"OK, Pasang La. I hope her boyfriend won't kick me out from *nangma*," I said, laughing. They also laughed.

We drove down the valley on the other side of the hill following the twisting road, which went ahead through the houses and passed two or three smooth bends and entered another valley. Again the flocks of sheep grazing on the side of the road; the shepherd and herdsmen; a few houses and a few Tibetan faces; the terraced fields in the winter barrenness, and in those fields two or three silo-shaped wooden structures, tall, as much tall as the poplars in the thin wood beyond the field and fresh-looking haystacks stacked on those wooden platforms (were they Tibetan-style silos?); and a little down, a little away sinuously flowing river and around the river the ruddy shelducks: the view offered a virginal country flavour. We continued until a narrow road split away from the main road and after a narrow bridge merged onto the highway. The highway led to Nyingchi, a prefecture in eastern part of Tibet; I was informed by Pasang during our drive on this highway weeks ago.

Here, our drive turned right, to Lhasa. On our way, we halted at a lone resort for drinks. I had noticed a few resorts in this part of the valley on our earlier drives. We had halted in a few of them to have drinks. Pasang knew all of them. This time, we halted at a resort nearly a mile away from the highway towards a mountain. As we got out of the Land Cruiser, a mastiff, unhitched, looked at us with its stern eyes, making me sick to my stomach in the same way as I had felt in Pradip's house on the very first day of my arrival in Lhasa. I tried to hide from its furious look and walked in between Pradip and Pasang, who did not care much about it. With an old yet impressive edifice in the middle and many other small open cottage-like or gazebo-like structures around the edifice, newly built, a few colourful tents pegged to the ground, the bare willows, the rustic benches, and the web of recently gravelled paths in the ground: the cottage presented a mixed feeling of newness and rustic country flavour. We walked towards the backside scrunching the gravel under our feet. Even in winter, a little greenery was maintained at the resort, mainly at the back of the edifice, which had a small lake, a little bigger than at the Lees' place. There was not a stream or rivulet to let in and let out the water. Might be, underground culverts were fixed for this purpose.

A girl came out of the edifice and with her *tashi delek* asked us where we preferred to stay: inside or outside.

Pradip asked her to set the table just beside the lake. She disappeared to come again soon with two other girls, who set the table under a leafless willow in such a way that allowed us a wider prospect of the lake and beyond. Little away from the lake was a low slatted fence, beyond the fence a farm, past the farm a small village, then the mountain climbing up at first smoothly then abruptly.

"*Kayrang gi mingla karay ray?*" Pasang asked her name in Tibetan, closing the menu.

"Yudun," she responded in her shyness. Her cheeks flamed as three pairs of eyes looked at her. Her small figure, black wavy hair, light green eyes, shining teeth, and a red hat on her head brought to my mind the similitude of Tenzing's look. Almost the same. A bit roughened by the country habit – a habit of carelessness for one's own beauty – she possessed a young country woman's dash.

"Where're you from?" Pradip asked.

Blushing more, she pointed her index finger towards the small village nestled in the lap of the mountain.

"Do you have boiled potatoes?" Pasang asked her.

"Yes."

"We'll have just boiled potatoes and Lhasa beer. Bring three bottles. I need a matchbox too," Pasang said, taking out his cigarette case.

"Let's take a meat item as well. Can you make *gong bao chicken?* How long will it take? I'm bit hungry," Pradip added.

"About twenty minutes," she said and scurried to the edifice.

Meanwhile, we skirted around the lake and went beside the slatted fence. From there, the village could be seen in more detail: a few houses, the whitewashed walls with pasted yak dung, a few wooden platforms with silage stored therein, and a thick cloud of smoke billowing from a chimney of a house, the biggest one. The smoke must have emanated from the burning of dried yak dung – the main source of energy in rural

Tibet. The smoke soon dissolved and disappeared into the sky. On the roof of a house, a few men and women were hammering down on the flat roof, repairing it or making a new one, and while doing this, they were doing a rhythmic duet. I guessed Yudun's house must be one of those. A few feet away from the fence, there was a yak, gazing at the mountain. A thick coat of brown-and-black fur, pointed horns, a bunchy tail, and a docile look: I was seeing a yak from so near for the first time. Indifferent to our presence, it continued to ruminate and gaze at the mountain.

"You know? The yak prefers to graze than being fed by humans. While grazing on the mountain slope, often it goes on and on. After it reaches scree, or a point from where there's no way to move ahead, it tries to turn, but it can't. Most often it loses its footing and hurtles down the slope to become the carrion of the vultures," Pasang said. "This animal! It can survive days just by chewing on the scrub twigs and licking the stones."

"Shoo," he shooed the yak. The yak lumbered away towards the village without looking at us.

As we sat for the drink, a few ducks swaggered to the lake and progressed ahead.

"Weihong called me yesterday. She's coming next week," Pradip said, inhaling the smoke deeply and then raising his glass. "*Sapta.*"

"*Sapta,*" Pasang and I reciprocated.

"Her absence is boring," Pasang said.

"She's the one who makes our group lively. I'll organise mah-jong in my restaurant once she comes," Pradip said.

The evening breeze swept the surroundings. The ducks were taken to the pen. We uttered our last *sapta* and left. Before leaving, plucking up enough courage, I asked Yudun whether she would invite me to her house sometime in the future. With shy red colour on her face, she said, "You can come during Lhosar."

I smiled. Pradip and Pasang smiled. The whole valley smiled.

Soon we were driving back along the highway. On our right, swaths of land had been turned into the greenhouse farms, and the farm lanes in those farms were snuggling down under the thick quilt-like cloths to keep the vegetables warm and growing. A little down, a little away, the Lhasa River was flowing.

Six

At the beginning of February, the winter was still in its full strength. The dry, cold wind blew continuously through the valley, frequently in dusty gusts. Thousands of ruddy shelducks reigned over the rivers and the marshland with their orange-brown body, plumaged whitish head, and white wings with black feathers. But they had begun to look north with curiosity; they were waiting for their retreat to the northern lakes and swamps. The nomads still basked in the sunshine in the yards and pursued their *kora* around the monasteries.

The absence of greenery was stark. The level of oxygen went down to the minimum. The precipitation was rare and mostly in the form of a few snowflakes, which were quickly absorbed by the dryness or were flown by the strong winds. Just once or twice, I saw tree branches giving under the weight of snow. That too did not last long. I hardly saw an accumulation of snow in the valley. The accumulation was limited atop the mountain ridges and in the ditches and hollows on the slopes. The effect of the chill and dryness, combined with the lowered level of oxygen, were acutely felt in my daily activities. The most difficult times for me were the late nights and the early mornings. The cemented structure with no sources of heating was extremely cold. One would feel as if sleeping in an open icy field. In bed, I would use as many as four hot-water bottles to keep warm; I would wear more than an inch-thick cotton trousers, a full cotton vest of similar thickness, two pairs of socks, gloves, and a beanie down to the ear lobes and eyebrows, yet I had to snuggle down under two thick quilts, which I had bought at a cheap price at Barkhor Street. The exposed parts of the face felt as if they did not belong to me. The acuteness of cold was even sharper inside the toilet, the window glass of which was cracked with a hole in the corner. Bidur had put a thick paper on the crack to block the cold air. He had also put shims to fill the gap between the cheap plywood slabs in the toilet door. The cold wind, however, somehow would find its way to the room. It would turn the upper part of the water in the bucket into a skin of ice. We had to use hot water to defrost the frozen water inside the tap. It was my first winter in Lhasa. Perhaps, therefore, some kind of suffocation, dryness, and gasps, even in slow walking or little labour, were not uncommon.

Yet I continued my routines. I continued the *kora* around the Potala. Each morning, bundled up in the layers of warm clothes, Thakur and I would come out for *kora*. Afterwards, after *kora*, Bidur and I would go to the restaurant. In the late evenings, we would walk to our room predominantly following the same route, the route that skirted the Potala from the right and, on a few occasions, following another route, little shorter and darker. Then, during Sunday off, Thakur and I would walk along the fence around the marshland and go to the river or for a drive with Pasang, sometimes to the resort, sometimes to the Lees' place, and, infrequently, to the monasteries. Every Sunday, I found a little time to sit on the rustic bench under the willow. Occasionally, I joined the *circle* during their drinks and mah-jong. Life, thus, took a routine course to follow; in a way, it was settled within a boundary.

But was it actually settled?

It had already been nine months. I could say it was my second year in Lhasa. It was difficult to ascertain whether time went by quickly or just dragged by as it was difficult to say whether my life was settled with the working in the restaurant and following a routine path of life or was unsettled with this working in an alien place without the warmth of Narrow Flatland, with no idea how long I would be working in this city. Superficially speaking, my life settled, but the very idea of living a settled life in Lhasa was deeply unsettling.

One Sunday, as I sat on the bench in the park, some sort of confusion about my stay in Lhasa, a sibylline dilemma, overwhelmed me.

Practically speaking, the nine-month period was not a long time. But I was feeling I had not seen Sushmita and children for years. The children must have grown up a few more inches, I would often think. The brief phone calls to them could not satisfy me. Sometimes, I thought to briefly go back, just for a few days. But it was not easy. It would cost money, another couple of thousand rupees, which I was not in a position to bear. I had yet to pay the loan to Pasang. The buying of another buffalo had cost twenty-five thousand rupees, my wife had told me; I had yet to pay that. She had to take again some more from Uncle for fixing the slides in Big Plot caused by the havoc of the monsoon and for other trivial necessities. I had yet to pay that amount too. I could not see any possibilities of going home at least until another Dashain, after another eight or nine months.

That Sunday, after some account work, I had walked to the park and sat on the bench. The bench had the strong effect of the season. It was cold. The bare willow branches hung brown. But there was no water in the pool to reflect them. It had been drained and had been turned into an ugly concrete hollow with rotten plastic, papers, rags, shoes, and dried twigs at the bottom. I did not know the reason for the draining. The purpose might be for the cleaning or maintenance, or it was because of disturbances in the supply of water, but it was drained as were drained away my hopes that I, together with my wife, had imagined before I came to Lhasa: working abroad for four, maybe five, years and saving money and buying some fields or to engage in a small business, then pursue the rest of life happily. The fantasy, in its extreme, had reached a dream of making a small house in the bazaar or in Pokhara. For such purpose, my stay in Lhasa could be extended for a few more years. But the experiences of the first nine months indicated that the reality was different. The dream we had seen seemed to be disappearing. After nine months, I did not have any savings. The income expected in the coming few months had been booked for expenses that had already occurred. With initial experience as a waiter, a labourer, it had become clear that making a fortune abroad was not easy as I had taken it to be before leaving the hamlet.

It was obviously not that I was living an extravagant life as my wife suspected, and indeed, her suspicion was growing and growing. Phone calls to her had been narrowed either to listening to her suspicions or convincing her rather than talking about the children and other matters. My life as a waiter, unlike many others, was narrowed to the work place, the room, the park, and the books. I did not go to karaoke or *nangma* or for drinks except for on the occasions when I was invited by Pasang or Pradip or Weihong. It was just once that I went with Bidur, Tenzing, and Pema. As Thakur had said, I spent the whole salary of a month. I was aware that I did not have the luxury of an extravagant life, but once you are in a group or crowd, it would become difficult to isolate your ideas and actions from the whim of the group or crowd. The remaining rationality was absorbed by the drunkenness. So it was thus; I spent a month's salary in a single night. And to be honest, it was just for once, and I deeply regretted it, like Thakur.

It was also not that I was engaged with girlfriends like Jaya or Bidur or Prahlad. Somehow my relations with women or girls became in a way rather superficial, maintaining a distance. I never entered into the depth of sentimental relations. During the initial days, I had a slight feeling that there was something – something extra than the sole distanced friendship – between Pema and me. However, the revelation of her boyfriend and my wife on the riverbank during the *linka* at the Lees' place and her indifferent attitude towards me made me think differently that there was no possibility of any romantic relationships or any such things.

It was only once that Weihong had put me in an awkward situation during a drink at her house – elegantly decorated with Tibetan and Chinese decorations – a few days after she returned from Nanjing. I did not know I was the only one there. She had told me that she had invited two or three other friends as well, but they did not come. As she drank a few glasses of whisky, she became titillating, difficult to ignore. Her sensuality was amorous and tempting. I realised she was making advances; nevertheless, it was somehow averted. It was averted by a phone call from someone who initiated a long conversation with her. After the conversation, after she put down the phone, she looked serious, tensed, and irritated. I concentrated myself on the pictures pasted on the walls of her room. We drank a few more glasses before she dropped me off at my place. That was it with Weihong.

Thus, it was not the case that I was spending money on girls and drinks. Expenses, however, came in different forms; they came in trivial necessities: enough to soak up the little money.

And thus, after nine months of stay in Lhasa, on occasions – after I called my wife from the public booth on Yuduo Road, or when I sat on the bench under the willow looking at the northern mountains, or when I sat by the window before sleeping, looking at the dark or silvery nights, depending on the position of the moon in the sky – I began to develop serious doubts whether I could stay for long thus. I grew to question the very purpose of staying. The fascination, the excitement of coming to a foreign land had eroded. The erosion did not come because I no longer liked the city, the valley, and the people. Always, they had charmed me to the level of fascination. The solace offered by the brown mountains, the sinuous river, the ancient city, the monasteries, and the people were still overwhelmingly existent inside me. But the erosion came because I could not believe that it was possible to achieve the very purpose of leaving the motherland. The little money I was saving did not offer the sense of certainty or security for my future. And with this awareness of insecurity, I saw the future of my children also being insecure.

About this awareness of insecurity, about the uncertainty of future life, sometimes I would share with Thakur. After sharing with him, I would become little relieved. As the days passed by, Thakur became closer and closer to me. We were from different backgrounds – he was from Madhesh whereas I was from the hills; our mother tongue was different. He loved his culture and I loved mine. Yet we had certain similarities. We were both from the same country, working far from our motherland. Our financial situation was somewhat similar – overawed by a kind of perpetual dearth. Our ancestral vocation was the same: little farming, directly related to the soil and the monsoon. Both of us possessed a responsible sense of a father and a husband. Such similarities of our situations had framed our mindset in a similar way; talking to each other brought solace to our despondency.

It was during our walk, he had said he too did not want to stay abroad for long. He told me that whenever he went to Nepal on his annual holidays, he always thought he would not return. However, the choices were rather limited. The situations – the limited options or no options at his disposal – compelled him to pursue the path to the alien land again and again. The case with other colleagues also must be the same. It was not difficult to guess. No one would have willed to leave the family without obvious reasons and compulsions. Whenever I talked to Thakur, my anxieties always lessened. I was impressed by his simple logic, without any hypocrisy.

The stream of my thoughts was disrupted by the sameThakur, "I knew you're here."

I had not even noticed at what time he came there and stood beside me.

"I waited for you for a while. But later thought you might have gone to the restaurant. So I went for a walk," he said again.

"I had gone there for some account work," I said.

"It's too early to go to the room. Let's go to Barkhor. It's a while I haven't been to that side. What do you think?"

"Why not? Let's go." I stood up. In fact, I also had not been to Barkhor for some time.

We came out of the park and walked along Beijing East Road and turned right on the crowded narrow alley, near Pradip's house. The alleys, as always, were full of men and rickshaws and smells. The shops were crowded with groceries and other stuff. We could see beheaded full size yaks lying and hanging in butcheries. The alleys and streets in Barkhor were geared up for upcoming Lhosar.

"Lhosar is the greatest festival for the Tibetans. They celebrate for a month. This year is the Ox Year. The next one will be the Tiger," Thakur said to me as we walked along, his voice being muffled by the voice of the crowd.

Lhosar approached. The valley and the tops of the mountains or foothills that were accessible and provided a vantage point for celebrants were decorated with prayer flags. The eight auspicious symbols, the moon, the sun and other images were carved on the walls of the monasteries and houses. The altars were adorned with Buddha's images, *stupas, thangkas,* the seven offering bowls, and the *chemar bo,* full of *tsampa* and barley and wheat. Candies, cakes, fruits, breads, and *chhang* were put on the side of the altar. Not only the houses, but also the streets and alleys smelt of the festival specialities: *torma, momo, chhang,* and *guthuk.* The people visited the monasteries, invited relatives, drank *chhang,* and exchanged greetings.

Perhaps it was on the seventh or eighth day of Lhosar that Thakur and I were in the little hamlet, Yudun's village. The day was the seventh or eighth day after Lhosar, the middle of February; I could say so because the previous night the half-moon had appeared from the middle of the sky even before the waning of the afterglow and also because that year the Tibetan New Year fell on the eighth of February.

We got off the old bus about half a mile away from Yudun's resort, walked along a dusty road before entering the little hamlet of six houses fenced with a stone wall, which had crumbled in places. Yudun was there to greet us with white silken *khada*s, murmuring in a sweet voice, "*Tashi delek.*" She must have already taken a bowl of *chhang*; her voice sounded melodious. Her eyes looked a little intoxicated. She was adorned with her Tibetan dress, a white shirt and green robe printed with cup-sized white flowers, and a blue hat, matching the colour of the sky.

"*Tashi delek,*" both of us reciprocated.

Hers was the biggest house, the biggest in the hamlet, which I had seen two months back from the fence of the resort. A few children, five or six, all newly dressed, appeared in front of us with their curious smiles. They curiously gazed at us, more at Thakur, at his trimmed beard. For them, it was new, to a degree, amusing too, to have two Aryan faces in their solitary hamlet. A young lad, a slender figure, came out from the inside and exchanged *tashi delek*. He was her younger brother, Dawa. Introducing us to him, she led us to an elderly man, sitting on a cushioned chair in the yard, "He's my pala."

"Pala, *tashi delek,*" we said almost together with our hands in the position of *namaskar* and gave him a packet, which we had taken with us as a gift for him. Inside the packet were a few packets of cigarettes, chocolates, and a small box of fruits and a bottle of whisky, which Pradip had given to me.

He stood up, saying, "*Tashi delek.* I'm Nima." He mimicked us and raised both his hands in *namaskar* posture and asked us to have seats in the chairs beside him.

His seamed face and ripe hair spoke of at least sixty or more than that. Yet in the depth of his eyes, there was a shine. He still had an impressive degree of agility. His respectable straight height yet to start bending with the effect of age added a distinct impression to his personality, making him deserve the respect from anyone who came across him. We too addressed him as *Pala*. He was in a brown hat, a double-layered robe with stripes, and boots up to his knees.

"Yudun said you're from Nepal. Where from Nepal?" he asked us.

"I'm from the hills in the western part near Pokhara. My friend, Thakur, is from the mid-southern part of Nepal. Pala, have you ever visited our country?" I asked in broken Tibetan, which I had learnt over the months.

We sat on the chairs. Yudun, meanwhile, brought a *chogche*, which she put in front of us. The children were still looking at Thakur, his beard especially.

"Yes. But it was long ago, nearly fifteen years back. I visited Lumbini. We travelled via Pokhara. I don't remember too much about the road. We had followed a narrow, curvy highway through the green mountains, full of trees. There were many rivers running at the bottoms of those mountains," he said, straying away his eyes somewhere else.

After chatting for a while, following Yudun, we went inside, the darkness of which required a few minutes for the adjustment of our eyes which had just been in the bright light outside. The altar and the decoration, although they were not as lavish and equipped with stuff as in the houses in the city (where we had been invited to celebrate the festival, earlier), spoke of enough care and faith of the person whoever had built it. *It must be Yudun*, I thought. After the death of her mother, she was the one to take care of most of the household things and religious rituals. She had told me this during the second visit to her resort. We picked up a pinch of *tsampa* and offered three waves with our thumb and ring finger – for the sky, the water, and then the earth – and put some into our mouth. We had learnt the ritual of offering from seeing other people doing the same during the celebration at Pradip's and others' houses. We did not know whether we learnt the rituals in precise details or if there were omissions or additions. Nevertheless, we were satisfied that we were following the rituals with all our respect to their culture.

We came to Pala. Yudun had brought many dishes of Tibetan cuisines and put them on the *chogche*. She had also brought a big jug of *chhang*, the bottle of whisky, a few plates and bowls with silver lines, and silver-coated glasses. The house, the decorations, the furniture, and the cutlery suggested Pala lived a comfortable life, perhaps a life of the upper-middle class.

"How do you find Lhasa? It must be difficult for you. You're from the lowlands." His question with *the lowlands* was perhaps to Thakur.

"At first I had difficulties. Now I'm used to it. Winter is hard for me. I often get headaches. But summer is OK. And people are friendly," Thakur responded while I looked at Yudun pouring *chhang* into our bowls.

"Let me taste the whisky," Pala said. "You should take local products to survive here. They help you to adjust to this hard climate."

"I didn't ask you whether you preferred *chhang* or whisky. We Tibetans prefer *chhang* to other drinks. It's only in recent days they have started drinking beer, especially in *nangma*. I'm taking whisky just to taste it. Later this evening, I'll take *chhang*. Enjoy yourself. This is our festival," he added. "*Sapta*."

"*Sapta*," both we said.

"I also prefer *chhang*. It tastes smooth," I said.

Pala did not stay much; he took another bowl of *chhang* and left us saying, "I need to go to see my elder brother in the next village and will be back in the late afternoon. You'll stay here tonight. I know you have nothing to do in the city during Lhosar. They'll show you the nearby area."

Thakur and I looked at each other, undecided on this suggestion (somewhat authoritative) to stay overnight there, at his house. When we had left, we had not planned to stay in the hamlet. We were planning to take the last bus to the city.

Dawa added, "We'll show you our dance, the circle dance." His intention was obviously to lure us for an overnight stay.

"Why not, Pala?" I said ending our indecision.

He walked away in his agile gait, showing yet another feature of his activeness, and vanished in the distance. Yudun and Dawa, until now looking hesitant to talk to us due to the presence of their father, joined us. Dawa seemed interested in whisky; I guessed as he poured a hefty measure into his glass. Yudun did not take drinks, just sat next to us offering more drinks and snacks.

"You had said you would come earlier. We had prepared many more dishes. Many of them had already been finished," Yudun said.

"We wanted to come but had to visit other houses. Dawa, do you go to school?" I said, sipping at *chhang*, which had already grown to give me its effect, slightly. I seldom drank with an empty stomach before the sunset.

"In the ninth grade," he said, taking a deep sip. His face grimaced at the taste of whisky. "It's too strong."

"You can add water," Thakur advised. The drink and our chatting, which never concentrated on a single issue, went for another hour. The boy's interest was varied and had no patience to stay on.

The children disappeared just to appear soon after. Their disappearance and appearance and gazing with their curious eyes and glowing cheeks had been continuous ever since our arrival in the yard. Sometimes, they even ventured to nibble at the snacks. But they could not gather enough courage to talk to us up until Thakur said to them, "*Tashi delek.*" They blushed and vanished away, then again appeared and one of them courageously replied, "*Tashi delek.*" Thakur then became engaged with the children.

A female voice, which sounded familiar, came from a neighbouring house, "Yudun."

"Coming." Yudun scurried towards the direction of the sound.

And as she came appeared with another lady, I was astounded to see her. Astonished was she too, to see me. It was Pema with the same emerald eyes and elegant neck. She was flawlessly decorated in Tibetan dress.

"Ashok La, you're here?" she exclaimed.

"And you're here, Pema?" I mimicked not knowing how to respond to the sudden encounter.

"Yes, this is my village where I live. But tell me how you're here, all of a sudden, beyond the city and without any books."

"Although you didn't invite me, Yudun did. I'm going to spend a night here at her house in your village," I said with slight cheekiness as I often used while talking to her.

Yudun looked at us, surprised to know that I already knew Pema. She got more surprised once I said we worked together. The entrance of Pema on the scene made our further hours in the solitary hamlet more comfortable. Three of them took us to every single house in the hamlet, introduced us to each and everyone, including the rheumy-eyed mastiff. As the resort was closed, its boss from Sichuan had asked her to take care of the massive mastiff.

The houses in the hamlet stood closely, except for one, which was a little away from the rest and looked desolate and old. The ruins suggested the house had been abandoned for years. At present, it looked tumbledown as though waiting for a final tumble down to the earth. It was Pema's grandmother's house. She had died of her old age, Pema told us while we walked along a narrow alley. The house had remained unoccupied, and the harsh seasons had hit it ruthlessly, withering it fast. At night, the children were afraid of the old house. Pema herself was afraid of the possible encounter with the ailing apparition of her dead grandmother. A little later, we stepped up and down a wooden stile in the fence, stepping into the farm, which abutted onto the hamlet towards the west. The farm was ploughed and sown, but the grain had yet to sprout, still in their dormancy. I was aware of the lengthy lifespan of the crops in Tibet, the drastically slow growth process, slowed down by the altitude and cold.

"The climate is very harsh for plants in Tibet. Wheat plants often struggle to adjust to the variation of temperature between the night and day. They take almost nine months from sowing to harvesting. In the daytime, irrespective of the seasons, green plants and leaves wilt due to the harsh sun," Thakur said while we walked through the fields.

We then followed them to a place a little up in the mountain where a few feet of scrubbed and rocky slope had flattened and developed into a little spur. The climbing was not more than a few hundred feet, and they were there within minutes, but for Thakur and me, it took more than half an hour. As we trudged up, each step felt like climbing a high mountain without oxygen and finally, as we, clambering through the scrub, reached the point with drumming heartbeats and bellowing gasps, they looked at us laughing. We just sat there looking at the prayer flags and cairns. The people of the hamlet had chosen the spur for their religious offerings. A little farther a few sheep scampered about and a few yaks lumbered along nibbling the scrub twigs. Pema set about making a cairn whereas I snapped off a twig and tried to shoo away a yak, coming near to us. In response, it gave a dismissive shake of its head. Another round of laughs erupted from them and this time from Thakur too.

"Ashok Ji, the yak doesn't obey you," he said.

I kept quiet. Pema shooed away it with her authoritative sound. The ladies of the land were far better than us in every aspect required for living in that land. We sat nearly half an hour there looking at the serene environment and adding stones to the cairns. Then we came down to the fields and walked to the resort.

The resort was closed for maintenance purposes. The owner had left the responsibility of looking after the resort to Yudun. The compound looked untidy with construction materials – the gravel, stones, sand, bricks, and iron rods – piled up here and there on the ground. Ambling along in the compound, as we reached the lake, a few ducks came out of the lake shedding water from their white feathers.

"Who takes care of these ducks?" I asked.

"They don't need much care as long as there's water and mud and weeds in the lake. Twice every day, I come here to pen them in and out and to give them fodder. We don't have cats in our hamlet, and there're no wolves in this part of Tibet. *Dakinis* are fed with human corpses and stay around the sky burial places. It's only the mastiff I need to worry about, which has never pounced on the ducks," Yudun said. "Have you seen our sky burial places?"

"Yes, I have. The one in the city. With Pasang, you know him. But I wonder why the corpses are given to the vultures," I said, although I already knew the reason.

"Because we believe *dakinis* are angels. They take our souls to the heavens. We stay there until our reincarnation. I'll also be fed to *dakinis* once I die."

"You believe in reincarnation?" I asked her.

"Yes. Why not?" she said confidently, once again, making me amazed at the plain trust and faith in the Tibetans. Whoever they I met, they showed their complete faith and wholehearted trust in their religion and culture. There was no room for doubt. That must be the reason behind their happiness and satisfaction from what they have.

Pema and Thakur were ahead of us already in the fields. Dawa was walking with us.

Tired from hours of wandering about and climbing up and down, we came to the house and sprawled on our beds in a tiny room. A shaft of the late-afternoon light was piercing through the gap of the window and slanting into the room. Dust particles were dancing and twinkling in the narrow lighted space that reminded me of my childhood: lying on a narrow bed in the little room and watching the shaft of light coming in, in a cone shape, through a small gap in the roof and the dust particles shining and dancing inside the cone-shaped light. Thakur too was gazing at the dancing dust particles; perhaps he was recalling the similar reminiscences.

We woke up before sunset to find the others busy with the evening preparation. Pala was already back. A few more tables and chairs were added in the yard. Heavy smoke was billowing from the chimney. We could smell the tempting smell wafting from the kitchen. The mastiff, attracted by the smell, was sitting in the yard with its rheumy eyes, gazing at the kitchen side. The children again came and engaged with Thakur while I talked with Pala. The people from other houses in the tiny hamlet and purlieus converged in the yard. The feast started, accompanied by drinks, talk, and the ripples of laughter: the mirth of the festival. Thakur and his beard looked to be the focus of the evening. In addition to the impression of his beard, another reason for his quick absorption with the locals must have been his fluent and idiomatic expression of the local language, I guessed.

"I was born in the Ox Year on Sunday. This is my sixth Ox Year," Pala said in response to my curiosity about his age. "I don't know whether I'll see another Ox Year, but before I die, I wish to visit Lumbini once again."

My assumption of his age – at least sixty – was right. (I was aware of the counting of the years in Tibet: each symbol of the year rotating every twelve years.)

"You're most welcome, Pala. We can go together. And you have to stay at least a night at my house," I said and proposed *sapta*.

The more I talked to him, the more impressed I became. He was a man of experience.

The half-moon – until now faded by the daylight – appeared and brightened in the sky and poured its faint mellow silvery lights in the yard. And as they all, including the children and the aged, danced the circle dance with their unmistakable steps and as they sang with their melodious voices – all their sounds sounded in perfect harmony – I realised Pala was right. He had said, before joining the dance, "The love for dancing and singing is deep-rooted in the Tibetans. In Tibet, we say those who can walk can dance and those who can talk can sing."

The smoke and smell of smouldering dried yak dung, which Dawa had put at four corners of the yard before the sunset, were warm and pervasive.

"Ashok La, come. Dance," Pema whispered in my ear with a husky and slurred voice and pulled me and Thakur up for the dance.

Dance had never been my subject. I could never dance, never had courage and the knowledge of moving my steps according to the song or music. So I soon retreated to my seat and sat.

In the sky, the stars faintly twinkled. The mountains feebly glittered in the dim lights. The ambience beyond the hamlet was quite solitary. I did not know how far the voice of the song emanating from the yard echoed, yet it reminded me of the nights in my birthplace when I would hear the muffled sounds of the *rodhi song* and *madal* that travelled from Gurunggaun, up in the mountain, all the way down to Narrow Flatland. The faint music, the melodious sound of the song, would always help me to have a sound sleep after the brief awakenings in the middle of the night. Had I heard this song from half or a mile away from here, from another nearby village, I would have had precisely the same feeling as I used to have after hearing the remote *rodhi song* in my childhood. The human nature, the aspirations, the hopes, and the desires deep down could not be varied much despite the socio-cultural differences or differences in living standard or despite differences of geography. Even if they varied, the variation must have been just a matter of degree. That night too, the sounds of the *rodhi song* and *madal* must have been echoing in Gurunggaun and Magargaun with the same enthusiasm and gusto as was being reflected in Pala's yard in Tibet.

Thakur was still dancing with his odd steps. Pema was trying to teach him the steps. I poured *chhang* into the bowl and emptied it. I wished I could have learnt dancing.

The dancing, the singing, the drinking went on until late night, until the half-moon traversed the distance for that night and glanced off its last smile from the horizon before disappearing. The people then dispersed. Thakur and I also snuggled down under the soft, thick duvets in our beds in the tiny room.

The next day, in the late afternoon, before we left the tiny hamlet and got on the bus, Pala raised his hand and said *"kha leh shu"* (goodbye – said by the person staying). Lhosar, the hamlet, the locals, our wandering about, the drinking and dancing in the yard became an unforgettable part of our life in Lhasa or maybe in our whole life. The ownership, the affection, and the nearness we received from Pala were difficult to forget.

"The Lhasa River looks as big as the Bagmati in winter," Thakur said, gazing at the river a little away on our right on our way to Lhasa on a public bus.

Seven

In early June, the Land Cruiser was heading north, upstream the Tilung River. The speedometer was showing ninety, which felt a little excessive on the bent and nearly empty highway: the emptiness supporting the solitariness – disrupted only by occasional appearances of the grazing sheep and very infrequent tiny hamlets on the sides of the highway. The high mountains on both sides stood bare. The sun, as usual in early summer, was shining brightly. The green barley and wheat plants in the fields had shrivelled even before noon. The early summer had already made it being felt in the valley along with warming days and nights. The cerulean sky above the river was circumscribed, narrowed by the high mountains. Inside the Land Cruiser were the five of us. Dorje was driving. Pasang, relieved of his driving job, was singing. His song, the *so ya rie lo*, had begun soon after we left Lhasa. Thakur was enjoying the outside view. Sprawling in the front seat, Pradip was snoozing, his head nodding slightly towards the window. We were heading to Namtso Lake.

The idea of visiting the lake had sprung from one of our get-togethers. Pradip, slamming the mah-jong tiles down on the table, had proposed the outing to Namtso. Perhaps the imminence of tourist season had spurred him to have a relaxed trip before the beginning of the busy time. He had been busy immediately after Lhosar. There were things to be fixed, to be replaced, and to be newly arranged in the restaurant, which had literally taken the whole spring season. During those fixations, renovations, and new arrangements, he was quite busy. He would wake up early in the morning, circle his *kora*, observe every patch of work cautiously and continuously, check and recheck the authenticity and accuracy of the works. If necessary, he would trawl many shops for the construction materials, engaging in vigorous bargaining. Sometimes, some of the days, he would even skip his regular *kora*. After the renovations, he and his wife had gone to the border to bring groceries.

Once he came, he became engaged for the tourist season. Whenever he was in the restaurant, he would give us instructions about our duties for the upcoming season. During one of such instructions, Chhawang had reminded him that the salary in the restaurant had been the same for last three years. Patting Chhawang's shoulder, he had assured the increase would be made before Lhosar. We all had wryly smiled at his assurance that would possibly be implemented nearly after nine months. Afterwards, after he left, I was told by my workmates that he had promised the same the year before too, which was not realised and was eventually forgotten by Pradip himself. Anyway, we all admired him for his friendly manners towards us. He never did let us feel that we were not part of the restaurant. I had heard about the rudeness shown in other restaurant towards the employees. We were lucky at least in that sense, Bidur had said to me.

I looked at him. He was still snoozing with his hat in his lap. And even in his sleepiness, he looked extremely careful about his neatly combed hair.

Further up the river increasingly became smaller and smaller. We had crossed many tributaries. After each tributary, the amount of water in the main river decreased. The bareness of the mountains deepened and darkened. The scrub became thin and eventually disappeared. The tiny hamlets, the fields with green sprouts, and the flocks of sheep had ceased to appear miles back.

"What a terrifying barrenness," Thakur murmured. He was continuously looking at the mountains. It was his first trip this far up from Lhasa. At first, while I mentioned about the trip, he did not look interested. It was only after I gave a few details about the lake – one of the holiest lakes for the Tibetans, some sixteen thousand feet above sea level, a rare chance to visit for people working like us – he had agreed to join. Nowadays, he looked more worried. He had not been to his birthplace for almost two years. So he had put in his request for a one-month leave to his boss. However, the *arrogant lady* had quickly spurned his request. She had been holding his two-month salary. She was afraid if she gave him all his salary, he would go and not return. It was the same with the others working in her salon. At one point, he was thinking of quitting his job. Later, after giving careful considerations to his thoughts with his dispassionate brain, he had given up the idea of quitting. The idea could not simply square with his situation. He was equally worried by the quarrels between Jaya and Prahlad. After Bindira and Prabha returned, the honeymoon period of intimacy between Jaya and Prahlad waned rapidly. The animosity and quarrels again erupted. The quarrels, at first were sporadic, but later they became regular, almost nightly, disturbing all of us staying in the house. Once we were awakened by angry shouts in the middle of the night. I came downstairs to their room to find them, both drunk, snarling at each other with slurred words as though ready to punch each other right away. Thakur was trying to control Jaya, while Bindira and Prabha were holding Prahlad. We hardly managed to calm them down.

"Ashok, take yak meat." My thoughts were disrupted by Dorje's bellowing voice.

Pradip was still dozing. Pasang too, exhausted with his song, had dozed off in his seat. I took a piece of dried meat and put in my mouth. Thakur continued to stare at the mountains. He rarely ate the yak meat. The bright sun became brighter with the maturing of the day. Again, I plunged into my thoughts. Bidur and Tenzing sprang to mind.

The details and the depth of the relationship were scanty and yet to be turned out to me fully; they were not fully revealed. Nor was it my business to delve into that. Yet I could sense they loved each other to the level of acute romance. I knew they had been going out together for a long time. And now it was being revealed increasingly. The relations between them had reached a romantic level. At least it appeared so to me. I had seen Tenzing many times in Bidur's room. Bidur, on his days off, disappeared until late night. One day, on our way to the room after wandering about along the marshland and the Lhasa River, Thakur and I had seen them cuddling and kissing each other in the park. The deep intimacy between them could be starkly noticed even when they were at work in the restaurant. The three others in the restaurant often gossiped about their romance. Occasionally, I had to ask them rather harshly, with the managerial authority with which I was entrusted by my boss, to work properly during the working hours.

It was perhaps a month ago, Tenzing, sobbing, had come to me, asking whether Bidur was married or not. Pasang had cautioned her that he had got a wife and daughter, which had created a considerable amount of distress in her. I could not respond to her outright. It was not only Pasang, who had a suspicion that Bidur was married, Bindira too had talked in the same way. She had told me that once she saw him in Kathmandu with a young woman and a child, walking together, holding the child between them. So my conviction that he was not married had become somewhat shaky, and I could not respond to Tenzing outright. I, however, assured her that I would find out and let her know. Tenzing tried to distance herself from him. But later, he somehow convinced her, or maybe it was difficult for her to tolerate the distance with him. They, after a short hiatus, became close; their romance went on to a higher degree.

Pema, after Lhosar, became a good friend of mine. The oddities in our behaviour were cleared up to a great extent by the events in her tiny hamlet. Thakur and I went to the hamlet four or maybe five times within those nearly four months. Taking a bus, we would go to her hamlet, talk to Pala, visit the resort to see Yudun and watch the construction works. The resort compound had become a hive of activity. There was a hum and hiss of workers' songs and the screaming and scrunching sounds of gravel, cement, and machines. Electric wires were connected to the resort as well as to the hamlet. "Now, probably, we don't need to struggle with the scarcity of fuel. It's very difficult to find firewood in here. It's only yak dung to provide us with heat and energy. But it smokes a lot," Pala had said during our visit. In the late afternoons, we would again take a bus to the city. At least twice, Pema had accompanied us.

"You slept a lot, Pasang La. I'm tired," Dorje again broke the silence with his bellowing voice.

A bit confused with the sudden interruption of his nap, Pasang, rubbing his eyes, said, "Then let me drive."

"Not now. After we take our snacks. I'm looking for an appropriate spot for the break."

Dorje continued his driving. A little farther, the Land Cruiser swiftly swerved towards the roadside and came to an abrupt halt. His driving was fast and sometimes scary. Pradip's doze also came to an end. While getting out of the car, he managed to look at the side mirror to ensure if his hair was intact. The top and the sides were intact. On the back, however, a few strands had been tousled at which we laughed. Pradip tried to tame the rumpled and oily hairs, yet again and again, they stubbornly rose. He gave up and put his brown hat on.

We sat on a wide flat stone on the bank. The water on the river had drastically decreased. From there, both the road and the river course went up: the river course went up straight and the road sinuously.

"During the tourist season the highway is full of vehicles. Now it looks so lonely," Dorje said. "I don't know why Pradip chose this time. We should have come here at least two months later."

"Can I see you after two months? You'll be either in your *kora* or with your wife or inside the shop. You won't have time for us," Pradip said, trying to take out a handful of water from the river.

"You don't need to try to be a monk. I know you. It's you surrounding your wife. Always," Dorje said, taking out a lunch packet from the Land Cruiser. "Especially after Ashok came to Lhasa."

"It's only me who finds enough time for friends. Isn't it *Aashok*?" It was Pasang, splashing the cold water on his face.

"There's no doubt, Pasang La," I said.

"You see, this Ashok! He's working with me and supporting Pasang. It's not fair, Ashok," Pradip said.

After a playful stay by the riverbank, chatting and sharing the lunch, we resumed our journey, driving uphill, towards the brow of the mountain. This time Pasang was driving.

"Pradip La, you know *Aashok* has become a good friend of Weihong," Pasang said. Perhaps he wanted everyone us to be awake and was trying to find a topic right to engage all of us. And nothing else but gossips about Weihong could serve the purpose. She was dragged just for the sake of our conversation, which was not for the first time. In her absence, she was dragged into our conversation very often. It offered a kind of fun and amusement. Dragging her, a sexy woman, in our conversation probably offered us – the males – a kind of satisfaction: a natural satisfaction of hidden sexual appetite. But this time I too was dragged. My ears pricked up at her name combined with mine.

"Serious?" both Pradip and Dorje expressed their surprise, seemingly in a conversational tone. "Congratulations, Ashok."

"What for?" I asked.

"For being her good friend. She's a beautiful lady," Dorje said. "Sexy too."

"If so, many, many congratulations to all of you. Her friendship is much deeper with all of you, except with Thakur Ji," I said.

"Thakur is also her favourite. He's the one who decorates her hair. And makes her a beauty queen." This time Pradip said, "If her head doesn't get his massage every other day, she can't sleep."

"She's my regular customer. Apart from her tips, I have nothing to do with her," Thakur said.

"And she gives hefty tips to you, doesn't she?" Pasang laughed.

"*Aashok*, tell me what were you doing in her room that evening?" he added with his enquiring voice.

"Which evening?" I asked.

It was only twice that I had visited her house in the evening, once for the drink, when I was alone there and she had made amorous advances which were later averted by a phone call. The second occasion was on her birthday, celebrated with all lavishness and lushness in a series. The day before the birthday was a long get-together at the Lees' place for which she bore all the cost by herself. Then evening drinks in our restaurant was also borne by her. On the day of birthday, there was mah-jong during the day and heavy drinking at night at her house. Such was her birthday celebration: oddly unique to a person like me, who hardly cared about his birthday. I had joined the celebration in the late evening after we closed the restaurant. By the time I wished her *happy birthday*, she was already drunk and gave me a long hug. The other members of the *circle* were there too. All drunk.

How did Pasang know about my first evening at her house? I had not told him, nor had I told any other men. How did he ferret out this information? Did she tell him? I knew that Lhasa in those days was not a big city and relations and acquaintances in that ancient city somehow engulfed the whole locals or at least many of them in a web. Any information that originated in a part of the city reached the other parts, albeit taking its own course and in an altered or exaggerated form, sometimes entirely different from the original version. Pasang had a huge web of relations and friendships. There was nothing that he did not know about the city and the locals. Yet I could not find any clues.

"Don't try to be innocent. Lhasa isn't a big city. I know you were with her the whole evening in her house. Only the two of you."

"Are you talking about the evening she invited me for a drink? Way back? If it's that, I drank a couple of glasses. Then she drove me to my place. *Kunjo, satya,* I swear to god. I had nothing to do with anything else," I said, swearing in so many languages. They all laughed.

"You're panicking without a reason. I didn't say you had anything with her. I know you're afraid of women," Pasang said, continuing driving while slanting his eyes away from the road.

Such was our drive to Namtso Lake, yet another earth of serenity and virginal impression and the feeling of being not far below the heavens. As if this world ended there, and from right there, another world began, similar to the Elysian Fields.

We sat on the side of the lake, looking at the vast expanse of the turquoise waters rippling and gleaming in the afternoon rays. Across the lake, a long way away, the faded mountains loomed, offering mysterious sensation.

Eight

The things and events appeared as mere repeats. At least to me, they appeared to be mere repeats after a full year and another quarter year in Lhasa. They lost the romance of newness, the feeling of strangeness. The present occurrences could now be perceived or compared with those of the previous year. The repeats must have occurred long ago, as soon as early May, once I had completed a whole year in the restaurant. The waning of spring, the sprouting of wheat and barley in the fields, the greening of the city with the poplars and willows had already occurred much before. The greenery around the valley had become rich much before. Much before, the vegetation in the marshland had changed its colours. The flowers on the side of the streets and in the parks had already become fragrant. Days back, the daylight had begun to linger until nine in the evening and the temperature had increased, some days feeling like the thirties. Weeks back, tourists had started pouring into the city and walking around the monasteries and the yards, often in thin clothes, especially the young women. All these I had seen and experienced a year before too. Yet I was somehow unaware of the repeated events. This unawareness continued until I saw Mark in August.

Yes, it was in the first week of August, on a Friday afternoon, when the illusion of novelty about new life which I was experiencing for last more than a year at once wore off and the awareness of the repetition was at once realised.

"How're you, Ashok?" As I turned around I saw him standing with the same look – his bearded face, serious eyes, a hat on his head, a book in his hand. His face was suntanned.

"Oh, Mark?" I exclaimed.

"Yes, it's me. You know? This time I travelled by way of your country. That's why I arrived here a bit late."

He added that he had come to Nepal two months back. There he did the Annapurna Trek. A month-long trekking and the lengthy visa process delayed his visit to Tibet. He had just five days in Lhasa. This time he had travelled from Kathmandu to Lhasa by road. On his way, he stayed in Dingri Valley for a week and visited Mount Everest base camp from the northern side. The road journey was fascinating, he further said. He flew to Kathmandu after a five-day stay, along with the promise of yet another visit the next year. During that period, he regularly came to the restaurant for his long sitting and drinking while reading. Before he left, he gave me a few books.

Thus, Mark again came and went. His visit was yet another pursuance of a series of regular visits to Tibet, which he had been doing for years the reason of which was not known to me. He could not discontinue the continuity he had been pursuing for years. But to me, his arrival and short stay left an awareness of the completion of a whole cycle and the repetition of the other one. His short visit reminded me, with a greater strength, that I had already spent more than a year in the city, away from the birthplace.

"But, Ashok Ji, even though we say the mere repetition of things or events, isn't this repetition new in a deeper sense?" Thakur revealed yet another truth or even philosophy by his simple words. He revealed that as I expressed my feelings of repetition during our usual walk along the fence around the marshland. The poplar and willow leaves had already turned into slight pallid colour, an indication of creeping winter. There was a projection that, that year the cold would start earlier in the valley.

The trees, the grasses, the birds, and the yaks: everything in the marshland appeared in the same way as they had appeared in the month of August of the previous year and gave the impression of the mere repetition. However, understood in Thakur's way, thought out in a deeper sense, it was not the mere repetition. They were new – the grasses were new, the leaves were new, the trees had produced new branches, the flocks of the birds consisted of a new generation or at least the feathers they possessed were new. The yaks were a year older than the year before. Thakur was right. The things or events were new in a false impression of repetition, or there were changes and newness difficult to be distinguished correctly, to be delineated precisely. Thakur once more gave me a new way of looking at things in his simple words.

It was more intensely revealed to us during our visit to the Lees' place for the *linka* towards the end of August. I had visited the Lees' place almost a year back for the first time, then afterwards many times: sometimes with the *circle* in the Land Cruiser and sometimes with Thakur, taking a public bus, until the carved image of Buddha, and then walking through the metalled road, crossing the bridge and walking along the rutted muddy road. All those times, I had not thought about that place in terms of repetition or change. This time as we drove down there – fifteen of us, crowded in two Land Cruisers – I tried to take in the things in that way, in Thakur's way.

The ruts, the furrows in the muddy road, were deeper and wider, maybe the season had witnessed much rain, or maybe the ruts were never fixed up or never filled in, or the flow of traffic on that muddy road had increased, causing the ruts to become deeper and wider. The Lees had developed a few more sunburns and lines on their faces. Their daughter had gained a few more inches height – a hefty growth for a year – than I had seen her the year before, during the first *linka*. Two or three sheds, open and thatched, had been built. A few more poplars and willows had been planted on the side of the narrows-like structure and those two small lakes, overgrown with the weeds. We walked over the springy grass following the Lees' daughter and went to the greenhouse farms across the narrows-like structure. Inside the warm and damp greenhouse farms, the vegetable species were different than those of the previous year. I could see the growing stalks of eggplants with broad leaves, supported by wooden stakes, could see green vines of beans with tendrils attached to jute-ropes, whereas the previous year, there used to be cucumbers and tomatoes. The rotation of vegetables offered better produces, Mr Lee had responded to my curiosity about the change.

That day the two of us spent most of our time with the Lees' daughter, Xiaodong, whom we called *xiao fengyo* (little friend in Chinese). Thakur could communicate with her, and I too had learnt a little bit of Chinese. While the others played mah-jong, we walked around following her little steps, went to the enclosure and watched the nervous sheep with rheumy eyes and wet noses. Walking with and talking to her was far more enjoyable rather than drinking alcohol in the group. We skirted the lakes looking at the floating ducks and then sat under a willow on the side of the narrows-like structure watching the fish and water striders. We joined the group late in the afternoon.

The changes were even starker at the resort, where Yudun was working. In late September, during our visit to that place, it appeared starkly different than it used to be earlier. We had not been there for the last three months. Now the changes were massive.

It had been wholly restructured, remade, and in that process of remaking, the old things had been done away. The road from the highway had been pitched. The old willows in the compound, including the one on the side of the lake under which we would sit to have our drinks, had ceased to exist. The edifice, the main building, had been coloured. The old open thatched cottages had vanished. They had been replaced by new concrete structures, inside each of which were the lavish mahogany furniture and mah-jong table. The low slatted fence had been replaced by a high iron fence. The compound had been well-gardened. The parking area and the walking paths had been paved. On the side of the paths, the rose plants had flowered in different colours. The grass had been evenly mowed. One more mastiff had been added, now both of them hitched to the iron posts on the two sides of the lake, which was the only thing that remained intact, that had been allowed to survive in the compound.

It had remained there somehow untouched like a vestige of the old resort. The water in the lake, the tussock weeds on the side and the floating ducks and ducklings reminded us of the previously existed resort. The weeds had grown even in the deeper part of the lake and had stuck up out of the surface. The naturalness of the lake was perhaps left intact to offer the natural views – among those modern facilities – to the customers, whoever came there, and to provide the different varieties of fishes with an exact feeling of a real lake, among those reeds, I guessed. I also guessed the owner from Sichuan obviously was very rich and had invested a lot for the demolition of the old and the construction of the new.

After the completion of the new constructions, just before the season started, he had organised a lavish party inviting high-level politicians, officials, businessmen, and renowned travel agents in the city, Weihong said that before we entered a wide room of one of the concrete structures following Dawa, Yudun's brother, who had joined the restaurant after he left the school, the reason for which he told no one. The Land Cruisers parked at the parking area, the packed rooms and busy waiters and waitresses suggested the business was running very well.

Despite the fact that the newly reconstructed resort had given employments to Dawa and a few other locals, Pala was not happy with the new look of the resort, the look that did away with the rustic charm of the old resort. To him, the modern structures of the resort looked odd in the countryside. The changes had been slow and gradual in the hamlet and the ambience for decades. The existence of the modern buildings, the flow of cars and people alien to the place did away with the ancientness and seclusion. The lavish construction was unnecessary or even absurd in that solitary place, he told me, while the others were busy with mah-jong. The change, the extravagant decoration, the artificial beauty added to the resort also struck me, to some extent. It felt imported and unnecessary in the secluded countryside.

Beyond the fence, in the fields, the wheat stalks were baled. I did not see the yak; it was not even on the mountain slope. Perhaps it had gone to the other side of the spur or a little away where it could hide itself from the colourful modern resort. Perhaps the yak had found it difficult to adapt to the massive change.

In fact, not only the resort, the whole city was massively changing. Lhasa was expanding unevenly in all directions, to all corners wherever the valley reached. The expansion, while looking at it from the heights, was like an octopus. The old houses were being torn down. The new ones were being constructed, according to new standards, with new materials and new methods. To that end, for the construction purposes, heavy machines – rollers, cranes, excavators, concrete mixers – and men had been brought in great numbers from the mainland. The loud screams, the clinking and clonking of the machines, the hiss and hum of the labourers, the sounds of gigantic trucks had become regular phenomena and would come to us from every side during our walks or drives. The conveyance of construction materials and people in such large numbers would often shake parts of the city. In places, we could see thick clouds billowing from the construction sites and spreading in the azure sky. The scrap and remnants of old constructions lay around in heaps. The calmness of the city was steadily being snatched by those new sounds and constructions. Was it developing or decaying? It depended on the judgements of the viewers. It came along differently to different people. To some, it was odd and unnecessary to do away the serenity. To the others, it was a perfect pace of development.

It became cold. As had been projected, the winter came even before the autumn ended. A cold breeze swept through the valley. The willows showered the last leaves. The poplars had become bare much earlier. The flocks of ruddy shelducks came from the north and settled in the valley. Soon the rivers, the marshland, and the parks were overwhelmed by them. The nomads and the people from the countryside, from highland areas away from the city, came down to the valley for their annual leisure. They pursued their *kora*, did their small business, and basked in the winter sun in the yards. The narrow streets and alleys smelt of country people and the herbs which they had brought. A few tourists, who had lately come to Lhasa with no idea that the cold would start so early, were seen often bargaining and purchasing the *yarchagumba*. The swords glittered when the nomads took them out from the sheath hanging in their waist. Both the tourists and country folks were amused at this encounter. Both exchanged smiles. Around the valley, the high and brown mountains stood with deepening nakedness.

And Thakur and I, one Sunday, rummaged around the wooden rack and through a tin trunk in our room for our warm clothes – those thick trousers and vests and woollen beanies. We checked whether the Thermos was working or not. We checked the hot-water bottles to ensure they had not got leaks. We checked all the doors and windows in our rooms and toilet, then put shims, clothes, or papers in all gaps and holes to block the chill. Once satisfied with our preparation for the cold, we wrapped ourselves up in the layers of clothes, put the beanies on our heads, and pulled them down to our ear lobes and eyebrows. Thus, fortifying ourselves against the weather, we walked out for the evening walk.

It was during this walk Thakur said to me, "Ashok Ji, I spent yet another Dashain without going home. Diwali is coming soon. I haven't seen my family for three years. I have been asking my boss for leave, but she always gets an excuse to stop me. This time she says she'll increase my salary and will give me a month paid leave along with a two-way bus ticket if I stay until Lhosar. This is November. December, January, February. Still four more months before Lhosar. I wish time would fly," he said, counting the remaining months with his fingers. "I hope this time she'll allow me to leave. I have made it clear even if she won't let me, I'll go without the salary, which she's keeping, and will never come back."

He looked convinced that he would see his family soon. Thakur, like Jaya, was brilliant in his profession. This must have been the reason his boss had not allowed him to leave the salon. She must have become worried if he went to Nepal, he would not return. As an owner, she was more concerned about her business. Naturally. Now Thakur had told her if she would not give him leave this time, he would leave the job even without the withheld salary. I thought she would accept his leave application, perhaps with more assurances. Losing him would not be in favour of her business.

So Thakur's chance of seeing his family within a couple of months was almost a certainty. But what about me? When would I see my wife and children? I did not have an exact idea when I would have that opportunity. Despite my desperateness, I had not thought about the exact timing or dates. I had not talked with my boss.

"Why don't you talk to your boss? He'll certainly let you go. He's far better than my boss, the *arrogant lady*. The restaurant won't be busy that time. We can go together," Thakur said as we walked along the fence around the marshland.

It was not that I was not in a hurry to go home. Every time I called my wife, the passion of missing would grow so much that I wanted to go back right away and never leave them again. The previous Saturday, during my usual call to her, Sushmita had given me disturbing news: Uncle's health, which had been delicate for almost a year, had become much more precarious in recent days. The doctors had suspected some malignant tumours in his stomach and had advised him to see a specialist. He had been confined to bed for weeks, and he wished to see me as soon as possible. The whole day, thoughts about him ran through my mind. He was a bit greedy, selfish and, to a certain extent, unfair, when it came to money. But at all other times he had been helpful to my family. Whenever we needed help, we had to ask him. He never said no, although he often knitted his brows. Whenever we needed cash, he was the one on whom we could depend. He never returned us empty-handed, the interest was high though. More importantly, whenever I needed the role of a father, he was always there with his proud eyes. During the marriage ceremony of my sister and in mine too, he had been there, at our home, during the whole ceremony in a red turban and white *kachhad* in a fatherly role. During my mother's death, it was he who had guided me throughout the rituals. He had been as my guardian and had given me a continuous sense of protection. So as I was informed of his sickness and his wish to see me, as the bedridden posture of a fragile body came in front of me, I became sentimental. All his humanly weaknesses were at once dwarfed. A still small voice told me that it was time to return home; I felt an urgency to see him.

I was sure that if asked, Pradip would not stop me. In fact, it was he who, months back, had asked me whether I wanted to have leave. His wife Bayang had always been encouraging me, in a tone of authority, to take leave and go back. She always insisted on me bringing my wife.

One bright morning, sometime in June, when I had gone to their house for account briefing and Pasang too had come there for some reasons, my leave had become a matter of discussion. Kneading *tsampa* and butter, Bayang had asked me, "Why don't you take a short leave and go to see your family? Did you forget your wife?"

"*Aashok* is in love with a Tibetan girl," Pasang had laughed.

Thank goodness he did not utter the name of any girls, especially Pema, as he would do often.

"Yes, Ashok. It's more than a year. You better go right now and come before the peak season begins. I'll arrange the permit for you," Pradip had added.

But at that time I was not ready; I did not have any savings. I had just paid the loan to Pasang and did not have money even to buy the bus ticket. So I had tried to segue into another topic. "I'll go in Dashain," I had said. "Pradip Dai, we need to arrange some wine before the season starts. The remaining bottles won't be enough even for a month."

And at this abrupt and deliberate change of the topic, Bayang had said, "Ashok *hyaku mindu.* Ashok isn't good."

I had said I would go in Dashain. Dashain came, I did not go. I told my wife that I would come home soon, a vague conjecture. I myself was not sure when that *soon* would come.

Now, as Thakur informed me about the high chances of his going back, I remembered the sickness of my uncle and intensely felt I needed to see him.

December passed by; January approached. I received yet another call from my wife with more information about ailing Uncle.

It was only then I talked to Pradip, and I talked to Pasang before I talked to him; the talk came suddenly.

In January, in the dead of winter, Pasang drove me to the narrow gorge up in the mountain, where we had been long back, with others. As we passed the extension of the city to the north, leaving the sky burial place on our left, and as we passed a secluded northern suburb, the road became gravelled and sloped up, upstream a small rushing stream. The houses and bare willows were left behind. We reached high up in the mountain and parked the Land Cruiser on the stream bank. We sat on a cold boulder. High up on the slope there was a monastery. Only a narrow outside view was visible; everything was obstructed by the mountain slopes; the sky was confined. A few vultures were circling in that confined sky. It was bright and cold.

Pasang lit a cigarette and said in his solemn voice or almost declared, "Somebody is going to die." The declaration brought back the posture of bedridden Uncle.

And it was at that moment I said, "I want to go home for a month."

He asked, "What led you to this sudden want?"

"Uncle is seriously ill."

"Then you must go," Pasang said as he ground the cigarette stump against the boulder on which we were sitting. We sat there until the late afternoon until the keen breeze pierced through our warm clothes and made us shiver.

In the restaurant, as I stepped up the spiral stair and entered the reception, I found Pradip. I was so overwhelmed by the idea of returning home, I could not hold it back. With no background, in a hurried and gasping way, I told him that I wanted a month leave. He, too, was a bit surprised at the sudden revelation of my wish to go back. Perhaps my voice was a little bit louder and excited; Pema and Tenzing, who were playing noughts and crosses at a table by the window, turned their heads to look at me. The sudden revelation of my desire, the way I expressed it, had surprised all of them. I knew and was sure that Pradip would not have any problems. Yet the way I expressed my desire made him ask me the question, the same which Pasang had asked me, why I suddenly wanted to go. I repeated what I had said to Pasang, upon which Pradip, right away, asked for my passport so that he could initiate the process, which could take another two weeks. Later that evening, I talked to Thakur.

From the next day on, we became busy in the preparation of our travel back to our country.

Nine

As soon as we started, before the sun came out, in a Land Cruiser along with an elderly couple, Thakur said, perhaps, to himself, "Hope, we'll reach Old Dingri today."

"If the road isn't blocked by the construction works, we should be there by six in the evening." It was the driver's surmise.

Thakur's eyelids soon drooped. Perhaps the previous night he had not slept well. The elderly couple did not speak much. They murmured twice or thrice once we started and then kept quiet. The driver – from Qinghai whose name was Chhako, Thakur's preferred driver (Thakur had said he always looked for him whenever he went home), a tall, beefy man with black eyes and freckled face – also seemed to be a soft-spoken person. I also kept quiet.

I kept quiet, partly because out of my own habit; I never talked much during the travel, both long and short. I would prefer to watch the views outside: constantly moving and changing. That day also as we moved ahead along the highway in our pursuance to cover 500 miles or so within one and a half days, I sat watching the outside views, faded in the pre-morning darkness. I preferred not to speak.

And partly because, that day, my mind was not inside the vehicle. It was in Narrow Flatland, where I was going after almost two years and, simultaneously or even more frequently, in the restaurant, the city, the streets, the marshland, or the river where I had spent equally the same period. I knew I would be coming back to Lhasa. It was arranged in such way. Pasang, after a month, was to travel to the border for the business purpose and was also to drive us to Lhasa. It was the arrangement planned by Pradip. I was given the exact date and time of arrival at the border point, which I had conveyed to Thakur as well, who, pleased with his increased salary and hefty gift items offered by the *arrogant lady*, did not utter even a single word of not returning. We had decided the date to meet in Kathmandu after a month. Thus, I was again to come to Lhasa, yet I became somewhat desolate when I left, for there was always a possibility of the things going differently than planned.

"Will you come back?" Just a day before leaving, Pema had posed the question, expressing intimacy and sadness through her tone and eyes.

"Of course, I'll be here next month," I had responded. I responded to her so easily, but after that, after she posed the question to me, a slight possibility of not coming to Lhasa, not having the opportunity to see her, was bothering me. I became a little desolate. I felt I was missing the city and the restaurant, more prominently her. Until the previous day, I was missing my birthplace and family. However, as I departed from Lhasa, and as my being in the hamlet within another two days became sure, the subject of the missing shifted from the birthplace to Lhasa.

I stayed, lost in solitary thoughts.

Before the first rays of the sun struck the earth, we had already left the Lhasa River and taken the road that followed upstream the Yarlung Tsangpo, the Brahmaputra, towards the west through a deep gorge. The mighty river had narrowed down, had shrunk to a few feet. A few miles downstream, where the gorge was wide, the river had stretched nearly to half a mile, but now it was confined to a much narrower width. The geography of the rivers – the illusive depth and shallowness irrespective of its width – always came to me as an illusion. I could never estimate the depth, width, and drift of the rivers. The Yarlung Tsangpo, so narrow in that stretch, widened itself many times a few miles downstream. Once it absorbed the Lhasa River – almost the same size and the same amount of water – it did not change its size; it looked the same before the merging. I never understood the geography of the rivers, of the big ones in particular. Once, when I was in mid-teens, I was visiting, along with Gopal, the natal home of my grandmother. On our way, we had to cross a river, big for us. The river with its illusory nature had narrowed and broadened frequently. Unaware of the nature of the river, we thought it would be easier to cross where it had narrowed, the crossing would take lesser time by way of the narrow stretch. But before we reached the middle course, the tenuous hold of our feet, inexperienced in walking on the slippery stones, gave out, and we were swept downstream. The men in the fields across saved us and helped to cross the river. They advised us never to take a narrow course in the river. On our return, we, depending on the suggestions of the men who had saved us earlier and a bit on our own changed judgement, took the wider course. There was hardly any movement of water visible on the surface. The river bed was silty. But before we walked a quarter of the distance, the water appeared to be flowing with force under the surface: there was a strong underneath drift. We were again swept a few feet downstream. We somehow crossed the river, but we lost our bags, in which we had put our shoes. We returned the hamlet barefoot. Grandmother told us to always follow the course which the other people had been following for years. Since then, I never used my feeble and tentative judgement about the rivers or lakes, just followed fords, the traditional paths – used and secure.

The drive along the Yarlung Tsangpo evoked the pre-teen memories.

More up, the river widened, revealing again its unique geography. We had entered Xigatse Valley. Thakur was still dozing. The elderly couple too.

"We'll take our lunch in Larche," announced Chhako – both his hands attached to the steering. His eyes? Inside the black eyeglasses (which he had put on just now, perhaps to block the bright sunlight), I could not see whether they were focused on the road or slanted elsewhere. But obviously, his announcement was addressed to me because I was sure he could see, through the mirrors, the drooped eyes of the rest of the passengers, or he could assume that because of the quietness on the rear seat.

"How far is it?" I asked just to continue to carry on the conversation.

"We'll be there at around two o'clock." A brief response, as brief as the question, then again silence.

The valley widened more ahead. The outside views were wearily bright, too bright under the open sky. Our journey progressed ahead through the valley, through the city – Xigatse, another ancient city, the seat of Panchen Lama – then again followed the river.

The valley ended and gave on to another valley. The whole day we travelled along the dusty and bumpy highway. We travelled through valley after valley, mountain after mountain; we drove up, crossed the passes, then drove down again; we travelled the whole day looking at the browns, at the grazing herds and flocks of yaks and sheep, and at cowboys and shepherds in their ancient-looking nomadic dress. The ancient-looking views continued throughout the journey.

At around eight o'clock, two hours later than his prediction (we had taken two hours for lunch), Chhako parked his Land Cruiser in front of a restaurant or a lodge or a family house turned into a restaurant in Old Dingri. The daylong journey had turned out in both ways: it was tedious as Thakur had said and was enjoyable as Mark had claimed; tedious in a sense that, at the end of the journey, I was completely worn out. When I got off the Land Cruiser, each and every part of the body ached. The pain was sharp in the leg joints. Thakur had developed a headache too: the effect of a long travel and more than thirteen thousand feet height of the valley, higher than Lhasa. The long journey along the dusty and bumpy road had taken a lot out of us. It was enjoyable in a sense that it was a wholly new experience for me. Such a long journey along such a typical and fantastic landscape! Throughout the journey, I enjoyed the views offered by the Tibetan earth.

The views, as soon as we crossed Lhakpa La – a pass, the 'La' connoting pass in Tibetan language, yet another meaning apart from Mr or sir, Thakur had told me that, on our way – more than sixteen thousand feet high and drove down to Dingri Valley, became more ancient and secluded. The valley was unique to me. I had read about it in history books. I had heard many myths about it.

After crossing Lhakpa La, we drove down to the valley and passed a small army check post, showing our papers to a young army officer with a very indifferent look, almost stern. The valley appeared precisely in the same way as I had fancied it. The late afternoon sun slanted through the western sky and a rivulet in the middle of the valley offered golden glints as we drove ahead. As we drove ahead, the yaks and sheep grazing beside the rivulet gave our Land Cruiser their tentative looks. In places, not far away from the highway, there were *chipis*, so common to the plateau, swivelling little heads around the earth from their burrows and two or three black kites circling in the limitless cerulean sky, directly above those *chipis*, perhaps looking for a chance of good feast. The black kites fed on those little *chipis*, Chhako had told me. I could see the less frequent views of remnants of ruined houses, seemingly burnt (the soot-covered walls suggested that), but with no idea what used to be there, why and when they turned into ruins. Were those structures burnt down accidentally? Or was the burning purposeful?

As we drove ahead, the ancientness grew deeper.

I forgot the exact date, but one day during our mah-jong or *linka* many months back, Dorje had said something interesting about the valley, which had created a curiosity inside me to see it. He had said he had heard from his father that it was written in an ancient book that when a white crane would perch on a branch of a tall tree in Dingri Valley, the people from Kathmandu would go to Tibet for shelter. I had never heard that before. A tall tree in such a barren valley? Not even the others in the *circle* had heard that before. They did not argue with what Dorje had said. Among them, Dorje was considered as the most knowledgeable person about Tibetan culture and geography. Many times he had shared how he travelled on foot, during his childhood, along with his father and the other traders, from Lhasa to Kathmandu and back, and how he had spent days in the valley and how they, in the valley, would start their long and weary journey immediately after midnight and settle under the tents before noon to avoid gusty winds. Many times he had shared the myths, stories, and the accounts of the travel, which had survived among the lineage of his ancestors. Those stories and accounts of adventures in that valley were amazing. I was taken with what Dorje had said about the valley. And now, as I travelled along the valley in the Land Cruiser driven by a freckled-faced Chhako, Thakur, and the elderly couple in the back seats, the stories, particularly the story of the white crane in a tall tree in the barren valley, felt like ancient tales. Amusing. They felt much deeper as the sun went behind the mountains and the full moon rose.

I did not know the authenticity of his adventure stories and myths. It was, in fact, difficult to take in those stories in the same way as he had told them. There might have been twists and exaggerations. The storytellers, his father and forefathers, would certainly have made deductions and inductions on those stories at their wishes and given them the present form, which I heard from him. Yet I was aware that the history of the valley stretched back to centuries. Throughout the history, there had been interactions and exchanges between the cross-Himalayan people, cultures, and the authorities. There had been cross-border movements, trades, exchanges, and strife and wars in the long history. Many must have fallen in those strife and wars. And certainly, the valley had been used for those movements, trades, strife, and wars. Many paths would have been carved, shelters would have been created, fences would have been constructed, and tents would have been pegged to the ground to serve those grand purposes. Dingri, I guessed, must have been the valley to offer shelter to Bhrikuti and Araniko and many more scholars from both sides on the way of their long journey.

As the Land Cruiser continued to move ahead – its yellow headlight somewhat resembling the mellow moonlight – the stream of the thought and imagination about the mystic valley continued. The highway we were travelling on, or part of it, must have been based on one of the paths used by humans and animals for centuries, until the highway was constructed. Or maybe a completely different line, a technically viable line, was chosen for the construction purpose. And once the highway was constructed, once vehicles started to move on the highway carrying humans and animals and goods, the earlier paths would have lost their importance and would have become obsolete. The ancient constructions and structures would have lost the relevance, the purpose for which they were built. Those paths, over the years, would have been retrieved by nature, by the grassy land. The earth there would have returned to the original texture, the texture of the pre-construction phase – bit by bit, piece by piece. Now there were no other paths except a few trails for the yaks and sheep. Ancient constructions would have been taken down and would have crumbled in the course of history. At present, they did not exist. Where they existed, they existed as remnants and ruins. The valley remained ancient and grand. The highway, a few new buildings, and the limited human construction could not challenge the vastness of the valley and gigantic mountains. They could not diminish the ancientness, the mysticism, the sanctity, and the grandeur, I realised as we drove ahead.

The silence was still prevalent. In fact, it was prevalent throughout the drive along the valley except for the few details about the valley given by Chhako. And in that silence, my brain was enormously engaged with so many imaginations. It was travelling, travelling to the remote past – to centuries back, hundreds and thousands of year back, to aeons back when the plateau originated out of the Tethys Sea. The valley must have been formed then. It was amazing to realise how old the valley was, yet much of its virginity was still intact, away from human encroachment except for the line of a highway and a few settlements.

"Mount Everest is there," Chhako said, breaking the silence and pointing his finger towards the south, on our left. I saw a grand object, an immense wall, standing up from the ground and touching the sky on the southern horizon. That was the Himalaya. The highest mountain in the world was somewhere there. With the moonlit Himalaya in its lap, the valley felt even grander.

And now, at the end of our journey for the day, as I got out of the Land Cruiser in front of an old house in Old Dingri, I was physically worn out and emotionally overwhelmed. Outside, it was bitterly cold. Gundum led us inside her house. I knew her name from Thakur. Before we started our journey, he had told me that we were to spend the night in her restaurant and also that she and her parents were from Amdo, Qinghai, and had a restaurant at Khasa until a few years back.

Giving me additional information, he said they had moved to Dingri three years back. The sudden move was necessitated by Gundum herself. He told me that in his murmuring voice as we entered a big, hall-like room, making me curious to know more about her. On all sides of the room, except the entrance side, a narrow mud-and-stone platform was raised against the wall, and thick carpets were laid on that platform. In the centre was a big hearth. The smouldering dried yak dung in the hearth made the room warm. An elderly couple – Gundum's parents, I guessed – were sitting beside the hearth. Gundum and her parents were tall and strong-looking persons with fair complexion, the general look of Amdo people. Beside the hearth, there was a child. Was Gundum married? Did the child belong to her? Or was he their relative? It was not easy to guess, but I saw that Gundum's mother was wholly taken up with the child. As we had planned to start at four the next day, we did not stay there much. We took our dinner, settled the bill, and went to a tiny room at the rear of the house, following Gundum and her shadow. That was it, the end of my meeting with her. It was short, but what Thakur said about her made me interested. Before going to our beds, Thakur also said Gundum was married in her teens. Her husband died in an accident. Later she fell in love with another man and eloped with him to Chengdu. The man, after making her pregnant, disappeared in the vast city of Chengdu. She came back to Khasa with a small baby in her lap.

"Was that the reason they left Khasa?" I asked Thakur.

"I think so. It must have become difficult for them to stay there after that episode," Thakur answered before he closed his eyes.

The room was ice cold. So was the bedding. It smelt foul and musty. My body was tired and brain occupied with many imaginations. It was hard to distinguish whether I was sleeping or not. Perhaps I was half-asleep and half-awake. In that state of half-sleepiness and half-awakening, many images, surreal images came to me: a grand valley with snow-capped mountains in its south, caravans of ancient-looking people, fences and shelters, little Dorje and his father – looking like him – pegging tents to the grassy land, nomads driving the herds of yak and flocks of sheep along wide and dusty paths and trails, a tall tree and a white crane settling on its branch, the construction of the highway and vanishing of the paths and trails, the put-upon face of Gundum and her son; every image came to the half-awakened and half-slept mind.

Those images, in different forms, continued to appear as we started our journey ahead through the dusty and bumpy road the next morning.

With silvery views of the Himalayas in the south, the valley was smiling in the moonlight. The surreal images ran through my mind, even when the first sunrays touched the Himalayan peaks, turning them into gold from silver. They continued while we, after driving up the Tong La, took the slopes down the mountains along the rushing river: the river sometimes on our right and sometimes on our left. The colour and texture of the land changed as we drove down. The vegetation became stratified. First the mountains with brown barrenness, then different types of grasses, bushes with scattered trees, and then green forest.

The images of Dingri Valley, to a certain degree, continued until I reached Narrow Flatland.

Thakur and I had said goodbye in Kathmandu. He had taken a bus to the east, and I had taken a bus to the west.

Ten

As I touched his feet and sat beside him on a rumpled bed in the granary, a new structure in front of his house built after I left for Lhasa, one room of which was used as his bedroom, Uncle said, feebly, "May god bless you and keep you always happy! I thought I would never see you again." He had been reduced to a skeleton. His cheeks had sunken, the eyes had been hollowed, and the lips trembled when he spoke. All agility, the liveliness and the activeness he possessed throughout life, had vanished. He looked much older than his real age: nearing sixty. He was reclining on a pile of old pillows, which was laid on the bed against the wall, looking outside through a door-sized open window, the frame and planks yet to be fitted. The window gave on to a wide southerly view.

"Why didn't you come in Dashain? I was expecting you. You didn't come. I thought I would never see you again," he added before I spoke.

"Uncle, why do you say so? I'm here with you. Everything will be all right," I said.

"You're talking the same way as Gopal talks. He didn't tell me, but I know I have got cancer. It kills people. I still remember your grandfather, my father, had died of the same sickness. I have the same symptoms. Those days we didn't know about this killer disease so we thought he just died, died of his age or something else. I still remember my grandfather, your great-grandfather also had died of the same symptoms. I don't think I'll be spared. It's just a matter of days or weeks. I wish death would take me away soon. I'm not worried about myself. I'm just worried about your auntie," he said, pointing his shaking hand towards Auntie, who was sitting on a straw mat on the floor, spinning bales of cotton into the wicks with her hands, which frequently moved to her eyes to wipe the tears. She was crying. In fact, she had been crying all the time, from the moment I stepped into her courtyard and bowed to touch her feet. She began crying, first with a faint smile, afterwards with tears, the smile for seeing me after two years and the tears for being aware of the illness of her husband: she was completely absorbed by the gloom caused by the possibility or even sureness of losing him within a few months.

Gopal had said this before I met Uncle. He had told me that the doctors had said the cancer was at the last stage; they could do nothing much. Even if he would be treated, he would just linger on for a few more months. Not more than six months. Aware of this reality, Auntie was continuously crying. She had changed a lot since I had left her. She – a woman of small stature – looked old, untimely old. Most of her hair had turned grey. Her eyes and cheeks were depressed. The red *tika* she had put on her forehead had smudged in the continuous course of wiping her tears. She herself looked sick. Obviously, it had been difficult for her to endure the sad news, the saddest in her life.

"Why are you crying so much? One day everybody dies. Nobody is immortal," Uncle said in his irritated tone.

"Mother, please don't cry. Nothing will happen to him." It was Gopal.

"Yes, nothing will happen to Uncle. I have brought some Tibetan herbs with me. You know Gopal? They say these herbs can cure those diseases, which can't be cured by modern treatments. These are full of magic," I said. I said so even though I myself was not sure about it, about the effectiveness of the herbal medicines to cure the disease that was not cured by modern treatments. I was not sure about the clinical effect of the herbs. Yet before leaving Lhasa, I, with the help of Pasang, had arranged some *yarchagumba* and other herbs, the peppermint-sized black round pills. I mimicked what Pasang had said.

Uncle's eyes momentarily shined.

I asked Gopal to bring a glass of lukewarm water, prepared the dose, and gave it to Uncle, which he drank and gave me a look of gratitude. The rest, I gave to Gopal along with the administration instructions.

"I have read about Tibetan herbs in *Muna Madan*. I still remember how Madan survived by the herbs and the treatments by a Tibetan. I know they're spiritual people. I have more faith in these herbs than in those medicines given by the doctors. They just suck money. I wish I had these herbs earlier," Uncle said.

What he said, the great faith he had shown in the herbs I brought, delighted me. I should have come as soon as I had heard about his sickness.

"Daddy, mummy is calling." It was Rabindra, my son. He came in and sat on the straw mat. Uncle gave him a stroke on the head.

"He looks exactly like you," Auntie said, trying to take Rabindra on her lap. "He loves his grandfather. Don't you, Rabindra?"

"You must be tired. Have some rest. We'll talk later," Auntie said.

"Yes, we'll talk later. I'm happy, at least you're here. I wish to see the other sons as well before I die," Uncle said.

"Uncle, please don't say anything about the death. Nothing will happen to you. I'll come later, Gopal," I said and followed Rabindra.

Outside, on the veranda, Pooja was sieving the maize flour. Her son, Prakash, was feeding the goats. He was dressed in camouflage.

"Uncle, how're you?" he enquired, touching my feet. He was tall.

"Prakash? You're grown up. And this dress? Where did you find it? You look like a soldier. A child soldier," I said.

"Dai, this boy is giving us trouble. A few months back, a few people, both women and men, came to the primary school wearing this type of dress. Some of them were carrying guns and cane sticks. Inviting all villagers, they organised a cultural programme. They gave long speeches. They said they were Maoists. Since then many lads in the villages are wearing this dress. This boy sometimes doesn't even go to school. He disappears for days, and when he comes back, he doesn't share with us where he went. I'm worried about this boy," Pooja said, pulling her shawl over her head as she saw me.

"Is it? Is your mother telling the truth, Prakash?" I asked.

"Uncle, she doesn't listen to me. She doesn't try to understand what I mean. Why does she insist on me going to school for that bourgeois education? It's better to work for the liberation of the country and development of society. I want to contribute to the great efforts of our great party in liberating all exploited, backward and downtrodden people. Uncle, what did you achieve with your education? I know you were good in your studies. What did you get with that bourgeois education?" Prakash commented.

"Prakash, you're too young to talk about these things . . . I mean . . . politics. For you, it's time to go to school to read your books." I supported Pooja.

"Uncle, I'm reading, but not the textbooks, I'm learning in our party's programmes, which is far better than those traditional schools." Prakash defended his deeds.

"Look, Dai, he listens to nobody," Pooja complained.

"Come, Rabindra. I'll take you to the wood. Uncle, I'll talk to you later," Prakash said and left with Rabindra.

I was surprised, a bit taken aback. Not by what he said, but by the way he expressed himself, immaturely confident. At such little age, before his teens, how could he become blindly convinced about what he was saying? How and by whom was his little brain being bred with such ideas, with such fanciful thoughts? Was he moving in the right direction?

Sushmita and the daughters were waiting for me on the veranda, curiously.

I was new for them, having returned from abroad after a long.

Earlier that morning, after stepping into the yard and putting the bag, in fact, two bags, on the veranda, as I had called my daughters, Sushmita had appeared from the cowshed. It had been difficult for us to adjust ourselves to a long-awaited yet sudden togetherness in the yard, my own yard, after almost two years. We both did not know how to respond with that pleasant encounter. For a moment, we looked at each other, gazed at each other with straight eyes; then I suddenly hugged her. It was the first time in our married life I hugged her in the open, so tightly. Within a few seconds, she tried to free herself from this unanticipated hug. She could not take it easily. She glowed.

In our rural areas, hugging was not common among our generation – a generation yet to adapt to the culture of hugging and kissing in public. Not only hugging, the other simplest means of expressing love were also not socially permitted, at least not in the open. They were considered almost as offensive acts. It had taken months for us to talk in front of our seniors. We never walked in parallel. Either she followed me or I followed her. Mostly she. My brief affectionate looks and occasional concerns about her petty issues – if she was tired, if she was fine, or if she ate anything – were enough to assure her of my love. Romance was possible only at night while we were in the bed. That also to a limited scale. So she blushed and freed herself in response to the sudden hug. Quickly. It was in that haphazard attempt of hugging I sullied the blue jacket, which I had bought in Pasang's store at a discounted price, solely for the occasion, for the arrival in the hamlet after two years. I was sure the jacket fitted me. I wanted to impress her and later to the others as well. I wanted to walk around the village in that blue jacket. But in that ridiculous attempt of hugging, cow dung smeared on its arms and the side. Only later, I came to know Sushmita was yet to wash her hands after cleaning the shed.

"Look at your Jacket. You spoilt it." Those were the first words of my wife. After two years!

"It's not me. It's you," I said, smiling or rather laughing and taking off the jacket.

Such had been our encounter in that early morning after a long separation. Such were our first conversations, a bit funny and perhaps dramatic. It was only after the children came out, the normalcy returned. We became normal.

"Rabindra, touch your father's feet," Sushmita said.

Rabindra looked at me: his look tentative and confused as if trying to fit the image of his father he had developed in his little mind with the real image, standing in the courtyard.

I swept him up into my arms. He was nearing three when I had left.

Both daughters were looking at me with their curious eyes.

"Daddy, I can count from one to hundred. I can also say *ka, kha, ga, gha*. I can also write," Rabindra said, touching the buttons of my shirt with his little hands.

He was trying to be intimate with me, to win fatherly affection. What I enjoyed was his childlike bass voice, at first somewhat faltering and croaking as if he had a sore throat or was speaking for the first time after he woke up, then becoming normal – a normal child voice. He had just started off school. The girls were in the fourth and third grade respectively. That day, they were released from school as their father was to come from abroad.

"But your writing doesn't look nice. You just scrawl on the paper. Daddy can't read those scrawls." Sarita tried to be smarter.

"My writing is better than yours. Daddy, Sarita Didi always hits me." Rabindra not only defended his writing but also blamed his sister.

"No, Daddy, I never hit him. It's he who always teases me," Sarita retorted.

"They always quarrel," Madhu said in her gentle, shy tone.

"I know all of you. Don't disturb Daddy with your nonsense chats. He must be tired." My wife silenced them.

Such had been my first encounter with my children after two years. I enjoyed their little talks and their childhood psychology of competing among themselves for fatherly affection. I was fully taken up with them. After having a cup of tea, the tea prepared with fresh buffalo milk, I had gone to Uncle's house to see him.

Now, as I stepped into the courtyard, Sushmita said, "You must be hungry. The food is ready. Freshen up yourself."

Following Sushmita, I entered the house. The narrow and dark inside at once offered me a warm sensation. The trusses, the rafters, the wooden pillars, the mud bedstead, the hearth, the little inside door that led to the attic, the *gagris* and *ghaitos*, the *amkhoras and karuwas*, the cauldrons, the tongs and *dhungro*, the haphazardly laid utensils: all at once smiled. The spout of the old tar-coated kettle on the hearth was spouting steam. It was the same kettle that had been with us from the days of my mother. Sitting on the old *pirka* on the side of the hearth and having the food – rice and curry and chutney – along with Sushmita and the children was like an occasion of regaining the home and hearth.

The rest of the first day, I went around the hamlet to see the fields and woods.

At first, Sushmita took me to the cowshed to show me the buffalo she had bought a year back for twenty-five thousand rupees. It was a shiny black buffalo. The udder was engorged with milk. She told me that even after six months of calving, the first time it calved, it was producing not less than two litres of milk twice a day. The young female calf was tethered a little away, at the other side of the shed so that she could not reach the udder of her mother. The buffalo bellowed as it saw Sushmita.

The goats bleated inside the pen. Mali, our beloved cow, gazed at me with her big glistening eyes, inviting me to stroke her.

The place for manure heap was vacant. The manure had obviously been taken to the fields. In the small patch of the land beside the place there were tall succulent mustard stalks with wide green leaves. I had seen similar mustard stalks and leaves in front of the yard. A bamboo platform was erected for tomatoes. Even after the season, the tomato plants were studded with the green and red fruits. At the back, in the orchard, I saw many eggplants and chilli plants, dried. They would come again in the season, she said. Every part of the land around the house was used and was cultivated minutely. Sushmita was green-fingered.

She had patched the dilapidated part of the thatch roof with chestnut leaves and had staked bamboo posts to brace the slanted wall of the cowshed. The cowshed had been constructed years back, before I was born. It should have been repaired or a new shed should have been constructed years ago, long before I went to Lhasa. There were, however, other priorities, more urgent than that. So despite its dilapidating condition, it had fallen into disrepair for all those years and now had begun to fall apart. The time had come. It required urgent attention. In such condition, it would not see the coming summer out. It would soon crumble down and might invite a huge loss, the possible death of the cattle. It scared me. Even though I did not say anything I decided to start renovating and restructuring the shed before leaving for Lhasa.

The ambience of the house witnessed that Sushmita had toiled hard in the earth, alone. And herself? She was simple as always. A simple blouse and cotton sari, a red *patuki*, a dot of red *tika* on her forehead, a small stud in her nose, a pair of earrings in her ear lobes, and a few bangles around her wrists: this was the sum total she wore most of the time after she was married to me. Except for these things, she had just a few extra clothes bought for her marriage and given by her father and a few pieces of family jewellery given by my mother to be worn on special occasions. I had not been able to give her much. Yet she never complained; she never demanded. She did not have any personal desires. Even though she had, they were subjugated to the needs of her children and her husband. Even now, even when she was getting something, the little cash, from me, she never wished an extravagant life. She was living totally up to my expectation, the selfish expectation: always wishing her to be dominated and subjugated.

Big Plot was furrowed two days ago, she said. We walked on the ploughed earth. The earth had a fresh smell. Big Plot had suffered many little landfalls. I could see them in more than a dozen places, a few of which were old, but the majority were new. Before going to Lhasa, I had tried to control rats, which, during the harvest, dug holes in the plot. During summer those holes filled up with water and caused landslips. I had planted the wormwood plants on the slopes. I had, many times, requested Little Uncle not to dig out the corners of his field deeply. Yet nothing worked. Rats always appeared in seasons, avoiding the traps and poisons I had put in their holes and walks. They survived and used new routes and dug new holes. They turned out to be cleverer than I had thought. The wormwood plants could not grip the soil in summer; the roots did not root long and deep. And Little Uncle never listened to me or never cared about my request. His digging became deeper and deeper. All my attempts became futile. Every summer, whenever the green rice paddy was watered, whenever there was a heavy rainfall, the landfalls occurred quite often. With these landfalls, the continuous process of decay, I became worried about the future of Big Plot.

Little Uncle's house and shed had vanished from the scene. There were a few remnants of stone and mud heaps covered in weeds and wild grasses. After he had migrated to somewhere in Terai, there was no one to look after the house so the house had tumbled down. It had taken on a forlorn look, even before I went to Lhasa. In the absence of any men to stay and smoke there, termites, ants, and mice had been competing to establish their colony in the empty house. This time the house and the shed were absent from the scene.

"Does Little Uncle visit this hamlet these days?" I asked Sushmita.

"Not often. He came during Dashain to have *tika* and also two months ago to see Uncle and to sell his remaining property. He was asking about you."

We kept walking. Nothing was much changed. The mountains, the terraced fields, the scattered houses, the *chautari* with the tall trees, and the little streams: they existed in the same way as they had appeared before I left.

But there was something striking my brain. As soon as I stepped into Big Plot, I felt something was missing. What was that? What property was missing from there? As I walked along with my wife, I got to know what was missing from there. It was the *simal* tree that had disappeared from the view. The absence of the tree was striking. To me, the huge tree, the branches of which had enormously stretched out wide and high above, was not only a tree; it was something more deeply associated with my childhood memory. In our childhood, we had played and spent plenty of time under the giant tree. We had seen so many birds nestling on its branches. The red flowers with thick petals and the floating fibre cottons from the tree would allure us so much. Moreover, the tree fitted a fairy-tale tree of a story, the story about a carpenter trapping the death itself inside a tree house. The story, I later found, had spread across the countries in one or another form. I had imagined the tree and the setting of the story to have been precisely the same as this huge *simal* looked. The tree had left an indelible impression on me. As I went to the place where the tree used to stand, I saw a stump, a wide stump, the relic of the giant tree and on the top of the stump unevenly yet artistically crafted circular rings, telling the years of the tree. A crack had developed in the centre of the stump. Numerous small cracks with irregular patterns radiated from the centres towards the edge. Sushmita told me that Little Uncle, whose property the tree was, had sold it to a carpenter the year before. The tree was cut down; the stump and branches were sawn apart; the tree was turned into furniture and firewood. Quickly. Sushmita told me as we walked along. What would have happened to those birds which had made the tree their home for years? When they came back to find their home missing, all of a sudden, how helpless they would have felt?

Gopal, too, was struck with the absence of the tree, he told me later during our roaming around the hamlet. It had been almost five years since we met last. He had gone to Dubai five years back, and I had left for Lhasa before he came on leave. Therefore, the desire for walking and talking to each other was immense within us as we met after years. In the late afternoon, as we, after having a purposeless walk – around the fields in the hamlet, over leaves-strewn trails in the woods and along the dusty trails that we would use to drive our cattle in our childhood – sat on a flat flint in the little foothill, looking at the barren slopes, he said the giant tree should have been allowed to survive as the tallest tree in and around the hamlet. He had said so looking at a small, poorly grown pine tree.

The barrenness of little foothills was intact. The effort to turn them into thickly forested hills, which had been initiated years ago, almost as a campaign, had failed. Perhaps it was a part of a national or a wider campaign. Hundreds of pines and willows had been planted all over the barren slopes. One of my cousins from the village down the foothills had been appointed as a forest guard, a paid job, to take care of those little plants. We were asked not to graze our cattle on the slopes. But the plants could not grow, partly because of the carelessness of the guard, partly because of the negligence and unawareness of the villagers, and partly or chiefly because of the infertility of the soil itself. The young plants died one after another. They became pale and were trampled down by the cattle's hooves. (The strict instructions were obeyed for a couple of weeks, but later they were defied, at first the cattle were grazed on the periphery; then within another few months everywhere.) So all plants – except very few in between big rocks, out of the reach of the cattle – vanished away within a few years, before I went to Lhasa. Thus, adamantly, the little foothills preferred to stay barren and stayed barren. Those very few pines and willows – in between big rocks – were now struggling to grow. They appeared like bonsai. Gopal had expressed his wish to see the giant *simal*, looking at a bonsai pine, struggling to grow.

Across the stream a vulture flew down from the sky and perched on a tree branch, which had poked out of the cliff. The lean bare branch began to give under the weight of the vulture. The vulture took a short flight to its home on a cliff ledge. It was right then Gopal asked me how long I was going to stay in the hamlet.

"One month," I replied.

That one month passed by very quickly. It gave out even before I felt at home, even before I went to the villages around to see the aged people as a matter of courtesy, and even before I was sated with the pleasure, the pleasure of embracing Sushmita at night and the pleasure of playing with the children. Perhaps it was after three weeks, one night Sushmita requested me to stay back at the hamlet. The realisation at once came to me that a month's time was about to exhaust. Was it possible to remain at home, as she had requested at that sultry night? Was it possible to find other options to earn for living to support the lives of five persons? I did not see any convincing options in sight.

A big part of the savings I had made was demanded by the urgent necessity of constructing the new shed. After Gopal and I had a close inspection of the slanted wall of the shed, we reached the conclusion that it could not be repaired; a wholly new one should be constructed. The only things from the old shed that might be used for the new structure were the stones and a few rafters. So I had commenced the construction after a week or so of my arrival, which consumed a lot of money.

It was not possible to start a small business with the remaining money. I did not want to take a loan. For the first time, our family had become debt-free. I had paid all the money I owed. I still remembered how Aama always tried to come out of the burden of debt, which was never realised throughout her life and how she had died in that status of indebtedness. So the idea of taking a loan to venture into a business of which I was not sure was not a good idea.

There were no other options to avoid Lhasa. The only options were either to go to the Gulf or to Malaysia, which were not the options understood in Sushmita's way, in the sense not leaving the hamlet, not leaving the country. Gopal had once again told me about the allure of Dubai, tempting me to go there to try my luck. However, the temptation did not last much. I was reminded of the cost, the one and a half lakh rupees; of the possibility of being cheated by the agents at both ends, in Nepal and in Dubai; and of the possibility of exploitation. The temptation subsided. Eventually, having considered all other options, I had decided to go back to Lhasa.

So when Sushmita, in her sultry voice requested me to stay at home forever, I said to her, "Don't worry, I'll come soon." In a further attempt to convince her, I promised her I would call her every week, promised her I would be back in the following Dashain. I promised her I would stay in Lhasa genuinely and would live a straight and narrow life. She understood me.

The understanding of the situation, of the compulsion of leaving the hamlet had been easier for her for yet another reason. At least I took it in this way. The young men (almost all) and women (in significant numbers) had left the villages. The villages were youth less, the fields did not find strong and young people to dig them, and thus remained barren. It was not the case of a single house. It had become a general phenomenon. Gopal had told me that there were hundreds of thousands of Nepalese working in the Gulf. Here, the villages were empty. Every doer man left at one stage or another. This generalisation of the situation helped both of us to understand the reality. The village had changed.

Indeed, it had changed a lot. Initially, I could not feel the change, could not notice it. But later it came upon me, quickly and extensively. I saw a young lady, a teenage girl, in camouflage – a shirt and pants – ploughing her field. It was strange to me, both the dress and the act of ploughing by a woman. Even more surprising was her addressing me as *sir*, which was not familiar in the villages before I left the hamlet. The address was used normally for school teachers. She had asked me, "When did you come back, sir?" Her tone was polite. Later, I came to know she was from Gurunggaun, the youngest sister of my friend, Yam Bahadur, who was in Indian Army now. With her grown-up body and the camouflage dress, I had not recognised her. Further later, Sushmita said she had become a Maoist. I now realised the reason behind her dress.

The movement that had begun before I left for Lhasa had since been growing and growing. The people in camouflage, some of them with guns, would come to the villages, would sing revolutionary songs, and would give speeches. They would try to mingle with the villagers and convince them about their *great party*. Some would seem polite and would talk logically. Many were arrogant and spoke arrogantly, often threatening the poor ignorant villagers.

They would talk of total changes, sweeping changes in all spheres of society – political, economic, social, and cultural. They said they were fighting for the poor and depressed. And when they left, the villagers talked about them, the children mimicked their songs, slogans, and styles.

The camouflage became popular. Some agreed with them, many did not, yet no one spoke against them. No one dared breathe even a word against them when they saw the guns and when they heard, and, in some cases, even witnessed the arbitrary action against those who could not and did not follow them. Sushmita always wondered if those arbitrary, sometimes inhumanely brutal, actions against humans were necessary to bring the changes. Were all other options exhausted? She told me that one time a few of them came to our house and asked for shelter for a night. She was afraid to deny. She had to give them food. They talked about so many things, many of which she did not understand. The next morning they left, saying what they were doing was for the people but again making her more confused. Devaki and her husband both were adamantly opposed to this new intolerant political force, so they had to move from their village. They migrated to Pokhara to make themselves feel secure, to stop their daughters being compelled to carry guns for the sake of sweeping changes! Anyway, the movement was spreading fast and had already engulfed a big part of politically vacuumed and economically backward countryside for whatever reasons.

And now, with Prakash influenced by them so much, I became worried about my children too, especially about Rabindra, who had already begun to mimic those speeches and songs in his childish tone. What future was it heralding? Such an unusual influence at easily manoeuvrable formative years of childhood!

The final two or three days, the last week of my stay, I spent mostly with Uncle. His situation after I met him had not improved nor had it deteriorated. Was it the effect of the herbs? Or was it the very nature of the killer disease? I did not know. I said I would send him the herbs regularly, which I knew was expensive. I was expecting Pasang would help me to find them at a cheap price. I was also expecting Pradip would find some ways of sending those herbs up to Kathmandu. From

Kathmandu, Gopal could bring them. One day, in the last week, at his request, I walked him to the *chautari* and sat there under the banyan shade. We sat there for hours. Even under the status of sedation caused by the drugs, he was talking; he told me about his early life, about my father and grandparents: the things I knew and knew not. He revealed many things to me as if he was aware of the fact that he was talking to me for the last occasion. I was aware that he was suffering from cancer, and he might (or would) die after a few months. I was talking with a person having knowledge about the imminence of his death in the near future. It was clear to me that every human being was aware of the sureness of death. But what would be the feeling of a person with the knowledge of the tentative dates of his death in the near future? I wished he would survive.

The next day, I left before the children woke up. Sushmita bade me a sad farewell. Gopal came to the bazaar to see me off. I was supposed to catch the day bus to Kathmandu in order to meet Thakur as we had planned.

Eleven

"Ashok La, you! I didn't think you would come back. I thought you already forgot us," Pema said, quizzically lifting her eyebrows.

She was surprised and happy too. Her expression showed the warmth of welcome. Surprised were the others too. They had not believed I would be back. They had not thought I liked working as a receptionist-cum-waiter. From the very start, they had taken my being in Lhasa as an unwanted course of life, a path mistakenly chosen. So they had not believed I would be back. It was the reason why Pema, before my departure, had asked me if I would return to Lhasa. Maybe I had already been out of their memory or at least faded.

"How can I forget such a beautiful lady? How's your boyfriend?" I tried to be as casual as possible.

But without caring about the casualness and question about her boyfriend, Pema said, "Pala always remembers you. How's your uncle?"

"He's suffering from cancer. The doctors say he won't survive more than six months, from now on five months."

"It's so sad. I'm so sorry." Apparent sadness ran through her face. "What about your wife?"

"She's fine. But she wants to see you. She wants to know how cruel you are."

"What do you mean by cruel? I'm not cruel. I don't think you talked about me to your *beautiful* wife, with whom you're always afraid. Where're your *books*? You didn't bring them?" she asked. And her eyebrows arched and lips quirked when she asked. The others laughed at her mentioning books.

"I'm not afraid of her. I love her more than any other women on earth," I said, with clear intention of teasing her more.

"Then love. Who cares?" she frowned.

"How's the road, Ashok Dai? I heard there was a heavy snowstorm at the border," Bidur chimed in.

"Oh, it was terrible, almost deadly. Such a heavy snowfall and those howling gales! We were stranded hours, just below Tong La pass. A huge mass of snow had been blown into drifts on the road. Thanks the courageous those Tibetan drivers. Thakur and I myself were shivering with cold. The chill had got into each and every part of our bones. But those gallant men came out with shovels in their frostbitten hands and cleared the road. Oh, that height and that cold! I had never experienced such elemental forces of nature. And this Pasang? He was leading them," I said, giving them a few details of my travel. "And Dingri was even colder. And over that, the lack of oxygen. The whole night I spent shivering and suffocating. I wonder how Mark managed to spend a week there."

"And I am sure while our Tibetan men were shovelling the snow, you must have been reading a book there or recalling your wife." Pema threw in yet another satire.

"No, dear, I was thinking of your dreamy eyes," I said, looking straight at her emerald eyes, "honestly speaking."

Her cheeks flamed at this unusual address for her, which was not usual for me either.

"How's Pradip?"

"He has gone to Nyingchi." Tenzing gave a twisted answer to my question.

"Oh, now I understand why you're playing cards during lunch time. Let him come. I'll see all of you." I sat behind the reception.

"We're not afraid of your favourite boss," Pema said.

At a table near the window, there were two monks in maroon dress counting the prayer beads and looking at Jokhang Temple in all their solemnity. The yard of Jokhang was full of nomads basking in the afternoon sunshine. It was cold both inside and outside. The arrival of the month of March had not brought the spring in the city yet. It still felt wintry.

It was cold when I stood in the yard near Jowo Utra in the evening, looking at thousands of illuminated lamps offered by devotees. The winter-beaten park behind the Potala, despite newly put up sprinklers, looked withered and felt cold.

Prahlad and Prabha had shifted to another place; Bindira had gone home, and Jaya was planning to return forever. Bidur told me about those new developments in our old building, the developments taken place during my absence. A fight had erupted between Jaya and Prahlad for reasons Bidur did not know in detail – though he had conjectured it must be about Prabha – in which Prahlad had got a bruise on his lower lip with Jaya's punch. After two days of the incident, they had moved to a new place. Prahlad wanted to inform the police about the incident; however, the others advised him not to do. They were afraid it would create problems for them as well. He, nonetheless, talked to the owner of the parlour. She decided not to renew the contract of Jaya. She was afraid that, despite his professionalism, his misdeeds would ultimately invite trouble for her business. She, therefore, had decided to get rid of him as soon as possible. She was just waiting for Thakur.

Jaya also had made up his mind to leave Lhasa. There was no option; the authorities were too tight for any illegal stay. Yet when I met him, he told me that he got tired of staying in Lhasa and wished to leave the city. He did not give me the reason for his leaving and did not tell me anything about the fight. From quite early on, I knew he was the sort of a personality who never accepted or exhibited any of his faults or weaknesses or things showing embarrassment or guilt on his part. He never exposed himself fully. I had rare chats with him and that also in a very distanced or, in a way, a detached manner. Our chats were confined to the brief mentioning of a few things such as family, the weather, the loneliness we experienced abroad, or such other matters, which did not contribute to establish intimacy or whatsoever between us. I was, many a time, told that he was fond of consorting much of his leisure in drinking and chatting with girls, and despite many requests, he could not come off that. But he never talked to me about those things. He had his unusual style of life, his character somewhat sibylline: mysterious to read, always busy on his own, content with what he had, some kind of privacy which he preferred to keep intact, and to an extent, arrogant and sullen. But he was unerringly professional in his work. When the scissors in his calloused black hand ran on the customer's head, the snaps were fast, rhythmic, and accurate.

Anyway, he left Lhasa. He left within a week of our arrival. And this, his sudden leaving, saddened Thakur. The personalities they possessed differed to a vast extent, and their stay, their togetherness, was full of squabbles on petty issues, but despite these, they were close friends and relatives; they had spent much of their life together. So the departure gave Thakur a feeling of losing a companion from his village carrying childhood memories. For days, the shadow of loneliness showed in his dark face.

Jaya left. But the Nepalese community in the city was growing. The ever-thriving tourism and restaurant businesses in the city had paved the way for more Nepalese to come to the city, primarily as chefs or waiters in the restaurants. The growth in the Nepalese community, negligible it was though, had offered them the opportunity to gather more frequently. At such gatherings, often served with cheap alcohol, they talked about their family, about their salaries, sometimes about the girls who invited passers-by to sleep with them even during the daytime in an undeclared red-light area. Of course, one of the topics of the discussions would always be about the political system and the leaders back in the country. There was an agreement, a unanimous conclusion, among them that it was the corrupt system and the leaders who ruined the country, compelling them to leave their beloved country. Such gatherings would sometimes end, due to the effect of the alcohol, with squabbles or fist fights for nothing. Thakur and I rarely joined those night gatherings. But we would know about whatever happened there from Bidur who, along with Tenzing, never missed such gatherings. Nonetheless, the increase of the Nepalese in Lhasa, as a matter of fact, was comforting us too.

The older generation, who had been in Tibet for years, whose roots had started centuries before, was, however, a bit hesitant in accepting the newcomers, the sweated labourers. This older generation had been blended with the local culture, had assimilated into society; they had developed considerably high social status. At times, they used to be addressed by the locals as *jindala* or *soktala*. Now, when these newcomers arrived in Lhasa, with very little knowledge of stratified society and cultural sophistication therein, and freely moved around the city enjoying their freedom to the fullest possible with their rather casual dress, the informality and hi-hello, the older generation felt a bit offended. They were worried that their social status, the status of being *jindala* or *soktala*, of which they were proud, would be jeopardised by the newcomers. Worries had been added to this by the singers and dancers who came to work in *nangma* or bars. The business of the bars where the young Nepalese sang and danced, almost naked, thrived more. Those bars were often crowded with young and drunk lads and lasses. At times, late at night, the fighting with swords and smashed bottles erupted there. Pasang and the others talked about this declining image of the Nepalese in Lhasa.

The sole person in the *circle* who was not bothered by this feeling of decline was Weihong. She was happy to spend time with young and smart boys. No one knew why, but she was fond of the Nepalese. She had named a few of them after the names of Bollywood heroes of those days. She could be seen in her comely appearance and come-hither look each time with a different person.

"Why are there so many tourists this year? I'm having a hard life in this kitchen. It's baking hot and there's no fan or air conditioner. We must talk to our boss. Sometimes I hate this job," Bidur grumbled as he poured the spices into the chicken curry. "Cooking for hours over hot stoves is making me sick."

Drops of sweat were shining on his dark face. He was wiping his sweat-sodden face with his handkerchief to avoid the drops falling into the dishes he was preparing. The narrow kitchen was indeed hot with as many as four stoves burning for hours without a halt. It was hot even for me who came there infrequently, and Bidur was working there for hours. And it felt even more so as there was a strong hangover left from the previous day's *linka* at the Lees' place.

I came out to the bar and started to prepare cocktails as per the order slips, the memories of the *linka* in mind.

Pema came, saying, "Ashok La, there's a call for you from your beautiful wife."

Whenever my wife came up during our conversation, it was usual for her to use the word *beautiful* with an added emphasis, which I never took otherwise. But the call from my wife at this time was not usual. It was not expected. I had asked her not to call me at the restaurant's number, unless there was an urgent matter, and it was the first time she called me during the busiest moment. Why did she call me at this time? With an unknown premonition on mind, I received the call.

"What happened?" Pema asked. Perhaps she had already read the changing colours on my face by the time I put down the receiver.

"Uncle passed away," I said in a low voice.

"Oh, so sad," she replied.

The restaurant was busy. There was no time for further talk or expressing emotions. I knew she was sympathetic to me. Her look was consoling, but she was a bit confused for not finding appropriate expressions to be conveyed at such a moment.

"Pema, can you handle the bar? I want to go to the room."

"Certainly," she responded.

I walked down the spiral stairs with heavy feet, walked heavily on along the streets, reached the park behind the Potala, then sat on the rustic bench under the willow, looking at the brown mountains. I felt tired mentally and physically. The news of death evoked memories associated with Uncle: from the childhood to the last time I had talked to him under the banyan shade just before my departure after the holidays. As I sat under the willow, listening to the monotonous cooing of a pair of doves, he appeared in my memory in different forms: first a faded memory of his figure in his thirties as soon as I had known him as my uncle, such an agile figure, a person of medium height, but amazingly active; then in between years steadily aging, first a few wrinkles on his face, skin, and neck, a few grey streaks of hair on the temples. Down through the years, those wrinkles turned into lines and the greyness expanded to the other parts of the head, the change slow and difficult to notice, almost invisible if one saw him every day. But when I saw him, after a two-year gap, the change was so visible, so noticeable: almost striking. The cancer-struck aged body looked pitiable. Now, when I got the news about his death, his last figure, the cancer-struck one, dominated all other previous figures.

His death was not unanticipated. Medically qualified doctors had already predicted it with anticipated dates. It was just a matter of days or weeks. But once it became a fact, it was emotionally painful. I had lost the last vestige of fatherly love. I lay awake the whole night.

The next day, Pasang came to my room.

"Pema told me about the news," he said. "It's sad, but life is short and unpredictable. Death is beyond our control, *Aashok*."

"He was like my father."

"I can understand your sentiment. I'll take you to Sera Monastery to pray to Buddha for the peace of his soul."

"Pasang La, first I want to go to the river to wash and shave my head. I have asked Thakur. This is our culture. If you don't mind I want you to go with us."

"Why not?"

We went to the riverbank. At our usual place. The river was flowing with its usual rhythm.

"The water in the river is too cold. I have brought warm water for shaving," Thakur said, taking out his shaving kit and Thermos.

"No, I want to take a bath in the river."

"But don't go too far. There's a drift," Pasang cautioned me.

I was not much aware of the religious rituals to be followed in detail on such occasion, but I knew I was supposed to have a thorough bath in a river, and though, not being his son directly, I was not supposed to shave my head, I wanted to shave it out of my respect to him. I stripped down to the waist and dipped into the shallow part of the river twice. The water was cold, cold enough to give severe shivers to every part of the body, but it gave me a sense of satisfaction.

Later that day, after praying to the colossal statues of Buddha at Sera Monastery, we sat under a paling poplar, looking at *chipis* with their fast-moving little heads. On our way back, Pasang drove along the road that passed the sky burial place and pulled in his Land Cruiser from where we could see the big boulders. A great number of vultures were around feeding on human carrion.

"At least half a dozen corpses have been fed to the vultures today," Pasang said, lighting a cigarette. "Once you're born, death is natural. It's just a matter of time."

"Yes, Pasang La," I agreed.

A few more weeks passed by. The winter had already approached in the valley. One Saturday, during *kora*, I came upon Mark surprisingly in front of the Potala, near the cave-like restaurant. More surprising was that before I saw him, I saw Gundum and her son, holding Mark's hand.

There had been unusual gusts and rain throughout the night. I had heard the wind-driven raindrops against the window glass the whole night. The unusual rain had added an unusual cold to the environment. Thakur and I, wrapped up against the unusual cold, had come out for our *kora*, our daily routine.

"Thakur Dai, namaste." A familiar female voice came from behind, compelling both of us turn back.

"Did you forget me?" It was Gundum, in whose restaurant in Dingri we had spent the night on our way to Nepal and back. She was standing there with her elegant Amdo complexion, her teeth glistening as white as virgin snow. She was with her son holding the hand of a tall guy. Who was he? Mark? But what about his beard, which would fit his face so perfectly and would draw an immediate attention from those who saw him? Yes, it was Mark with his beard shaved off. He was in Tibetan dress, which gave him a different look than I had seen him earlier.

All of us were surprised with this unanticipated encounter.

"Hey, Ashok! How're you? I was just planning to come to your restaurant this afternoon. Is everything all right?"

"Mark? It's you? I hadn't expected to see you here in this season," I said.

"It's a long story."

We pursued *kora* together: Thakur talking with Gundum, and I myself talking with Mark, Gundum's son in between, holding Mark's hand.

He told me everything. How he met Gundum during his trip to Dingri, how he fell in love with her, how they pursued their communication, and then how they decided to get married. He quit the professorship in America and owned a bar in a newly established star hotel in Lhasa.

"But it's not for making a lot of money. I need to do something to run the family," he laughed.

During our conversation, he said he always loved Tibet and its serenity and finally found someone to live his life with among the barren mountains.

Oh, Mark! What a passion for Tibet! What a love for this serene land. And Gundum? You and your son found destiny, I was thinking as I said goodbye to them, inviting to come to the restaurant.

My life continued. It continued with the repetition of my routine: *kora* with Thakur; the daylong work in the restaurant – six days a week; solitarily (sometimes with Bidur) walking to the room along the empty roads in the late evenings; on Sunday, tiring yet satisfying walks with Thakur along the fence and on the shingle riverbank; the peaceful sitting on the bench in the park behind the Potala; and then on occasions, when Pasang was free, the drives along the highways. Calls to Sushmita, occasional visits to the Lees' place or Pala's hamlet, and very rarely carousing with the *circle* were also part of the routine. Furthermore, the visits to Mark's bar in a newly established hotel and talking to him, sometimes helping him to prepare drinks, were added to my schedule.

Life took a scheduled and rhythmic path, and I was, in a way, adjusted to this uneventful cycle of my life. The feeling of missing the family and birthplace was always there, although not as intense as it used to be in the first months. Sometimes, I felt an urgent need to return. However, I had adapted myself to the reality, the reality within the reach of life. The dream of earning a lot of money and making a house in a city or town had subsided. The fantasies, dreams, and ambitions had found their practical level, which I had accepted.

With these, I was thinking to stay a few more years in Lhasa, until at least I had a little saving for the future or to start a small business. Pradip had increased my salary, almost another one thousand Chinese Yuan more than what I drew earlier. It had given me some comfort. I was saving little by little. There were no debts. The children were studying. Sushmita, as usual, was committed to the well-being of the family.

Amidst these, I was thinking to stay a few more years in Lhasa. I had spoken to Sushmita about it, which she had accepted on the preconditions that I would visit the hamlet every year for one or two months. So, according to the plan, I was planning to go on leave for a month. I was just waiting for Bidur. This time, I was planning to go with Mark up to Dingri, of course together with Thakur.

But I did not know life was to take another course, its own path.

Twelve

Lhosar was not yet over; people were still in festive mood. There was still a shivering chill in the air. The yard in front of Jokhang was full of nomads. Tourists had not yet arrived. The business had not yet picked up. Chhawang and Dolma were on leave. Pradip and Bidur had not come back. Pasang, Dorje, Mark, and I, on one of the cold afternoons, were brewing tea in our restaurant.

"How's your business going on?" Pasang asked Mark.

"This year I was busy establishing the bar and making contacts. I hope it'll pick up in the coming season. The hotel is getting reservations," Mark said, mixing his words with his newly learnt Tibetan. He was trying to grow into his new life, so different from the previous one. Interestingly enough, he had become a part of the *circle*. He had grown interest in mah-jong and *linka*.

"The hotel is in a good location. I think the business will surely pick up," Pasang said.

"But, Pasang, I need a barman. A professional. Like Ashok."

"Why don't you talk to him?" Pasang said, sipping at his tea.

"And Pradip will kick out all of us," Dorje said, laughing out loud.

"No, no, no. I don't want to fight with Pradip. I'll find somebody else."

Tenzing and Pema came in, perhaps after their afternoon *kora* around Jokhang, and, despite our request to stay there, they went to the kitchen. Tenzing had worn a sad look. I had been reading a woebegone expression on her face for a couple of days, as soon as Bidur went. And it was growing every day. She had stopped caring about herself. The texture of her complexion looked rough; her lips were cracked; and streaks of unkempt hair strayed into the air. She had stopped humming songs while working. In response to my queries about her worried look, she always said everything was all right, or it was simply a headache. But I was certain there was something else behind her sadness.

Leaving the others with their tea, I went to the kitchen to find Tenzing crying, beads of tears trickling down from her face. Pema was trying to console her, but the more she was trying, the louder the sobbing was becoming.

I asked, "What happened, Tenzing? Why are you crying?"

She did not speak, rather sobbed even more loudly. Caressing her hair, I asked again, "What happened to you, my sister?"

"Bidur cheated me."

"What did he do?"

But she did not tell any more, did not reveal what actually had happened between them. After sobbing a few more minutes, she came to a halt and wiped her tears with the back of her plump hands. The shaft of sadness was still in her eyes. Pema was standing beside her and trying to soothe her.

"What did he do, Tenzing? Tell me. I'll see him once he's here." I tried to know what was troubling her.

"He won't come. He should have come the day before yesterday. But he did not. He cheated me." She sobbed again.

"It's too much, Tenzing. Don't cry. Be a strong woman," Pema said.

"Will your friends have dinner here?" Pema asked, trying to segue to a different matter.

"I don't think so, Pema. Isn't it Butter Lamp festival today? Mark says he'll stay to see the lamps. I'll let you know." I came out, without knowing what was the matter troubling Tenzing so much; how Bidur cheated her and why she thought he would not come. He did not tell me he would not come. Maybe he was stuck for some business, but I was sure he would come.

I came out. Chats were continuing. They were planning to visit the monasteries before the business season started. Mark was interested in visiting monasteries in the countryside, chiefly those built on steep, craggy slopes. He showed his great interest in the secluded environment of those monasteries, and it was Dorje who knew all about such places.

After a while, once Pasang and Dorje left for their homes for the preparation of the festival, Mark and I sat at a table by the window, drinking and chatting.

Even before the sun's purple afterglow ended, the full moon appeared in the east in its complete size and cast its silvery light over the mountains and the city. And from the earth – the Jokhang, the wide yard and Jowo Utra – innumerable lights, the butter lamps – prepared in different shapes of gods, plants, flowers, beasts, and birds – flickered. The two lights, from the sky and from the earth, mingled in between, offering colourful hues.

"The Tibetans are as equally aware of the aesthetic part of life as they're religious. They're fond of colours and brightness," Mark said, looking at those lights. He had much wider knowledge about Tibet and the Tibetans; he understood them philosophically. "Did you manage to travel some in Tibet?"

"Not really. In fact, not at all. Except for going home by road and to Namtso Lake."

"You must travel more. You'll be amazed."

"But you know, Mark, it's not easy for us. I mean for the people working in a restaurant."

"That I can understand. But you can visit at least the nearby towns and villages," he said and poured whisky into both glasses. "*Sapta.*"

"*Sapta,*" I responded.

"What would you like to eat?" Pema asked.

"I'm tired of *thukpa*. Can we have rice and curry today? What about you, Mark?"

"A fantastic idea. I haven't had it for quite a while. Oh, that spicy dal and curry!" Mark clicked his tongue.

"Pema, do you need help in the kitchen?"

"No, Ashok La," she said.

Yet I went to the kitchen, leaving Mark to watch the lights alone.

Inside, Pema was soaking lentils, the pink ones, my favourite taste. Tenzing was chopping onions, her eyes filled with tears.

"Are you still crying, Tenzing?" I asked.

"No. It's the onion." She smiled a faint smile.

"Tell me, my sister, how can I help you?"

"You can just continue with your drink."

"Let me grind *jeera*. I want to have spicy and hot dal," I said. "Why were you crying, Tenzing?"

"For nothing. I just got nervous Bidur won't return."

"I assure you he'll be here within a week."

After I came back, Mark poured another hefty measure into my glass.

I did not know why, but that day, Sushmita and the children were coming to my memory more sharply. The children must have grown some more. What about Sushmita? What about her health? What about her headaches, which she had had most of the time and which she always tried to hide? Last time, when I had gone to the hamlet, I had seen her hands pressing her temples. When asked, she had just shaken her head to say *no*. She always endured pains within her.

Bidur did not come. After another three days, Pradip came back. Alone. He said he waited at Khasa for those three days, but he did not come. One more week passed by, then another week and a month, yet he did not come. Tenzing became restless. Her sadness increased. With the passage of the days, it turned into anger and hatred, probably towards Bidur or towards the Nepalese in general and even towards me. I could sense the anger in her voice. I was told by Pema that Tenzing had been pregnant already for three months. Bidur had assured her that they would get married as soon as he came back. So far, she was hiding her pregnancy from other people, except for Pema, but now, with her growing belly, it became difficult to hide. It became more and more visible, firstly to us, working in the restaurant who already knew about the fact and later to everyone who saw her. With her woebegone look and odd-looking stomach, before marriage, she became the centre of sympathetic expressions. When Gundum – who would often come to the restaurant with Mark and, leaving him with us, would chat with the girls – knew this, she said, "A poor and unfortunate girl." Dorje said he had, long back, cautioned her not to trust *the bastard guy*. But sympathies did not come with solutions, which she needed. Rather, sometimes, they came together with comments of blame, the apportioned blame in her part. As the days passed by and her belly became bigger and bigger, she looked more irritated and frustrated. The pregnancy, the seeding of a human being in the womb of a mother, which would have been a cherished dream of a married woman, became such a problem for her. Her parents were not happy. Once her brother came to the restaurant with his friends, all with glaring eyes, and said to Pradip, in his cold, steely voice, that it was his responsibility to find Bidur. While saying so, he was touching the handle of the sword hung at his waist and was looking at me glaringly as though I was also responsible.

Pradip was in an awkward position. The tourist season was creeping up, but Bidur – the chef upon whom his business largely depended – had disappeared, fornicating with a staff, making her pregnant. He tried his best to trace Bidur. He sent his brother in Kathmandu to Bidur's village.

He asked his friends to find him in the border, but all his efforts went in vain. Bidur had just gone out of sight, leaving no trace. Tenzing's belly was growing and growing. Her parents were hesitating to take her back, a pregnant daughter without her husband. In such situation, he could not tell her – who had worked with him for so many years – to leave the restaurant until she could find any assured shelter. He rented a separate room for her and Pema near my place. But he was worried about his business. Many awkward and sympathetic looks slanted to her when she walked heavily and entered his restaurant for her daily work.

One day, on my day off, Thakur and I were sitting on the rustic bench in the park, chatting. We saw Dorje, along with his wife, coming to us with his strutting gait. After a chat, he laughed and said to me, "Ashok, how's the girl doing? Are you taking care of her? Bidur and you stayed and worked together. He didn't come. Now it's your responsibility to take care of her belly." He left, laughing. Perhaps he said these words with no motive to hurt me or without any intention to blame me. He was always humorous and informal in his chats. It, however, gave me almost a shock. Did the rumours go like this? I was suddenly alarmed. Were the others blaming me? What if Pasang and Pema also thought in this way? What about Thakur? He was with me when Dorje uttered these words. I did not know what his thinking was behind the words; he did not mention it. But Dorje's uttering of such words buzzed in my ears for some time.

After some days Pradip was able to convince her to stop working, promising that he would be paying her salary every month. A little later, when I had gone to her room with Pema to say hello to her, she was preparing to go to her parents' house. After a couple of weeks of sadness and frustration, she had come back to a status of normality. Amidst emotions and her anger or even hate for Bidur, she had grown to love her unborn baby. The motherly love had won out over all other emotions. She was determined to take care of her child. Poor Tenzing! She had at once become mature. Her single mistake, a young emotion, had changed the course of her life. She never thought one natural mistake would cost her for her whole life. She was going to be another Gundum. Would she find a person like Mark to take care of her along with the baby?

Pradip had a shortage of people. The business had started, but the chef he had found in Kathmandu had not arrived yet. The visa process could take another one or two months. So I could not leave. He requested me to stay until the new chef would come; I could not ignore. When I told her this, the voice of my wife sounded worried and suspicious.

Six months afterwards, that Sunday, I did not go for a walk with Thakur. Rather, stayed, turning out the room, arranging the untidy things: the old stove and utensils, smudged with smoke and messily lying in the room. The wall, the one against which I had put the stove, was layered by the smoke, all the way up to the ceiling. There were thick cobwebs in the corners, beneath the window ledge, at the back of the door and around the electric bulb on the ceiling. So that Sunday, I did not go walking; just stayed in the room, cleaning it. And after that, exhausted, I lay on the narrow bed, splaying legs out and looking out lazily through the window.

My fourth year in Lhasa. Yet another September. Yet another autumn. The days were closing in. The last leaves were falling from the willows. The city was browning, resembling the browns of the mountains. Dashain was less than a month away. I was all set to go to Nepal after two weeks. But I wanted to see Pala before leaving.

The next day, as I spoke to Pasang about my desire, Pasang took a long puff, stubbed out his cigarette, and said, "Why not to organise *linka* at the resort? We all can go."

"That's a marvellous idea," Mark, who had just joined us, said.

The programme was set for the following Sunday.

We took two Land Cruisers. In one, I sat with Pasang, Pradip and Pema. The others were in another. Weihong could not be contacted. We took the narrow road, the one on the northern side of the river.

The sweeping road snaking up and down the mountain spur, the extensive view, the glints of water, the small structures of cairns (some intact, some crumbled), the small valley in the shadow of the mountain spur silhouetted against the afternoon sky, the grazing yaks and sheep, the curious eyes of the country people, the bales of freshly harvested wheat and barley, the bare poplars and willows: all they, repeated though, gave me an enjoyable sense of freshness. Even more enjoying was Mark. It was his first drive along that road.

As we stopped at the parking lot of the resort and got out of the Land Cruisers, Yudun ran to us to offer a smiling greeting. She was wearing a white shirt, tight jeans and a sky blue hat, allowing her wavy hair to cascade over her shoulders. The resort looked well managed. The colour of the building and additions had a fresh shine even after a year since they were painted. The pavement was neat and the garden green and mowed. The lake had been expanded to almost double what it was previously. Two Chinese men were fishing. Not far from them, a few swans were floating. The mastiffs were lying down near the fence, indifferent to our arrival. But this time also, I could not see the yak grazing on the slope past the field, now vacant.

After a few minutes of strolling around, all others settled in a mah-jong room while Thakur and I went to Pala's house with Pema.

He was perching on a flat stone on the ridge of the yard, smoking and looking deep into the sky.

"Pala, why do you look so down?" Pema asked before we greeted him.

"You just frightened me. How're you, Pema? Ashok and Thakur, how're both of you? It's long since you came here. Sit," he said, showing a wooden bench in the yard.

"*Tashi delek*, Pala." We sat on the bench.

"Pala, talk to them. I'll just change and come." Pema went to her house.

"How's your health, Pala?" I asked.

"It's all right. But not as good as it used to be. Sometimes I get pains in the knee and finger joints. I'm getting older. The old age is a house to all illnesses, you know."

"You still look young and strong," Thakur said.

Pala laughed. Showing his glistening teeth, he said, "I *was*. At your age, nobody could challenge me in this whole area. I could carry a grown-up calf on my shoulder and walk without gasping." Despite the wrinkles around his eyes and on the forehead, he still looked agile. "I forgot to ask. Do you want to drink anything? Dawa is away."

"No thanks, Pala. We came here just to say hello to you. The others are at the resort," Thakur said.

"Why didn't you tell me earlier? I would have already joined them," he laughed again. "Pema, take care of your guests. Why don't you offer them *chhang*? It's fresh."

"All right, Pala." Pema appeared and said.

"I'll go. I'll see all of you at the resort later," saying, Pala walked towards the resort, following a trail, a seasonal trail, used when the field was vacant. I watched his long, firm steps until he vanished under the willows.

"What do you drink? Don't say no. It's an order from Pala."

"Whatever you give us," I said. "Even poison."

"How can I give you poison? I don't want to kill you," she said and brought two bowls of *chhang*, thick and smelly. "But today, I want to see your drunken face."

"I'll fulfil your wish," I said and emptied the bowl in a single draught. "One more."

After having two bowls of *chhang,* I was a bit tipsy.

We walked around. This time the children did not follow us with their curious eyes. We were no longer new. Thakur's trimmed beard had become familiar to them. They just continued their own life and their little games. Not much change had taken place. Not many constructions as compared to the city, not any new additions. The sole change was the disappearance, the vanishing away of Pema's grandmother's house. Altogether. The whole structure had been torn down almost to the level of the ground. Weeds had come out from the rubble as if the earth, nature, was regaining its authority over that little man-made construction.

Later that evening, while the others were busy playing mah-jong, the two of us – Pema and I – sat on a bench under a bare willow, beside the lake. The full moon hung over the sky and cast a mild glow. I asked, "Pema, do you still remember your grandmother?"

Thakur and Yudun were on the other side of the lake.

She answered, "Yes, sometimes, when I go to her ruined house."

Her response was calm, without emotion. She had not drunk. But I was drunk and had become emotional. The ruins of the house, the full moon in the sky studded with faint stars, the solemn prospect of the mountains had made me more emotional, had made me recall my childhood, my grandmother, the little foothills, myself, and Pema: everything appearing so sombre yet so atmospheric.

My emotion grew more as I looked at her, in the striped glow of moonlight – the stripes created by the bare willow. I did not know what to say and what not to. I just uttered, "How's your boyfriend?" To me, her boyfriend was an evergreen subject matter to talk to her if I did not find any other matters.

"I don't have a boyfriend."

"What? What happened to him?" I was little taken aback by what she said. "Did you fight with him?"

"No. I never had."

"What? But you always said you had."

"It was a lie."

"But why did you lie?"

"Because I knew you were married, and I did not want to see you in your married status. Anyway, will you come back? Or you'll disappear like Bidur?"

"I'll come. Definitely."

I did not know how to react to her last expression. I had been with her more than three years, but she never let me know her real feelings towards me. By saying that, that she did not want to see me as a married man, what actually did she want to say? Did she want me in other ways, as a member of the opposite sex? Or was it another joke, which she always threw at me and which I always absorbed? I knew she was beautiful. Her emerald eyes, her elegant neck, and curly hair always attracted me to the level of sensation, sexual sensation, although I always controlled myself.

And in my tipsiness, under the moonlit sky when she expressed herself in such way, I became a bit romantic. Emboldened, I took her hand, kissed it twice or thrice, and held it tightly. This boldness reached up to the level of kissing on her forehead and keeping her head against my chest and whispering, "Pema, I love you."

She remained quiet, her head against my chest, and I myself stroking her hair. We remained in that position for almost four to five minutes, until Thakur and Yudun walked to us.

The next morning, I found myself in a soft bed, burrowed under a blanket, in a cosy twin-bedded room. On the next bed was Thakur. I could not remember how I came to the room. The last thing I remembered was that, after sitting outside, beside the pool, we went to the mah-jong room where I drank a few more bowls of *chhang*, looking at Pema. Everyone was encouraging me to drink. Once more! Once more! I was enjoying it. I could not remember anything after that: what I did afterwards; what I ate; who brought me to the room.

The hangover was unbearable. Thakur was still sleeping. I continued lying in the bed for one or two hours, burrowing deep inside the blanket. When I came outside, there were not any other people except for a Tibetan waitress who informed me that we were supposed to leave in the afternoon. I strolled around the pool. I saw a tractor, a red tractor coming to the resort. And the person in the driver's seat? It was Mr Lee. He had come to the resort to deliver fresh vegetables from his farm. We were surprised to see each other at the resort and chatted a while. He did not wait much. He had to deliver vegetables to other resorts and left, inviting me to visit his place.

"How's your daughter, Mr Lee?" I asked before he left.

"I have put her in a good boarding school in Chengdu," he said in response. He said so with a distinct smile across his face and brightening his narrow eyes. A satisfied fatherly pride was being expressed from his face and from the way he answered. He left in his red tractor.

We left the resort in the afternoon. It was there, on our way to the city, on the sharp bends, the blind curves near the bridge where the terrible accident took place. On our way back also, we – Pasang, Pradip, Pema and I – were in the same Land Cruiser. Pradip was in the front seat, as always, his head nodding towards the window. I was sitting on the rear seat along with Pema. The last night's conversations and the romantic moods were still dominant in mind. She was looking outside. Pasang was driving along the right lane. As we were passing one of those bends, a truck came from the other side at a high speed almost taking up half of our lane. Everything was quick and sudden; Pasang could not control the steering. We all screamed, and the Land Cruiser swerved towards the edge of the road and fell down, then, rolling head over tail twice or thrice, settled upside down on the riverbank: the doors open and the glasses broken.

I was inside. There was no pain at first, but my left hand did not have any sensation, as if the nerves were detached. I somehow crawled out. The hand was bleeding from the wrist. I saw Pradip moaning, his left leg pressed by the body part of the Land Cruiser. Pasang was a little away on the bare ground, silent. Thick red blood was streaming from his head and face, soaking the sandy ground. Pema was nowhere in sight. Within minutes, my hand and other parts of my body began to pain and soon became intolerable. Desperately I looked up to the road. A red tractor pulled in on the roadside from where our Land Cruiser had left the road. An old-looking Chinese man got off and peered down. Was it Mr Lee? I pinned all expectations on him. Everything became shadowy. Everything went dark.

Thirteen

As I came around and rolled my eyes; I found myself on a bed in a narrow white twin-bedded room, the door of which was left ajar. From the light coming from the door and windows, I could take it that it was around midday. A strong smell of medicine was pervading the room, almost nauseatingly. My left hand was in a plaster cast and felt heavy and painful. There were bandages on the neck, left armpit, and right leg. Dull pain was everywhere on the body, difficult to pinpoint. I was in a hospital. Which hospital was it and how I was brought there, I did not know yet. Perhaps it was Mr Lee, whom I had seen before I went faint. On the next bed was another person, a young Tibetan with closed eyes and blood-soaked bandages on his face and stomach. In between our beds, there was a low table on the side of which two intravenous stands stood: one for him and one for me. The saline, the mixture of medicine and glucose, was dripping through the intravenous pouch and being dissolved into my veins drip by drip.

The door creaked, and there entered a doctor, a middle-aged Chinese man with a white complexion and thin receding hair and his glasses falling down the bridge of his small nose. He was wearing a white coat, black trousers, and shining black shoes. A stethoscope was hanging over his chest. A nurse was following him, also a Chinese. Her white nursing uniform matched her whiteness.

The doctor checked my heartbeat and blood pressure while the nurse put an infrared thermometer into my eardrum for a short time, until it made a beep.

"Ninety-nine," she said in English.

The doctor scribbled something in a paper and gave it to the nurse.

It was after she left the room, he said in heavily accented English, difficult to come across. "You're in Tibet People's Hospital. Some army-men brought you here. They said you had got in an accident. Your left hand was broken at the wrist. We operated on it. There're wounds and bruises on the body, but not serious. The only thing is that you lost a lot of blood, so you're a little weak. You need to stay here about ten days. Thereafter, you may be discharged, depending on the situation. You'll wear a sling until the full recovery, and I'll suggest physiotherapy also. But for now, take a full rest. Don't worry. Everything is all right. I'll see you this evening."

"Thank you, Doctor. Thank you a lot." I tried to give a smile to him.

The nurse came back. The needle getting into the vein was painful, but her soft touch and voice *it won't hurt much* was comforting. I was administered painkillers and sedatives. I soon fell asleep.

As I opened my eyes, I found myself put in another room, with more beds partitioned by green curtains. Thakur was sitting on a wooden chair beside the bed, looking at me worriedly.

"How're you now?" he asked.

"It's better," I replied. I did not know how long I slept or went into unconsciousness, but this time the pain was less severe than earlier.

"They brought you here just now. They say your condition is improving," he said, but his face was serious as if unwilling to share something.

A little later, the doctor, the same one with another nurse, came and started checking up on the patients from one side of the room, and finally approaching my bed, asked me, "How're you feeling, my friend from *Nibo(r)*?" He used his own pronunciation for Nepal.

"I feel better, Doctor."

"Good. You're making progress. But you must thank this gentleman. We didn't have enough blood to match your group. It's your luck that his group matched yours," he said as he put the stethoscope on my chest and back, checked my blood pressure, and took my temperature.

I threw my eyes towards Thakur. Dark face, glistening eyes, trimmed beard: he had not changed much over the years. Even if he had changed, it had not been known to me. He was the same Thakur whom I had met during early days in Lhasa and with whom I had consumed much of my time. As I was told he saved my life; his blood was running through my body, it was difficult for me to choke back tears.

"Everything is in control. I want him to start eating. He can start from liquid, any juice or soup," the doctor said to Thakur.

Thakur went out and came back with a few bottles of juice and milk, then went out again, saying he would come the next day.

"Where're Pasang and the others?" I asked Thakur when he came the next day.

"They're in other rooms," he replied, turning his eyes to other patients.

Later that evening the Lees came with a bunch of flowers, red and blue, grown in their farm.

"I wanted to come yesterday, but something urgent came up," he said.

"It was Mr Lee, who, in fact, saved your life. By the time of the accident, we had already crossed the bridge, unaware of the accident. Mr Lee, after he saw you, drove fast to the bridge and reported to the army at the bridge post, who brought you here," Thakur said.

"Thank you," I said. I was struggling to find appropriate compliments for him.

Mrs Lee insisted on me taking the Chinese soup, which she had brought, hot and sour – my favourite one – but this time less hot. The Lees watched me slurp the soup.

I spent another nine days in that room. There were patients of all ages: from the children to the elderly, they had different illnesses and injuries, some of the injuries frightening. The room smelt of medicines and of something like urine. Was it the real smell of urine? Urinated by the aged patients, who could not manage to go to the toilet? Probably. I spent a suffocating nine days in that room, listening to the snores and moans of patients, which became louder at night.

Thakur came every day, twice – before and after work – brought food and wished me an early recovery. Mark also came occasionally.

Each time, after checking me, the doctor would smile and say I was making fast progress. Especially his words after the morning check-ups mixed with the twittering of birds, coming from outside, and his smile mixed with the morning light soothed me, helped me to relieve. I was gradually recovering. After a week, as per his advice, I stopped taking the painkillers. The pain had become mild and tolerable.

But what about Pasang, Pradip, and Pema? I was not aware of them. I did not know why Thakur had not told me about them and about their status. My questions about them were not responded to properly. The only response I got from him was that they were in other rooms, upstairs. I was desperate to see them. We had that terrible accident together. I wished to know about their status.

"Thakur Ji, I'm tired of lying down on the bed and changing my position. I want to stretch my legs inside the hospital. Can we go to the room of our friends?" once more I requested to Thakur on the evening of the seventh day.

"Let me ask the doctors if they'll allow this."

He soon came with a negative response that patients were not allowed to visit other patients. I could meet them once I was discharged. Two days after.

The next day, the day before discharge, two nurses took me to another room and undid the bandages. The doctor came, smoking a cigarette, checked the wounds, and asked me to move my fingers. Then asking the nurses to apply the medicines and bandages, he told me, with a satisfaction in his voice, that I was going to be discharged the next day.

The information was relieving: I could at least get rid of the suffocating hospital room and go to my place. At the same time, however, the medical cost I incurred was constantly worrying me. Up until now, I only knew Mark had deposited the necessary amount for the treatment. I did not know how much. Thakur had said the medical treatment for foreigners in Tibet was expensive. Everything was charged double compared to the locals. During the day of discharge, the hospital invoice came to me as a shock. Thirty thousand Chinese Yuan! The amount equal to my ten months' salary. The accident cost me so dear. I broke my hand – I was sure it would never be like before; the doctor had already indicated that, given the age factor, it might not be perfect – and lost the ten months' salary!

"God saved your life. It was a terrible accident," the nurse said, helping me to put the heavy plaster-cast hand in a black sling.

"And if so, wasn't it the same god who caused this accident?" I said. My response, sounding somewhat atheistic, made her look at me with an arched lift of her eyebrows.

"Now shall we meet the others?" I looked at Thakur.

"Let's go to Pradip's room. Pasang and Pema have been taken to another hospital," Thakur said, making me more confused.

Why were they taken to another hospital? Why did not Thakur say that earlier? I did not speak, just followed him, with the plaster-cast hand hanging in the black sling.

Perhaps it was a private ward: neat and clean and no other patients. Pradip was reclining on a pile of pillows on the bedhead, looking at the ceiling. His wife was sitting in a cane chair beside the bed, knitting.

"*Tashi delek*," I greeted them, sitting on the bed. Thakur stood.

The plaster cast on Pradip's left leg and the wheelchair, beside the bed, spoke of his broken leg. Few other bandages were put around his body.

"Did they discharge you?" Bayang asked.

"Yes."

"It was bad luck for all of you. The doctors say Pradip needs to stay here a few more days. The cast will be taken off after two months. His leg is badly broken."

"This hospital? I don't want to stay here for even a single minute. I want to go home. But these doctors don't listen to me, just want to keep me here," Pradip fussed.

Our conversation ended with this brief exchange. We did not know what else to say.

Later, as I walked out with Thakur, I was reminded of Sushmita and the children, the upcoming Dashain, and the hospital invoice.

"Tomorrow, I want to go to see Pasang and Pema," I said.

Thakur did not speak.

The day after, perhaps, was Sunday and was dark. Heavy clouds rolled from the eastern sky and hung over the valley, casting shadows. The mountains looked brown; the wind moaned and swept away the remaining leaves in the willows; and before noon, it rained, heavily, almost unusual for Lhasa.

I was desperate to see Pasang and Pema, but the rain was torrential.

"Are they in Military Hospital?" I asked.

Thakur kept quiet for a while, sat on the bed beside me, then said in a low but heavy sound, "Ashok Ji, I wanted to tell you earlier but didn't have enough courage. They're not in this world. They couldn't survive the accident."

The valley became darker. The mountains browned more. The Potala looked faded and dim. The leafless trees in the park offered me a terrible sense of loneliness. My mind became thoughtless and mouth speechless. I was trembling. Why had that day, that particular moment, cost me so dearly with no possibilities of turning the clock back? Why did god, if he existed, punish me? I never thought I would lose them in such a tragic way.

Pasang was so nice to me. He always appeared as a monk: his attitude so positive, his face so calm, his expression always soothing, passionless, his life so simple and his thoughts so pure. Those long drives, those visits to monasteries, those solitary stays under the poplars and willows, those stops by the sky burial place. And Pema? Such a beautiful figure, leaning out of the window with her elegant neck and emerald eyes, her love for cairns, her little jokes directed at me and her sudden revelation of not having a boyfriend and of not wishing to see me as a married man. She left the world. The relations remained undefined. I never thought destiny would snatch them in such a ruthless way. It was very difficult to believe.

"Death always comes early to good people," Thakur said.

I continued to look through the window. The black clouds were rolling and rolling. The winds went almost ferocious, sometimes carrying the rain droplets into the room.

The gloomy weather continued throughout the day and the day after that. I stayed inside the room, remembering them and, very frequently, uttering a stream of profanities, unusual for me. It was only towards the late afternoon, the pale sun, before it sank behind the mountains, appeared. Breaking the clouds, the faint rays fell slanting in the valley. Another few days, until all my bandages were taken off, I did not come out.

And after nearly a week, with the broken hand hanging in the sling, I went for *kora* around Barkhor and the Potala and, while moving the prayer wheels, prayed to Buddha. Another day, I went to Sera Monastery and stayed under the same poplar where we would sit together. The earth was still damp there because of the rain. A *chipi* came out of the burrows and looked around. I walked to the sky burial place to see those flat stones where the dead bodies would be cut into pieces and given to the vultures. There were a few vultures perching on the stones. Pasang and Pema must have been taken to those stones before dawn and must have been fed to those vultures, the angels from heaven. Their souls must have been taken to the heavens.

The restaurant looked deserted. There was no Pema to crane from the window and look around. She was not there to welcome me with her satires. Tenzing was not there. Pradip was at his house, worried.

I lost interest in the restaurant. I lost interest in *kora*. All the time I was overwhelmed by memories associated with them. I lost confidence that I could stay in Lhasa any longer without Pasang and Pema, with the knowledge that I would never see them again. So I called Sushmita and informed her about my decision of returning to Narrow Flatland, once and for all. I did not tell her about the accident. I did not want to make her worried.

I talked to Thakur.

"I'll also go with you," Thakur said. His voice sounded determined; the note of finality was clear.

But it was not easy to tell Pradip about going back. Looking at him, in the sitting room, with a splint on his leg and in a wheel chair, was painful. He looked pale. His face and body had shrunk. His eyes did not glisten as they would. He had lost more than I had lost: his friends, his leg, and his business. My wishes and sympathies went to him. He would be struck down by the accident for his whole life. Yet I had to speak. I was feeling my own life was dwindling.

"Can't you stay more? But . . . I understand your situation. Go and meet your family. Anyway, when do you want to go?" he asked me.

"As soon as this plaster cast is removed."

"Will you come back?"

"I wish I could. But now I can't say." I could not lie to him and give a false assurance.

Bayang made butter tea and *balep* for me. I recalled my first sitting in that room, three and half years ago.

"Don't forget us. Once you get better, come," Bayang said.

"I wish I could have gone to the airport to see you off," Pradip said.

Bayang followed me as I stepped down the wooden stairs. She was saying, "Don't forget us."

The mastiff was looking at me with its affectionate look. Over the months and years, we had developed a friendly relationship. I went to it and stroked its head as Pasang would do. It stood, waving the tail. It looked a little aged, three and half years older than I saw it first.

Thakur and I left Lhasa in Dorje's Land Cruiser. The sky was as blue as I had seen it first. The sun came out from the east, offering the bright golden rays in the valley, in the mountains and on the river. We passed Drepung Monastery, crossed the Tilung River, and reached the cliff with Buddha's image. On the left, across the Lhasa River, I could see the Lees' farm. I looked at the valley, the Potala, and the mountains for the last time. Every moment, every occasion, all images with Pasang and Pema became vivid.

The road continued and entered the long and narrow valley. On both sides of the road were the poplars and willows and then a little away, the Tibetan houses.

The road went on ahead. The first fleets of ruddy shelducks had already arrived and begun to float on the river, to graze on the bank, to perch on the stones and to stretch their wings, which were shining in the child sun.

The road continued. The Lhasa River merged into the Yarlung Tsangpo – the Brahmaputra, the Lauhitya – and from there took its course towards the east. The road followed the river and reached the small area – the traditional Tibetan houses below the steep cliff of the mountain where Pradip, Pasang, and I had halted on our way to Lhasa for the first time and had taken butter tea and *tsampa*. The houses stood in the same way as they had stood earlier. The stream flowed downwards, and a few yaks grazed on the slope. But the young girl with whom Pasang had conversed three and half years back was not there. Her shack itself was disappeared.

The airport and the little township, a white plane with blue stripes and *AIR CHINA* written on it: everything looked the same as I had seen it three and half years back. Our eyes were wet when we hugged Dorje and said goodbye.

It was thus I left Lhasa after three and half years in that serene land, in that solitude amidst the brown mountains. I left with Thakur, leaving all other friends. I did not know whether I would meet them again or not.

The plane took off and flew over the brown mountains. Reclining in the seat, as I closed my eyes, I saw Pema, adding stones on the cairns. I saw Pasang and me, staying under a poplar tree in the monastery compound and looking at *chipis* coming out of the burrows, swivelling their little heads around.

Far Beyond the Hamlet

One

After a few sips of *desi tharra*, a kind of stiff local alcohol, Kapil seemed to have got drunk. The strain on his face, the redness in his eyes and the frequent utterance of loutish words were witnessing his drunkenness.

"I won't spare him. I don't care he's my relative. Fucking cheater," he said as he took one more sip.

It was almost nine in the evening. All of us – Kapil, Tenzing, Thakur, and I – were drinking *desi tharra* in a small room of a so-called *hotel*. Venkateshwar, a man from South India whom we had met in that very room on the very first day of our arrival, was lying stripped down to his waist on the bed. He had a limit of drinks, just two or three glasses. With that, he would sleep, often snoring. It was a small room with two beds, a cheap carpet, wall-to-wall though, and a small mauve flower vase sans any flower. The room did not offer the comforts to be called a room of a hotel as claimed by Khem, a close relative of Kapil, our agent in Kathmandu, who had said we would be lodged in a nice hotel in Mumbai until we would fly to our destination, France. But here we were dumped in a cheap hotel in a slum community somewhere in Jogeshwari, Mumbai. Anna, the agent who received us at the airport, had said he could not find any other hotel in Mumbai: an easy excuse, an unconvincing reason. We did not complain, although we were cheated. Perhaps we, all four of us, had learnt from our past experiences about the meaninglessness of any complaints in such situations. Or more accurately, our past, most of the time without options, had taught us to keep quiet or to put up with the situation forced upon us either by the destiny, or it be by a human being. When we reached the room of the so-called hotel, Venkateshwar was already there, dumped for almost two weeks by the same group of agents, he had told us.

That day too we sat on the carpet on the floor under the faint light from the single low-watt bulb and started to drink *desi tharra* with pickled onions. Drinking alcohol, smoking, and scolding the agents in a loud voice and, on occasions, quarrelling among ourselves had become part of our daily life. In drunkenness, we felt comforted and forgot anxieties about our loans, about the miserable condition of our families at home, the uncertainty of our futures, and our difficult condition, for a short period though. After that short period, the next morning, the reality of our life reappeared in its exact or higher degree.

So we sat for our drink that day too. The room gradually filled with smoke and the smell of cheap alcohol. And after a few fast glasses, Kapil, as usual, got drunk.

"I won't spare Khem. I have spent more than three lakh. If I don't get the visa for France, I'll kill him. I don't care even if I go to jail. Bloody cheater," he exploded and gulped yet another glass.

"Don't drink so fast. You're getting drunk, Kapil," Tenzing said, blinking his eyes quickly, three or four times. He always blinked his eyes whenever he spoke.

"Do you think I'm drunk? I never get drunk," Kapil said, taking the bottle and making a funny attempt of posturing himself as sober.

"Khem had told us that the visa would be stamped within less than a week. It has already been twenty-two days, but there's no sign of the visa. Anna didn't even show his face today. We have to do something. Why not report to the police? How long are we going to wait like this?" Tenzing suggested, blinking his eyes.

"But will this solve our problem? Will we get our money back? I know the police and the people in power. They're just blood suckers,"

Thakur expressed his suspicion, putting a slice of onion in his mouth. "What do you think, Ashok Ji?"

"We'll talk tomorrow about that. Let's enjoy our drink now," I said and took a sip, pretending to have forgotten everything. But I did not know why the alcohol was not affecting me that day; so many things were coming to mind and making it fresh.

We had been dumped in that narrow world for more than three weeks, unaware of how long we were yet to wait. Anna, who was supposed to arrange our visa, rarely appeared these days, and whenever he appeared, he had easy excuses: the consul, the visa officer, had an emergency meeting; the traffic was so heavy that, by the time he reached the consulate, it was already closed; the consul was waiting for the response from Paris; and so on. Each time we met him, he uttered an excuse so easily as if his mouth chewed paan.

Perhaps Tenzing was right. We had to do something. But again, Thakur's suspicion? He was also right. By informing the police, would we get our money back? Even if we would get it, when? The process might take years. We would have had to spend a lot to bribe the authorities. By threatening the agents, we would have threatened ourselves. We were hemmed in by the tricks of agents and were left with very few options – either to follow their advice or to forget about our money and return home with empty hands.

I gulped at once a large glass and lit a cigarette – a habit learnt in Lhasa and grown here in Mumbai.

By treading this path, the path to a foreign country for yet another time, I had made a mistake. After coming from Lhasa, I ought to have stayed in the hamlet and pursued the farming as Sushmita had suggested. But I was tempted to go abroad again, the temptation, to a large extent, caused by my greed for a wealthy life and, to some extent, fuelled by the reality: the stark reality of poverty being exposed through the clothes of my wife and children. Not long after I returned from Lhasa, I was thinking about leaving the hamlet again, and this time, the temptation was for Europe to earn euros and dollars. At the cost of the little ancestral jewellery, so dear to Sushmita and Big Plot! Now, after spending so much money, I found myself dumped in a small room in a slum area of Mumbai.

The room became hazier. Chats became rowdier. Venkateshwar turned to the other side and scratched his belly. I ground the cigarette on a plate.

It had been pretty difficult to convince Sushmita about the idea of going abroad again, to convince her to sell her jewellery, to mortgage Big Plot for the money, to make her realise the plain realities of poverty-struck life, the dearth, the rarity, and on the other hand the possibility of earning a good living. It had taken many nights to convince her.

The day we had, after a series of formalities associated with the mortgage, deposited the *lalpurja* in the bank in the bazaar, was the gloomiest day in her life. In mine too. Would I be able to pay off the loan and get the earth back again?

I lit another cigarette and gulped one more glass.

The conversation became wilder. Tenzing accused Kapil of having connections with the agent and just pretending to have become angry with him.

"How can you blame me? You know he doesn't even receive the phone calls. Don't blame me. You're drunk." Kapil got provoked.

"You're drunk too. He's your relative. It's you who introduced me to him," Tenzing said, pointing his index finger at Kapil.

"Don't point at me. You have lost your sense," Kapil responded.

"Why not point at you. If it was anybody else in my place, he would have already punched you."

"What did you say?" Kapil was clenching his fist.

The convivial drinking seemed to be taking the form of a hot discussion.

"It's too late. We'll talk tomorrow. Now let's sleep," I tried to calm them down. They would listen to me, even in their drunkenness, for I was the eldest in the group.

The next day, as I opened my eyes, I found a total chaos in the room. The scattered plates, the glasses and napkins, the ash and cigarette stumps, the burnt-out matches, and the bottles lay here and there on the floor. A miasma of slate alcohol, cigarette, spice, dampness, and sweat from our own bodies was hanging around in the room. The others, except Venkateshwar, were still sleeping. After consuming almost two bottles, we had somehow managed to spread the sheet and pillows on the carpet and to sleep there, what time I did not know. The sheet looked crumpled.

The waking up was difficult and lousy. Venkateshwar had already left the room. He had the habit of waking up very early, having a quick wash, then visiting Jogeshwari Temple in order to pray to the gods and goddesses for his visa. His regularity never gave him away, rain or shine.

After visiting Jogeshwari, he would go to a tea shop, the nearest one in the slum, and would have tea, and sometimes teas, especially when the lady, the shop owner was there. In such lucky days, he would sit on the bench outside the tea shop, drinking his teas, looking at her face. On the very first day of his arrival in Mumbai, he had found a kind of attraction in her charmless yet coy face, which had amused him. He had liked her. By the time I met him, after two weeks of his arrival, he had already become a great admirer of her, he was already in an impression of her love, though false it might be (or for sure). He never thought about the very possibility of the woman already being in a relationship with another man more handsome than him or the very possibility or maybe the certainty of the woman not liking or even disliking him – a middle-aged man with streaks of grey in his hair, big belly, shadowed eyes, paan-rotten teeth, and lacking sex appeal. He never allowed such ideas to appear and dwell in him. He was sure of her love for him. He had an impression that she always looked at him with her smile and would prepare the best tea for him: a gesture of love. He had great faith in her, as much as he had in the gods and goddesses in the Jogeshwari Temple.

He must have gone to the tea shop to comfort himself with the illusion of love along with cups of tea that morning too.

I woke up lazily and looked outside through the window, which gave on to an obscured view of the sky, the facade of the hotel, an outdoor toilet, the weathered and mottled wall of the next house, and, atop the wall, a pair of pigeons – one, probably the male, dancing with its puffed-up bluish plumage around the neck whereas the other, probably the female, preening its feathers as if not yet impressed by the courting male. A little away, beyond the fence, was a section of the asphalt road with heavy traffic, across the road the massive slum, and beyond the slum area, tall buildings, real Mumbai: Mumbai as I had fancied.

Before I came to the city, I had developed my own idea about it: a picture far different from the one I was faced with at present. Mumbai, which I had seen in Bollywood movies, had read about in books and seen in magazines, was an entirely different city. That Mumbai was clean, full of tall buildings, with wide roads and branded cars, with a picturesque view of the sea and the sunset and with Bollywood actors. But here everything looked different and opposite of the city I had envisaged. I was confronted with a straggly view of a massive slum, a chaotic view of crowded shanty houses and vehicles. I was come upon with the view of many things: plastic and aluminium utensils messily lying outside shacks, clothes haphazardly hanging, cycles, rickshaws, auto-rickshaws, scooters, gaudily painted old vehicles, and hoarding boards here and there.

For a while, I stood glancing into the distance, towards the tall buildings where I could never go. Then, having a quick shower, I stepped out of the hotel and walked to the asphalt road, without a destination in mind. Outside, the sun had already matured. The weather – the March-weather of Mumbai – had become much hotter in the last two to three weeks. The humidity was always existent.

On the roadside, at the same point from which I used to cross the road on other days, I stood waiting for the traffic to become thin. The commute was heavy. Across, a few feet away, the old banyan tree with dense foliage and hanging roots around the trunk was standing offering a shady bower under it as always. I stood there, for a while, but the heaviness intensified. I then walked along the roadside to find another point to cross. A little ahead on the side of the road, there was a dog: dead and rotting. Flies were buzzing around it. It must be a stray dog, a pie dog – unattended and neglected and always wandering about in search of rotten food and at times in search of a mate – and perhaps the smell of rotten food coming from the other side of the street or the appearance of another dog might have attracted it, and perhaps, while crossing the road, it had been hit by a vehicle. The stains of blood were still there on the road. The view of the rotting carcass of the stray dog on the roadside, almost at the same point from which I had crossed it so many times, was scary. The day before I myself had been almost hit by a vehicle. It had missed me by inches. Today the stray dog did not survive. It just died there and was left unattended. This view, the view of a dead dog, which at once reminded me of my crossing of the road the other day and of being nearly hit by a vehicle, was scary enough to make me sick to my stomach. It was just a matter of a few inches and seconds between life and death! Morbid thoughts of death scared me.

Dropping the idea of crossing, I went down the pavement and took a gravelled road – rutted with wide and deep ruts filled up with filthy water coming from the nearby slum houses. I had never before taken this road. On the sides of this road, the slum houses were not dense. Unoccupied lands could be seen. I walked along with the tabloid of the rotten away carcass of the stray dog in mind. Perhaps the carcass of the stray dog would be left there for a while. Or it would be hit by other vehicles and would be smashed and scattered. After walking a few more minutes, I found a tea shop where, to my surprise, Venkateshwar was slurping tea.

"Namaste, Bade Bhaiya," I greeted him. I always addressed him as *Bade Bhaiya*, an elder brother.

"Namaste, how're you? You're drinking a lot these days. Why do you drink so much?" he said, asking the owner of the tea shop to prepare *badhiya* tea for me, putting stress on the word *badhiya*.

I did not respond to his question, rather asked him, "You didn't go to the temple today?"

"No, I couldn't cross the road. Did you see the dead dog?"

"Yes," I answered, sipping at tea.

I did not talk much about the dog. I did not want to. But the scene was still fresh, leading to scary thoughts – the heavy traffic on the road, the crossing, the moment of being nearly hit by a car the other day, the family at home, the loan, Big Plot, and being dumped in a slum in Mumbai.

Venkateshwar too did not speak further, just continued drinking his tea and smoking. He must have thought about his grown-up daughters, the dowry, the broken marriage, and the loan. During our walk around the slum the other day, he had shared with me that he had two grown-up daughters, who had already crossed the marriageable age. A few boys had come to see them, but there was no agreement on the dowry. So there was no marriage.

We – both of us possessing different cultures, different backgrounds, yet both of us ruthlessly hit by numerous unpleasant situations in life; our expectations always thwarted; the vanity of our wishes to have always come in the face of bitter realities; now dumped in a little room of a so-called *hotel* in the slum in Jogeshwari, Mumbai; and both of us once again reminded of the meaninglessness of our lives by the view of a dead stray dog, unattended and unnoticed, in the crowded city slum – preferred to remain silent or became too afraid to say anything about the dead dog. We just slurped our tea.

"This bloody agent is playing too much. The day before yesterday, I made it clear to him if he doesn't arrange our visa by Friday, I'll go to the police and lodge a complaint against him." He broke the silence after a while.

"But are there any chances of getting our money back? We have already spent almost four lakh rupees. I think we would better wait for a few more days," I said in the tone Thakur had used the previous night.

"I don't know whether I'll get back money or not. But at least, that bastard goes to jail. How long are we going to wait? It's already more than a month since I arrived here, and every time I meet him, he promises the next day. *Saala ka dusara din kabhi nahi aya*, the bastard's second day never came. I'm going to kill him," he added.

"Bade Bhaiya, I can't return home with empty hands. I can't show a gloomy face to my wife and children. I have sold her jewellery. I have mortgaged my farm. How can I pay that loan? I have no option but to wait. Why not to give him a few more days. Then we'll think what to do," I expressed my apprehension again.

"Let's meet him today and talk seriously," he said, calming down himself. Perhaps he was reminded of his own problems: the grown-up daughters, the dowry, and the loan.

"Let's go to the hotel and talk to other friends," I said.

"*O saala bhi koi hotel hai*? He just dumped us in the slum. Now look! He even didn't appear yesterday. We should meet him today anyway."

On our way, we did not take the road we had taken before, rather followed another road, more rutted and with fewer settlements on the sides. Venkateshwar, due to his frequent walks, had become acquainted with the locality. We walked until we reached a four-way crossing, where I would often come to buy small necessities like soap, toothpaste, drinks, cigarettes, and matches; to make phone calls to Sushmita; and sometimes just to chew paan, which I had learnt from Venkateshwar. The sun had matured enough to make us sweat even with unhurried walk. The crossroads was as busy as other days. Life, at that four-way crossing, had once again appeared in striking contrast.

From the very first day of my arrival at the airport in Mumbai, I had realised life in here appeared in greater degrees of differences. Differences in appearance, walking, dressing, eating and, in so many other aspects, than in Narrow Flatland, than in Lhasa and Kathmandu. The views were so varied – a well-dressed *babuji* inside a dark-blue Mercedes looking very much content and almost indifferent towards the world outside his car; a little away, a young couple moderately dressed up, getting in a taxi; near that, people in auto rickshaws, on motorcycles, and cycles; not far from there, a crowd of people in different appearances waiting for a public bus; beside the bus stop a few beggars wrapped in rags and tattered clothes or in near nakedness; and among them, a young mother with pallid complexion begging with her old aluminium bowl and her baby just lying on the earth beside her. Then again, a few feet away, a stray dog chewing a bone and suckling her newborn poorly fed puppies. Such a diversity of material availability! Mumbai offered lives in contrasting degrees of sophistication.

We bought paan – *jarda* for him and *mitha* for me – and walked towards the hotel, chewing it. In the hotel, just in front of our room, to our surprise, was Anna in his usual dress: the cream kurta and pyjama, a pair of red leather sandals, a pair of glasses, a thick gold chain around his neck, and, as always, chewing paan. He never looked like an agent, his style of dress and tenderness in his manners did not match with his profession. He was much different than Khem in Kathmandu. He was talking to our friends, all of them with gratified looks.

He said, before we greeted him as we used to do, "Congratulations, your visa and tickets are ready."

"Really!" we exclaimed together. It was great news for us, news that would eventually rescue us from being stranded.

"Yes. Tomorrow, you're flying to Antananarivo, Madagascar," Anna said in the same calmness.

"What? Antana . . . Madagascar?" we again exclaimed, this time with confusion. We could not pronounce the name correctly.

"Yes, Antananarivo. The capital city of Madagascar. Here you can get only the visitor's visa for France, not the working visa. There, you'll get that. Until then, you'll be staying in a nice hotel," he said with extra stress in the last phrase *a nice hotel* as Khem, almost a month ago, had promised *a nice hotel* in Mumbai.

We did not speak.

"If you want to work in Madagascar, you'll get a good job there. The salary won't be less than 500 dollars a month with an increase every six months. You can do overtime."

Again, we kept quiet, with no idea about Madagascar.

Anna went on, "Somebody will pick you up at the airport in Antananarivo. You have a couple of hours in transit in Nairobi. Stay inside, in the transit-area, until your next flight. The flight from here is at around eight in the morning. You need to be at the airport by five. I'll send a vehicle to pick you up at three thirty in the morning. Be ready by then. I'll see you at the airport and give your passports and tickets there." He walked away in his usual gait, an unhurried walk.

He left in his usual gentle gait, but his mentioning of Madagascar as our next destination made us pretty confused. We were hoping to fly straight to France, to Paris. However, he was giving us the visa and ticket for the country of which we did not have any ideas and about which we had never heard before.

We looked at each other.

Venkateshwar said, "I don't think we'll find a job in Madagascar with 500 dollars. The French visa which we couldn't get from here, how will we get it there? This fellow must be tricking us again. He's planning to dump us there."

There was logic in his doubts. How could a place, about which we knew nothing, offer us a job with a good salary? But were there any other options? Were there any chances of withdrawal from this journey? Seemingly not. The single option other than to follow Anna's suggestion would be to forget our dreams and our money and return to our hamlets. And we were not yet ready for this option. We could not return with our bare hands and gloomy faces. Our movements, our decisions, and our lives were being wholly controlled by Anna and were predestined by the agents. The deprivation and the very impossibility of fulfilling the trivial necessities in case of our retreat had left no option but to continue to tread along an unsure path of life Anna had suggested.

And, therefore, we started to pack up our belongings in preparation for the departure from the so-called *hotel* somewhere in the slum community in Jogeshwari, Mumbai, and for the beginning of one more step of our journey towards an uncertain destination.

The next morning at thirty minutes past three, exactly the same time as given by Anna, a man came, dumped us in an old van, and took to the airport. We flew. The hassles at the airport in Mumbai before flying and exhausting and worrying transit hours in Nairobi, the worries coming in several forms: we all were exhausted. So exhausted was I that I fell asleep before the small plane took off.

When I woke up, perhaps after an hour, and looked below from the small window, I saw the dark-blue Indian Ocean with white spots – the whiteness of the glints formed by the afternoon sunrays and the ocean froth, possibly – the calmness of which was only interrupted by oceanic waves. The faraway view of the land was approaching.

The land view first commenced with an artistic view of a virgin beach. The absence of any ships or yachts or boats in the sea, of any constructions or activities on the shore, the absence of settlements in the nearby land spoke of the virginity of the beach. I was not sure, but from above, it looked like a long, wide beach with dried and wet sands, the sands – I supposed – deposited by the tides and parts of it already dried and the rest still wet. And in the process of drying itself, the process of turning into the dryness, a process of change, a splendid piece of art was created there. Again, I was not sure, but the picture, the abstractness, and the beauty of that art somehow matched with a picturesque picture sketched in a Chinese or maybe Japanese or Korean art style, which I had seen somewhere in Lhasa or in a restaurant in Kathmandu. It was a bare tree, or say, a late autumnal or an early wintry tree with hundreds of small leafless twigs, sparsely and minutely entangled and intertwined together against a grey background and under that bare tree a picture of a phantom-like appearance of a lone woman with windswept hair and clothes sketched in a sepia-coloured piece of cloth. It resembled precisely that picture, finely sketched with nature's hands. I was aware that the picture would not last for long. In the process of change, it would vanish away soon or would be swept away by another tide or would be changed into another picture. Fascinated, I looked at the picture until it was photographed clearly and embedded securely in mind and heart.

The plane was now moving above the island of Madagascar. Venkateshwar, on his side on the aisle seat, was dozing off. At times looking at the wing of the plane, half of it shadowed and half glinting, I continued to enjoy the outside view below, which changed along with the progress of the plane. After the beach, small grey hills sparsely forested, otherwise barren, came into the scene. Soon after the view of flooded rivers and rivulets with red muddy water; a few roads with similar colour, looking like a contour map with curvy lines; then terraced fields and scattered settlements on the smooth slopes of the hills; ahead, more roads and settlements.

Then everything was obscured by a thick layer of clouds. In the sea of the clouds, there was a swiftly moving shadow, the shadow of our own plane. Far away, here and there, above the surface of the clouds, huge masses of cotton-shaped white clouds stood solid high above casting their shadows on the surface of the clouds. The view also soon exhausted. The plane entered the layered clouds. The frightening bumping for a few minutes, then the plane was under the clouds, close to the ground offering the view of the city, Antananarivo, the capital city of Madagascar. Buildings, houses, roads, narrow and crowded with old vehicles; electric and telephone wires hanging in the air not differently than in Kathmandu; scattered trees, rice paddies, and people working in those fields: the view the city offered was talking more of a paucity and plainness than of availability and luxury. I thought Venkateshwar was right. The city would not be offering the jobs with salaries as Anna had told us about.

The plane halted. We got out. It was almost evening, but there was still enough light coming from the translucent pink sky in the far west.

Two

As we crossed the immigration control with our pounding hearts, in front of us was a neatly dressed young man.

"Namaste. I'm Rakesh from Nepal," he said, giving us a gentle smile and his hand to shake. The grip was soft, not very confident. "How was your flight? You must be tired."

"I'm Ashok. Indeed, it was a tiring journey," I said, the piercing eyes and suspicious looks of the immigration officials still in mind.

Outside, it had already grown dark. Dim airport light did not allow us to have the faraway view.

"I have arranged a place near here for your stay," Rakesh said, walking towards the parking area.

"Is it a hotel?" Thakur asked as we squeezed ourselves, the five of us, in the rear seat of an old car.

Rakesh spoke to the driver something impossible for us to understand, then, turning to us, said, "It's an apartment and it's nice. The locality is also good." He again began to talk to the driver as the van sputtered bumping along the road.

"Which language are you speaking?" Thakur asked.

"Malagasy. English isn't popular here. They speak either French or Malagasy."

"How long does it take to understand it?" Thakur asked, adjusting himself slightly moving forward from his sitting position. The rear seat was not enough for more than three passengers, and here we were five. Venkateshwar had gone dozing off, spreading himself out over almost half of the entire seat.

"You can learn to speak quickly. By the way, did you manage to learn a little French before leaving?"

"No."

"You should have learnt, at least a little."

Rakesh then engaged in conversation with the driver who spoke spluttering.

Our place was not far. Within twenty minutes or so we were there, *a nice apartment*: a square hall on the third floor of an old-looking house without any furniture, not even a carpet. The windows did not have curtains. In a corner of the bare, cemented room, stain-layered cooking utensils and a paraffin stove lay on the floor along with a sack of rice, a packet of pink dal, some green vegetables, rotting potatoes and onions and spices. Opposite that corner, on the bare floor, lay a heap of bedding. The bedding sans the bed.

"This is your *nice apartment*," Venkateshwar, already annoyed for being awoken from his dozing and for being asked to walk up the stairs up to the third floor with his heavy baggage, threw a stern look towards Rakesh as he saw the room.

"If you don't like it, I'll find another one. The owner of this apartment is a thorough gentleman and can speak English. Upon my request, he gave the bedding and these utensils. And these groceries, I purchased them. Sometimes I'll join you for a meal, but not today," Rakesh said and unfolded the bedding. We plonked our bags on the floor and, spreading the thin blanket on the floor, threw our tired bodies on it.

"I'm staying not far from here. It's getting late. I must leave now. Before leaving, let me introduce you to the owner of this house."

He went down, perhaps to the second floor, and came back with two aged people: a male and a female, maybe husband and wife. The man looked fragile. His bald head – with a line of hairs on the side and the nape of his head and with a few hairs on the bald area, funnily spiked up, which could be virtually counted – shaking hands, almost staggering walk, and wrinkled face spoke of his fragility. "Welcome all of you in my house. I'm Dominique, a retired government officer," he said, swallowing hard as if he had a pain in the throat yet with a slight stress on the word *government officer*. Did he have a throat problem? Or was he drunk? The woman was conceivably younger than the man, but not much. She had decaying teeth and stringy hair. Such were our landlords; the profile of the aged couple demanded a kind of pity and humane behaviour from those who came across them. Trying to smile, they stood there for a couple of minutes, maybe waiting for us to talk. However, tired and hungry, we did not have the energy or interest in talking to them at that odd hour. We remained almost stolid. It must have been due to this stolidity or our disinterested attitudes that they soon left with their staggering steps as they had come. Before they left, the man waved his shaking hand and said, "Goodnight."

And Rakesh too. "I'll come tomorrow before eight. Have your rest. If there's anything, just call me," he said, giving his phone number.

"We don't even have a SIM card. How can we call you?" I said.

"Oh, sorry. I'll bring one tomorrow."

"*Mr Rakesh*, also don't forget to bring news about our visa to France. I don't want to stay in this *nice apartment* for long," Venkateshwar said sternly, adding *Mr* before his first name.

Rakesh went out, stepping down the stairway; we heard the receding sound of his footsteps.

"*Saala, nice apartment bolta hai*. I knew it would happen. Friends, I'm tired. If you can prepare anything, wake me. Otherwise, let me sleep," Venkateshwar added before he sprawled on the bed in a supine position, splaying his legs apart. Soon he was snoring.

The rest of us set to preparing food. We had not had a square meal for the last two days.

The next morning, the first morning in a new city, a strange place, I awoke to a sound of a crow – *caw, caw, caw*. A dazzling light had entered the room through the bare glass window, which looked east, and spilled all over the floor. Except Venkateshwar, all others were sleeping. He must have gone outside to find a tea shop, like in Mumbai. Outside, the sun had come up a few feet high above the contour of the faint hills in the far-east. I did not know in which part of the city we were. Nor was it possible to get even a crude idea about the city from the view that the window offered. The southerly aspect of the house consisted of motley views of many things all around: the houses differently shaped, the roads narrowly constructed, the vehicle mostly old, the people leisurely walking in the streets, and the electric wire and telephone lines, which hung loose in the sky not high above the ground. Apart from those views, there were, to my curiosity, the patches of the terraced fields with swaying rice plants in different places. In the distant south, I saw the faint profile of a few tall buildings against the sky. Towards the north of the room, a balcony projected out. From there, I could see a small patch of land, vacant and walled by a single-layered brick wall. Beyond the wall a bamboo grove had spread thickly. Mother stems had put forth sturdy baby shoots. After that, the land, forested with tall pines, sloped up forming a small hillock, not much taller than the building we were staying. The western side was blocked by the building itself; I could not see anything. To the east, before the compound of another house, there was a patch of vacant land, an orchard, in which banana plants and a few other trees, the varieties of which I did not recognise, had thrived. It was there the crow, the pied one, glossy black in other parts of its body and bright white around the neck and under the chest, so new to me, had perched on a wooden electric pylon – which stood on our side of the vacant land and slanted towards our building – and was crowing, *caw, caw, caw*, looking at our room, as if heralding our unsure future. I unlocked the window to see it clearly.

However, it flew away and perched on the roof of a nearby house, still looking at our room and crowing.

"You haven't woken up, lazy guys? We're in a terrible situation, and you're sleeping?" Venkateshwar came in, gasping. "Ashok, I walked around a little bit. Now I'm hundred per cent sure the city won't give us the jobs we're looking for. Either we need to go to France or we have to go back."

"How can you say that?" I drank water from a plastic jug.

"Look at the houses and shops, look at the streets and vehicles, look at the people. Do you think we'll get 500 dollars? I bet we won't," he said. "And you know? There's nobody who can understand the English we speak. I tried to talk to them. They look at you as if you're from a different planet. I did not find even a tea shop. And this Rakesh? He hasn't arranged milk and sugar for tea. We're finished."

"Maybe we're in the suburban area of the city," I tried to keep his hopes alive. Or, to be honest, to keep my own hopes up, though false they might be.

"I don't think so."

"Why are you talking so loud early in the morning?" Kapil woke up, screwing up his eyes against the rays, which now spread on the pillow side of the bed. Thakur and Tenzing also woke up.

"It's not the early morning, *ladsaheb*. You know where we are? It's not your father's house where you can sleep until midday snoring and breathing your rotten smell. We're at a place the name of which we never heard before we came here. Get up quickly. We need to make some plans." Venkateshwar almost exploded.

We all sat on the bed.

"Look, our visa is the visitor's visa!" Tenzing blinked his eyes, looking at his passport.

"That's the reason I'm worried. We're here on a one-month visitor's visa. I think the French visa is nothing but their drama. Had I known this in Mumbai, I wouldn't have boarded the plane. That bastard Anna didn't give us our passports until the immigration point," Venkateshwar said.

"Let's wait for Rakesh. I don't think there's another option in our hand. We can't do anything without his help. We don't know anybody here. We don't even have enough money to go back," Thakur said.

He was right. What could we do in an alien city where we did not know anyone? In fact, deep inside, I had grown suspicious ever since I boarded the plane in Mumbai that we were cheated and that the assurance of French visa was merely a story. After coming to Antananarivo, and after being faced with the first views of the city (although the very limited views might not have been enough to make a full judgement about the city), I realised that getting a good job in that city was impossible. Yet I could not give up hopes, without which our lives would immediately turn into darkness. I was afraid to accept the reality. Probably the others too.

No option was left to us except waiting for Rakesh, which took not less than six hours. To see if he had come, we came down, frequently, and standing a while in the yard went back to the room to wait him again. Each time we came down, we saw the old man in a cane chair, basking in the sunshine and looking at a newspaper.

It was a big house, the biggest in the vicinity. It looked old, as old as the landlords themselves. The yellow colour of the house was faded and in places completely washed away; the windows and door frames were left unpainted; the narrow yard, fenced in with almost a man-high brick wall from three sides, was layered with bricks. The bricks in the yard and on the fence were full of moss. At one end of the yard, there was a water tap, a common tap for drinking water for everyone staying in the house. That morning when I came there to fetch water, I had seen two men filling their buckets. The house must have been constructed many years back when the landlord was in the service, and as he retired from service, it also looked retired and neglected; it could not get the attention it needed.

Rakesh did not come until noon. After eating rice and pink dal followed by loud belches, we walked off our heavy meal. As Venkateshwar had said, there were no big restaurants or shopping centres or hotels around. The streets were crowded with sputtering old vehicles. We tried to talk to the people who sat on the sides of the streets selling cigarettes, candies, and fruits. The language sounded incomprehensible. The figure and the colour of the people, although resembling the people of the Terai in Nepal or the people in Uttar Pradesh or Bihar, the northern states of India, to some extent, appeared in complete strangeness to us with that incomprehensible chatter. Once we saw a few policemen standing under a tree in the middle of the crossroads; we walked back hurriedly. At our place, Rakesh was waiting for us in the yard, talking to the landlord.

"I'll talk to him in straight language," Venkateshwar whispered, poking into the side of my stomach.

Up in the room, he said, "Look, *Mr Rakesh*, I have already spent more than a month in Mumbai. I don't want to stay in this city for a single day. I have spent four lakh Indian Rupees for the French visa. They have paid almost the same amount. We want our visa at the earliest. Before we left, Anna had said it would be stamped within a week."

"We're new in this city and don't know the language. I was not able even to ask tea. I'm so addicted to tea that, without having it, I can't even go to the toilet. Why don't you stay here with us until we leave? It would be really helpful to us. At least, we'll have somebody who knows the locality," he added.

"Well, I'll try to secure visas for all you as soon as possible. But why don't you consider working here?"

"Ours is the visitor's visa. Won't it create difficulties? And how much will we get?" Thakur asked, sitting on the floor beside me reclining against the wall.

"Well, there're many people working without papers. The salary? I think it should not be less than a hundred dollars if we find work in textile factories. We'll see." Rakesh also sat on the floor, at the bedside.

"But Anna had said it won't be less than 500 dollars a month. And what do you mean by *we'll see*? I knew all of you were just tricking us. I won't let you go from this room." Venkateshwar latched the door. He moved towards Rakesh and firmly gripped him on the two arms, and then said to us, "Friends, don't let this guy escape from here. Otherwise, we won't see him again. Tenzing, search his pocket and take whatever things he has got."

"What are you doing? It's criminal," Rakesh said, trying to free him from the grip.

"And the way you cheated us was not a crime?" Venkateshwar tightened his grip. "Tenzing, what are you waiting for? Search his pocket."

Tenzing took out a wallet, a passport, and a small phone book from his pocket.

Venkateshwar released him and keeping his passport with him said, "*Mr Rakesh*, it's not that I want to give you any trouble, but let me make you clear that I'll give this passport back to you at the time of our departure for France."

Rakesh looked green and tried to give a sheepish grin.

To me, what Venkateshwar did was a wise step. At least, Rakesh was to stay with us.

Later, he went to his place to bring his things. Venkateshwar and Tenzing were with him. Venkateshwar was careful not to let Rakesh slip away even for a single minute.

On the same evening, in his drunkenness (he himself had arranged a bottle of alcohol and a kilo of chicken), Rakesh said he was not the real agent. He was working for Anna for a small amount of money. He said he did not know much about French visa, and it was difficult to find a job in Madagascar. His duty was to accommodate the newcomers like us until they got a job, often low-paid, and this could take months. There was another Malagasy agent who had connections with companies which could hire labourers for low levels.

Information came out gradually in his drunkenness that he himself was dumped in Madagascar for months while the main agents were enjoying themselves in Kathmandu and Mumbai. He wanted to go back, but he did not have even enough money to buy the air ticket. If he did not obey Anna, he felt his security was at stake. Smirking, he said he was happy to see us. At least, he found someone to share his difficulties. I did not know whether he was telling the truth or was trying to be smarter so that we would stop expecting from him and would try to find something on our own or was just trying to cotton up to us, but what he said called forth further ire towards him.

"I don't know anything. You cheaters have gulped my money. Either I need a visa for France, or I need my money. Otherwise, I'm going to kill you. *Saala, chutia*," Venkateshwar shouted and clenched his fists as if he wanted to hit Rakesh. He was shaking with anger.

"Bade Bhaiya, be calm. Anger doesn't solve the problem. We're in a difficult situation. We need to think calmly. I think he's just a pawn." I tried to smooth things over.

"What's left to think now? They cheated us." He was staring at Rakesh, his eyes filled with anger.

"Are there any people from our countries working here?" Thakur asked.

"There're very few Nepalese. I know the factory where they're working. There're a few Indian people, doing business and working here, in the city centre," Rakesh responded, looking at Venkateshwar nervously, whose stern voice panicked him.

"How far is the city centre?" I asked.

"It takes almost half an hour by bus. But if there's traffic, it takes much more. You can't tell."

"Why did you put us so far, *saala*," Venkateshwar again exploded and swallowed his drink in a single draught.

"Bade Bhaiya, the city centre is too expensive." Rakesh found an appeasing word to address Venkateshwar to calm down him. He then did the dishes in a bucket. It became obvious to us, at least to me, that this poor guy was merely the pawn, who was working for others, the real agents. If he had been a real agent, he would not have washed our dishes.

For a week or so, we tried to adjust to the vicinity. We would wake up at dawn and walk to the nearby crossroads, in the middle of which stood a tall tree the name of which I did not know. But it was tall. The branches were thick and dense. The place was like a junction, a meeting point of four roads from different side. The four of us – Venkateshwar, Rakesh, Thakur, and I – would visit that place and would have tea at a shack on the side of the street, which Rakesh had shown us. Drinking our tea, we would watch the comings and goings of the people and would listen to the honks of the minibuses, the public buses at the stop near the junction and would buy vegetables – often potato, watercress, cassava leaves, or roots – and would return to our room to find Kapil and Tenzing preparing the poor meal. We would spend the daytime playing cards or talking. In the evening, again we would go to the junction and come back with a bottle. Rakesh would try or pretend to call his friends to find work for us. But there was no progress. Rather the little money, which we had saved for the emergencies, was being spent each day, reminding us of an imminent danger of being penniless. Frustrated, we would sit for the drink in the late evening, regularly.

We spent another week or so. I wanted to talk to Sushmita but was afraid what to tell her? Tell her I was still jobless? Give her the information about our helplessness in foreign soil? Give her extra worries?

One day, looking at the pied crow, Thakur said, "I need a SIM card and airtime. I haven't called my wife since I left Mumbai. She must be worried."

Sushmita came sharply to my mind. I had called her before leaving Mumbai. Listening about a new country I was about to travel to, she had expressed her worries, "Call me once you reach there." There was a panic in her voice. Now, with Thakur talking about the SIM card, she came to my mind strongly. I was pining for her.

I asked Rakesh, "Can I make a call from your mobile?"

"There's not enough airtime."

"Let's go to buy some," I said.

"I'll also go," Kapil said.

"Then, let's all go. After all, we all want to talk to our family," Thakur proposed.

"Call rates are very expensive in here. I think banks are not open yet. Let me talk to the landlord if he can change some dollars for us. Let's change 500 dollars for now, one hundred for each of you," Rakesh said.

We looked at each other at this new demand, a matter associated with our family with whom we were desperate to talk. None of us argued. I took a hundred-dollar note from the inner pocket and gave it to Rakesh. This was the third last note I had saved. He went to the downstairs and came back with a bundle of local currency, Malagasy Ariary.

Anyway, I managed to call my wife. The connection was poor. But I managed to convey that I was fine and to know that they were fine.

It was raining. In fact, the rain was always there since we reached Antananarivo, sometimes heavy and sometimes just a drizzle, intermittently. But that day it had been raining the whole night. The rain had set in after we went to sleep. Throughout the night, I heard the rain spattering on the roof, against the bare windows and on the wide banana leaves. The rain continued with intervals. The sky thundered occasionally.

"March and April are the end months of the rainy season," the old landlord said one day in his slow French-toned English, holding his knees.

"My knees pain a lot during this wet season," he added.

Dominique, the old landlord, had developed arthritis. Walking upstairs and downstairs in the house would pain him on the rainy days. To adjust his feet, to avoid the sudden attack of pain, he had to briefly pause on each stair, holding the wooden handrail. So most of the time, he looked annoyed at the cloudy sky. He was waiting for the end of the rainy season. I did not know what Rakesh had told him about us, but so far, it seemed to me that he had not taken us as foreigners coming into his country in search of jobs. During our brief meetings on the staircase and in the yard, he would often show his curiosity about us and our country, the name of which he had never heard. It was only after mentioning the name of Mount Everest, he had nodded his head up and down, many times, uttering, "Oh." On another occasion, I had to use the name of the neighbouring countries to give him a tentative idea about the location of my country.

The rain continued for another couple of days, reminding us of the monsoon season in our own country. Mostly we stayed inside, playing cards, waiting to a brief halt of rain so that we could go to the nearby areas to buy groceries. It had been clear to us that we were not going to

France. The only thing what we were hoping was to find a job, whatever it would be, and collect some money for the return ticket.

Rakesh would call to his Malagasy counterpart every day in order to know if he had found jobs for us. While playing cards, we would listen to him talking to his friend in the language incomprehensible to us, and when he would put his mobile down, we would try to read his face if there was something new, and then we would keep quiet to know nothing was new. At times, he would try to call the few Nepalese he knew in order to find if there were vacancies in the factories they worked. But his calls were rarely received. Even if they were received, the responses would be negative. In many instances, the respondents would scold him for cheating them. The sounds of those scolding would be so loud; we could hear them clearly. Rakesh would abruptly end the conversation by switching his mobile off. He also called Anna and the agents in Kathmandu the details of which he did not share with us and after which he looked more frustrated. His call to his friends did not bring the succour to us. Kapil too tried to call Khem but received no response. Consequently, our situation was worsening day by day. The passage of each day was reminding us of the tenure of our visa and the possible illegality of our stay, which would definitely put us in jail. The jail in a faraway country, in an alien country! The thought itself was scary.

And now it was raining, raining, and yet raining, making the days gloomier.

"Ashok Ji, how long are we going to stay like this?" Thakur asked one morning, washing his face with the tap water in the yard. The rain had paused, although the patches of heavy clouds were rolling around in the sky, presaging a downpour any time soon.

"What shall we do? I'm so frustrated with our situation," I said.

"We can't stay this way. I know this Rakesh is worthless for us. We need to go around and look for jobs."

Later, after talking to our friends, we took a public bus and went to the city centre to hunt for work. After that day, every day, we travelled to the city centre on the crowded bus, looking at the rice paddies on both sides, a view unique to a city. We walked along the streets, some of them well-laid, sloping uphill, and then falling downhill. Looking around the places for work, we walked until our feet gave in. In the evening, after those failed attempts, we would come back again looking at the paddies.

We stayed hours in front of the textile factories, waiting for the crowd of people to come out, and when it came out, like an army of ants, we tried to trace someone from our country. In the evening, we came back, prepared our meal, and played cards to console ourselves. We tried to sleep, often sleeplessly. Even if sleep came, it came for a short period and with scary dreams. The routine continued as did continue the rain and as did continue the pied crow to caw early in the morning, perching on the slanted electric pylon and giving us a bad omen, every day, no matter we scared it away. The clothes we wore started to fade due to the everyday wash. Each one of us had no more than two or three pairs of clothes, and we had to wash them every day. Otherwise, they would smell of sweat and damp. Our toes poked out from our smelly socks, and shoes wore out, yet we did not find any jobs. We stayed in that strange place with our hopes going badly adrift as each day passed.

And one day Tenzing cried. We had just come back after yet another failed attempt: Venkateshwar lying flat on the bed; Thakur and Kapil chatting; and Rakesh and I myself preparing the rice and potato curry. Tenzing began to cry. I saw him burrowing his head in his arms. At first, I thought he was having a rest or pondering over his situation, but as I noticed his sobbing, I asked him, "What happened, Tenzing?"

He broke down, "I want to go home. I want to go back to my village."

We looked at him, helplessly. The situation became sombre. None of us could ask him not to cry. We did not have enough confidence to calm him, to assure him that everything would be all right. We did not know about our own future, so we could not ask him not to cry. Rather, we ourselves wanted to cry like him, like a child. The sombreness remained in the room for a while. Then, all of a sudden, he woke up and hit Rakesh at the nape, knocking him down on the floor.

"Why did you bring us here, *saale*? Buy a ticket for me. I want to go tomorrow," Tenzing said, his fists still clenched in anger.

And this time, it was Venkateshwar who tried to calm Tenzing, "Tenzing, my brother, relax. Come. Sit down. This poor guy can't do anything. I saw his passport. His visa is expired. *He is as pitiable as we are*. The people who took money from us are in Kathmandu and Mumbai. Enjoying."

"Now, brothers, I think we should inform the police about our reality so that we can go back home safe. At least, we have got the visa for another week. We need to leave this country before our visa expires," he added. "Rakesh, tell me. Are there any ways to extend our visa or can we change it into other categories?"

"I have heard the visitor's visa can be extended for one or two more months and is expensive," Rakesh said. He was sobbing.

"I'll try to contact my relatives in India tomorrow. Let's see what we can do. Let's prepare the food. I'm hungry." Venkateshwar tried to comfort us.

The next day dawned with open sky, promising a sunny day. Was the rainy season over? I did not know. April was not yet exhausted, but it was a bright day. That day, we did not go to the city. Venkateshwar called his relatives to arrange the ticket for him. Kapil and Tenzing called their fathers, giving every detail of their difficulties. Assurances came from their parents that they would go to Kathmandu and talk to the authorities concerned. At least they had their fathers. But Thakur and I?

Whom to tell? Should we tell our wives who pinned all their hopes on us? Obviously not. It was not a good idea to add further to their worries.

After lunch, Thakur and I wandered through the sloped wood with tall pines to the north of our building. Never before had we been to that side. The striped sunlight falling to the ground on the dried pine needles, the rustle of the wind in the trees, and the cooing of the doves gave us the impression that we were not in the city. We ambled up, following a narrow trail covered with fallen pine needles. As we breasted the crest, we saw a wide valley on the other side. The hillock had stood between the two valleys, two flat lands, one on the side of our building and the other on the opposite side. The two valleys looked different, possessing different properties. The one gave the peripheral view of the city, whereas the other had a clear impression of rural views, more natural: a small lake right at the foot of the hillock; then a small patch of marsh; past the marsh, paddies, and a few houses; and beyond, a prospect of a wide vacant land with scattered trees.

The slope on the other side of the hillock was bare, covered with nothing but grass. We walked down and sat on the ground, a little above the lake, on which lily pads floated and reeds stuck out tall. Among those reeds and pads, white swans, followed by their progeny, progressed along the water. Ducks and ducklings dipped their heads into the water. A little away on the wetland, a few herons stood on their single sticky foot. There was a flat rock jutted out into the water on the side of the lake. On that, women were washing clothes. Further up, a few men were getting in something from the water and marsh which we did not recognise from afar. Was it watercress? Maybe. We always saw bunches of watercress in the vegetable market.

"Ah, it reminds me of the lake next to my village," Thakur said and threw a small stone (or was it a clod of earth?) into the lake. The surface of the lake rippled smoothly to all sides.

Three

"We don't have money to go back. Nor can we find work here. What are we going to do?" Thakur asked. He threw yet another stone in the lake, this time a little bigger. The ripples emerged and spread wide before they subsided.

"How much money do you have, Thakur Ji?" I asked and took my shoes and socks off. The socks were torn in the toes and had lost the grip on the tops. They smelt. The sole of the right shoe had little detached from the upper and had a hole under the ball of my foot. The shoes required urgent repair, or I needed a new pair.

"Around 600 dollars. A hundred-dollar note is torn almost in half from the middle. I don't know whether the money changers accept it. It's not enough even to buy the air ticket."

"I have got just 200 dollars. But I need to buy airtime and a pair of shoes."

"With this approach, I mean, the approach of all of us walking together, I don't think anybody will give us work. Don't you think that five men walking together for finding work sounds a little weird? Why don't we split up ourselves at least into two groups and look for work separately?"

"Our other friends, I suppose, won't stay here. I don't think they'll walk any more in search of jobs," I said. "Thakur Ji, do you still hope we'll get jobs here? I have lost all hopes. Sometimes I think we also need to tell somebody about our situation. If we don't find work, what are we going to do? I'm scared."

"Then we'll do as luck would have it. Let's not give up. I have seen some hairdressing salons. I'll go there tomorrow to try."

I did not speak. After failed efforts of almost three weeks, I had lost all hopes of getting work.

The whole day remained calm. We stayed there until the red sun cast its last glows and disappeared. The women and men on the other side of the lake went back. The herons flapped their white and brown wings, flew up and planed away. We returned, walking up the hillock and then down through the darkening pine wood.

Thakur's idea worked.

Our friends were all set to go back; they had asked their relatives to buy air tickets for them. They had stopped going to the city centre in search of jobs, rather they would play cards the whole day, discussing as how to get their money from the agents. Thakur and I extended our visa for one more month, paying a large sum of money. We did not know whether it was a visa fee, or Rakesh put the money in his pocket, but at least we got the visa. We began to look for work, any types of work. It was after a week or so we, just the two of us, started to walk, Thakur got a job in a hairdressing salon near the city centre. That day also we were walking on the brick-layered narrow streets in search of work. We saw an Indian-looking guy in a salon on the corner of one of the streets.

"Let me talk to him," Thakur said and went in, leaving me outside to walk from this end to that end of the street. When he came out, his face was bright.

"He has asked me to start from tomorrow," he smiled. "The owner is originally from India."

"Really? How much is he giving?"

"I didn't talk about the salary. I was too afraid."

"Oh, yes. Anyway, you have got a job which we needed. Let's celebrate today."

"Why not?"

Thakur changed some money. He wanted to celebrate. Obviously, this finding of a job had come to him and, to me as well, as a great relief. At least we could survive, would not be left unfed, until I would get for myself. Hopes grew in me that the owner of the salon must know about a restaurant where I could find work.

"The soil must be fertile in Madagascar. You see those clumps and panicles. Just like in Madhesh," Thakur said as we travelled back on a crowded bus, showing the paddies, a little away from the road.

Indeed, the yellow clumps looked sturdy with rich golden panicles bowing down towards the earth. They were almost ready for harvest. Even from the initial days, despite our sufferings, the views of those scattered paddies in the capital city, along the roads and amidst the houses, had pleased me and obviously the others as well, but we had never before talked about those fields, those yellowing rice plants. Up until now, we were always overwhelmed by the worries about work, about our survival. Now, as he found a job and became free, to some extent though, from the worry of survival, the lovely views of those fields, which resembled the views of the rice paddies in his homeland, struck him.

He was in a jubilant mood. "Today, I'll ask Rakesh to buy a special drink," he said as the bus pulled up at its final stop near our place.

"That's what I want," I replied.

We bought chicken at the vegetable market and walked towards our place, not more than ten minutes away from the market, gossiping.

But at our place – the big, old house – the scene was not usual. There was a police van outside its gate. A few policemen were entering the house. Our feet halted. Why were those policemen there? What was their presence about? Were they after the landlord or after our colleagues? Did they discover that our colleagues had not extended the visa? Did they know we were in Madagascar to work, not to travel? Or were they after Rakesh who might have involved in other crimes? My brain flooded with millions of questions and doubts. The heart was pumping. My mouth dried. Thakur's face darkened.

"Why are they here?" he whispered.

"I don't know. Let's not stand here, go somewhere before they notice us," I said.

We crept out to the wood and, reaching atop the slope, positioned ourselves behind a huge pine in such way that we could see them while hiding ourselves. We saw our friends, coming out of the gate, handcuffed to the policemen. The old man, the owner of the house, was standing in the yard.

As the police van pulled away and disappeared leaving a plume of dust and smoke behind, Thakur asked, "Why did they take our friends?"

"It must be because of the expired visa," I conjectured.

"Are they putting them in jail?"

"Maybe."

"They're in trouble!"

"We too. I think this place is no longer safe for us. I'm sure the police will be eying this house. The old man will certainly inform them that we're here," I said, sitting on the bare ground, looking towards the other direction, towards the lake.

"But we have extended our visa." Thakur said as he sat beside me.

"It doesn't make much difference. It's a tourist visa valid just for a month, which I think isn't good for work. After a couple of days, we'll be in the same situation. They'll arrest us as soon as they find us," I said, picking up a dry pine needle from the ground and chewing on it.

"God, what shall we do?"

"Did the salon owner ask anything about your visa?"

"Yes. I told him everything."

"Let's request him to help us, I mean, to arrange another place for us. He might understand our situation. We must keep ourselves away from the police."

"And tonight?"

"Let's stay here until the old man is asleep. Then we'll go to our room. We can climb over the compound wall. And I know he doesn't lock the channel door."

"If he locks today?" Thakur expressed his suspicion.

"We'll come back here," I responded.

The evening rays fell over the slope and the valley, slanting. The striped shadows of the pines spread long and disappeared along with the setting of the sun. Below, on the side of the lake, the men packed their stuff and walked away. The swans dipped their beaks and heads once again and swaggered towards the vacant fields, the rice plants there had been cut down. The herons flew away. The frogs croaked and jumped into the water. The doves cooed for the last time and rested on the lateral branches. A pair of squirrels, so far playing with the pine cones, disappeared; they returned to their drey. The bugs and insects buzzed and cried the bizarre forest sounds. The pine needles sighed in the evening breeze, almost ghostly. The evening matured. The stars twinkled high above in the sky. The faint electric lights glimmered, up to far away. We sat under the pine, listening to eldritch sounds of the night, waiting for a total gloom to come to the house, the lights on the second floor of the house to be switched off, and the old man to sleep. The Stygian night grew dark and darker.

I was worried about my colleagues. Would they have anything to eat? Would they find bedding for the night or would they have to spend the whole night on the bare, cemented floor? I also might be caught by the police and would be eventually thrown into prison. Would there be anyone to rescue me? Who would inform Sushmita? What effect would the information have on her? Scary thoughts reeled through the brain. Thakur too must have been thinking in the same way. He was silent. How long we stayed there I did not know. It was late and completely dark when the lights were turned off in the house. We lumbered down the slippery slope covered with pine needles, and then climbing over the compound wall, we crept up into our room. Luckily, the channel door was not closed, but we were too afraid to be noticed by the landlord. We slept without eating. We kept the chicken we had bought in the corner of the room.

The next day, we slipped out before the old man coughed his morning coughs and before the pied crow cawed. At the bus stop in the junction, the traffic and the crowd had already built up even at that early hour. The streets were increasingly being filled with the people, selling and buying the groceries. The public buses were honking and throwing warm and thick clouds of pungent-smelling smoke. We got on the one going to the city centre and sat on a smelly, cold seat.

"We must do something for our friends. I think we should inform their relatives," Thakur said, wiping his running nose with a handkerchief, which he always put in his pocket. The morning breezes were cold.

"I think so. Let's call them from a public booth and talk to our landlord as well. He must have known the matter well," I said, looking at the fields. The cold window glass steamed up with my warm breath.

"Won't it be risky? I mean . . . the landlord may inform the police."

"We have to take that risk. We can't be mean to our colleagues."

We found their mobiles switched off as we called from a public booth.

Thakur's boss, the owner of the salon, turned out to be a thorough gentleman and a helpful person. After listening to Thakur, he not only allowed me to stay with Thakur in a small room behind the salon, but also assured he would try to find work for me. He offered me hopes to cling to. We did not tell him anything about our friends. Nor did Thakur talk anything about the salary.

Thakur commenced his work the same day. And when he was asked to deal with a customer who had just entered the salon, the scissors worked well in his dark, calloused fingers.

Leaving him in the salon, I strolled through the streets and markets, the name of which I could not decipher. All they were written in French or Malagasy. In fact, even after more than a month in Antananarivo, I did not know much about the city. What I knew about it was narrowly confined to the purlieus of the place where we stayed, the bus route for Tana, the city centre, the rice paddies we saw from the bus, a couple of streets in Tana, the canals (built everywhere in the city centre), and Lake Anosy. I was not aware of any other places beyond those places.

After a little walk along the open canals, I sat by the side of Lake Anosy, looking at the Monument aux Morts, a monument to the dead or the war memorials. A few days back, Rakesh had told us the name of the monument. I sat there, strolled around the lake, and again sat, looking at the lake and at the paling leaves of the jacaranda trees, some of which were coming away and, dancing in the air for a few minutes, were settling down on the ground. A light breeze was sweeping around moving the emerald-green waters. A little away, in their business stalls, the locals were pushing hard to sell their goods. I spent the whole day idly. It was already evening when I reached the salon. Thakur had just finished his duty.

The room given to Thakur was not a big room. But small though, it was a fitted bedroom with a single bed and bedding, an attached shower and toilet, and a paraffin stove and cooking utensils. It was enough for us. More than our expectation. The little window of the room looked onto a brick-layered street.

"You're lucky, Thakur Ji," I said, sitting on the bed.

"I'm sure he'll find work for you. Until that, we can stay together. Or even if you work somewhere else, why not to stay together. In fact, I prefer that," Thakur said. "But what shall we do for our friends?"

"I'll go to our place and try to find out what actually happened," I said before we slept.

The next day, when I spoke to the old landlord, he said, in his slow and angry voice, "The police were looking after that guy, Rakesh, for long. When they came here, they found all others were staying here, in my house, without any visa. The police are looking for the two of you. I don't want to see you. Why didn't you tell me before?"

In his puffy eyes, almost prolapsed, I saw hate for us. In his cold, stern voice, I heard a frightening sound of anger. Certainly, he had disliked us. I did not stay there long. It was not safe at all. Dominique could inform the police. I came back and told Thakur everything. We called Kapil's relatives to give this information.

The days passed by. Thakur's boss found work for me in a restaurant, a few streets away from that place. It was a waiter job, but if any customers ordered Indian food, I was supposed to be a cook. At times, I was asked to wash the dishes and to mop the floor. So I did not know what my position was in that restaurant. The salary was low, less than a hundred dollars. Yet I had to continue; I needed money for the ticket, for paying off the mortgage, and for buying some clothes for Sushmita and the children. I was unaware how many more months or years I was supposed to work to collect that much amount.

Nearly after three months, we heard our colleagues were rescued and sent back by some international organisations. Thakur and I continued working, hiding ourselves from the police. Our visa was said to have been changed to working visa. But we were not sure whether they were genuine or false, so we always hid from the police and lived constricted life in Antananarivo.

The weeks and months passed by. The seasons changed. The jacarandas around the lake browned and became bare. In October, they bloomed in purple bunches. The rice paddies changed their colours and textures – watery to green to yellow to brown to vacant. In the park, Riva, lemurs – so unique to see and which I had heard to occur wildly only in Madagascar – hung on the tree branches. The sky opened and grew clouded, according to the seasons. The dry season ended, and the rainy season came. We continued working in Madagascar in the hope that one day we would return home.

And in December, almost after nine months, a well-suited man came to the restaurant. Talking to me softly, he proposed if I preferred to work in his restaurant in South Africa. Yet another temptation, yet another venture, yet another twist in life. I called Sushmita. As always, she pleaded with me to return. I talked to Thakur; his face darkened. It was not easy for him to spend time in Antananarivo alone. For me also, it was not easy to leave him. But the temptation prevailed. Soon I left Madagascar; I left my friend, Thakur. We waved our goodbyes. As I crossed the security check-in, frequently turning my head to see him, my eyes were wet. Was I crying?

Four

Some seven years elapsed since then.

It was in late September. In Pretoria, South Africa.

"Cheers!" We clinked glasses. Vinod had not arrived yet.

"Jo, this man is always late," Hemanta said, looking at his mobile. "And once he gets here, he'll blame traffic."

Hemanta, originally from the western part of Nepal, was now running a business in Centurion – a business selling a wide variety of things, ranging from bedding to furniture and from electronics to electrical appliances. He had a long nose, a little crooked. Down through the years, his brown silky hair had gone grey, almost half of it. He was irritated with this premature greyness. His deep eyes would crinkle when he laughed. Though younger, he looked older than me. Yet he possessed a lively personality, always loving to talk or, to say more appropriately, to argue with what the others said.

"Oh, Friday traffic on the highway?" I said, stoking up the braai stand with some more firelighters. "It's terrible, especially before the long weekend."

The blaze caught the coals; thick smoke billowed.

It was a bright Friday. The sky stretched wide. The greenery had already darkened. The bougainvillea and other flowers had already blossomed in colours. The jacarandas, however, were yet to sprout; they were awaiting the first rains of the season.

John, my gardener, had just left. The whole compound was filled with the smell of the freshly cut grass. The lines, the even stripes made by the mower, looked virgin, not yet trodden. He had trimmed the branches hanging over the fence, had done away with the fallen twigs and leaves, had swept the pavement and had applied weed killer to the weeds, which occasionally found their way through the gaps of the paved bricks. Behind him, he had left a clean garden as always. I loved him, loved his style of working and his passion for gardening in his sixties.

Varieties of seasonal birds – helmet shrikes, sun birds, thrushes, grey-go-aways, sparrows, true weavers and others – were busy chirping, hopping, darting from this to that tree, pecking at the ground, and weaving nests. Butterflies and dragonflies were flapping their tiny wings through the branches and over the pool. A few hadedas, the African ibises, were grazing on the lawn.

And we had planned to have a braai at my place as we often would do on Fridays; it was my turn to organise.

"You know, Hemanta, what this city fascinates me most is its open sky. You can enjoy the sky without a streak of cloud for weeks and weeks. Just like in Tibet," I said, pouring whisky and putting ice cubes into both the glasses.

"Here he comes!" As I opened the gate, a dark-red car entered the compound.

Inside was Vinod. Cropped hair, medium height, Mongol colour, and complexion with moustache and beard: he was dressed up in his branded old clothes. He never allowed his moustache to grow. Nor did he shave it neatly as I would do. He always presented himself with stubble on his face, which to other people, to the people like me, seemed to be a carelessness about one's own self, a lack of sense of neatness, but to him, it was a style. Years before, during an evening at his place, he had said he believed he looked handsome, strong, and sexy in that rugged style. Since then he had not changed his style; he never failed to have stubble on his face. Did he shave in the evening to have that particular length of stubble and to maintain his style for the next day? Or did his hair grow so fast on his face? He did not tell me. Nor, in spite of my curiosity, did I go to the extent of asking him.

Anyway, he got out of the car with the same stubbly face and cropped hair. He had a smile and a ready-made excuse as Hemanta had presumed.

"Sorry, guys. You know the traffic during the weekend."

"I knew. I knew he would say this. I know this man. For him, traffic is heavy even in the middle of the night if he finds a reason to delay," Hemanta said.

"Especially if he finds a girl," I added.

"Hey, guys, do you want me to leave before I come," he said and lit a cigarette, Marlboro Gold. "Ashok, did you marinate the meat with the spices I had told you? You put in too much coal! You guys are here for these many years and don't know how to braai meat." Vinod filled his glass and clinked with ours and took a sip. He took out some coals from the braai stand before fanning it with a piece of cardboard.

He loved meat. In our get-togethers, which came about every weekend or at least the alternate weekend, it was he who showed interest in braaing meat. It was he, even though braai was organised at my or Hemanta's place, who instructed us which meat to buy, what spices to use, how long to marinate, and when to take it out of the fridge. He would trawl the stores or would go through almost all magazines of the main groceries – stuffed in bundles in the letter box, which, in my case, would have been thrown into the bin, unopened – particularly to see where the braai chops were being sold at sales or promotion. Hemanta and I could manage just with bare drinks or with snacks or whatever we found. Vinod, however, always needed chops. He had the feel for braai and for drinks too, but even so, he never lost his sense, his behaviour always balanced. He was difficult to come across when he drank; it was not easy to comprehend what he was about on, yet he never became offensive. And his driving? It was fast and rough, but always in control, very similar to Dorje's driving in Lhasa.

Puffing his own brand, Hemanta asked me, "Ashok, are you really serious about settling in Nepal?"

"I'm staying away from the children for long. They need me."

"Why don't you bring them here? Schools are good here. Your business is running so well. What do you get going there? Just crowds, traffic, smoke, and dust. I had also thought to settle in Kathmandu. But last year when I went there, jo, I couldn't stay even two weeks."

"I don't know why I always miss it, and my heart always asks me to go back. And my daughters prefer to study there."

"Just go, see yourself. Once you're there, you'll know what I mean. You better bring your children. There's no future there," he said and refilled his glass.

It was almost seven years ago we had met first. That time, seven years ago, we were the only three Nepalese in Johannesburg. There might have been more, but we did not know. We had heard about a few others working as professional doctors in other provinces but not nearby. Over the period, over those seven years, we had formed a close friendship. Later, the number of Nepalese coming to Johannesburg and working and engaging in small businesses grew. We established contacts with many of them. Yet we were the ones who would meet regularly. Despite the arrival of other Nepalese, the relations between three of us remained close, intact, as it had been earlier or even closer. We would call many times a day and would meet and drink every weekend or alternate weekend. On such weekends, we would chat and drink for hours and hours, until midnight, sometimes even after midnight, drinking glass after glass – glass for good health, glass for prosperous business, many last glasses and glasses for the road. The chats would cover a wide range of issues, segueing from social to political, family to personal business.

The following morning, with our strong hangover, we would commit ourselves over the phone to quit alcohol or at least to take a break. But once the weekend came, we would gather again. The glasses would clink until midnight, discarding our commitments.

"Guys, don't sit there folding your hands. At least prepare salad," Vinod said, putting braai chops on the grill.

"You're the one, who doesn't let us touch your meat," Hemanta said and began to chop the cucumber, tomato, and onion. I went in and put on the lights.

The dragonflies flapped their gossamer wings for the last time and disappeared in the evolving darkness. The weaver birds tried to catch the last insects and nestled in their lovely plant-houses hanging in the branches. The hadedas flew away high. Evolving from the east, the evening fell on the lawn. The sky slowly darkened, exposing twinkling stars, first one or two, then a few more, a little later the whole constellations. The evening breeze smoothly swept across. The coals glowed red. We stood around the braai stand having our drinks and chats, Vinod still busy turning over the braai chops from side to side.

Hemanta once again showed his discontent about my idea of going back and said, this time addressing Vinod, "You know, Vinod? Ashok wants to settle in Nepal."

"Serious? I never knew," Vinod said, putting braai chops on a paper plate.

"I haven't decided yet, just thinking," I said, although deep inside me I was determined.

"Why did such a stupid thought come to your mind? How can you pack up such a good business for nothing?" Hemanta said. A white puff came from his mouth and nose as he lit another cigarette.

"Settling in your own country isn't a stupid thing. That's my earth, that's my soil," I said.

"Hey, you don't need to be an idealistic gentleman. Be practical. Granted, that's your earth, but what has your earth given to you? Nothing. There're so many Nepalese, never accounted accurately, working in different cities in India. Equally in the same numbers are working in the Gulf Countries and Malaysia and Korea. Lately, the African cities are being explored as new destinations. What did your *earth* give to these people?"

"It gave me everything. Most importantly, the identity. The soil can't be blamed for everything wrong."

"What identity have we got? Who knows us and our country and for what? You just talk ridiculous."

"Mount Everest is in Nepal."

"They may know about Mount Everest. They hardly know it's there."

"The birthplace of Lord Buddha is in our country."

"If you ask where Buddha was born, either you get a wrong answer or they walk away shrugging their shoulders."

"We're known for rich cultural diversity."

"Now we have been fighting among ourselves."

"Not everyone is fighting. There're people trying to settle the fighting."

"The people around the world don't know us. Even if they know, they know us for poverty, for unemployment, for insecurity, for strikes, for crowds, and blah, blah, blah. They see us with pity, with sympathy."

"Isn't it our responsibility to promote our country, I mean, the dignity of our country."

"And when you're queued in the immigration and customs offices, you're expected to give them a bribe. When you go for any official business, you're embarrassed. When you go to politicians to express your dissatisfaction, you're neglected. All are just corrupt."

"Still, there're non-corrupt people with vision and sincerity."

"Hey, what the hell are you arguing for? Chops are ready, just grab them. Ashok, put some in my glass," Vinod said. "These guys talk always about political nonsense."

"Jo, this Ashok is too principled. I don't know what on earth he's going to do in Nepal. There's no sense talking to him. I better take the braai chops." Hemanta took a chop.

I followed him.

Hemanta and I would often enter into endless arguments, of course, without offending each other. Over the years, we had become aware of each other's limits of tolerance.

He had exhibited a friendly impression from quite early on, from the very moment when I had first met him in Midrand, Johannesburg. A week or two after, I had met Vinod. The gestures he exhibited – the way he spoke, the way he laughed, ha . . . ha . . . ha . . ., showing his shining teeth, and the way he shared with me, frankly and honestly, how he had developed his childhood fantasy to become a politician or a senior bureaucrat, how he had studied and spent all his time on books, keeping himself away from all types of fun for his age, how he had secured high marks – all were appealing.

"But nothing happened as I had thought. My dreams were dashed. I was not able to pass the bureaucratic exams. I tried to join politics but only to hate it because of nepotism and numerous malpractices therein. I found even the most democratic parties being run by whimsical decisions of the leaders. Frustrated, I started, with a loan from a bank, a small business, the business of construction materials that, due to my inexperience and inability to compete with the established businessmen and syndicates, soon sank. Then you know, Ashok, the people from the bank came to my land which I had mortgaged for the loan and posted a notice about the non-payment. All of a sudden, I came to the footpath," he had said to me so frankly and honestly when I met him first. Seven years or so back.

"My father wasn't satisfied with me for not being able to do anything. Every moment he met me, he would give me a lecture that my friends had already sent this and that amount of money from abroad and blah, blah, blah. I was lucky that, around the same time, the eligible Nepalese were invited to apply for a working visa for South Korea. I learnt the language for a few weeks and appeared in the interview. And look, I was selected. It was the happiest day of my life. Wasn't it ironical that a man with a determination to serve in the country would become happy when he was selected for a labour job in a foreign country?"

"It was the LG Electronics branch in Changwon, a city near Busan, to the far south from Seoul, where I started the job without any training. The labour job would not require much training, I was told. It was a hard job. Eight hours a day. Wearing three pairs of gloves, I had to move the hot metal frames from one place to another, atop a forklift. I was supposed to put the frames in my hands not more than six seconds. Otherwise, the gloves would start to smoke. Jo, at the end of the day, you become so tired that all the flesh of your body would pain. And your hands? They wouldn't hurt. They would feel detached from the body. Even if you hammered them, you wouldn't feel it."

"Then eight o'clock evening in the kitchen, the restaurant-kitchen. The smell of Korean food," Hemanta had continued. "It was absolutely strange to me. It wasn't my palate, especially the smell of *kimchee*. It took days for me to adjust my taste. Before sleeping, drinking Korean alcohol! The next morning, I would wake up with painful muscles and swollen hands and would start the work again. And those Korean people! When it comes to work, nobody can compete with them. One Korean would accomplish what we two, my friend and I, couldn't do."

"You know what happened one day? It was after almost three months, I found a half frog in the vegetable stew, cut in half from the middle. The leg still intact and that one eye? As though rolling and staring at me! I showed it to my friend. Jo, he ran away to the toilet. I too. Later, when we told the manager, he said we were being fed frogs for three months. Ha . . . ha . . . ha . . .," he had laughed out loud. "We requested the manager to give us money and a place for a separate kitchen. It was so difficult in the earlier days. But everything became smooth as time passed by. I stayed there for three years."

"I came back to find a different Nepal, a different society. During my absence much had changed. You couldn't find any youths in rural areas. Most had gone abroad for work. The remaining had joined security forces or the Maoists or had left the villages. I stayed for another half a year. Then I couldn't stand it. I was already drugged by foreign stay. I contacted an agent and this time for Canada, Australia, or the USA. I paid almost five lakh rupees, in addition to the ticket. He promised me the visa for Canada. Once I gave him the passport, I never got it until I flew from Delhi to Nairobi, where I met Vinod, cheated like me. We spent months in Nairobi, then travelled to South Africa through all those forests and savannahs, hiding ourselves from all those dangerous animals and police. How we came here, I'll tell you later sometime or you can ask Vinod. We have the same story from Kenya."

He had completed his long narration by saying, "Sometimes it comes to me that we are meant to work for other people. First, we worked for the British as Gurkhas, then for Indians as *bahadur* and *chowkidar*, and lately for the Arabs and Malaysians as labourers and domestic helpers. We're meant to be exploited and destined to live in a desperate plight. Always and always."

Those were the words he had told me seven years back in his sunny apartment in Midrand, the windows of which looked out onto a wide expanse of a grassy land. In that wide grassy land, somewhere in the middle distance, there was a tiny settlement of uniformly built houses, the colours of which were uniform greyish blue. Hemanta had ended the brief narration of his past, looking at those blue houses amidst the wide grassy land dotted with mid-sized trees in places. His words sounded friendly and authentic.

Not long after, on our second meeting, he had taken up his story after Nairobi.

"For our journey ahead, we had to travel days and hours by bus and had to walk following the agents along the trails in savannahs and forests, those trails probably being used only by smugglers and poachers. One day, you know, Ashok, we were nearly trampled down by elephants. It was in a jungle in Zambia. We saw a parade of elephants just crossing our way. Suddenly, one of the elephants stopped there, spreading its big ears wide and slanting its narrow eyes towards us. Luckily, we were screened by trees and bushes. Jo, at that moment my heart almost broke. We were handed over from agents to new agents after crossing each border. And those agents? They knew every detail of those forests and trails. They could even smell animal's spoor and find how far the danger was. Once knowing the danger, they would lead us along another trail. They finally brought us here three weeks after we left Nairobi, and once they brought us here, they just disappeared. We had nothing: no money, no clothes, no contacts. We were just like beggars. And I was thinking, honestly, to stand at the crossroads and beg for change. Ha . . . ha . . . ha . . .," he had shared with me.

I still remembered vividly it too was Friday. We had gone for a short walk around the municipality building in Kempton Park, east of Johannesburg, and it had been drizzling. Perhaps it was the first drizzle for many months; the soil quickly absorbed the first droplets of rain and gave off the fragrances. I was delighted to smell, for the first time, the sweet smell of soil, the South African soil.

"I don't understand why we always prefer to work in a foreign country, under other's control. Why we can't be entrepreneurs and establish our own business," Hemanta had concluded.

The same day, Vinod had organised a braai party. It was on that occasion – outside drizzling offering a sweet smell and inside the coals glowing in the braai stand – the seed of the idea, the entrepreneurship and business, had come to our minds, which later was discussed in detail and eventually was worked out.

And this Friday too, seven years after that first Friday, we were having a braai. We talked about a wide variety of subjects. Especially Hemanta and I. Once we finished about Nepal, we began another topic. Vinod participated occasionally, only on his favourite subjects, for example, business, girls, fishing, or wildlife. Not politics. He distanced himself from the political matters. He rather would light a cigarette and would be busy over his mobile.

"I have customers leaving early tomorrow. My driver is on leave, and I have to leave them at the airport. I must leave now," Vinod said, pouring the last drink into his glass.

Hemanta also expressed his intention to leave earlier that day. Soon they left.

I continued drinking, the lone drinking, sitting beside the braai stand under the canopy of stars.

The air was still, and with that, the spring evening felt clement. The stars had come out in their full strength in the dark sky. The pale light coming from a few tall street lights in front of the house, pale and faded as if lighting in half power, hardly reached the lawn. A large part of it was absorbed by the tree branches hanging over the street before they fell on the land. I was always curious to know why, in this part of the locality, the street lights were dim. Was it a well thought-out effort to save energy? Or was it the neglected area? Or, might be, no one cared about the dim lights. I never came to know the reason behind it, but the street lights were dim, sometimes giving you the security worries. I had noticed the dim lights in the early days when I moved to this house, when I was much worried about the security. Over the years, the security perception came down to a tolerable level, and I stopped worrying much about the dim lights, but the fadedness remained the same.

I was gradually recollecting my initial days in South Africa as I stayed outside in that maturing, still evening.

Five

The initial days in Johannesburg were difficult for me. As I came to Johannesburg from Antananarivo, after saying goodbye to Thakur, I had found myself in a different world. It was strikingly different from all other cities where I had been so far. The speedy pace of people, their fast-moving eyes, the speed of vehicles, the well-established infrastructure, the criss-cross of roads, and overhead bridges were new to me.

I had not thought my destination was at such level of development. As I boarded the plane, South African Airways, I had taken the journey simply as yet another journey to yet another city like the cities I had already been. I had not worried much about the destination, which would have been the case in my earlier journeys. So, unaware about the real status of my destination, I, throughout the flight, two hours and forty minutes, spent looking the outside views, the miniature views below on the earth, firstly on the Madagascar side, the widely spread suburban area of the capital city, green and brown hills, the rivers that looked flooded with recent rains, solitary beaches and then vastness of the Indian Ocean. On the South African side, long white beaches, sinuous rivers (or ditches? So difficult to ascertain from high above), winding roads, green dams, shrubby veld and swaths of fields in different shapes, circle and semi-circle in particular. Some shapes were formed so perfectly as if Euclid himself had joined the farmers to give geometrical precision to those farms.

But, when I came upon the view at the airport, the people in their hurry, in their fast pace, I became a bit panicked and nervous. The panic and nervousness increased more as I did not see Mr Ajaya Gupta, my would-be boss. Mr Gupta, the owner of a chain of restaurants in the city – who, during his visit to Madagascar, after listening to my story, had offered me a job in his restaurant, who had sponsored the visa, and who had assured me that he would be at the airport to receive me – was not there.

Perhaps the confused look I wore was readable on my face and in my behaviour. People approached me from different directions offering a taxi, a hotel, or asking for my destination. They wanted to carry my baggage. But I did not know where I was going. The only information I had about Mr Gupta was his phone number. I wanted to buy a telephone SIM card. It was at that moment, in that process, I lost my wallet and baggage. Someone had taken it. I did not know who; it happened within minutes. I was asking someone where I could buy a SIM card. The baggage was beside me, but as I looked back, it was not there. I reached inside my pocket to find the wallet to have disappeared. Who took it out of my pocket without my notice? How? There were many people, watching and following me. I became penniless on the very first day in Johannesburg. Had I lost the cheap phone set, I would have lost the contact number of Mr Gupta as well. Fortunately, it was there. I approached the police (or the tourist information desk?) and told them rather embarrassingly about the incident and requested for a free phone call to Mr Gupta. I had to stay at the airport until a Pakistani man named Ahmed came to fetch me four hours later.

And this Ahmed? What a long and thick beard he had! He laughed out loud at my story, exposing his rotten teeth. And his reaction after listening to what had just happened to me at the airport? Unbelievable! He said, "You're lucky you didn't lose your life. Anyway, welcome to Joburg." He said so with his laugh, probably mocking, thereafter did not speak to me until we reached the restaurant. He drove very fast, at breakneck speed. The speedometer never came down below 140. Very frequently he came out with *fuck you* to other drivers, albeit the mistake was his own. Was it the single word he had learnt in South Africa, I was wondering? He perhaps was trying to impress me, to show me how much knowledge he possessed about the locality, how smart he was. Or maybe, it was his habit, his real personality. I sat beside him, nervous and quiet. All the time, it worried me what I was going to do with all my money and clothes stolen. How and with whom I was going to ask for the immediate necessities. Could I ask Ahmed? With this exhibition of unfriendly and indifferent attitude, it seemed that he would not lend me even a penny.

He drove fast, overtaking other cars from the lane he chose, no matter right or left, taking the bends and turnings fast, halting abruptly at red lights and then speeding again before the green signals, causing me to panic me more and more. Finally, he took me to a restaurant at Fordsburg in Johannesburg, a locality largely dominated by people from South Asia. This locality appeared to be untidy, to be starkly different from the views, the modernity, and the infrastructure, which I had initially seen from the airport and on the way to the city, with tall buildings on the right and different from the initial perception of the city, the whole of the city, I had made once I came across those views. Here, in this stretch of the city, at Fordsburg, I witnessed the same squalor, clumsiness, crowd, and the mess I was confronted with in Antananarivo and in Mumbai. I thought I was always destined to stay in the untidier part of the city.

Mr Gupta was not in the restaurant either. I was told he was a very busy businessman. He owned several restaurants in the city, and he came to the restaurant very rarely. I was given brief instructions about my work by the manager who spoke brusquely, although the way he spoke and the words he chose to speak spoke of his educated and professional demeanour. Despite his brusqueness, he seemed to be far better than Ahmed. And he did not have the beard! He asked me to have some food and to have a rest for the rest of the day at a place where I was supposed to stay with some other people.

Farooq, a Bengali waiter (he had introduced himself before we left the restaurant), led me to a place, a run-down three-storey flat-topped building, not far from the restaurant. The building looked like a perfect part of the locality, matching the untidy buildings in the neighbourhood. As I entered the compound through a sliding corrugated tin gate following him, I came upon the view of a dilapidated building with mottled exterior walls, advertising pamphlets and posters displayed on it. Beer and juice cans and bottles, perished tyres, metal scraps, bricks, and the clods of cement (probably detached from the compound walls and pillars) littered the compound. The plaster had come away from various parts of the walls. The windows were dusty. The paint was peeling off the door. Farooq led me to the upper floor where there were three tiny apartments. Before he opened the door to one of the apartments, I was faced with a small room offering a blend of odours, similar to decaying fish, tobacco, and strong spices. The room had a dirty kitchen and a toilet, the commode of which looked stained with yellow. The sink was cracked and the floor was soaked.

"This is where we stay. Including you, we're four to stay in this room. Rice and vegetables are in the kitchen. If you're hungry, you can prepare for yourself, otherwise wait for us. We'll come at around ten or eleven," he said and left me in that cluttered room, alone.

On one side of the room was a bed, not good for more than one man to sleep. A few more sheets and pillows and blankets were put on two thin mattresses, which spread on the floor. An old television was on a small table, positioned at such an angle so that it could be viewed from the bed, from the floor, and from the small kitchen hatch. The whole room at once gave the impression of how the migrant workers lived their life, no matter in whichever cities or countries they lived. It was not different in Lhasa; it was not different in Mumbai and in Antananarivo; and it was not different even in Johannesburg. It was not that I was worried about the standard of living. I had had the opportunity, the opportunity of living poor life, throughout the past. I had grown within me a realistic sense of livelihood of people like me. Yet when I came to Johannesburg, the richest city in Africa, it was my little presumption that the living standard of the workers must be better in this city. As I lay on the narrow bed, looking at the low ceiling with damp patches and pared-away plaster, I was reminded that the sophistication of a city did not have much to do with the living standards of the poor. I lay on the bed, splaying legs apart, and trying to adjust myself to the new setting, including the strong smell of fish and tobacco and of Ahmed. I lay there worrying how I was going to fit in with these new people. I wished Ahmed would not appear as my roommate.

After eleven at night, Farooq came. I heard his voice. I heard him open the gate and his footsteps come up. When I opened the door, I saw what I was not wishing to be the case. Ahmed was there. Before Farooq. He was chewing paan; the corners of his lips were smudged with red colour.

There was one more man.

"Masood from Pakistan." He offered me a strong hand to shake.

"Nice to meet you. I'm Ashok from Nepal."

"Oh, you're from Nepal! I thought you were from India." Ahmed, this time, came out at me differently, with a soft tone, much different from the earlier one. Was it because I was from Nepal? I did not know. But I felt comfortable with his changed tone.

"Does it make any difference? After all, we're workers here," Farooq said.

Indeed, there was no such difference. From whatever country we were, we were migrant workers detached from our country and family.

"Come, come. I'm hungry, let's eat," Ahmed said. "This bastard manager doesn't give even a samosa. *Saala haraami* says there's nothing left. I know him. He must have packed it for himself."

They changed and sat on the floor, inviting me to sit. Farooq brought some worn-away plates and bowls from the kitchen and undid the aluminium wrapper of the packets they had brought from the restaurant. It obviously was leftover.

"So how long did you stay in Madagascar?" Ahmed asked, tearing off a big hunk of garlic naan and dipping into a bowl, full of spicy, thick creamy dal. He seemed to have a great feel for food.

"Almost ten months."

"Was it a good place?"

"It was not bad. But the salary was too low. And there was a language problem. French is more popular there. Nobody speaks English."

"How much are you expecting here?"

"The boss had told me that it would be two thousand rand a month plus tips and free lodging and food."

"Look! He lied to this friend also," Ahmed said. "He has the capacity to convince people to work for him. He said the same to me when he brought me here from Kenya. He never gave me that much money. I know he won't give you either. You can see your lodging yourself. And food? There're rarely any leftovers in this restaurant. The manager hides it for himself. We're trying to find work in other places. And you're here."

Masood and Farooq did not speak much; they just took their food unhurriedly. Differently than Ahmed. They looked more tired than hungry.

Me too. I pecked at a piece of naan and cauliflower.

"*Khalo, khalo, Bhaiya.* Why are you so shy?" Ahmed said. "*Baggage to luta diya, ab kya karoge*? Do you have any money to buy your necessities? Don't worry. You can take a loan from me."

Saying so, he offered me a relief and the realisation about his actual nature, different from what I had thought about him during and after our first encounter at the airport. He was offering help so readily. Amidst his rough appearance and style of speaking, there was a gentle human being inside him. He slept on the bed. The rest of us on the floor. Sometimes he stepped on our bed while we were sleeping. But no one dared to oppose him. After all, he was the chief of the room, the boss of the narrow world.

This was the account of my first day in Johannesburg in search of employment, in search of means of livelihood. Yet another venture, new pastures strange to me. I was almost terrorised by the whole drama. Would I be able to survive in such a strange world? The question kept disturbing me the whole night.

I began my work. Ahmed was a driver for Mr Gupta. Whenever Mr Gupta would drive himself, he would work in the restaurant as a waiter or in the kitchen. Was he taking on this extra duty for the sake of tips, a little extra income, or just for the leftovers?

Mr Gupta came to the restaurant after five days. Until then, he did not receive even my phone calls. He was understandably a busy person and did not bother much about the calls from unrecognised numbers.

"Good afternoon, sir," I said politely, slightly bowing my head in his honour.

Without responding and looking at me, he walked to the reception where the manager was busy doing his business. He walked in such way as if he did not see me. He was in his elegant grey suit and grey striped tie, almost the same he had worn in Madagascar. Did he not see me? Or did he forget about me and the later correspondences? Or did he forget me? I became embarrassed for being ignored.

Ahmed came to me and whispered, "You see! He refuses to recognise you. He doesn't care about us at all. I don't like to work for him even for a single day. But what to do?"

I stood without speaking, just looking at Mr Gupta and the manager talking and looking at some papers. It must be important for them; they took quite a while. When he was about to leave, the manager called me and introduced me to him.

"Oh, here you are! You finally managed to come. I'm sorry I forgot your name," he said.

"Sir, I'm Ashok," I replied.

"Oh, yes. It's Ashok. I remember. I hope you're settled. If you need anything, just ask him," he said, first clicking his fingers, then pointing his right hand towards the manager.

"Thank you, sir," I said.

He left. Ahmed followed him, carrying his black suitcase, a Samsonite. While leaving, he again whispered, "This manager is just a bootlicker of Mr Gupta. Be careful of him."

I looked at him opening the door of a blue Mercedes Benz for Mr Gupta and himself sitting in the driver's seat. The car soon disappeared in increasingly building up traffic.

That was it. My short encounter with the owner of the restaurant, who had talked so intimately in Antananarivo and who had tempted me with his impressive words to come to work in his restaurant. Now, as I met him after five days, he appeared in a totally different way. His behaviour towards me was almost sardonic. He took me not more than as a labourer, not as a human being. Ahmed was perhaps right. I recalled my life in Lhasa, working as a labourer, yet with a certain degree of dignity. I remembered, Pradip Tuladhar, my boss, yet so friendly, so caring. Also, I remembered Thakur, who must have been feeling lonely in Antananarivo.

Though over the years, I had developed, to some extent, a skill necessary for any sorts of restaurant job, from a waiter to a receptionist to a cook and though I was ready to take any types of job, I had difficulty in comfortably fitting in. I was the most junior in the restaurant, not in terms of age, but in terms of working period there; I was a newcomer in the fast world of Johannesburg. Everyone working there was my boss. I realised all of them portraying themselves in that way. They would love to give me instructions. Ahmed had already shared with all of them about the event, the dramatic loss of my baggage and wallet at the airport. So, to all of them, I was a subject of a joke. They all took advantage of that for days to come. Equally bothering was the absence of any Nepalese in Johannesburg. In Antananarivo, at least, I had Thakur to share loneliness.

The restaurant was busy. We worked hard until late evenings, sometimes until midnight. As soon as I would return to my place, my eyes would glaze. Before changing and washing, I would drop on the bed. In spite of the fact that Ahmed turned out to be friendlier than I had expected and never behaved as he had behaved on the first day, at the airport and on our way to the restaurant; in spite of the fact that I did not have a deep misunderstanding with Masood and Farooq, except a few petty grudges on the matter of tips (most of the time both of them would put the tips in their pockets whereas the money was supposed to be shared among all workers in the restaurant); and in spite of the fact that, perhaps given my age, the manager never shouted at me using vulgar words as he – in contrast to his usual behaviour, the soft and politely spoken – would use with Farooq and the other young workers, I had difficulties in adjusting myself to the new environments. I found it pretty hard.

Within a month, I was robbed for the second time – in Pretoria in the middle of the day. Violently. Farooq and I had gone to Pretoria to make our asylum seeker permits, which would allow us to work legally. On our way to the concerned department, on one isolated corner of the road, we were robbed at gunpoint by five men. We were walking side by side, talking about our manager, or in fact, gossiping about him, those people appeared in front of us, all of a sudden, from where we had no idea.

One of them, pointing a gun at me, said in his steely voice, "Hurry up. Give me whatever you have got."

"What's going on? Who're you?" I said in a terrified voice.

"Don't talk. Just give me whatever you have," he said, punching me on my nose.

Farooq tried to come towards me, but two of them grabbed hold of him, roughly. He tried to fight back, yelling, "Help, help!" But no one was there. Rather, all four of them, except the guy covering me, beat him, on his head, on his stomach, and on his head also. He gave up as one of them took out a glittering knife from his pocket and held it to his throat.

As I said, *"We're just workers, we don't have anything,"* or something like such, the guy with the gun punched on my nose one more time, knocked his gun against my temple, and shouted, "Shut up. Do fast."

We gave in and gave them whatever we had. Fortunately, they did not take our papers. Throwing our papers on the road, they fled before passers-by came there. After they tore off down the street, Farooq yelled, loudly, "Fuck you, criminals!"

We exchanged a pitiful sight at each other, shocked and terrorised. In that pulling and pushing of less than five minutes, we got bruises. The right sleeve of Farooq's shirt was parted half from the armpit. My nose was bleeding.

"You see these criminals. This is the third time within a year. I don't want to stay here any longer," Farooq said in his trembling voice.

"Shall we report it to the police?" I asked, closing my nose with the left hand and touching my temple with the right from where too the blood was oozing.

"There's no use. I had tried earlier. You'll simply waste your time." He took out his handkerchief from his pocket and gave it to me to wipe out the blood.

The whole day as we queued up outside the office among hundreds of other asylum seekers from many other countries, predominantly from Africa and South Asia, the agents there, time after time, approached us claiming that they would get our papers within minutes if we gave them money. But we did not have any money. We stayed in the queue, waiting and talking about our fate and the poor situations in our countries, compelling us to flee and seek jobs in alien countries, putting our life in dangerous pastures, and cursing our leaders. Farooq somehow managed to borrow money from other Bengalis for the fees of our permits and taxi fare to Fordsburg. For days, we got the words of sympathy from our colleagues.

Time and again, Sushmita and children came to mind terribly, filling my eyes with tears. It had been more than a year since we parted. The picture of the weary faces of my wife and children was vivid. Her weak assurance – *don't worry about the house and children, I'll take care* – and my consoling words, not much convincing – *I'll call you every day and come soon* – would often come to my ears as whispers. When I had called her to tell her about the new country after coming to South Africa, she had become further worried. Thereafter, during each call, which was very rare (as it cost money), her voice sounded near tears. Each time I would try to give her weak assurances that the job here was good and that I would be back soon. But I myself did not know when I would go to my country. I had not paid off the loan from the bank against which I had put Big Plot as security. When I was about to leave Madagascar, I had sent a little money to pay the interest. The bank charged compound interest. If the amount remained unpaid, it would be doubled within a few years. There were other debts to be paid off. What was I going to do after going back?

And here in Johannesburg, life was so difficult, so insecure and so lonely. As Ahmed had forecast, I did not receive the money as was promised by Mr Gupta; it was set at one thousand, plus a few hundred rand from tips. Every month, or once in two months, depending on the tenure of the papers, almost half of the salary would go to permits and on taxis to and from Pretoria.

Another one third would be spent on other necessities. Hence, the saving was too little, not enough for an air ticket even if I wanted to go back.

Such had been my initial days in Johannesburg: monotonous, dull, difficult, and frustrating. Tired and lousy wakening amidst the foul smell; irritating waiting for the dirty toilet; lazy walks to the restaurant and almost twelve hours of work in standing position; weary returns late at night; then, travels to Pretoria by taxi and queuing up for the permit with strange people: life felt mechanical and anonymous. In my solitude, I would often think I made yet another mistake by coming here, yet another new destination. In fact, for a long time, it had begun to appear to me that the whole life had become a parade of mistakes.

Such had been the initial days in Johannesburg. Life was like a penance, trapped in a serious dilemma to go back or to stay a few more months. Had I not met Vinod, I would probably have continued my job in the same restaurant amidst the dilemma and confusion. But one day, during the lousy walk to the restaurant in the morning, as chance would have it, I came across him, a Mongol complexion with narrow eyes and a small nose. He was busy speaking over the mobile phone in Nepalese. I was surprised, obviously happy too, to hear someone speaking in my language in a strange place, where I had not thought of meeting any other from my country.

I stopped there on the road with my curious eyes at him. His head was shaved. He had stubbly cheeks and chin. After he finished his conversation, I asked him, "Are you from Nepal?"

"Yes," he looked at me. His narrow bright eyes squinted in the sunlight.

"I'm Ashok," I said, giving him my hand.

His handshake was friendly as if he had met a long-lost friend.

"I'm Vinod. Vinod Thapa. How long have you been here? What are you doing? I never knew you were here."

"It's almost five months. I'm working in a restaurant. Near here. Are there any other Nepalese in Johannesburg?"

"There's one in Midrand. Hemanta. I have heard a few are working in other cities. Not in Pretoria and Johannesburg. I'm working in a hotel in Kempton Park. Today is my day off. Where's your restaurant?"

"It's just a five-minute walk. Let's go there to talk."

It was thus I had met Vinod, in a way all of a sudden. This sudden meeting with someone from my country, from my own area, gave me a kind of energy, freeing me, to a large extent, from the deep-seated loneliness.

That very day, in the afternoon, he took me to his hotel in his car, an old model Ford with dark-red colour. The hotel, a part of a reputable and busy hotel chain, looked full of business. The same day, he took me to his place in the back of the hotel, an apartment with single bedroom. It was a bright apartment facing north.

"How much are you drawing?" Vinod asked me as we sat for a drink the same night.

"One thousand rand and a few hundred extra as tips."

"That's too little. I'll find a job for you, if possible in this hotel, otherwise in another restaurant or hotel. One thousand is too little money for your type of job. I'm also alone. If we stay together, I'm sure, life would become easier and more comfortable," he said, stubbing out his cigarette on an old plate. Probably there was no ashtray in the room, or it was mislaid somewhere.

"Please, Vinod Ji. I don't like to stay there," I said.

"Why are you adding *Ji*? And please for what. We're friends. We need to help each other. Just call me Vinod."

The days appeared differently after I met him. The loneliness and frustration lessened. I laughed more, talked more, and came out during the day off. I walked along the busy streets with Ahmed, chewing paan, talking to his friends, buying samosa and pakora. Ahmed was seemingly popular in the locality. He would exchange *assalamualaikum* to almost everyone he came upon.

The following week, Vinod took me to Midrand to see Hemanta, who worked in a restaurant and who had shared with me about his stay in Korea. The same day, the Friday evening, Vinod organised a braai at his place, the first braai during which the idea of business was seeded.

Not long after that first braai, I got a call from Vinod about my new work in a restaurant in his hotel with an attractive salary, four thousand rand a month plus tips. I called my wife, whose voice sounded chocking as if she was trying hard to control herself from crying.

"Ashok, you're lucky. You found a good job. And we? I don't know how long I have to suffer from this Gupta and his manager," Ahmed said, putting a sweet in his mouth after we dined on our leftovers. I had bought some sweets.

I came away with the impression that within the short period of time I had grown to have enough friendly feelings towards those strangers in what was a strange city. Probably in their innate nature all human beings would behave in a similar way. The religions, the cultures, the traditions would always come after the humanity.

"Please speak to your friend to find a job for me too. Do come by whenever you're free," Ahmed said when we hugged and parted.

I moved into the new place. It was a waiter job, but it proved to be better than in all other restaurants I had worked earlier. After a long time, after I suffered much in Mumbai, in Madagascar, and in Johannesburg, I enjoyed my working. It seemed the loan I had taken from the bank could be paid. Our Big Plot would remain with us. The children could continue school. Festivals could be celebrated with something nice to eat and new to wear. Above all, the sadness cast on my wife's face for so long would come off, I thought. Thus, after I met Vinod and a little later, Hemanta, my life changed. Perceptions about Johannesburg changed. I grew to like the country. At first, the South African weather grew on me, such mild weather. Even in summers it was far cooler than what I had thought, out of ignorance, about it to be. Then grew on me the lands, the cultures, and the people.

Was it luck smiling on me? After I met Vinod and Hemanta, it felt so. Success and prosperity became finally known to me. Hemanta's idea of beginning our own business worked out. It was Hemanta who seeded the idea. But it was Vinod who pursued it, vigorously. He forced us to start the business. First, he changed the status of his visa into a business visa, which was obviously not easy. He brought investments from Nepal, a little though. He persuaded the officials, sometimes politely and, at times, assertively according to the circumstances, to change his visa status. He registered the company in his name first and included us – Hemanta and me – as shareholders, later. He worked out the plan, he studied in detail, he consulted with others, and finally we bought a bed-and-breakfast with ten rooms near the airport. He made the majority of investments and

Hemanta made the rest. To me, I did not have money. So I was supposed to pay off my share every month from the salary and bonus whatever it came.

We divided our responsibilities as per our knowledge and experience. Vinod took the responsibility of marketing and finding guests. Before the sunrise, in his dark-red Ford, he would go to the airport and would stand in the arrival area with Mount Everest or Buddha's eyes printed on his T-shirt. He would convince tourists to come to our place. He made friends at the airport, at the information desk, the tourism desk, and the police desk and requested them to send tourists to us. The commission he promised them worked. I was assigned to take care of guests when they would arrive, take care of their room, their necessities, including breakfast. Hemanta took the responsibility of purchasing the necessities and handling the reception. We did almost everything ourselves. Except for hiring two local women for cleaning purposes, we did all work ourselves.

We would wake up at four o'clock in the morning. If not, Vinod would shout at us, "Hey, lazy guys, it's too late. Get up now."

We would work until late at night. We promised trust and understanding between each other. We cut out alcohol except on rare occasions. We were at great pains to achieve success. And it paid off. Our bed-and-breakfast never went unoccupied. At times, the occupancy was a completely full, compelling us to refer the guests to other places we knew. Within two years, we had yet another restaurant in Centurion.

It was after that we stopped sharing the business and divided the property among ourselves, with no problems. There were no grudges, no divisions, and no misunderstandings. The partition was just for the sake of avoiding possible difficulties in the future, and along with our own interest, a thoroughly discussed and well thought-out step. Vinod owned the bed-and-breakfast. In my share was the restaurant. Hemanta took cash as his share. He opened a shop in Centurion.

After I took over, the restaurant ran even better. I asked Ahmed to join me, to look after the day-to-day business of the restaurant, which he agreed.

I was thinking of inviting Sushmita and the children.

Six

I was still in the bed when I heard the doorbell ring. It was Amanda, my housemaid. Like every other Saturday morning, that morning also was lousy and difficult. Lazily, I woke up, drank three or four glasses of water, and pushed the button on the remote.

"Good morning, Amanda. How're you?"

"I'm fine, sir. How're you?"

"Can't complain. Except a mild headache."

"That's not new for you on Saturday. I can imagine you drank a lot. Eish, when you drink, you're a dolphin. I don't know why do you drink so much? Look at your garden. What a hell of a mess you made," she fussed. "Sir, I can't tell you not to drink. I know you don't agree with that. But at least, don't make such a mess. Please. It looks as if you organised a huge ceremony, inviting hundreds of people. It'll take the whole day for me to clean."

There were bottles and glasses lying on the lawn. The remains of the braai, paper plates, coals, and bone pieces, littered everywhere: on the lawn, on the pavement, on the veranda, even on the floor inside. Colonies of different types of ants had gathered around to have their preferred feast. The uneven marks, suggesting tentative shapes of the soles of the shoes we wore the previous evening, during braai, were printed throughout the floor, beginning at the braai spot, then spreading around and leading to the kitchen and the toilet.

"Sorry, Amanda. Let me help you clean."

"No, no, no, don't interfere. I'll do it myself. You'll mess up it," she said, putting water and cleaning stuff in a bucket. "Don't step into the floor until I finish it, and it dries up. Otherwise, you're going to print your big steps everywhere."

"So you want me to stay outside at least another two hours," I said, collecting the empties from the lawn. "I don't mind. I'll have a walk inside the compound to get rid of this damned *babalas*!"

"There's no reason to swear the *babalas*. You invited it. It's just a result of something that you did yourself." She began her cleaning job, crooning a Zulu song in her euphonious voice.

Amanda, a woman with deep religious faith, in her fifties, had been working with me from when I moved into this house. She would travel all the way from Mpumalanga – her hometown – to Waterkloof, Pretoria, every day for her work. She worked at my house every Saturday. She had proven herself as an honest maid, as a kind woman, sometimes offering me a sense of guardianship. I never had problems with her. In turn, I was always cautious not to make her feel slighted upon any account.

It was almost noon. The spring sun was bright in the sky. Trying to avoid prolonged exposure to the rays (I was told that the sun here carried excessive amount of ultraviolet rays), I went beneath the leopard tree, around the trunk of which John had padded the soil and put a few big flat stones to erect a small platform, similar to a *chautari*. I sat on one of those stones, looking at the flowers. Flowers in that patch of the garden – which was always under the dark shadows cast by thick branches of the leopard tree inside the compound and the jacarandas outside the compound on the street, especially during summer when the sun would reach the farthest south – were of the species that produced very tiny flowers, negligible in comparison to the wide leaves of the plants. It was John himself, who had chosen the species with the ability of surviving in the tree shade, with little sun. He had brought small flowers in his *bakkie*, saying, "This grass from Zimbabwe is fast grower but requires a lot of sunshine. I'm afraid it'll soon die in this shadowed part. So it's better if I plant these flowers here, in this shadowy patch." He was true. Not long after I moved into that house, the perpetual shadow on that patch of the garden stunted the grass. The grass became thin and thinner and eventually died, exposing the naked earth. The only things left there were those flowers he had planted. Every year, he watered those flowers until late autumn, until they stopped flowering.

There was one more thing about that patch of garden. When I came to this house first, groundwater came out of a hollowed spot near the leopard tree and made the earth around there damper, in one particular area just like a swamp. In that swampy ground, he had planted a few elephant's-ear plants, maybe three or four tiny seedlings, which over the period grew and grew and gradually stopped the water, although the ground, the soil without grass, always looked a little bit damp. Now, the place looked like a bush with wide-leaved tall plants. Birds sometimes perched on those leaves and left their droppings.

Soon after I stayed there under the leopard tree, the shadow made me feel a slight cold. In spring and autumn, it always happened to me. If I stayed under the sun, it felt hot and if I stayed in the shadow, it became cold. I had to change my sitting location: from sunny to shadowy and shadowy to sunny after every few minutes.

I went to the backside of the house. The garden there was more open. The grass saw more sun. No big trees shadowed there as they did at the front side. Just one small aloe, a white pear and a juniper stood there still in their infancy, growing unhurriedly. The shadow of the branches of the gnarled oak tree never fell on the grass; it stretched on the pavement, not on the grass. The trees in the compound of the neighbouring house seldom shadowed my lawn. So the grass in the back garden was greener and thicker. John loved it. He had told me that all those trees were planted there a few months before I moved in. He did not want to let them grow after a certain height so that they would not stunt the growth of the grass.

Against the fence on the eastern side of the lawn, there was a wide old mulberry trunk, not taller than five feet. During winter, it would look dead as if it would never come back to life again. However, interestingly enough, in season, many branches would sprout from the stump. Those branches would rapidly grow with wide dark-green leaves, and each of them would bear the fruits, the purple and black. Every year. It never died. I had never seen such a wide mulberry trunk. It was much wider than those I had seen in my hamlet. Yet the leaves and the fruits looked similar. Certainly, the soil in the garden was fertile, which allowed the mulberry to grow to such a huge size. And perhaps the owner of the house was afraid of the size, was afraid it would damage the fence, which must be the reason he had cut it down. It was not what I had heard from John but was my own conjecture, which was possible to surmise given the size of the trunk and its position against the fence. Past the mulberry tree, in the neighbouring compound, the frangipani had come out in white flowers, a few of which were blown to my compound to stud the lawn.

And it was that compound from which a melodious tune, either from a flute or from a clarinet or any other instruments belonging to the woodwind group, had begun to sound in the atmosphere for a few days. Almost continuously. The tune would normally begin at noon and would continue the whole day with infrequent brief interruptions. On Saturday and Sunday, it would begin to sound from as early as the morning. Perhaps a flutist or someone with a passion for music or music student had moved into the house as a tenant whom I had not met so far. The tune was not much familiar to me – it sounded somewhat like the tunes from a Peruvian traditional instrument, which I had listened some time back somewhere in Pretoria. The tune came in pieces with different notes, in changing rhythms suggesting he or she must have been harnessing his or her skill, yet it was euphonious and soon appeared to be an addition to the solitude of the backyard of the house, bringing back the reminiscences of the remote past when I would sit on the veranda of Padam's house and would listen to him playing the flute so melodiously.

To the west, near the shaded garage, a few tendrils of a climber (the name of which I did not know) had come from the compound of my other neighbour and rambled all over the fence and the shed, now with red and pink flowers. My daughters had directed a few tendrils, which had appeared on the top of the fence from the neighbouring compound, towards the asbestos shed made for daytime parking. Those tendrils now had rambled over the whole shed. John had not minded it.

Amanda was still busy with cleaning the floor. The house was big, and the floor was tiled in all rooms, except one or two. So much of her time would be always consumed in mopping the floor.

When I had come to this house four years back, it had charmed me. It was spacious; it looked new, and it had extensive grounds both in the front and back, a built-in garage for two cars, and an outside garage for yet another two cars, then a swimming pool with the shape of the Caspian Sea. Over and above, it was in a peaceful locality. Every part of the house: the roof tiles, walls, doors, and windows, the supply system of the water, the gutters and drainpipes, the inside rooms, the kitchen with enough inbuilt cupboards, the fresh colour on the walls and the yellowish curtains resembling the colour of the walls spoke of the newness of the house. The moment I had seen it, I had decided to rent it and had thought to call my family.

But I later noticed the house was renovated or founded on the old foundations. The old palisade with three pointed iron palings between the house and the back garden, a few cemented and iron posts in the middle of the back garden, a narrow cement platform there (the purpose of which I never knew; sometimes I sat there to drink teas or drinks), the old wires, hardly noticeable but poking out from different corners, and the mulberry trunk: all those indicated that the house was either renovated or erected on the old foundations.

"Sir, your mobile is ringing," Amanda said, giving the mobile to me. "I'm done with the floor. You can go in."

"Thank you, Amanda," I said, looking at the number.

It was Devaki, calling from Nepal, "Dai, namaskar. Are you fine? Why didn't you call me and didn't send any emails for such a long time?"

"Devaki, how're you? Is everything all right? I was just about to call you."

"You always promise but never call me. Everything is all right. The children want to see you. Dai, did you book your ticket? When are you coming?"

"I haven't decided the date yet. But I'll come."

"*You have to come.* You know, Dai? It's almost a decade I haven't put *tika* on your forehead, and I haven't put any garlands on you. Every year you say you'll come, but you never come. This year you must come. I have planted the *sayapatri* and *makhamali*. They're about to blossom. Please, Dai, come this time." Devaki was almost crying over the phone, making me sad.

I had Bhai Tika from her last time was before I left Nepal, in anticipation of going to France, but only to be dumped in Mumbai and later in Madagascar. Now, when she reminded me of Tihar, Bhai Tika, approaching soon, I dreamt of myself in Narrow Flatland, in the northern hemisphere. It must be autumn there, just the opposite of the season in South Africa, yet with the same balmy weather.

I closed my eyes and travelled to the homeland. I saw the terraced rice paddies with golden plants whispering in the smooth autumnal breeze and giving off sweet fragrances. I saw a long flock of *karyangkurungs* flying high up in the sky towards the south, and the squawking green parrots with curved beaks, so peculiar to my hamlet, flying from the south and roaring just over the yard and settling on the green millet fields. And I saw a large group of women, with cane baskets on their backs, walking through the path overgrown with dew-wet grass before sunrise and coming back at sunset with *geru, kamero,* and *kalimati* in those baskets. Numerous wet gossamers gleamed with the first rays of the sun in the millet fields, on the sides of little paths and trails and in the meadows. Red and purple *malati* flowers bloomed in the untamed hedgerows. I saw children around the hamlet, taking great pains in searching for chestnuts in the striped afternoon light in the wood and filling their little pockets. I imagined myself sitting cross-legged facing north-east in front of Aama and getting her blessing along with *tika* and *jamara* in Dashain. On the day of Bhai Tika, my sister prepared a rainbow-coloured *tika*. After anointing my head with oil, she put the *tika* on my forehead and around my neck the fresh smelling garlands of *sayapatri* and *makhamali* flowers: I saw it in my imagination. Once again. Autumn happened to be so beautiful there in the homeland.

"Sir, I'm done. I'm going." Amanda was in front of me, expecting her wage. I took out a two-hundred rand note from the pocket and gave to her.

"Thank you. See you next week," she added. "Sir, I think you miss your children a lot. I can read that from your face. Why don't you go to Nepal for a while and see them?"

"I'm going next month, Amanda," I said with a firm determination.

That evening I was surfing the Internet for the air ticket.

Seven

The spring had reached almost the halfway. With the first rains of the season, the bluish purple jacaranda flowers had blossomed, canopying the streets. When jacarandas blossomed in Pretoria, the purple dwarfed all other colours, at least for some three weeks, albeit the beauty was associated with the mess created by the fallen petals, especially after the rain.

It was Sunday. I could hear the peals from the church two blocks away from my house. I informed Ahmed that I would not come to the restaurant. Sunday, it was not busy, and Ahmed could handle it. He could handle even during the busy days. He had won my trust, both for handling the restaurant and taking care of cash.

Taking out a photo album, my only album, I sat on a flat stone under the leopard tree. The album possessed a few pictures, mostly family photographs, the rare ones. Rare in the sense that I did not have many photographs. By the time I left for Lhasa, photography was rare in the villages, still a matter of an expensive hobby. The peasants could not afford cameras. Even my uncle, the richest in the hamlet, did not have one. Therefore, whenever we wanted to be photographed, we would go to the photo centre in the bazaar and take our picture, our lips a little tight and curved with smiles as instructed by the photographer, with an artificial background. The background often consisted of a lake or a river with lily pads and a fleet of swans, some floating on the water with their strutting heads in an upright position, some others preening their wings, and a few of them flying in the blue sky with patches of clouds. As I turned through the worn pages of the old album, among a few others, I came upon a picture of my wife and myself, sitting side by side on a bench, in the background a similar view: a small lake with lily pads, the floating swans, and the azure sky with patchy clouds. The picture had been taken many years back, perhaps soon after our marriage. Faded though it was, it showed the youth, the radiance, and dreams on our faces. She had slightly slanted towards me in a smiling pose.

Now, after so many years, as I sat under the leopard tree and looked deep into the picture, it carried me back to our life. Years back while we had been together.

Even in the scarcity and inability to fulfil the trivial necessities, life seemed to have been so happy, so peaceful. The daylong work in the fields, in the woods, in the pastures, and in the evening, the gathering of all the family around the hearth, a little chat, a little grudge, a little smile and simple food; at night a warm sleep: life was far more enjoyable in a true sense. However, I left the hamlet, the home and hearth, in search of material pleasure, material adequacy which I could not earn for years, and once I earned it, it had already been too late to give happiness to my family. And I felt awfully guilty.

In fact, a deep sense of guilt – about not listening to my wife and not giving much attention to her, about ignoring her advice and pleading not to leave the hamlet, about leaving her behind alone with the small children – had begun to appear in me much earlier, as soon as I left her for the first time to find greener pastures, a long way away, out of the homeland. Down through the years it grew, steadily and strongly. Whenever I remembered her, the feeling or even the realisation that I should not have been away from her, that I should have found some ways of living in Nepal, that I should have cared more about her health, her necessities, her happiness and her life consumed much of my thoughts. I always lived with the burden of guilt. Her watery eyes and choking voice expressing her untold sorrow and emotion, her hands stroking Rabindra's head, and my daughters' gloomy, unwashed yet delicate faces: those images of my wife and children during each of our partings never faded. I always lived with those pictures and unbearable pains. Each time after calling her, after hearing her painful voice, I found my eyes dewy. And the pleasure I got each time after meeting them, after going back to the hamlet, which was very rare and brief, was incomparable, difficult to measure in hedonistic terms.

She was a common woman, a part of the rural peasantry, devoted solely to her family, with her personal wants always suppressed for others. She worked hard every day from dawn until dusk. Every day, rain or shine, she woke up before the east became bright. In the dim light of the paraffin lamp, she swept the kitchen, veranda, doorsteps, and yard. She gave a fresh coat of red clay, dung, and water to the hearth and threshold before she lit the fire, blowing hard on the remnants of fire left in the log, burrowed under ashes, during which process the ash scattered on her hair and brows. She cleaned the cowshed, gave fodder to the cattle, milked them, and prepared food for the family. Each her day was occupied with the work in the fields or with the collecting of the firewood or with the gathering of the fodder for the cattle or with grazing them. Her evenings were again for looking after the cattle, preparing food, and many other chores. And the rest? It never came into her life unless she was taken seriously sick.

She was a rural woman, beautiful yet simple. I never saw her apply any additions, except *tika* and *sindur*, to add to her beauty. Later, the years of hard labour and perpetual exposure to the sun and the rain and wind aged her before time. Lines developed on her forehead. Crinkles gathered in the corners of her eyes prematurely. The corners of the fingertips of her hands and feet cracked and skin went roughened. The whiteness of her teeth slowly yellowed. Rough knots developed in the palms of her hand. Yet she hardly cared about those things.

She loved her children immensely. She sewed the hanging hems of her daughter's frocks. She sewed back on the undone buttons on Rabindra's shirt. Every Saturday, during winter or spring, she would take them to the stream bank. Then putting three stones triangularly, she would make a small fireplace in the middle of a vacant field and would warm a full cauldron of water with the help of dried maize stems and twigs gathered from the firebush plants and bamboo grove just above the stream. She would bathe them thoroughly. Then sitting on a wide black flat stone on the stream bed, she would set for rinsing the covers of quilts and pillows, while the children played in the fields. Whenever she went to the bazaar, she never forgot to bring peppermint, doughnuts, and sugarcane, which the children would chew, sitting on the berm of Big Plot. Whenever she went into the woods and the fields, she barely missed to bring for them wild berries, particularly wild raspberries and barberries, chestnuts, guava, or whatever she found according to the seasons. When they got sick, she sat beside them, putting her palm on their forehead to measure the temperature.

Her world was narrowed to the scenes and sights seen from the yard. She had never travelled beyond the bazaar or the bank of the Kali River, where she would go for religious purposes, or her birthplace, the natal home. It would be the most enjoyable part of her life when she stepped into the yard of her father's house in the evening after a tiring journey, most of the time with her children, carrying at least one of them on her back. It was once or twice she travelled to the cities. She was afraid of the city life. She preferred to be narrowed down among those surrounding mountains and hills, to be nestled in her hamlet in the lap of the south-facing mountain, warm and bright. Sometimes she would wonder how the earth beyond the Oxbow Hill would look like. She had heard it was a flat land in the far south of the country. On occasions, at dusk, when the sun was about to dip down into the mountains and the patch of the western sky became pinkish, reddish, and yellowish, she would gaze in wonder, being curious what the country would look like beyond those mountains, yet she was never tempted to go beyond that point.

I always felt lucky to have such a life partner. Time and again, I questioned myself was I suitable for her? Did I take care of her as I was supposed to do? Did I fulfil the responsibility given to me by Vedas, during our marriage, during the *saptapadi* around the sacred fire amidst the chanting of mantras, and during the pledge which I made while putting *sindur* on her *siundo*? Did I listen to her inner voice? Did I ever ask her or myself whether she had her own dreams rather than mine and the children's? Honestly, I did not. As a part of our male-dominant society, during the initial days of our marriage, perhaps, or for sure, I tried to behave dominantly, perhaps dominated her or perhaps tried to impose my will on her. I took her niceness, her simplicity, and her virtues for granted. On her side, she just surrendered. From her childhood, she was taught, was trained by her parents, by her elders, by each and every segment of society, to submit to the will of her husband. The notion given to her from her babyhood, from the tabula rasa status of her brain, later became her habit. She never complained about her life and about her scarcity-struck days; she never thought of herself. The rare few moments she thought of herself was the moment her head pained intolerably and went on for hours. She would put a shawl tightly around her head to absorb the pain. She hardly uttered anything about it.

I always behaved irresponsibly with her and her health. In between years, I ought to have gone to see her, ought to have taken her, at least, to Kathmandu for better medical attention. I could have done that. Once the business thrived, I could and ought to have done that. But I did not do it despite knowing that her headache problem was increasing with the passing of the days. Once the pains went unbearable, she would tell me, but I did not listen to her even when my business succeeded to the level of affording to have a proper check-up for her.

Three years ago, when I came to know – that she, while milking the buffalo in the hamlet, collapsed and had to be taken to Pokhara and then, after the doctors failed to diagnose and cure, to Kathmandu – I broke up.

"Dai, Bhauju is seriously sick and is in a hospital in Kathmandu. Please come." Those were the words from Devaki, enough to give a sense of seriousness of the situation.

Now, after three years of the terrible incident in which I lost my wife, as I sat under the leopard tree looking at those old faded pictures, once again the memories came back sharply.

A pair of hadedas landed on the lawn to graze. They, like all other hadedas, were black and brown in colour and had bluish or greenish glossy feathers in their wings. They did not seem to be afraid of me. They were certainly used to seeing me sitting like that, in that position under the tree, quite often when I was at home. Or was it the character of all hadedas? I was not sure if they were the same birds which came every day on the lawn. The hadedas I saw on my lawn or that I saw in other parts of the city had similar features – sticky legs, black or brown body, glossy on the back from where the wings came, a stringy neck, a long beak, and the same harsh sound *ha . . . ha . . . ha . . . .* They all looked alike. In my garden, they mostly grazed near the elephant's-ear plants, on the damp patch.

The pair grazed there not long. One of them preened its feathers with its long beak and in that process one of its feathers, probably, already slacked before it landed on the lawn, came out of its wing. The feather was glossy and solid. Such must be the feathers to have been used for writing in ancient time, including those sutras in golden letters in Drepung Monastery in Lhasa. A section of the feather, the inner vane, was bluish or greenish dark – so difficult to differentiate – and the other section was brownish dark. On the root part, the spiny side, it had thin white downy hairs, swaying gently. The feather was still warm. And with the feather in my hand, I again plunged into my past, three years back.

Devaki did not say much and did not give the details about the illness. She just told me that my wife was seriously ill and was in a hospital. Yet I could understand the urgency in her voice. When I reached Kathmandu, after a hurried and almost unconscious journey from Johannesburg, I came to know that she had collapsed because of brain haemorrhage, and there was only a slight chance of survival.

I saw her with tubes in her nostrils, needles in her veins, and her eyes closed. I stroked her face, ran my hand through her awry hair, and arranged them to her back, touched her eyes and lips. With faint hopes that her consciousness would come back again, that she would see me in front of her, and I could tell her that I would never leave her again. But she did not come about. She lay on the bed in the same position.

Responding my question if she would survive, the doctor said, "Mr Pandey, the report shows her brain is seriously damaged. All systems in her body have slowed down. It would be very difficult to predict at this moment."

The next day she died. The world became dark to me; everything in life just perished. My whole purpose of living sank all of a sudden. I could not think what I was going to do.

Devaki was there in the hospital. Rabindra, Gopal, and a few other relatives too were there. Gopal had come to the hamlet on his holidays. Her dead body was taken to the hamlet in a van. I just followed them. I was so saddened by her death that doing anything was beyond my capacity. I just told them that I wanted to see her in the yard of our house at least once. She wanted to be always in the hamlet, not in the cities, even after her death.

"I won't come there. You come here. I'm too afraid to be away from this hamlet," she had said a year back over the phone in response to my desire to invite her and the children to Pretoria.

So despite some of my relatives' advice to cremate her in Aryaghat, Pashupati, I asked Gopal to take her body to our house. Both the daughters were in the yard. They had already got the news of their mother's death. As the van entered our hamlet through a recently carved narrow trail and I got out, both of them came towards me crying deeply: the tears brimming over and falling on their young cheeks. It had been a long time since I last saw them. But now, when I saw them, I saw them under those circumstances. Grief-struck, I took them into my two arms, held them tightly, sobbing.

People gathered to mourn. My wife's body was wrapped in a yellow shroud and tightly tied to a green bamboo bier. They decorated the bier and body with flowers and sandalwood. Sympathetically, I looked at Rabindra being shaved by a mourner. He looked small and pitiful with his bald head. The whole day I remained quiet. Those participating in the funeral process were consoling me and were telling me about my wife: she was a good woman, a good wife, a good mother, and a good neighbour.

On the bank of the Kali, I perched on the big boulder – the same one on which I would often perch whenever I came there during the funeral processions or during religious occasions along with my mother and, later, before going abroad, with my wife – looking at the ripples. The river had widened and the greyish waters, as always during summers, were hiding everything beneath the surface. On the other side, the wide white sand shone in the sun. Away the white sand, there lay a cropped land and past that land stood the Oxbow Hill, looking at my wife's dead body.

The mourners piled the sun-dried firewood in an oblong shape and put the dead body atop the pyre, while I sat, looking at her for the last time. The fire burnt quickly. A pall of thick smoke billowed and spread into the heavens. Her body vanished, turned into ashes. Rabindra collected a little remnant of the body and a speckle of ashes in a bronze urn as I had done many years back when my mother had died.

Once the fire gave out, we washed the place. The remaining ashes flowed into the Kali. The place looked like before, a little blackened, which, I knew, would turn into its original colour within days, the sand colour. But my life changed forever. Later, after we came to the hamlet, I went to Big Plot and scattered the ashes, which I had managed to pick up from the pyre (avoiding the mourners' eyes because I did not know whether it was ritually permitted). She had once told me if the religion would permit, she wanted to be buried underneath the soil of Big Plot.

The after-funeral ceremony commenced. Narayan, the pundit, performed his part. He came with the bundle of books wrapped in a piece of the old white cloth, more yellowed and blackened. He instructed my son and us what to do. Unfolding the bundle, he took out the same leather-bound old books, the edges of which had been eaten by worms. The books this time looked older than I had seen them earlier, during the funeral ceremony of my mother or grandmother. He chanted the mantras. He told us the same stories about the surety of death, about *moksha*, reincarnation, heaven and hell and, of course, about the importance of charity. He said authoritatively what Rabindra was supposed to do for his mother's *moksha*. And while telling the stories, he spoke phenomenally, rather philosophically – using both deductive and inductive methods. He was a good orator. The art of speaking and twisting stories according to the level and interest of the listeners and giving them a philosophical and vague insight must have been passed down to him from his father. Down through the years, he had further developed his oratory skill, the skill of storytelling. He could speak with evangelical fervour, with uneven tones, high-pitched and low-pitched, as the story demanded.

Rabindra listened attentively; he followed all the instructions. I did not think he understood the religious exactitude of the vague mantras and contradictory stories told by the pundit; they were too deep to understand. Nor could I think he did that piously. Yet he obeyed faithfully what he was asked to do. He wanted the soul of his mother to be at peace.

He wore a dhoti and put a black blanket around himself. Every morning, he would be taken to the stream, the same place where he would go with his mother during his childhood and would be bathed by her. He was fed rice and ghee on the banana leaves, once a day. He slept on hay on the floor. At times, my eyes met his, but both of us were hesitant to talk. We had not got much time to mingle. So we did not know what to talk about in that deep grief.

One day, after the completion of daily ritual, I sat outside the threshold of his room and asked, "Rabindra, how did it happen all of a sudden?"

"Daddy, I also don't know much. She had been complaining of terrible headaches for a few days. I was in the orchard when I heard a loud bellow. I rushed to the shed. She was lying on the floor. The milk had spilled all over. I cried. Gopal Uncle came there. Later, others also came from the villages. We called Devaki Didi and took mummy to Pokhara. Doctors advised us to take her to Kathmandu," he said. His voice had broken to a male voice.

He was slim and tall. The people who saw us would say so; they would say he looked exactly like me. Perhaps Aama was right when, many years back, she would often say, exposing her toothless gum: *He looks like Ashok, natikuti, exactly.*

"Are you feeling cold?" I asked him to build up our intimacy.

"No, Daddy. I'm fine," he said, burrowing himself under the blanket.

I could sense he had difficulty in feeling comfortable with me. I had been away from him for so long. Rather, he could behave comfortably with Gopal who would frequently visit the hamlet, at least once a year.

For my daughters too, it took time to open up to me. The grief had struck them more than Rabindra and me. Most of the time, during the after-funeral ceremony, I saw them sitting on the veranda, sobbing and looking at Rabindra perform rites, quietly. Devaki would try to console them. I heard her often saying, "If you cry too much, your mother's soul can't go to heaven. Dai is here. Don't worry too much."

And me? Detached from the village and the family for years and now broken with the death of my wife, I did not know what I was supposed to do. All the time, she came to mind. I dreamt of her trying to persuade me not to leave the hamlet. I pictured her and me, together, working in the fields, hammering the clods, sowing maize seeds, planting rice, and gathering them.

"Na jayate mriyate wa kadachinnayam bhutwa bhawita wan a bhuyah.

Ajonityah shasheswato ayam purano na hanyate hanya mane sarire."

(The soul is not born and nor dies at any time. It does not come into being and will not cease to be. It is permanent, eternal, and is not destroyed even when the body perishes.)

Pundit Ji was trying to console us by excerpting quotes from Bhagawad Gita about the immortality of the human soul, whereas I kept remembering the physical being of my wife. I was wondering whether she would come again as Pundit Ji was claiming,

"Wasamsi jirnani yatha wihaya, nawani grihanati naroaparani.

Tatha sharirani wihaya jirnanyanyani samyati nawani dehi."

(As a human being wears new clothes discarding the old ones, the soul similarly enters a new body giving up the previous one.)

Mali, which had grown old and feeble, was lowing long and loud in the shed. She had been lowing in this way, in this sad way, ever since Sushmita died.

And Pundit Ji was telling with an effective degree of certainty about the immortality of the soul. He looked so certain that, at times, I myself – who, detached from religion and culture, had grown a very flexible and neutral faith towards religion and all those religious fictions, almost a kind of agnosticism – was wondering whether the soul of my wife would exist and would see us. A pious hope. I wished that she, like a phoenix, would reappear from the ashes that I had sprayed in Big Plot and would comfort us and would stroke Mali.

But it was not possible. The idea of reincarnation must have been just a faith, a technique, created to console the bereaved persons after the death of their family or relatives or friends, which later would have found its proper place in religious books and social beliefs. The belief in the existence of the soul after death must have been the most effective and easiest way to console the bereaved families.

Here, I did know Sushmita had gone forever. And all the time I felt that had I not left her alone and gone away in search of material pleasure, things would have been different. I had earned money. But for what? What was I going to do with the money? Would she come again? Could I bring her back to my children? I thought my whole struggle had been in vain.

The rituals came to an end. Rabindra put on the mourning attire: a white shirt, white pants and shoes, also white. On my request, and of course after receiving some extra alms, Pundit Ji reduced the time of his mourning to forty-five days. The regular arrival of Pundit Ji came to an end. Before leaving, he said he would come on the next *tithi*. As a part of the offerings, I gave him my wife's beloved Mali whose long and loud cries would make me and my daughters sad. Someone had told me that offering the cow, the holy animal, to the pundit would ease the way to heaven. So I offered her to Pundit Ji. But, as I unhitched her and gave the tether to him, I was almost crying. Confused and sad, she followed him.

But, not long after that, Madhu told me that she heard the old cow died. We were doing something in front of the shed. Staring with her sad eyes at the post to which Mali had been tethered for years – as long as Madhu could remember – she said the old cow had fallen down the slope of the mountain while grazing. The shed was still giving off her smell.

Anyway, the coming of the mourners came to an end. Our family was left alone. Elegiac though it felt, life had to continue. Days and weeks passed. Even a month. Each day after the sun set, I would go to Big Plot where I had sprayed her ashes and would spend hours in solitude. Sushmita would appear vividly in those moments. It would feel she was with me in that Big Plot. (Perhaps I was overwhelmed by the pundit's preaching.) Deep in my soul, I realised it was time for me to return to the hamlet. Shouldering the burden of the future of the children had come solely to me. The motherly love and care which they had basked in throughout their childhood no longer existed. I was supposed to be with them, if possible, forever, otherwise at least to pick up the pieces. They had all gone to pieces.

Yet a hasty decision was not possible. Before returning, I had to think about the business, which was running so well. I had to find someone to buy it or at least to buy the management at a reasonable price. I had spent a lot of labour and time for the restaurant. It was the sole property I had made. Although my greed for amassing the property had come to a virtual end after my wife died, the future of the children heavily rested on it. So after discussing with the children, I decided to bring them to South Africa, with the determination that we all would return home once the daughters had finished matric. I asked Gopal and his wife to take care of my house and Big Plot until I would return.

Such was my plan, and I was supposed to return the year before. The children returned. They did not wish to stay long away from their country. After my daughters did their matric all of them returned and stayed with Devaki. But I did not go back. I could not find a buyer who would give me the price I wanted for the restaurant or it deserved. Yet I was sure I would not be staying in South Africa for long. It was just a matter of time.

Now, when I sat under the leopard tree and went through the pages of the old album, the urgency of going back became even stronger.

Eight

"*Jayanti Mangalaakali Bhadrakali Kapaalini,*
Durga Ksyama Shiva Dhhatri Swaha Swadha Namastute.
Jaya Twam Devi Chamunde Jaya Bhutapharini,
Jaya Sarbagate Devi Kalratri Namastute."

Standing in front of the picture of Goddess Kali pasted inside a cupboard in the kitchen, I uttered Dashain mantras. My daughters had printed the picture from the Google and pasted it there. As long as they stayed in Pretoria, in every festival, they would search for the nicest picture of the deity for that particular festival and would paste it there. Sushmita had filled them with deep religious and cultural orientation.

That day, it was Dashain. Yet another Dashain away from home. My daughters, during the previous years' Dashain, when they were here, had asked me to utter the mantras. So after performing a few rituals, I uttered those mantras over the phone. In doing so, I could sense brightness on their faces.

Again, I uttered the mantras to Rabindra,

"*Aayu Dronasute Shriam Dasharathe Shatrukshayam Raghawe*
Aishwarya Nahushe Gatishcha Pawane Maanancha Duryodhane.
Shaurya Shaantanawe Balam Haladhare Satyancha Kuntisute
Bigyane Bidure Bhawati Bhawatam Kirtishcha Narayane."

Then I talked to Madhu.

"Madhu, sorry I couldn't be with you today, but I'll be there within two weeks. I have already bought the ticket," I said loudly. The phone connection between these two faraway countries was poor and had not improved at all despite all technological advancements in communication. The connection was hard to get. Even if got, it was to be disconnected soon. Besides that, I had to speak loudly to reach the other side, which later had become a habit. Once Hemanta had cautioned me that my loud voice on the phone would almost irritate him.

"We're waiting for you, Daddy," Madhu's voice came. "When are you coming?"

"After two weeks."

"Daddy, I haven't been to the hamlet for quite a while. Once you come here, we'll go there together."

"That would be a fun, Chhori."

We were disconnected before I completed the sentence. I could hear them, but they did not hear me.

"Daddy, I can't hear you. The line seems disconnected," Madhu said.

"Once you finish your talking, it's always disconnected," Sarita expressed her dissatisfaction. I could still hear them.

"It's not my fault," Madhu protested.

The girls would not usually fight. Yet they had petty differences and would argue frequently, especially if the matter was associated with getting the fatherly affection.

"Madhu, Sarita," I tried a couple of times to be heard. The line got disconnected on my side too.

Anyway, after blessing them over the phone and after talking to Madhu, for a short while though, I felt light-hearted. It felt I celebrated Dashain with them.

Later that evening, I was at Vinod's place along with nearly a hundred Nepalese to celebrate the festival. The number of the Nepalese had grown in South Africa and the nearby countries over the years. The agents had found yet another destination for the poor: different African countries. It was not difficult to lure the unemployed, desperate for the job, no matter wherever in the world. The agents used different techniques to convince the people. They would show the pictures of big cities. They would show well-established infrastructures around the cities. They would give them fake data about the economy, the situation of the employment, and salary. The techniques they adopted proved sufficient enough to lure the people not only with a limited level of knowledge but also those with a certain level of education. Paying a large amount of money to the agents, the nation's youth travelled abroad as far as to South Africa in search of employment.

"Not only here, I have heard there're many in other African countries. Even more than here. I don't know how these agents convince the people so easily," Vinod said, putting firelighters in the braai stand. The fire blazed. His bald head shone.

"They convince in the same way as they convinced us. You forgot how we were cheated?" Hemanta said and sat beside me.

"That time we didn't have much information. Now people can retrieve any information they want from the Internet," Vinod said.

"It's easy to say, sir. But once you're trapped by the agents, there're hardly ways to come out. Once you start the process with them, they give millions of promises. You're no longer in a situation to think rationally. You just follow them. And you always lose. If you're a little lucky you end up in a difficult situation in a foreign land beyond your expectation. But if your luck doesn't favour you, you find yourself aimlessly walking the streets in Kathmandu with worn-out shoes and a sad face, for you have spent all your money. This is the reality," Malla Ji said. "You see all these. They have been cheated in one way or the other." He lifted his right hand to show all those gathered there, while resting his left hand on a chair beside me.

His first name was Resham, but to us, he was popular with his surname *Malla* added with *Ji*. He had not been here for long, but due to his personality – an attractively built body and impressive complexion and his capacity to express – he had become famous within a short span of time. To those with whom he spoke, he would address as *sir*. If it was a woman, he would use *Didi* or *Bahini*, depending on her age.

"Anyway, I'm happy to see so many friends from my country," Hemanta said.

"But if you think the other way round, sir, it's not a situation at which we can be proud. The villages in the country are being vacated, farms are idle, and festivals aren't celebrated as they should have been. These days, you can't find people even for a marriage ceremony or a funeral procession," Malla Ji said. He was a good speaker. What he spoke, spoke clearly. The way he adopted to express himself, a kind of authentic and confident yet polite way, the enunciation in his speech impressed the listeners and made them listen attentively to him. They had rare reasons to chime in. Apart from being a good speaker, he was a good listener too. He listened what he listened carefully and patiently. His background was teaching. He had fathered three sons, but the two of them were killed.

That day, he was in a mood to share with us more information about himself. He said, "My village is on a steep mountain, almost a four-hour walk from the district headquarters. It's located amidst the fields and woods. On clear days, you can have the amazing view of the snow-capped mountain peaks in the north. You can hear the twittering of birds, the gurgling of mountain streams streaming down near my village before merging into the river, which arises in the Himalaya and winds through the mountains and hills towards the south. After school, I used to engage myself in the fields. On days off, I used to go to the curved and sloped pasturage just beyond the stream with the cattle. Putting out the cattle to the pasture, I would enjoy the books and the views. Occasionally, I would go to the bank of the river. In the valley down by the village, it has slowed down and widened its course. There I would sit with my sons under an old banyan for hours, looking at the river and watching the fishermen throw their nets and haul them back. I wasn't rich, but I was living a satisfied life."

"But everything changed after the Maoist movement began in the country. It badly affected my life. At first, the effect came sporadically. It was confined to regular checking, interrogations, and sometimes brief arrests by the state authorities for being a Maoist and giving them shelter. Then again, being kidnapped by the Maoists for not being a Maoist and spying against them. I myself didn't know whether I was a Maoist or anti-Maoist. To me, political theories never became more important than human life. I believed and still believe all theories are for human goodness and aimed at human happiness. Only the difference is how to get that, the difference is the choice of an appropriate way. The theories themselves are not supposed to be the reason for fighting. It's possible to change society through peaceful means, without violations and without the killing of the people. It should be changed through education, through awareness or other peaceful means."

"As you know, the movement went on, took its height, and gripped the villages. Due to the confrontations between the two sides, life became terrible. I lost two sons. Both of them were killed, one by the security forces and the other by the Maoists for reasons I never knew. I was told one had joined the Maoists and the other was spying for the security forces, which I didn't believe. How could I believe that at such a young age, at the initial teens, they did any harm to the state and the Maoists to be killed in such a torturous way? So inhumanly. The killing shocked me and my wife. My faith in humanity began to dwindle. The parade of events wasn't over yet. The attacks and counterattacks were going on. It came to me that the remaining son was also a target. I was a suspicious character to both sides. In one of the series of arrests, an army colonel, with his stern voice, asked me to cooperate with him. He didn't believe I wasn't with the Maoists. The next day, a few Maoists came to my house.

They threatened me saying that if I wanted to see my son alive, I must join them. After a few days, it was still dark when we slipped out of the house," he said and paused for a while to take a sip.

He continued, "You know, how you feel when you're compelled to leave your home, where you have seen so many dreams together with your family. Especially when you don't know where you're going and for how long, it's scary. I still remember, when we left our yard, how my wife was frequently looking back until the house was obscured by the bent pasturage beyond the stream. I myself was blinded by tears. I was trying hard to control emotions, not to let my wife and son panic. I went to a city in the south. Life there wasn't easy either. I didn't have savings. I had lost the job. My request for transfer had been rejected by the authorities on the assumption that it would set precedence. Therefore, before leaving, I had resigned from the nineteen-year service in expectation of one-time gratuity. The money I was given soon gave out. I sold my wife's jewellery. Without a regular source of income, it became impossible for me to provide a simple living for my wife and son, let alone his education."

"After a few months, I was aboard Air Malaysia, along with many others, travelling to Kuala Lumpur in search of employment. I worked in a construction company there for three years. You know how labourers live their lives abroad. That's not life. You work more than twelve hours, six or seven days a week. You become so tired and feel so lonely that, without being drugged with alcohol, you can't sleep. Life becomes just a repetition: waking up before the sunrise, working for the whole day, cooking and doing the dishes, and, after all those things, drinking the cheapest alcohol, not easily available in a Muslim society, and then sleeping. There're no other means of amusement. On the payday, what you receive is just a pittance. What do you do with such little money? The dream you had seen before leaving your country dies away within a few days of facing the reality. You're lucky if you can save anything to work off your loan. I was lucky. In three years, I saved almost two lakh rupees, a little more than I owed."

"Then . . .," he paused for a while to chew a braai piece, which Anuradha, a Nepalese woman, had put on our plates. Excluding him, we were five at our table – Anuradha, three others, and I myself – listening to him. All tables became full; the gathering became livelier and livelier.

"Then I returned to Nepal," he went on, taking one more glass of whisky. "By then, the peace accord had been signed among the political parties. We hoped the new political changes would bring peace and prosperity. I was desperate to go back and settle down in my own village. But you see, when I went there, I was informed that it didn't belong to me any longer. No other justification was given. I just came to know that it was taken by the party. I looked at the house. Old and ramshackle, the roof sagged, the coat of the walls fallen off, and the yard and ridge covered with tall weeds. Yet I wanted to move back into this house. It was my house, the property handed over to me by my father. But the local leaders said the house, along with my land property, belonged to their *great party.* Pending the decision at higher levels, I couldn't be allowed to move in. My son, in his early teens, had dropped of school and joined the Maoist combatants in one of the camps readied for them, solely for a job. He was told he would be integrated into the security force. He didn't know when and how."

Malla Ji had got the art of speaking during his career as a teacher; he spoke fluently, without much pause.

"I tried to do a small business, but I couldn't be successful and again had to hunt for the agents. I met one who promised to send me to Poland. I was supposed to pay four lakh. Half of that in advance. When I expressed apprehensions about paying in advance, he said sorry. I compared my life in the country and in a foreign land, a European country, a high salary, a high standards of living, and with all possibilities of slipping into other

European countries. He showed me with a colourful dream. I saw my life far better in Poland. I agreed. I borrowed money from my relatives. Fifty thousand from a person, fifty thousand from another person, and another lakh from the other one. Thus, I gathered the required amount and left my wife and country for the second time. My son was still in the camp. I asked him to support his mother until my return," he said.

"The clever agent had already said that the Polish visa would be issued in Kenya. I think, here I made a mistake. I knew there was no Polish Embassy in Kathmandu, but I should have enquired why the visa couldn't be issued from Delhi. I didn't ask him. I was overwhelmed by the thoughts of Poland."

"We flew to Nairobi by way of Mumbai. The Kenyan visa was supposed to be issued on arrival. I was the first in line and got a visa for thirty days. But my friends behind me were denied the entry for the reasons I didn't know. I dared not talk to the visa officer about that. I was afraid they would cancel my visa and lock me up. With the enormous feeling of guilt, I slipped from there and somehow called the Kenya-based agent whose number was given to me by the agent in Kathmandu. He came there: a tall and lean guy, walking as if one of his legs was wounded or disabled. I asked him about my friends. He told me not to worry about them and just to follow him. He took me to a place, a small house at the corner of a dimly lit street, where I met four of these Nepalese," saying, he pointed his hand towards a group of people sitting at a corner table and continued again.

"They had been brought by the same nexus of the agents and had been put there for more than a month with an assurance of a Polish visa. Now I had been added to. The hope was dying away. Every day we would call the agent in Kathmandu to get a vague answer. This agent in Kenya always came back with false guarantees, each time giving a date for the visa and on that particular date coming empty-handed and again giving another date. The money we had was soon spent. We had difficulties even in getting food. The tall and lean agent would always assure us that the visa would be issued. But when? We got frustrated. One day, our colleague, that one," he said, showing a fellow at the corner table, "the one with the red cap, who earlier served in the army, slapped the agent hard on the face and threatened that he would kill him if he didn't arrange the visa within two days. The lean guy practically cried and said it was beyond his capacity to arrange the Polish visa. My friend called the agent in Kathmandu. Luckily, he was connected. He said with the same angry voice, 'You see, bastard, it's too much. I don't care about my life and my family's life. If you don't arrange the visa for us, we'll come to Nepal and rape your wife and leave you lame. And until we get the visa, your pawn will be here with us.' He put the mobile in his pocket and gave another hard slap to the agent. I tried to calm him down, but this fellow, saying, 'Malla Ji, these bastards are playing too much' slammed the door."

"His anger worked. Though it worked out differently, it worked out and relieved us from that situation. The following day, a woman came to us with our passports and the three-month visa for South Africa. We didn't know whether the visa was fake or genuine. But we were allowed to enter South Africa from Zimbabwe. Now, you know, we're working without a working visa. Life is always at risk. There's a huge amount of loan to be paid off with high interest at home. Even if I save the whole amount of the salary, I need at least five years just to pay the loan. When to save for the future? I don't know," he said.

Finishing his glass, he poured another one and popped some ice into the glass, concluding, "The country has gone through drastic political changes, but the much-awaited economic improvement still looks illusive. In effect, millions of us, the ordinary ones, are compelled to leave the country and eke out a pitiable existence in foreign soil."

Malla Ji finished telling his story, a story, which agreed with the stories of most of the Nepalese in South Africa and certainly with those of millions of Nepalese around the globe, working as low-paid workers: most of them having been compelled to leave the country solely for earning livelihoods for them and their family. While leaving the country, after paying a large amount of money to the agents, they would have certainly carried with them sweet dreams and hopes, but their travels ended up in unwanted and unperceived realities. Very few of them achieved success but most of them suffered a lot and lived a difficult life in foreign soil, humiliated, their very human dignity always denied. Each day, they dreamt of their country. Each day, they wished to go back. But it was not easy. They had left behind them a pile of debts.

Admittedly, Malla Ji was right. The country, after I left the hamlet for the second time, had gone through huge political changes. The whole royal family had been massacred, for what reasons and by whom mysterious and unknown to the common people. Ideologically contrastingly different political forces had surprisingly come together. The political movement – with the great and enthusiastic participation of the common people – overthrew the monarchy forever. The election of the constituent assembly took place for the first time in the country, ensuring the colourful representation of different and varied segments of society. People were expecting much from the epoch-making changes.

And socially? Our society went through enormous changes, both good and bad: good in the sense that the political movements did away with many of the obsolete and superstitious beliefs, harmful to society. The backward segments became aware of their rights to dignity and rightful share in society. Negative in the sense that along with those, many good traditions and cultural faiths, the tradition of mutual cooperation among the people, particularly existing in the villages, became weaker and weaker and practically came to an end, I had heard.

However, apart from those political and few mixed social changes, no other changes, including much-desired economic change, took place. The economy remained the same, stagnant: no industries developed and no employment was generated. People continued to leave the country daily, in great numbers, and continued to work abroad. They continued to be exploited everywhere: inside the country and outside the country.

Now, as a few of us met in a distant place, on the occasion of Dashain, a cultural festival (to us, an opportunity of gathering and talking to each other), we each had plenty to share about our own story and grief. Like Potapov's grief in Chekhov's story *To Whom Shall I Tell My Grief.*

There was Shyam Bahadur, who had come almost six years back, paying half a million rupees. Unable to find a job, he had started a small business, a business of selling second-hand things in Alexandra, a poor township in Johannesburg. He felt so insecure that initially every day he had to resort to alcohol to release himself from the anxiety and fear. But he was a man of determination and patience. He struggled. Now he owned three stores, selling almost all things. More importantly, he engaged another seven or eight fellow countrymen in his stores, some having shares in the business and some others working on monthly salary. Once I had been in his place. It was absolutely chaotic with sordid surroundings. I was taken aback how they had been doing business in such a place.

"What to do? This is our life," he had said to me, pushing hard, at the same time, his customer to buy a mobile set. "Bro, I'm giving you this at half price. You can't find this thing anywhere in Joburg at such a cheap price. I bet."

Outside, in the street, people were busy: some selling things in the street, some dancing, some whistling and singing, and some drinking. Their place to stay was messy. They, eight of them, had rented a three-bedroomed dark apartment on the ground floor of a two-storey house among the squalid houses.

"We're doing business without papers. Our business isn't registered. We're not paying any taxes. We don't know when the police arrest us and confiscate our stores," he had said to me before playing the *madal* at their place to stay, where they had offered me rice and *gundruk* cooked in black-stained old *dekchis*.

There was Bikash Bishwakarma, a handsome and energetic guy, almost like Adonis, who, after falling in love with a Brahmin girl – a girl from a family considered to be high-caste in stratified Hindu society – had been compelled to leave his village as an outcast. He had somehow managed to enter this country. He would cry every time he drank with us. He had been moving from this to that restaurant, but he was never paid on time and in full, for he did not have papers.

Laxman Lamichhane – who had worked in Dubai for five years and later was lured to go to Cypress on a fake visa and who was sent back to Nepal by the immigration authorities in Cypress and was put in an immigration jail in his own country to be released only after paying a hefty amount of money, as fees or as bribes he did not know – had paid six lakh rupees to come to South Africa. He gave his passport and twelve thousand rand to an agent for the extension of his visa, but the agent disappeared. He did not have documents. "I'm waiting for the documents, but it's almost two months since I applied. I don't know when I'll get them," he had said.

There was Angchhiri Sherpa who had bet all the money he had saved in Saudi, where he had worked more than five years, to come to South Africa. He was assured by the agents that he would be paid almost one thousand dollars a month. After he came here, he lived more than half a year without work. He found a job in a restaurant with the salary of a mere 200 dollars a month.

There was someone who had spent years abroad, and recently, his wife had eloped with another man with all properties he had earned so far. The small children were at home.

There was the other one, who, despite having a beautiful wife and two children in Nepal, had married a Zulu girl.

And this Anuradha? What a sufferer and yet what a courageous lady! Was she widowed? Or divorced? She did not tell us; she simply said she had two daughters and *no husband*. She said she owned a small beauty parlour in Kathmandu. She was brought to Kenya, along with three or four other ladies, with a firm assurance that they would be working in a beauty parlour in Nairobi. But after coming to Nairobi, they were asked to dance in a dance bar, also known – in fact, popularly known among the South Asian community in the city – as a *mujra* bar. Their passports were taken by the manager. Life was brought to a virtual confinement within the bar. They were not allowed to go out. Their calls were monitored. The most terrible thing, which she did not say to me, was that they were abused. Sexually. Life had become hell. I had heard from someone else that if they declined to sleep with men, with their customers, they would be hurt. One day, she and a Thai dancer took the risk and ran away from the bar, leaving her friends behind. It had taken almost three months for her to come here. She had travelled vast swaths of the African savannahs and forests with foreigners and agents, complete strangers to her. The path itself so dangerous for a woman. In many places, she fell down and got injured. Her clothes were torn by the thorns. She got wounds from the barbed wire fence while crossing the borders.

Her suffering in South Africa was not less painful. After many struggles, eventually she got a job as a beautician in a Thai massage centre in Fordsburg. Still, she lived in an insecure place. It looked scary.

Once she had invited me to her room to have the Nepalese food, and as I drove through a deserted street – the street itself petering out into a narrow and rutted road without street lights – and entered the old house, the outside of which was pitch black by two or three leafy trees the variety of which I could not recognise, I wondered how she was staying in that scary place. Even scarier was the presence of the two men there, in the yard, before entering her part of the building where she was staying with the Thai woman. They reminded of scary characters in horror movies: one, the older one with almost bald head and with a bottle in his hand, sitting on a wooden chair as if he had been drinking in that position for his whole life and the other, with thick and droopy moustache, smoking and looking drugged. The presence of those two suspicious characters in the yard looked scary to me. And more disturbing was his, the one with the bottle in his hand, uttering of almost incomprehensible words as I got out of the car.

"Why did you enter my private property without a prior consent?" he had asked in his stammering voice. I felt rather offended and angry, not with him, but with Anuradha. Why did she not talk to her landlord about our arrival if it was required? Anuradha came out and apologetically said, "Sir, don't care about him. He's always like that."

"Is that man your landlord?" I had asked her.

"No, he's not. He always says so. He's an insane person."

We did not talk much about him. The information given about the old man surprised me even more. If he was not the landlord, why was he claiming so? And with those two scary characters in such isolated area, how was she managing to live?

Later, just before I came out of her room, I had suggested to her, "Anuradha Ji, I don't think this place is safe for you. Why don't you move to other places where there're other Nepalese?"

She had responded, "Sir, where's safety for us, the women? You know, sir? My friend in the Gulf has written to me that she's raped almost every day by three generations of the same family: the grandfather, son, and grandson. If she rejects, she's beaten and threatened. For us, life isn't safe anywhere in the world. This is rented by our boss. If we move to other places, we'll need to pay ourselves."

So it was because of money that she was staying in that isolated part of Johannesburg with those suspicious characters.

Anyway, her security was at stake. The security of a Nepalese woman was at stake in a faraway country. Who was responsible for that? Was it her husband who divorced her or abandoned her? Or was it our society, which always ignored the dignity and rights of women? Or was it the state, which could not provide any means of living to such women in the country because of which they had to work abroad with such difficulties?

The party was going on. Vinod, relieved from the braai job, was now playing the *madal* and singing *sale jo*. Hemanta, I could see, was busy visiting every single table and talking to them, humorously, and pulling deep on his cigarette. He came to our table and looking at my plate, said, "Jo, Ashok can eat like a horse. Look at his plate. It looks like Table Mountain." A loud laugh erupted at his comment. After some time, he joined us with a plate bigger than mine.

"Now it's not Table Mountain. It's Mount Annapurna," Malla Ji said, causing another round of laughs erupt.

The party continued until late night.

Late that night, while I drove back along the highway – with vast expanses of savannah on both sides of the highway, bathed in the faint moonlight – I imagined myself being in the homeland, my country, after two weeks. Would all those get such an opportunity? And how long was Anuradha going to stay in that scary place with ghastly characters, far beyond her hamlet?

Mandakini

One

Driving in Kathmandu never felt enjoyable. Narrow, dusty roads with innumerable potholes and crowded with people, vehicles, cycles, and, quiet often, lumbering cows or bulls, all with blithe indifference to the traffic rules: driving in this city felt scary and exhausting. It always gave me a kind of anxiety, a kind of nervousness, and a kind of fear that a motorcycle or a cycle or a walker would appear in front of my car from nowhere in sight and would be hit by the car. Things were different in Pretoria. Driving would have become a matter of pleasure there. In Kathmandu, I never enjoyed it.

I drove along, passed Dharahara, which once would prominently stand proud to the sky as the tallest creation in the valley. Now, in its faded colour, it looked struggling to attest its very existence amidst the high-rise buildings and mushrooming shopping centres, a new but rapidly growing phenomenon in the city. I drove on. New Road Gate, Bir Hospital, Ratna Park, then Rani Pokhari. At Rani Pokhari, the level of water had shrunk; overgrown with algae and overrun with litter, it looked ruined and decayed.

It was not only Rani Pokhari, the whole city looked decayed, run-down. The Bagmati and Bishnumati had lost their purity. I had heard once there would be white sand on the bank of those rivers. Different varieties of fishes, including those with long whiskers, could be seen swimming in the clear water before snoozing for a while on the bed to swim again. This truth had become like a tale long back. Sundhara had lost the beauty. Thamel, Durbarmarg, New Road: all had lost the original attraction. The decay was everywhere, including in progressively westernising cultures, traditions and rituals and in deteriorating *Kantipure* orientation of Kathmanduits. Old alleys and yards had ceased to resonate with ancient stories; foggy mornings had ceased to blanket the valley; and patches of terraced fields with swaying rice plants had been lost to concrete constructions: plot by plot, *ana* by *ana*. In the process of turning into a metropolitan city, the valley had been more peopled and more concreted, but it had been more damaged, ruined and decayed. It felt so as I drove along. This time the feeling came out to me more intensely than ever before, to a greater degree of realisation.

At Bhotahiti, I turned right and drove onto Durbar Marg. The lines of cars on both sides of the road suggested the restaurants there had already grown to cater the evening joy to the elites even before the sun went behind the mountains. The dense foliage, which had come out from the trimmed stems of the jacarandas thinly lined on the sides of the road, was still green. The winter had not affected them yet. Those dense green branches, while looking from the ground at that particular moment of driving, offered the impression of an abstract art, the paling sky as the canvas of that art. A little away, at the end of the road, inside a big wide gate, stood Narayanhiti Palace Museum in its usual quietness, bringing back a long period of unresolved history. The tall trees inside the tall fence, made of palings, stretched high around the Palace Museum. As I turned right, I saw another gate, on the other side of Hiti Pokhari. Two sentries were standing inside the gate, their quietness resembling the quietness of the inside itself. Past the gate, a high wall and thick bamboo groves blocked the inside views.

I passed Nag Pokhari, Bhatbhateni, and Bishalnagar and then reached my place, a two-storey house built on a narrow, sloped piece of land, the upper part of which I had been renting for almost a month. Defying the suggestion from my sister, Devaki, and the children staying with them in Pokhara, I chose to be in Kathmandu. I was thinking of buying a piece of land in the capital city and to make a house. I did not have much time. I was supposed to return to Pretoria as soon as possible. Staying in Pokhara might cause a delay.

It was not unknown to me that – as conceived the peace and happiness as a genuine objective of life, which I was always looking for – life in a decaying city would definitely not be comfortable compared to the simplicity offered by the rural life. The crowds, the narrowness, the foul-smelling piles of waste piled on every corner of the streets, the plumes of dust and smoke, the scarcity of water, the heavy load-shedding, and the perpetual fear of insecurity the metropolitan city offered were almost scary to cope with. Yet I was looking for a piece of land: four *anas* or even less, whatever I could afford. Why? I did not have a certain answer why I was hunting for such a small patch of land in the city, and why I was running after brokers daily for the last one month. I did not understand what the driving force was. Was I driven by our false social attitude that owning property in the capital city would make you superior to the others? Perhaps! Perhaps by building a house in the valley, I was wishing to join the so-called civilised group of society, distinct from millions of people living out in the sticks!

Anyway, I parked the car – a rented white Hyundai – in a low underground garage and followed an alleyway: narrowly lying between the house and the mossy compound wall. In a true sense, it was not a purposely built alleyway. It was a vacant piece of land left between the house and the compound wall, a leftover piece of land, yet the overhang of the house just above the vacant piece of land, the high walls on both sides (the wall of the house and the compound wall), and the paving laid there, on the ground, had given it the shape of an alleyway. The paving was cracked. Tiny weeds had grown through those cracks and had pushed out through the gaps of bricks on the compound wall.

Mandakini was there. Just after the corner, I saw her putting soil into the clay flowerpots lined on the side of the alleyway which she had brought almost a week back.

"What are you doing, Mandakini?" I asked her, although I could see what she was doing.

"Ashok sir? So early today? You almost scared me," she said, swivelling around to look at me. As always, her hair in a ponytail became her. Pushing stray hairs behind her ears, she stood. Droplets of sweat on her reddish white face glistened in the last streaks of rays. The soil was smudged in her delicate hands and on her shirt and pants. She was squinting her eyes to see me against the setting sun in the background, and with this squint, she looked even more beautiful.

"You came so early, today? You didn't enjoy your drink?" she asked, offering a cheerful laugh. Her white teeth gleamed.

"I drink just once in a blue moon," I said while putting my bag on the ground.

"And that *once in a blue moon* comes to you every other day," she laughed.

"So you think I'm a drunkard! It's not fair, Mandakini," I said, reclining against the wall.

"Don't recline there. You're going to spoil your jacket."

"It already needs a wash. Which flowers are you planning to plant?"

"Many. Dahlia, white lily, rose, periwinkle, geranium, iris and many others, I don't even know the names, but they look beautiful."

"More than you?"

She glowed. I myself was a little ashamed. Why did I say so when I knew she was beautiful? And certainly, she was aware of her beauty and maybe even cautious. Why was I telling her that? I felt ashamed.

"The papers are on the table on the rooftop, sir," she said, perhaps to gloss over the matter.

"Is there any new news?"

"Nothing. What could be new news in this country? Every day political parleys to sort out nothing, a few inaugurations and seminars in big hotels, news on crimes, accidents, the plight of women, then, of course, the death of the those working abroad. The same news repeats every day. Sir, let me finish my work before it gets dark," saying so, she began to fill the flowerpots with soil.

"You know about this country more than me," I said and went up the stairs to my flat.

Plonking the bag on the bed, I went to the kitchen and made a cup of black tea and went to the rooftop. The sun had dipped down the mountains, but the sky was still bright pink. The peaks in the north were bathed in the last dregs of sunlight, faded though.

"Sir, load-shedding will begin at eight today. Don't forget to prepare your meal," her voice came from down.

"All right," responding, I continued sipping at my tea.

Mandakini, along with her friend from her hometown somewhere in the far western part of the country, lived on the ground floor of the house hiring two rooms: a small room as the kitchen and the bigger one as the bedroom or the study or for any other purposes for them.

She was a student doing her Masters, she had told me almost a month back when I came there to stay.

"Mandakini?" I had exclaimed as I heard her name for the first time.

"Yes. Why? Is it a bad name?" she had asked, looking at me with her curious eyes.

"No. It sounds pretty," I had said.

As pretty as she herself, I had thought.

In fact, to me, it had been always a beautiful name! The word *Mandakini* – having connotations with the sky, the Galaxy, the Milky

Way – so brilliant to look at in the starlit night had always been a preferred word in my lexicon. Way back I had considered giving this name to my first daughter. However, something came in between. Perhaps I had to compromise with my wife's idea about the name of my first daughter. Yet the name *Mandakini* always remained in my lexicon. Now what a coincidence? I had met such a pretty girl with the same name!

And while helping me to take the baggage upstairs to my flat, she had told me that her friend's name was Kabita.

From quite early on, Mandakini had been frank with me. On the very first day, she had been curious to know many things about me: where I was from, what I was doing, why I came to Kathmandu, how long I was going to stay in that house and such like. She had put a series of questions, all with a remarkable easiness, yet at the same time, in contrast to her easiness, with frequently changing colours on her face – now perfect white, now a bit pinkish red and then slightly dark-red – and with changing looks – now confident, now a bit nervous and then a bit frightened – all within a minute. She was pretty yet so vague, so vast, and so enigmatic: difficult to understand, just like *Mandakini*, the Galaxy.

I felt ashamed again. Why I was thinking so much about her! I tried to distract myself, tried to read the papers but could not.

The January evening was cold. The people on the rooftops of neighbouring houses left in order to secure their meal before load-shedding. The nearby bamboo grove became crowded with hundreds of crows. Like other days, they were competing fiercely to secure their places in the grove: some of them to have found their places, some yet to find, some being displaced and some replacing the others. The scene was chaotic. My eyes stuck on a small crow, probably the smallest in the whole group. It was looking for its place, but wherever it tried to perch, it was not allowed. It was chased, was attacked ruthlessly by the others, the bigger ones. The crow-psychology was not comprehensible to me, a human being, yet I could see that not a single crow allowed it to stay. Was it because it belonged to the different group? Or was it because it was the weakest? It tried again and again, but it was always in vain. Desperate with its situation, with no space for settling in the bamboo bush, it flew away. I looked at it until it disappeared in the darkening sky.

"Sir, you're still here? Aren't you going to eat anything tonight? It's already seven. Go and cook, otherwise your rumbling stomach won't let you sleep the whole night. I have left some dal and tomato chutney in your kitchen." It was Mandakini, taking her clothes from the clothes line.

"Oh, thank you so much, Mandakini."

"Don't forget to eat."

The sound of her footsteps receded as she walked downstairs.

Downstairs, the lights were put on and the curtains were drawn in all rooms. It must be Mandakini, I guessed, or to be accurate, I knew. Most of the evenings, I would come back late, or even if I came back earlier, before the sunset, I would be on the rooftop, talking over the phone or looking at the surroundings. So mainly it would be she who switched on the lights and drew the curtains in my rooms.

In the kitchen, I saw a bowl of pink dal and the potato and cauliflower vegetable on a plate with tomato chutney on the side. All my favourite dishes! I put a cup of rice in the rice cooker and went to the bedroom with Mandakini in mind.

From the very first day, she had known many things about me. It was the same day of my arrival she had asked me whether I liked tea or coffee, with milk or without milk, with sugar or without sugar. The same day or maybe the next day, she had prepared black tea for me and had shared the vegetable curry she had prepared. Within a week, she had known most of my likes and dislikes, my hobbies, and my favourite books and dishes.

Throughout life, I had had difficulty in finding friends to share my inner feelings. I always tried to keep myself distant from the crowds. I found it difficult to open up. There were very few with whom I could share about not only my happiness but also the sadness. I did not know why, but I always remained, throughout life, as a quietly spoken person, hesitant to share the difficulties of life. And now this Mandakini? She became friendly towards me so quickly, although she was almost half my age and of the opposite sex. Why was it so? Why did I feel that way?

"Mandakini! What a pretty name you have got!" I realised I murmured those words in a bass voice as I finished the evening meal. Again, I felt embarrassed: why was she coming to my mind repeatedly?

I lit a cigarette, went to the rooftop, and tried to call Ahmed in Pretoria to know about the restaurant. It had been almost a week since I called him last. Over the years, he had won my trust in running the restaurant. I could leave him with the entire responsibility and had done so when I had come to Nepal during the death of my wife or when I had gone away from Pretoria on different occasions. He had never disappointed me. This time, however, I was far from Pretoria with no idea about the exact dates of the return. That must be the reason why I was a bit worried. I tried to call him but could not get through. Then I called Devaki in Pokhara and talked for a while.

The lights went out at once. The evening became cold and dark. I came down to the bedroom and burrowed beneath the blankets. From downstairs, flickering candlelight streamed through the half-closed door and poured on the lower part of the wall. Mandakini and Kabita were talking in a low voice or maybe discussing about their class at the university.

She was studying literature, my favourite subject, which I could not pursue. Once I had entered her room, and I had seen many poems printed in large bold fonts and pasted on the walls. There were poems by Laxmi Prasad Devkota, by Robert Frost, by Lord Byron, by John Keats, and other world-famous writers.

"You like poems?" I had asked her.

"Who doesn't like poems? And it's my subject."

"Do you also write?"

"Yes, I do. But just for personal satisfaction. I don't have a dream to be a poet."

Her passion for poems once again reminded me of my past, the adolescence when I had grown in me almost a fanatical revere, an intolerable adulation for poems. I had consumed much time in collecting poems and reading them. I had, in my fantasy, dreamt of being a writer, to be a poet. However, destiny did not agree with this fantasy; it dragged me along its own path, a different path. Destiny always compelled me to run after survival, after a little money. When the chase after survival slowed down, when there were little savings, the charm of being a writer, a poet, had already faded away.

Now, after years, when I found such a passion for poems in her, my liking for her grew colossally. She was as dainty as those poems.

I tried to concentrate on my breathing, the rhythm of breath, inhaling and exhaling. "*It helps you to go to sleep quickly,*" Thakur used to say to me this when we had to struggle to get to sleep while in Lhasa.

Two

I looked at the image in the mirror hung on the wall of the bathroom, the floor and walls of which were tiled with ceramic tiles, sparsely clouded sky coloured. In the mirror was a middle-aged man. The skin under his eyes had grown to slacken and shadow. Lines had developed on the forehead. Veins were apparent beneath the skin at the temples. His hair, once thick, soft, and silky, had thinned with streaks of grey. Muscles around the neck, in the arms and in the chest had gone flaccid. The texture of the skin on his hands was rough. He looked aged.

Certainly, I was not a young man any more. The mirror was clearly telling this. I had lost the physical charm which I used to possess until a few years back. It was not that I was not aware of this age-related decay in parts of my body. I had accepted it as a natural process. Never before had I taken my age – now aging fast – as a matter of concern. Never before had I worried so much about my outward appearance. I had rarely stood in front of a mirror, looking at myself deep. But now there was a beautiful girl: almost half my age. My age worried me all of a sudden. This standing in front of the mirror and observing my own image, closely, gave me the precise realisation of my age; I felt it.

I shaved my beard, trimmed the moustache, and cut the hairs poking out through the nostrils, applied the cream I had bought a week back to lessen the black shadow under my eyes and tried to pluck out the streaks of grey at the temples, and wore different kinds of make-up, those artificial things which I had never used in the past, but which, according to the advertisement I had seen on the television, might help me look younger than the real age: an unusual wish at this age. Why was I doing that? Why was I trying to look younger? Why was I curious to belie my age? Was it not to impress Mandakini? Perhaps! I thought as I came back to the bedroom and put on the new clothes: a dark-blue T-shirt with brown stripes on the chest, blue jeans, leather jacket, and canvass shoes. An unusual clothing sense, the sense of physical smartness, had developed in me since I saw her. And though I was not comfortable (to some extent even disturbed) with this new change; though I was aware of my age, of my status, of being a widowed middle-aged man, father of three grown-up children; though she never showed any such behaviour to be regarded as an attempt to attract me (her behaviour towards me, though extraordinarily frank, in every sense was decent and within the perfect parameters of socially accepted moral standards), I was finding myself attracted to her. At that time, I could not say it was at the level of sexual attraction, yet it was definitely beyond the simple friendliness. The more I was trying to control this feeling, the more bedazzled I was finding myself by her charm.

Downstairs, in the alleyway, I found her watering the flowers, some of which had already started off sprouting and growing. She was in her usual dress: a half-sleeved loose shirt, a brown sweater, cotton pants, and a black pair of shoes. Nothing more. As simple as she would always appear. The black leather bag hanging on her shoulder suggested she was going somewhere.

"Where're you going, Mandakini?"

"Oh, Ashok sir? You always sneak up and frighten me. I never notice you until you come up to just behind me and speak suddenly," she said looking at me with her curious gaze. "I never saw you wearing this outfit before."

She did not comment whether the clothes I was wearing suited me or not, her comment was simply confined to *this outfit*. The words, however, gave me a slight sense that she did not like my dress. Did the unusual dress that I was wearing for extra effect or to impress her have the opposite effect? Did she think of the dress as too informal and showy for my age? Thank goodness, I had not put on the sunglasses, the ones with those unusually fashionable big greenish dark lenses, which I had bought the previous day. A little abashed, I asked again, trying to appear as normal as possible, "Where're you going?"

"To the university. To collect the examination entrance card. Oh, it's already late. I need to leave. My friends are waiting for me at Ratna Park," she said, looking at her mobile.

"I can drop you there."

"No, no, sir. I can take a microbus."

"I'm going to Bagbazar to a bookshop. Why bother waiting for the crowded micro?" I lied. I was not going there. Instead, I was going in another direction to see a piece of land that the land broker wanted to show me, and, in fact, I was already late. Honestly, for many days, I had been thinking to ask her out for coffee or for a drive or just for a walk but was hesitant to ask. This was a perfect opportunity, I thought.

"I'm not working in a foreign country. I can't afford to use a car every day. The micro is fine for me," she laughed and followed me to the garage.

As I drove her through the streets, she did not speak to me. I could sense that she was feeling awkward sitting in the front seat with a middle-aged man with whom she did not have obvious family relations. I also felt some sort of uneasiness to have such a young girl with me. During the stay in that house over a month, I had made some friends (of my age) in the locality, and they knew I was a widowed father. What would they say about us if they noticed? What type of reactions would our constricted society make out of seeing two people of the opposite sex with such a vast difference of age and with no family relations sitting together? We did not converse throughout the drive. A couple of times, our eyes met each other's. Each time her gaze dropped on her lap and mine one slanted to the streets. We remained silent. She got out of the car at Durbarmarg, almost half a mile before Ratna Park. Perhaps she was afraid to be noticed with me by her friends. I pretended driving towards Bagbazar.

Later, in the afternoon, I met her with Kabita, reading papers on the rooftop. Trying to present myself as usual as if the drive was already forgotten, I sipped at the black tea.

"Do you want to read the paper, sir?" It was Kabita. She would rarely speak to me. Only at those moments when I talked to her first or when we three were together.

"Go ahead. I have lost all interest in these papers. They repeat the same superficial news every day. They write without knowing the details," I said and lit a cigarette, stealing a glance at Mandakini to find out if the silent drive had left any effects on her. She showed no sign, nothing out of the usual. She offered her chair to me and stood. I felt comfortable.

"When is your exam?"

"After a month. And this load-shedding is killing us. It doesn't allow us to read even a single chapter in the evenings," she said.

"What time does it start today?" I asked.

"It has already started and will end at four in the morning," Kabita said.

Mandakini swivelled her head towards me as if remembering something and asked, "Have you eaten your meal? I know . . . you have not. Anyway, you can share ours."

"But I'm a voracious eater, like Ganesh. If I eat, nothing remains for you."

She laughed. A great beauty once again radiated from her face, shadowing everything around.

Later, in her narrow kitchen dimly lit, by flickering light of candles, she gave me two cane stools, one for perching on and the other for putting the plate. "We don't have a dining table. You must manage with these stools."

"What do you think I am? Do you think I need a dining table to eat? I grew up in a remote village and even abroad, mostly I lived a worker's life," I said, putting aside the spoon she had given me. "And I prefer to eat with hands. Eating with the fork and spoon does not satisfy me."

"You're doing business in a foreign country for so many years. We thought you forgot our culture," Kabita said, putting a glass of water on the floor beside the stool.

"Nobody forgets his culture. Why don't you eat yourself? You're just serving me?"

"First, we want to feed Ganesh Ji to see whether there'll be anything left for us or not," Mandakini laughed. Her teeth and eyes gleamed in the flickering candlelight. Her face looked unmistakably beautiful.

That evening, I had had homely feel and food for the first time after a long time.

And later, in bed, I burrowed myself under the blanket, thinking about her, whose thoughts were overwhelming me for days. Had I begun to love her? Probably! Or even certainly!

But what about her? I had never thought about it. I had no idea about her family. I did not know whether she was already married or engaged or whether she had a boyfriend. I was unaware of her sentiments. Honestly speaking, I was afraid to find out the details. I was very aware of the large gap in our age. One of us still rising, the other fading fast. I had the full knowledge of her enviously beautiful figure and myself being of obsolete for her, for her beauty, so I felt secure to live with the ignorance about her feelings towards me. It was secure to remain in my own fantasy, as Venkateshwar had lived during our short stay in Mumbai. Years back. The very truth could have shattered the happiness and peace, which I had got from her nearness. Thus, I continued to live in that romantic fantasy, an impression of being loved, false though the impression might have been.

Almost equally disturbing another thought, yet another aspect of my relations with her, was nibbling at my brain. Supposedly, she loved me. But what result was it going to produce? Would it prove as a workable relationship? Would it be acceptable by social standards? Would it be long-lasting? Or was it just going to give both of us a torturous mental situation? Considered in that way also, I was afraid to accept the possibility or maybe the reality. There were social restrictions and limits which I did not dare cross and did not possess the courage. I was fully aware of them. So, as an adult man, was it not my responsibility to control myself? Was I supposed to behave like a teenager? But these emotions! They were so difficult to control. They were hard or even impossible to be erased. Was it natural? What the demarcation was between *could do* and *ought not to do*? I was confused. Deep inside me, there was a fierce fighting going on between two contradictory forces: an awareness of socially defined morality and a strong primal desire almost to the extent of sexual pleasure.

Initially, these two forces were working together: the one balancing the other, the one opposing the other, the sense of morality somehow obstructing the physical desire. But with the passage of each day they were closing in, or rather say, the awareness of morality was getting weaker and the primal force was getting stronger. Was I, as a human being, prone to evil thoughts than to social ones as Machiavelli had suggested a few hundred years back? Was my propensity for wickedness stronger than for goodness? Did I lack the eternal verities I thought I possessed throughout my past? I was in a serious dilemma. Sometimes I realised I was going in a wrong direction, and I must stop the emotions sooner rather than later. But more often than not, I tried to justify my thoughts whenever I found myself unable to control the powerful primal force. I tried to validate my sentiments towards the girl half my age, believing that the human being was primarily driven by biological and physical forces, after all. Then what was wrong in falling love with a girl? It was not unnatural.

Anyway, unaware of her private sentiments, of her feelings towards me – a man in his forties – I began to like her almost impatiently. With the passage of each and every day, she grew on me. It had become crystal clear to me that I had fallen in love with her.

That night sleep came to me with dreams about her.

The following evening, even before the sun sank and the crows settled down in the bamboo grove, the large round moon rose above the eastern sky, progressed gradually and grew to cast a soft glow on the mountains, on the valley, on the houses, on the nearby grove and upon us. It was a full moon. We three were on the rooftop. Kabita was sitting in the chair. Mandakini was staring at the northern sky, maybe trying to locate the Pole Star, which like other stars had become faint in the moonlit sky. I was standing, holding the railings, and looking at the moon and often at the right profile of Mandakini which I could see from my position. We were quiet and kept quiet. In fact, the appearance of the full moon had taken us to the status of quietness. We had found it more natural to keep quiet and observe the silvery light than to speak.

It was on that evening, for the first time, I asked her after Kabita went downstairs to her room for a short time, "Mandakini, do you have a boyfriend?"

"What are you talking about, sir? I haven't even thought about a boyfriend," she said, turning her head towards me. She never talked to me without looking at my eyes. In that process of turning, I saw her whole face lit in the moonlight. So pretty! So dainty!

I felt a deep satisfaction. She was unmarried. She was not engaged. Nor did she have a boyfriend. Until I went asleep, the melodious sound came to my ear: . . . *I haven't even thought about a boyfriend.*

Three

One day, however, I lost control. The primal force inside me completely defeated the social barriers on which I had rested until now.

It had already been more than four months in that house. Ahmed was expecting me in Pretoria. There were tax related papers, which required my signatures. My house was empty for a long time, so he was worried about the safety of the house. I was supposed to be back. Yet I was in Kathmandu and wished to stay there I did not know until when. I was enjoying staying in that house, with Mandakini downstairs. I had stopped running after the brokers in search of the land. My interest in buying a piece of land in the valley had died away along with the passage of the day. It had been pretty clear to me that the land in Kathmandu was too costly, with no justifications for its high price.

With nothing to do, I would often go around to wander about during the daytime. In the morning, after having a cup of tea, I had begun to walk. In the evening, I would stay on the rooftop with them. Once I went to Pokhara to see the sister and children but did not stay more than a night.

A couple of times, I took both of them for drives. Mandakini was less hesitant when they were together. During those drives, she always sat in the front seat, beside me, as though it was her right, which gave me a kind of romantic sensation.

After finishing their exams, they were preparing to leave for their village for a few weeks. And this was unsettling me.

The spring had matured enough with the summer temperature in the daytime, but the evenings were fine. The cool breezes would pass rustling the bamboo leaves and branches, audibly. As audibly as in the bamboo grove in Narrow Flatland, just beneath the *chautari*.

Many of the flowers had come out in the alleyway. Mandakini would water them twice a day. Each time the water was quickly absorbed into the dry soil. Had she not taken care of the flowers, they would have died away long ago, I was sure. But they did not die; they got her passionate care. Now, along with the preparation of going to her village, she was worried about those flowers. One evening, leaning down on the railings, she asked me for a great favour.

Just two days before their departure, she said to me, "Sir, I need a favour. A big, big favour."

"What's that *big, big* favour?" I asked, looking straight at her eyes. I wanted to say – *Mandakini, I can do whatever you say. I love you a lot.*

"These flowers."

"Don't worry. I'll take care of them more than you do. I'll weed. I'll water them four times a day."

"But don't touch them."

"I won't, except for a few touches."

"Please don't joke, sir. They're delicate. They'll fade with a human touch, especially with a man's touch."

"I'm just kidding. I'll take care of them. You don't need to worry at all." I wanted to say: *They are not more delicate than you.*

"Thank you. I'll bring a nice present for you from the village, your favourite *gundruk* and *maseura*," she said, giving me her usual laugh. Then she went downstairs.

I lit a cigarette and looked at the crows fighting in the bamboo grove. The smallest one was not there.

I lost my control. It was just a day after I promised to her to save the delicate flowers, putting the other way the day before they left for their village, I saw her, with wet hair and droplets of water on her face, in front of my door on her way to the rooftop. She was going up after a shower. It was right at that moment the primal force inside me became irresistible. I lost all rationality. I caught her in the arms, pulled inside the bedroom, hugged her tightly, kissed on her forehead, and both cheeks. My lips touched hers. My hands ran through her body underneath the clothes from this to that part. I could not think anything. I was shivering and gasping. Everything happened within minutes. Everything happened so fast probably she even did not know what was going on. She freed herself from my grip and left the room.

I sat on the bed with a blank mind. It took a couple of minutes to realise what a terrible mistake I had made. How I, despite the guardian-like age, tried to exploit her. My heart was pounding. I was filled with an enormous feeling of guilt and fear. What I did! What if she told Kabita! I went to the rooftop and came downstairs in front of her room. I saw her come out of the toilet, wiping her eyes, which looked smudged with tears. She was perhaps crying in the bathroom. An enormous feeling of guilt over what I did, and of love for that dainty girl, overpowered me. I wanted to wipe her tears and beg her forgiveness. She went to the room mumbling something and closed the door from inside without looking at me. Kabita was in the kitchen, unaware of what had happened.

Again, I went to the rooftop and stood, looking at the bamboo grove. The crows had not yet rested. Above, the sky came to be dark and soon studded with twinkling stars. But there was no Mandakini to watch the starry night and to remind me about the load-shedding and to ask me whether I had prepared the meal or not. "Mandakini, what did I do?" I closed my eyes, cupping my face with both hands.

I lay awake the whole night with my eyes open staring at the darkness. I spent the whole night, turning from this side to that side, thinking how to face her. It might be only in the morning that sleep came to me briefly.

I woke up and went downstairs. The doors were closed: they had already gone. Outside, in the alleyway, the delicate leaves of geranium and dahlia had hung downwards. Perhaps she had not watered them before she left. I brought a bucketful of water and watered them.

After she left without speaking to me, without letting me know about her state of mind after my sudden and unexpected deed, days came with sharp feelings of guilt and remorse combined with loneliness. I had shown her a Machiavellian side of human nature which at once thwarted all gentleness I had pretended to possess so far. Within minutes, the very foundation of the idealism on which I was trying to get her love and regard had crumbled. I had been exposed very nakedly to her. Now it was not difficult to presume that she no longer respected me as *Ashok sir*. She might have begun to hate me. Otherwise, why did she leave without speaking to me? Why, before leaving, did she not water the flowers she cared so much about? The days began to give me a strong sense of being hated by her, which, to me, was far more intolerable than being not loved by her.

How to face her? How to convince her that though I might have not been an ideal man, I was not too bad? How to prove to her that throughout life I had always tried to be an honest man and to live a straight and narrow life, even in foreign countries and even after the death of my wife? These and such questions were clouding my brain. I was desperate to talk to her but was afraid she might not accept my call or did not want to talk to me.

I lost interest in the walks and drives. I became a stay-at-home, apathetic to almost everything. Yet I cared for her flowers, plucked the weeds, dug the soil around the stem, and mixed the manure. I did not allow them to fade.

Maybe after two weeks since they had left, I called her. My heart was pounding as the call went through.

"Hello." The melodious sound came.

"Mandakini, how're you? It's me. Ashok."

She did not speak.

"Mandakini, I'm terribly sorry for what I did. It wasn't deliberate."

There was still no sound from her side.

"When are you coming? All of your flowers are flowering."

It was only then her voice came from the other side. "Serious? Even the roses?"

"Mandakini, do you forgive me?"

"I wasn't expecting such thing from you. I always took you as a thorough gentleman."

"I won't do that again."

"You *can't*."

The phone connection became disrupted or she deliberately ended the conversation, I did not know.

Mandakini appeared all of a sudden. I was aware she would come anytime soon. The exact date, however, was not known. I was not informed of the date during our short conversation over the phone. So her arrival along with Kabita felt all of a sudden, rather surprising and amusing. I was watering the flowers, leaving the gate open. Purposelessly. Or even if there had been a purpose which I forgot later, that must have been a minor thing, for example, just to look the street or to switch off the street light which hung in the nearby post, which was often forgotten to be switched off due to unpredictable load-shedding, or for any other minor reasons. Anyway, the gate was kept open. And Mandakini was there, along with Kabita, carrying a rucksack on her back and wearing a cap with a long peak. It might be because of this purposeless opening of the gate, her arrival felt sudden. With that typical appearance – the cap, the rucksack slinging on her back, her hair haphazardly strayed over her shoulders, her face a little bit tanned, supposedly due to the exposure to the country weather or the daylong travel on the bus – she looked slightly different. Yet delicately beautiful. The quirks of her lips, the changing colours of her face, and the deep eyes offered the same beauty, the same enigma as she possessed earlier. Still with the feeling of guilt, I could not gaze at her. On her part, she behaved normally as if she forgot about the episode that had taken place a day before her departure, as if she had forgiven me. She looked at the flower plants, touched them, and spoke to Kabita or to herself.

She said in her murmuring tone, "Aha! All of them are alive. I was really worried about them. You see these periwinkles. How beautiful they look!"

She looked at me with her usual smile and said, "Thank you, sir, for taking care of them."

I stood beholding her, the watering can still in my hand. Her addressing of *sir* to me gave me a feeling of joy that she had forgiven me.

"Sir, I have brought *gundruk* and *maseura* for you. Today, we want you to eat with us. We have brought some special from the village," she said before entering the house.

"Thank you. It would have been certainly fantastic to join you. But a friend has invited me to dinner tonight. I think you must be tired," I lied.

I was not invited by anyone. My acquaintance in the locality or in the city had not developed to the level of invitation for dinner. Yet I lied to her. I was not yet ready to face her in person. It was partly because the feeling of guilt was still fresh in me. And partly because I wanted to be far from her so that I would not lose control. More than that somewhere deep inside me, I wanted to pretend avoiding her so that she would know I did not value her, and in turn, she herself would try to be near to me. I did not know why, but I was feeling I was giving her too much importance, which she might have taken as my weakness and that might be the reason she did not value me much. Therefore, I lied to her by pretending to have been invited by someone to dinner, whereas I spent the whole evening at Durbarmarg, first strolling along the streets and thereafter having drinks in a restaurant. I came to the house late in the evening. In the kitchen, there lay an old plastic bag, its colour faded, the letters and pictures inscribed on it almost omitted. And inside the bag two pouches containing *gundruk* and *maseura* and a plastic container with ghee, which smelt fresh. She knew I was fond of ghee.

I slept questioning myself why Mandakini appealed me so much, why my adulation for her was growing to such an intolerable extent!

The next day, I woke up earlier than usual. I went for a walk and afterwards, after the walk, longer than usual, stayed in a coffee shop having strong black coffees and going through the newspapers. Once it was almost ten, and I could assume Mandakini and Kabita must have already left either for the university or for some other places, I came back. I took a quick shower and went out. I drove here and there, walked from this street to that street, took lunch and dinner outside in a restaurant, and came back in the late evening and crept stealthily to my room. They were already asleep.

I repeated the same routine the next day and the day after too. I began to wake up earlier and earlier and to come back later and later. At times, I had to face pie dogs barking at me. I tried to be far from her, to evade her or, truly speaking, to avoid her.

But this avoidance did not help me at all. It did not help me to get her favour as I had thought. Rather, in turn, my passion for her grew more, grew to the level beyond the control of rationality. I was desperate to see her, to look at her dainty face, and to talk to her for hours. She always came to my mind, every moment: while walking, while driving, while reading, or while doing any other things. So though I tried to be away from her, she, in fact, came nearer and nearer to me. Despite a growing awareness of the non-workability of the relationship, I continued to live in the romantic fantasy, which would often conflict with the reality. This confrontation would befog and hurt me.

Nevertheless, I continued to stay in Kathmandu, in the same house with her, yet without facing her. I began to drink more, sometimes to the extent of drunkenness. The alcohol would help me to feel the fantasies, those romantic feelings, coming closer to realisation.

One day, after two weeks or so since the new routine began, so unusual for me, particularly waking up such early and returning so late, I found her sitting in my bedroom on a stool near the door with a book in her hand. It was a late evening. I had come back as usual in tipsy condition. She was there, sitting on a stool.

"Mandakini?" I said, sitting on the bed. I was both amused and bewildered to see her in my room at that time. Did the strategy of avoiding her work?

"Yes, sir. It's me," she said, casting her eyes to mine.

"And I'm here to ask you," she added.

"What?" I looked in another direction to avoid her eyes.

"Are you angry with me?" she asked sharply, making me further nervous. *Why was I feeling so weak in front of her, a girl half my age?*

"No. Why should I be angry with you?" I said, trying to be calm as far as possible.

"You *are*. I feel so."

"No, Mandakini. I'm not angry with you."

"Then why are you trying to avoid me?"

"I'm not avoiding you. I'm just busy these days."

"I understand, sir. You're avoiding me. I don't know why. What's my mistake?" she asked in a slightly arrogant sound, shrugging her shoulders and quirking her lips as if she was mocking me, and I thought it a little offending behaviour.

"You know, how affectionately my mother had prepared that *gundruk* and *maseura*? And you're just ignoring. They're in the same place where I left them. For days, I haven't seen you. You come late. I don't know where you go until so late. You don't know the security in Kathmandu at night can't be taken for granted," she added. "And why do you drink so much? You don't know how dangerous might be a driving after getting drunk?"

I kept quiet.

"Did you eat anything? I have prepared rice and dal for you and put it in your kitchen. I want you to eat properly," she added again.

I had not expected to hear so much from her, from that dainty girl. Whereas I was, in fact, trying not to face her, she presented herself to me boldly, frankly, and yet so innocently. I was feeling weak in front of her, in front of her boldness in dealing with a man double her age. And how much she was concerned about me! How many people on earth had shown this much concern for me after my wife died? Had anyone asked whether I ate or not? Had anyone advised not to drink?

The tipsiness of the alcohol further grew with the feeling that she was so concerned about me. And before I realised and had a chance to go to the toilet to wipe them out (to hide my weakness), a few drops of tear rolled down on my cheeks. The care she had for me was emotional, enough to create sentiments.

Perhaps she was not expecting tears from a man, an adult man; she was confused how to respond.

"Did I hurt you?" she asked.

She came near to me and sat on the floor, propping herself on her elbows on the bed. Her palms were holding her cheeks. I stroked her hair. She allowed me to stroke. I allowed the tears to roll down; they had found their way out.

"Sorry! I didn't mean to hurt you," she said softly.

"Let me eat the food you prepared," I said, calming myself down, and went to the kitchen.

The next day appeared to me differently, as fresh as the flowers in the alleyway, as balmy as the spring morning, as clear as the blue sky. The morning fell heralding a pleasant sunny day. The conversation with Mandakini had offered me new energy. The feeling of guilt had lessened. I started off the usual routine. I went for my walk but not too early and not too long. Instead, I took a short brisk walk and came back to water the flowers, which had grown to flower in full. I had not noticed before that the same type of flower, except for roses, would flower in so many colours. In fact, my knowledge about flowers was awfully limited, confined to the *sayapatri* and *makhamali*, which would flower in autumn and would be wreathed as garlands or to those that would flower in the trees in my hamlet. Beyond that, I could hardly remember the names of flowers. I could not fit those few which I remembered in their exact figures: the shapes and colours of petals and pollen and leaves. For example, the flower with the name of the dahlia in my imagination would turn out to be a different one in reality. The geranium would turn out to be the lily. The garden in Pretoria was dominated by grass and non-flowering plants or plants with negligible flowers. Earlier I never had time for flowers. So I was not aware of the periwinkles and dahlias flowering in different colours and the lilies producing such beautiful bunch.

I arranged scattered stuff in the bedroom and kitchen before I took my food, rice and *gundruk* and *maseura*. Afterwards, I read a book lying supinely on the bed.

Perhaps it was Saturday. Mandakini and Kabita did not go outside. I could hear them throughout the day: cooking, washing, pegging clothes on the clothes line, and then reading. However, it was only in the evening I came across them on the rooftop.

"Sir, where had you been for these many days? I thought you already went to Pretoria," Kabita said as she greeted me. I knew she knew that I was still in the house. Yet her reaction came in that way, slightly as a jest, as she saw me on the rooftop after almost two weeks.

"Yes, I had gone to Pretoria and came back today. How're you, Kabita?" I too responded in the same tone and smiled.

"But I need to go," I added.

"When?" Mandakini at once swivelled her head towards me. Her voice sounded somewhat different than usual, somewhat emotional. Was she worried at the mention of my leaving Kathmandu? She was difficult to read with so many changing colours on her face.

"I haven't fixed the date. It's pretty long since I left the restaurant. I'm a bit worried," I said and lit a cigarette, fixing my eyes on the bamboo grove and stealthily looking at her. Her mysterious eyes were fixed on the far west.

They went downstairs saying, "Let's cook rice before the load-shedding starts."

Four

A few more days passed by and then a few more weeks and one more month. The spring was about to end. The streets were filled with more dust and litter. The tap water, which would rarely pour in drops, completely stopped. The load-shedding hours increased to almost the whole day. The flowers in the alleyway struggled to survive. The late May sun cast strong rays, shrivelling the delicate leaves and petals.

I was supposed to return to Pretoria long ago. Nowadays, Ahmed would give me frequent calls, complaining that it had been becoming difficult for him to handle the tax-related issues. Every time he called, he would request me either to return or to appoint an accountant and authorise him to sign on my behalf if I were to stay in Kathmandu for a few more months.

Yet I stayed in Kathmandu with unusual feelings of romance, the feelings that gave me sometimes great amusement and at times an utter affliction. With the further passage of time, Mandakini grew on me more fanatically, albeit at the same time she would come out to me, to a greater degree, as a more mysterious character than I had thought earlier. She became more elusive, difficult to define. Her smiles and unusual physical nearness, her soft touches, especially while we would see the papers together, her increased wishes to go for drives and walks with me gave the impression that, despite my age, she grew to like me. However, her behaviour at other times, in contrast to these – her fast attempts to move her hands somewhere else as I tried to touch them, veiled yet deliberate attempts from my side, her sudden drawing back from my nearness as if she realised her body came too near to mine and, during our evening chats on the rooftop, the sudden changing colours of her face and the fixing of her dreamy eyes at the faraway mountains and in the sky as if she was preoccupied by something else, not by me, and as if she forgot or neglected that I was beside her – bespoke that she was not filled with the same feeling, the same degree of romance I had for her. After all, I was not a young man. I was more than twenty years older than her. My projection (which came occasionally in my mind) that she loved me in the same way I loved her might not be true. My efforts to project the same feeling as I had onto her might have not affected her at all. The nearness of her might be merely coincidental. Her touching my body would have been without sensual intention. After I begged her forgiveness for hugging and kissing her, she must have been assured of my sobriety when she came near to me. Yet honestly speaking, her nearness, her soft touches, and her warm breath always gave me some sort of awkward awareness, a kind of primal attraction, sexually felt. I had to struggle hard to hide those feelings. She was beautiful, young, and attractive. It was difficult to ignore or set aside the beauty she possessed. So, in spite of the fact that I pretended to be a sober man, deep inside me, the hedonistic notion of physical attraction quickened my pulses, the Machiavellian selfishness of my own pleasures without regard to her feelings dominated my thoughts, and the paroxysms of primal forces heated my blood. Quite often.

Thus, as time moved ahead, I found myself plunged deeper into an enormous feeling of liking her (now progressively being mixed with the feeling of lust). I was dreadfully confronted with the dual face of my liking to her, a kind of dubious feeling, so difficult to ascertain whether it was a love or a lust. But her feeling? Up until now, I was unaware of her real feeling. I was living on my own, had got the fixation with her beauty without much knowledge about her feeling, about her reaction.

But one day, the reaction came to me as complete defiance, as an utter blow to my belief, at least to some extent though, that I was loved by her. *I don't like to be hugged*: it was the reaction as I tried to hug her yet another time. I felt embarrassed, rejected, and goaded.

The May sun had been baking hot throughout the day. Throughout the day, I had not gone out, had remained in the room reading the papers, which gave the news of those days: the fast-moving political developments, the social issues, the financial concerns, and so on. But oblivious or uninterested in such news, I was living in a confined world of romance. My thoughts were narrowed down to Mandakini. My interests were confined to a fanciful world of romance. *Whether Mandakini would love me or not* had become my only concern, existing all time, morning, noon, and night. And the response came: *I don't like to be hugged.*

It was just after I took a shower on that evening and stayed a while on the rooftop smelling the pungent taste of iron or some other minerals that came with the groundwater. (In fact, the smell had now become familiar to me though the water had made my hair stringier, had yellowed my teeth, chiefly the canine ones, slightly, and had toughened and stained my nails. More worryingly, all my white clothes would become yellowish after each wash.)

Anyway, I stayed for some time on the rooftop, drying my hair, and looking at the bamboo grove and came back to the kitchen to find Mandakini doing the dishes. She was in a pink T-shirt and loose cotton pants patterned with white flowers on a dark-blue background. She had undone her ponytail and allowed it to cascade over her chest. From the right. She looked beautifully pale and white in the dim kitchen light.

"Sir, are you really leaving us?" her voice sounded concerned.

"I have to go. I wish I could have stayed here for longer."

"Why?" she asked, fixing her eyes at me.

I thought it was an appropriate time to tell her about my feelings, to let her know what I thought once and for all. I hugged her and whispered in her ear, "Mandakini, I love you."

"Sir, what are you doing? I don't like to be hugged," she shouted.

The answer came as complete defiance to me. The distinct edge to her voice cut me deeply and painfully. The rejection from a young girl brought to me sharp feelings of pain and embarrassment and to some extent the feelings of anger towards myself. *Why was I running after her? Why was I giving so much importance to her? What extraordinary qualities did I see in her?* She could not be a paragon. I wanted to ask her what the hell she was thinking about herself, why she was ignoring my love for her, why she was giving me such a pain. Yet I hid the emotions. This time, after the hugging she did not walk off, which I was afraid of. For a moment, her face became puce and then returned to its usual colour. As usual, she did the utensils, did the dishes, cups, and glasses, and drew the curtains. She did all these without looking at me and left saying, brusquely, "Goodnight."

"Goodnight," I responded, embarrassingly. I was filled with pent-up frustration.

I was not moving in the right direction. It was a self-destructive path. At the age of forties, I was not supposed to show a teenage crush. Right away, I was supposed to stop growing further romantic feelings. These and similar thoughts came as I tried to sleep. I could not concentrate on the rhythm of breathing. Thoughts were too strong. I was awake all the night, both my mind and body heated: mind from the thoughts and body from the heat coming from the cemented roof that absorbed heat during the day and now passed to the room. In addition, the mosquitoes, with electricity gone and the Chinese mosquito killer having stopped working, had gathered in the room to start off their music. Outside, at the neighbouring house, a dog was barking, louder than other days. It might have sensed unusual movements, perhaps, of lumbering cows, which would have been the usual case, or of a drunkard who was staying a little away from our house and would often stagger back late at night. Or maybe the barking had sounded louder because I was awake. I spent the whole night tossing and turning in the bed.

The following morning, the first thing I did was to go to a temple after having a long, cold shower in mineral-smelling water. Contrary to my superficial or even irreligious faith, after the shower, I went to the temple and put my head on the feet of deities, one by one. (Throughout life, I had taken the religion merely as a part of culture rather than religion itself. In my whole past, I had rarely gone to the temples – except for visiting the Kali and few other temples in my birthplace and that also for childhood amusement rather than for religious purpose and having *kora* around the monasteries in Lhasa, which again was part of my walk or pastime.) I begged with all deities to help me from coming out of the frustrating situation. Then I went to a bookshop at Thamel and bought some spiritual books and CDs containing Buddhist chants. I was desperate to overcome my lascivious feelings towards her. I was desperate to do away with the romantic thoughts.

I tried hard. I tried it hard to take the feelings associated with Mandakini away and to come above the pleasures of the flesh. I listened to *Om mani padme hum*. I googled *how to forget the beloved one* and *how to overcome the romantic feelings*. I tried to convince myself that she was just an ordinary woman – nothing more than that. There was no reason to cling to her. But nothing worked well. I continued to experience the turmoil of being in love with her; she grew on me more and more. However hard I tried, the torrid feelings continued. But Mandakini? There was no change. She was as she had been earlier. The look and colour of her face changed frequently as it would change earlier. In the morning, she went to college as always. During the day, she stayed inside the room. Once or twice, she watered the plants. In the evening, she came to the rooftop undoing her hair and again doing it and saying, "I wish the monsoon would start soon."

She did not appear to be aware of my pathetic situation and changed routine. The sole thing she mentioned about this changed routine was a short comment on the Buddhist chant, which would nowadays play in my room. One day, poking her head through the door, she said, "Oh, it's you, sir, playing such nice music. I was wondering from where this music was coming. Why did you start to listen to such spiritual music?" Throwing a careless smile and leaving the door slightly ajar, she walked downstairs. What a surprising lady! I was suffering so much, and she was not aware at all!

I tried hard to accept the reality, to think rationally that I was old for such a delicate young lady. I should overcome the carnal desires. I should find other foundations of love. What would they be? It was difficult, almost impossible, for me to forget her. At the same time, it was not possible for me to pretend accepting her in any other forms of relationship, say a friend or a sister. She was a woman for me. The opposite sex.

With these changes in my routines and with my efforts to live a spiritual life – though it was not working well (the foundation of and conviction in spiritualism in me was too weak) and very often it felt I was living a fake and extrinsic life – I began to wait. How long did I have to wait? I did not know. Yet I was hopeful that time would ultimately heal my wounds. Somehow, I had developed a faith in the healing capacity of time, a conviction that all feelings and pains, whether they be physical or be mental, were not atemporal; they were temporal, with a possibility to be defined and confined by time.

Time gradually moved ahead. I tried to adjust myself to the understanding that Mandakini was too naive for these things. I should refrain myself from sexual feelings.

Then again one day, the same day when I had come across Thakur at Bagbazar, it appeared to me that she was not as naive as I had thought.

We were standing in front of a bookshop, turning the pages of a recent publication, our back towards the road. I sensed a man coming near and looking at me.

"Ashok Ji? You?" Thakur was there. The old friend of mine, standing. He had gone bald. His beard was shaved. With a thick moustache, black and grey, almost half and half, and power glasses, he looked a little different. Yet I could recognise him. In fact, I would have recognised him even if there had been other changes. Thakur! I had not met him since I left Madagascar. After Madagascar, our phone communications had gradually dwindled and eventually ended. And here in Bagbazar, after many years, after more than seven years, he was standing in front of me!

"Thakur Ji, you?" I was surprised to see him.

"Let's go to my salon. We'll talk there."

His salon was two minutes away from the main street, on the ground floor of a five-storey unpainted building on the side of a shadowy alley. It was a hairdressing salon. He had returned from Madagascar three years back and had opened a salon or rather salons as he had got three in other cities, he told me on our way to his salon. Mandakini was following us.

"Ashok Ji, I always wanted to establish my own small business, which finally worked. I have got a business and have a little farm and a fish pond in my village. Mostly, I stay in the village. It's just sometimes I go to the cities for the business," he said, offering us chairs and requesting *Sahuni* in the nearby tea shop to make two special teas.

"Why don't you do something here? A foreign country is always foreign. You may earn a little there, but you never get the recognition and satisfaction of being in your own soil. There're problems here, but, after all, it's your own country," he said after listening to me about my business in Pretoria.

"Tonight, we must take our dinner together. We have met after so many years," he proposed.

"Thakur Ji, I'll be here for two more weeks. I'll come later. But today I'm afraid I can't wait long."

"Why? What's so urgent that we can't sit together? Anyway, we must sit together sometime soon. I want to tell you about my life after you left Madagascar and want to hear from you too."

Exchanging mobile numbers, we parted. It was obviously a bit unusual to leave him, whom I had met after so many years, after that brief conversation. I ought to have talked more with him, ought to have shared more, ought to have accepted his invitation, and ought to have asked Mandakini to go back alone. But I left. I wanted to be with her as long as possible. What a selfish man I had become! I walked with a slight feeling of guilt.

As we walked to Durbarmarg, I told her about our stay in Lhasa and in Madagascar.

It was the same day, the same evening, I got yet another sharp realisation that she did not like me, that I had not understood her at all.

"Mandakini, shall we take some snacks? I'm a bit hungry," I proposed to her.

"Won't it be late? It's already five. Kabita must be waiting for me," she said. She was hesitating.

"Let's take some quick snacks," I insisted.

And she did not say no.

As usual, the restaurant was full with customers, and as usual, almost all of them were male. (In our society, until then, the restaurants, particularly in the evenings, did not have many female customers.) The waiter led us to a table with two chairs, almost in the middle, and took our order: two *momos* and a beer for me and a juice for her.

As I looked around, I could see covetous eyes staring at Mandakini from all around. I realised I made a mistake bringing her to a male-dominant restaurant. It felt awkward to be in the centre of prying eyes. More than that, it felt awkward with her unusual behaviour, which I had sensed sometime before in another restaurant. I had not said anything that time. But this time, it was more vivid. It came to me that she was relishing those prying eyes with clear sexual intention. Her face brightened. She looked unnecessarily cautious about her style and clothes. She very frequently pulled the sleeves of her shirt exposing her white arms, touched the collar, untied the rubber band at her nape, and, pressing the band with her lips, did her hair and tied it again as if trying to attract as many eyes as possible. And while doing so, she managed to look at all male customers from young to old with her hysterical gaze. I felt she was blanking me. Was she the same Mandakini, my ideal character? Or was she trying to fool me all those months? Was her behaviour known to me so far totally false? I felt awkward. Disgusted. Disgusted with her and with myself. It was difficult for the manhood within me to tolerate such a sexually taunting gesture: what did she find in them that I did not have? A stab of jealousy, sexual jealousy, ran through my mind to the extent of insanity as though I wanted to pick up a chair and break the head of that old man, almost nearing sixty, who was eyeing Mandakini from behind our table. I was sure his look was perverted. I felt as though I wanted to slap Mandakini's face down to the table. Why was she shooting sideways glances at the old man whose nose was so crooked and who was looking at her with a clearly visible sexual leer?

"I feel pain in my chest," I said and walked. Emasculated. Indeed, I was feeling a slight pain, which was for the third time within a year, but the reason I walked so suddenly was more of that feeling of emasculation than the pain.

"Sir, we have already ordered our food."

I did not speak; I just walked out, putting the money for our order on the table and giving a heavy tip to the waiter. She was following me. Outside, I signalled a taxi.

"Do you want to go or stay in the restaurant?" I asked her rudely, further exposing the paradigm of my egoistic side.

She did not speak. Probably she became afraid of me, of the angry manner I exhibited, which she was confronted with for the first time. She got in.

"Where to go, Dai?" the old taxi driver asked me; he was wearing a cap.

"Just move on, I'll tell you the direction. Why are you calling me *Dai*? Do I look older than you?" I was furious.

The driver turned to look at me and drove.

At my place, giving him an unreasonable tip, I went to the room and, without speaking a single word to her, slammed the door hard. I drank almost a quarter bottle of neat whisky and lay on the bed.

The next day was terrible. An unbearable hangover had crippled the whole of my body. The headache, the chest pain sharper than the previous day, the pain in the joints and muscles, the feeling of nausea, and acute dehydration, as though I wanted to sleep under the sea. Limp and exhausted, I woke up, but unable to do anything, I lay back on the bed. The previous evening's memories were painful despite the hangover. My life had become pitiable. It was dwindling. Why did I so obsessively want Mandakini? Why did I feel such a pang of jealousy and anger when any other man looked at her or when she looked at any other men? Why was I so afraid or worried about the possibility of losing her, whereas I had already realised there was no future of the romance or any other absurd fantasies I wanted to live with? How to get over this strong feeling of attachment? How to take her normally? I lay down until noon, pondering on my situation going miserable. Towards the afternoon, I went for a long sweating walk, took a long shower, and sat on the rooftop.

The monsoon had not arrived yet. The sun strongly struck the rooftop and the purlieus. It was almost three o'clock. The maize plants, which the owner of the neighbouring house, a little away from my house, had planted in his small backyard, had shrivelled. The bamboo grove looked withered. The whole environment was sun-struck and hazy, similar to my mind. What would have happened to the flowers in the alleyway? I leaned from the railings to see all of them dried up and drooping. Apparently, Mandakini did not water them. Why? My anger had settled to a tolerable level. The rationality was coming back.

Why did I present myself so angrily? It had already come out to me that our relation was not about physical contact, not about hugging and kissing and not about sex. So what was the reason for getting so angry and jealous about her looking at other people? It was her choice. I should have not been bothered. Why was I not able to go beyond the carnal love? Why was I disturbed now and again by the primal force, a strong desire to have physical relation with her? Was I a weak man, inferior to the others who would claim to have control over their thoughts? Or was their claim just a pretension, simply hypocrisy. And deep inside all they were alike, just like me? Or was it because of the dissociation from religion and spirituality?

I came down, poured water into the flowerpots, and sat on the ground at a shadowed part of the alleyway thinking about Mandakini and myself.

As far as I had understood, our society in which I grew up was never generous to women. It was full of unjustifiable and absurd ethics for women planted long back, culminated purposefully throughout centuries, and later rooted in society. I had vivid recollections from the villages of so many violent and criminal events. A husband would go to a tea shack in the nearby *bhanjyang* and would spend the whole morning drinking teas, smoking cigarettes, and endlessly nattering about political nonsense while his wife would do all household chores and prepare the food for the whole family. Then he would come back and sit for the meal, complaining that the vegetables were too salty or the meal was overcooked (because he had already lost his appetite to the teas and cigarettes). He would spend the whole day gambling, drinking, and chatting with coquette and losing his little property, while his wife would work on the farm or in the wood. He would stagger back to his home late, would accuse her of flirting with someone, would hit her ruthlessly almost every day, and would sleep snoring loud, his breath reeking of smoke and alcohol. He would father many girls and would blame his wife for not having mothered a son and would marry with another woman to have daughters again. He would boast himself as a *marda*, always unwilling to admit his mistakes and criminal deeds towards his wife whereas his wife would always live beneath her dignity.

And I was a *gentleman* grown up in that society poisoned with the double standard of morality, bred in that way, and, still now, after some forty years, adhering to those fixed sets of obsolete and conservative beliefs. How could I develop a sense of justice towards a woman? All I was reflecting was an example of a man who had been brought up in such society and had grown in him a narrow and bias attitude.

I should have been above the narrowness and bigotry. I should not have judged the character of a girl solely on the basis of her odd behaviour in a restaurant. The behaviour might have been resulted purely due to her unawareness, due to nervousness or due to curiosity, which was natural at her age in a new place with the new people. It would have not been unnatural for a man or woman to look at the opposite sex. How many times in life had I looked at women, knowingly or unknowingly? How many times had I, cautiously or incautiously, been keen to look at charming faces? How could I be judgmental about her character, such a sensitive aspect of life and her private matter merely on the ground of my narrow perception? I did a great injustice to Mandakini, showing my rude behaviour. Yet I was claiming I loved her.

What was I expecting from her? Sex? After that? Could I accept her in place of my deceased wife? Was I, a father of three grown-up children, socially and morally allowed to do that? Did I possess that much courage to go that far against the established social practices? Obviously not. Considered from her side, why was she supposed to love me? Supposedly, she loved me. Then how and what would she tell her colleagues and parents that she fell in love with an old guy having three children? How could she share that?

Sitting there on the ground for some time, I watched an army of ants carrying a dead grasshopper many times bigger than them and, by doing so, reminding me of the computer-animated movie *The Ant Bully* and its main character, *Lucas, the destroyer*, which I had seen during an air journey. I then went to the rooftop.

Mandakini was there looking at the distant west. She wore a worn-out look. Her eyes had become bleary, telling that she had not slept the whole night. I felt sorry for her, for that delicate girl. "Mandakini!" I called her.

"Yes."

"Are you tired?"

"Not really, it's just because of a sleepless night, which often comes to me. Sir, can we go to your room? I want to talk to you."

In the room, I sat on the bed. She sat on the cane stool as usual.

"Sir, why were you angry with me yesterday?"

"I wasn't angry. I couldn't stay because of the pain in the chest."

"You were angry. Please tell me the reason. I can't tolerate you becoming angry with me."

"I didn't like the way you were looking at the other people," I said, hesitantly.

"To whom? And in what way? I don't understand what you're talking about."

"In the restaurant. You were looking at so many people and the way you were looking was something as a bad woman looks at a man." I expressed my narrow thoughts.

For a while, she kept quiet, closing her eyes, biting the right corner of her lower lip and stroking her forehead from down to up for a couple of times and then cupping her face with her hands as if she wanted to say something but was not finding appropriate words to express.

"Sir, I'm from a poor family in a small village. I know nothing about the city people. I don't know whom to look at and whom not to and how to look at and how not to. I don't know anything about cars and restaurants. The first time I rode a car was yours. The first person I went to a restaurant with was you. Now you're blaming me for looking at somebody in a particular way, of which I myself wasn't aware," she said in a low tone.

"Sir, I'm a woman. You know how our society looks at a woman. I'm aware of my character and dignity. At the moment, I'm focusing solely on my career. I don't even think about those things, I mean, about indulging in a relationship with a man," she continued.

"After you came to stay with us, I saw in you a kind gentleness, a kind of man whom I can trust, a kind of sobriety. Honestly speaking, you were the only person with whom I became so frank and close. I don't know why I always wished you would never go back to Pretoria. I don't know how to cope with the feeling of missing you after you go back. I'm frustrated with myself. The person whom I trust this much, he doesn't trust me. Have you ever thought, sir, if you go without trusting me how I'm going to survive? Please trust me, sir."

Tears brimmed in her eyes and rolled down through her soft cheeks.

The room became silent. I did not know what to speak. Then after a while, I went near to her, wiped her tears and murmured, "Sorry, Mandakini. I know you're pure, as pure as your flowers. I'm so sorry."

What she said was definitely enough to make me think how narrow-minded I was, how narrowly I was thinking, and how impure my thoughts were. And in contrast, how broad her thinking was. How pure! Yet deep inside, honestly speaking, I wished if she had added a few more words to show she loved me.

Now it had clearly dawned to me that I had no romantic future with her. Though I had always difficulty in understanding her, or to say more accurately, I never understood her, what I assumed from what she had said that evening was that she did not love me the way I loved her. Her words were not explicit expressions of love. She had simply said she took me as a gentleman, a nice man. She needed only my trust. And for a person like me – in whom suspicion, the suspicion almost about everything, was rooted as an inseparable part of innate character – it was difficult to take her words as the explicit expressions of love. It was true that she had cried, and it might be true that she did not have a boyfriend until now. It might also be true that she had not even thought about that sort of relation. But it did not necessarily mean that she loved me the way I loved her. There was not compatibility between our feelings. She simply regarded me as a gentleman, as a nice man and needed my trust whereas I loved her deeply.

So once again, it appeared to me that it was not possible for me to get her love as I wanted. I had to change my attitude towards her or had to forget her. But how? Would it be possible for me? I would often question myself lying on the bed and listening to those Buddhist chants or some traditional music.

The remaining one week or so in Kathmandu, I stayed in the room, befogged and gloomy. My moods were swinging quickly. Despite the efforts to turn myself away from her, there was not a single minute when she became absent from my mind. Sitting inside the room and on the rooftop or lying on the bed, all the time I wished that she would come near to me and stay for hours, wished that we could go somewhere far from the city to sit in isolation and talk for hours.

What a pathetic situation I had created? I would become angry with myself. It was me, I myself, who seeded the seed of unusual feeling of love and romance, which was not possible to grow with a girl half my age. But why did I never think about the reality? I ought to have realised she was not meant for me. She was young; ahead was her whole future and her dreams to fulfil. And here I was disturbing her. I was longing and longing for her and pushing myself towards this situation.

On the day of departure, she came to my room and looked at me, sobbing. I put my arms around her and held her tight. She did not try to free herself from the grip. Instead, she nestled down against my shoulders. I wanted to kiss her, on her lips, but was afraid of possible withdrawal, of yet another rejection. So I controlled myself and began to arrange the baggage. Deep inside, I made a firm commitment to keep away myself from her, not to disturb her, to let her live her life on her own and fulfil her dreams.

Thus, I left Kathmandu, that house, and Mandakini pathetically, sadly – or put down straightforward defeated, unable to achieve what I had desired the most in that particular stretch of life – and perhaps depressed. Would I be able to forget that dainty girl? When would the time cure my mental wounds? How long would it take? I was wondering as I left the house. I had grown doubts about my conviction on the temporal character of the mental suffering. My future promised to be melancholic and dark.

Outside, the leaden sky was sprinkling a light drizzle.

Five

The travel back to Pretoria was a total blur for me. I did not know how I did the airport formalities in Kathmandu, how I spent the four-hour transit in Doha and those tedious hours on board, and how I picked up the baggage from the carousel at the airport in Johannesburg. I was consumed by the memories of the past nine months, was awfully overwhelmed by the thoughts surrounding Mandakini. Awfully, I remembered the dainty girl with changing colours and looks, the alleyway and her flowers, the rooftop and her eyes fixed on the faraway mountains, the evenings and chaotic views of the bamboo grove, the drives and walks and her doing things in my kitchen. I did not know how to cope with the separation and live a life without a convincing assurance whether I would meet her again or not. It felt as if I was parted from the very essence of my life.

In Pretoria, the winter had set in. The savannah grass on either side of the highway had browned with black patches, some of them smoking from the veld fire. Trees had gone predominantly bare. Those which possessed leaves did not look green. The afternoon sun itself looked pale. Everything appeared gloomily in my gloomy mind. Never before had this city become so faded to me. As Ahmed drove me inside the gate, the house looked as though it had been wrecked by a hurricane. The pavement and dry lawn were strewn with fallen leaves. The swimming pool had become a green puddle, full of algae and litter. The tree branches had hung down onto the electric fence. The flowers had disappeared or looked bare and thin. The elephant's-ear plants were the only greenery left on the lawn. The bird droppings – the black droppings which birds had passed probably after eating the small black-coloured berries fruited in a tree close to the swimming pool the name of which I never knew – had sprinkled on the pavement, on the veranda, and even on the wall where there was nothing to perch on. Did the birds manage to stand on the vertical wall and pass their droppings? Or was it the wind to blow the droppings onto the wall? Or maybe they were nesting under the eaves. The droppings were scattered massively on one side of the wall. The house looked ghostly and abandoned. The twittering birds around the trees and grazing hadedas on the lawn felt alien. Had I been in another situation, an ordinary situation, I would have definitely expressed dissatisfaction and would have sought the reason for the carelessness. But now my life itself was a total emotional wreck. The wrecked house did not concern me much.

"Sir, John broke his hand and decided to retire from gardening. I have found another gardener for you. He'll begin from tomorrow," Ahmed said, giving some justification for the chaos. Taking out the baggage from the boot of the car, he added, "I have put dinner in the fridge and have brought a bottle. If you wish, I'll come later. For now, I leave you to rest."

"Thank you, Ahmed. I feel tired. If I need you, I'll give you a call," I said. I wanted my own privacy.

"Amanda will come tomorrow, sir."

He put the baggage and left.

I spent the rest of the day and the whole night in a total gloom. The rooms felt strange. Sleep seemed afraid to come to me. The drink Ahmed had arranged did not have the usual effect. I could see Mandakini everywhere: in the kitchen preparing tea, in the bedroom sitting on a stool beside the door, and in the passage standing, looking at me. I was yearning for her terribly. I had to call her.

I had to call her. I had promised to keep myself away from her and not to call her. I had promised to hold back feelings, not to become passionate because I knew she did not have the same passion as I had for her. Yet somewhere in mind, there was a faint hope that she had the same feeling as I had for her. Perhaps she could not expose herself in front of me while I was in Kathmandu. Maybe the distance would let her express which she was hesitant to do in the nearness. Otherwise, why she needed the trust from me? Why was she crying when I left?

So I called her, not realising that the time in Nepal was almost the middle of the night.

"Hello," the sweet sound came.

"Mandakini, I miss you a lot," I said with a pounding heart.

"Ashok sir, at this time! Where are you? How was your journey?"

"I reached Pretoria. I couldn't stay without calling you. I miss you a lot, Mandakini."

"Sir, I feel your absence. Can we talk later? Maybe tomorrow or the day after tomorrow. I'm sleeping now," she said yawning. I could hear the sound of the yawning.

The response from her was not as passionate as I had expected. Why did she not say she missed me? Why did she not want to talk for long? Why was she feeling so sleepy whereas the sleep was miles away from me? I weighed every word she had expressed, the tone she had used. No, she did not love me. Not at all. A pang of anger and jealousy made me shiver. I threw the phone aside and tried to sleep.

The next day commenced dully. Amanda came with her usual greetings and laughs, asking what present I brought for her. I wrapped a pink pashmina shawl around her. She went to the mirror and smiled a happy smile. She cleaned the house, washed the clothes, hung them on the line, and left. Before leaving, she asked me if I was fine, if I had enough rest, or if I missed the daughters too much. Perhaps she had read the gloominess in my face.

Towards the afternoon, Joseph, the gardener Ahmed had arranged, came along with his mates, driving an old-looking *bakkie* filled with the garden rubbish. He looked around whistling and said, "Jo, it's a big compound and so many big trees."

Stretching his bony hand towards me, he added, "I'm Joseph. How're you, sir?"

"Good and you?"

"I'm fine. Thank you," he said. "What was the name of the bearded man? Oh . . . *Amaad* or something sounding like that. He had told me you were in your country, *Napad*. When did you arrive, sir?"

"I came back yesterday. It's not *Napad*. It's *Nepal*," I said, putting extra emphasis on *a*. "And it's not *Amaad*. It's *Ahmed*."

"Oh, yes, yes, *Nepaad*. Where's that?" he asked. He seemed to be curious. "You know Mount Everest, the highest mountain in the world? It's there."

"Is it? I had heard about it. But I didn't know it's in *Nepaad*."

"Yes, it's there."

"Jo, this compound! It's huge. Look at this tree, how big it is!" he said, showing the leopard tree. "The amount *Amaad* was talking is too little for this big, big compound."

"How much had he said?"

"Just 400 rand per visit. That's nothing."

"I'll give you another hundred rand. I hope you'll take care of the swimming pool as well."

"Eish, you're making my job difficult. Why don't you add another hundred for the petrol?"

"Let's compromise on five fifty. That's the final."

"You know how to bargain," he laughed wide and gave instructions to his men in his own language, Zulu. He himself set about trimming the branches with the heavy-looking shears. When the trimming was finished, they collected the rubbish and leaves in sacks. The sacks were limited, so they dumped the remaining rubbish and leaves (in fact, more than they had collected) around the trunk of the leopard tree and in the corners of the compound, saying if I could arrange sacks or garbage bags, they would collect the leaves next time. Or maybe the rubbish could be used as compost. They left.

Joseph was different to John, who had never asked me to arrange sacks for the leaves. He had never dumped the leaves under the trees and had never given me the idea of making compost out of the rubbish.

With Joseph gone in his *bakkie* outside the gate blowing a large portion of the leaves again into the compound, I found myself again lonely. Mandakini came back sharply to my memory.

I felt utterly lonely. It had not been more than two days since I left her, yet it felt to me as if I had not seen her for months. What would she have been doing? I wondered and then guessed she might have been watering the flowers, or staring at the faraway mountains from the rooftop. If I had been in Kathmandu at this time, she would have been doing something in my kitchen.

"Mandakini, where're you? I miss you," I said to myself.

And again, I remembered how she had rejected me, how she had tried to free herself from the hugging, how she had looked so many other people with her sexy look while I was with her. Why did she not love me? A stab of anger and jealousy overpowered me.

"Nonsense fucking woman!" I mumbled, picked up a stone, and threw at the grazing hadedas. Then again, I regretted having uttered those words, so unusual from my mouth.

She kept coming. No other thoughts blocked her. In futile efforts to distract my mind, I called Vinod and Hemanta and informed them of my arrival, talked to them with fake laughs, and fixed the date of braai: the following Friday at my house. I called Ahmed and inquired about the business in detail. I walked in the compound, went inside the house, and then came out again. I tried to engage myself in something. But

Mandakini remained in mind along with the mixed feeling of love and anger the whole day.

The chirping of birds came to an end. They rested in their nests. The grazing hadedas pecked at their last meals of the day, preened, and flew away with loud *ha . . . ha . . . ha . . . .* The bats came to dart through the darkening sky. The street lights, faint as always, pierced through the bare branches and fell dimly on the lawn. The memories of Mandakini became stronger.

I took a whisky glass and sat beside the window in the study room from where I could see the whole front lawn, the swimming pool, and the eastern sky. As always, the two tall trees a little away from the compound stood straight and high. Those two trees – their branches, leaves, and the texture of the bark resembling the features of *masala trees* in Kathmandu – were tall, the tallest in the vicinity or perhaps in the whole city. I was always curious about them. So strong was my curiosity that I had to Google to satisfy this, after which it was known to me that they were eucalyptus, *Eucalyptus camaldulensis*, precisely the same family, the same genus, and the same species as those *masala trees* in Kathmandu.

Mandakini continued to come. Every other memory became blurred by her memories. It was only in the late night, after putting away almost half a bottle of whisky, I staggered to the bed and lay down drunk to wake up the following morning with a bad hangover.

The routine repeated: late hour waking up, strolling in and around the house, inside the compound, sitting under the leopard tree, looking at the birds or gazing into space, into nothing, every evening drinking heavily and eating sparingly, and then lying on the bed.

I did not go out. I did not go shopping. I did not go for evening walks and did not go to the restaurant. My life became a life of a recluse. Ahmed was puzzled (or perhaps worried) with this enormous change in my life. He had time and again tried to find the reason why I was absent from the restaurant and why I had become indifferent to my own business. After a week, he came to see me carrying fruits, juice, roti, dal, and curry and asked, "Are you fine, sir?"

"Yes, I'm all right. I feel a bit tired."

"All right, sir. I'll bring the papers for your signature," he said. "But take care. If you need any assistance, please call me," he added before driving off in his car. Certainly, he was not convinced by my version of the problem.

Vinod and Hemanta were disappointed when I called them and requested to postpone the date of braai. "Is everything all right, Ashok?" Hemanta asked me. "Yes, it's just because I find myself a little busy," I responded briefly and put down the phone.

But anything was not right. I was weak, both physically and mentally. There was a pain, a continuous dull pain somewhere inside the chest and upper stomach, difficult to pinpoint. Maybe, I was developing gastritis or some other illnesses because of too much drinking and smoking. I had lost weight. Mentally, I was overwhelmed by the thoughts of Mandakini: love, anger, and jealousy. I was befuddled.

And the realisation came to me starkly once Amanda came to the house the next week. Right away after entering the house, she expressed, raising her eyebrows, "Eish, what happened to you, sir? Are you sick?"

"I'm fine, Amanda."

"No, no, no, you aren't fine, sir. Look at your face, how pale it is! Look at your body! It looks just like a rake. It's all within a week," she said, touching my forehead with her parental authority. "Are you eating well?"

"Yes," I tried to offer a smile, bland though.

"You must see *sangoma*," she declared and engaged in her work, crooning her song. She had found a new boyfriend. She had told me he was much older than her. But he was a man of sturdy build and could dance very well. So she liked him despite his age.

The realisation of my weakness came sharply to me.

I sat sunning myself beside the pool. In the cold of late August, the sunrays felt warm. Joseph had done with the gardening before Amanda came. But within two hours, the pavement and lawn had again filled with leaves. The trees would shower the pale and brown leaves even with a small wave of the wintry wind. Across the pool, in the tree (the one with black berries), birds were darting and pecking at the berries. The earth and the part of the pavement below had been liberally sprinkled with fallen berries and bird droppings. The pool still looked green. The chemicals Joseph had put did not work effectively.

I tried to feel strong. I must overcome the pathetic situation, must be a doer, must be a goer. I should deviate from Mandakini or at least, while remembering her, having recollections associated with her, I must do something. I should forget her. Or I should think positively. I should use my enormous love for her and the fact that she needed my trust as the source of inspiration, not as the source of the ruin. I thought as I basked in the sunshine. I should look after my business. I should call Devaki and the children. I should engage myself outside the house with my friends. I tried to feel strong.

I shaved, took a long shower, dressed up, took the car out of the garage, dropped Amanda at a nearby taxi rank, and went to the restaurant. There were not many customers as it was off season. Yet the restaurant looked well taken care of. The tables were neat and strewn with new tablecloths. They were decorated with new sets of plate and cutlery, silverware, and flower vases.

"Sir, these vases are from Pakistan. Whoever comes to the restaurant doesn't leave without commenting on these gypsum vases," he said with a slight emphasis on the word *Pakistan*.

"These are indeed beautiful. Where did you find them here?"

"One of my friends is doing this business in Johannesburg."

I took my dinner in the restaurant with Ahmed, forcing myself to talk to him. As soon as, however, I left the restaurant, Mandakini appeared more strongly and continued to appear until I got drunk and lay on the bed. The next day, the first memory, after I woke up with a terrible hangover, was of her.

The following days and weeks were no less gloomy. The winter gradually became weaker. The sun grew warmer. Frequently, the wind blew from the east and howled through the compound and trees, showering more leaves and pods from the leopard tree. The leaves and pods in turn swirled in the air and rustled on the ground before settling in the corners of the compound, in the lap of the tree or on the pavement where the bricks were hollowed. A few trees had put out the green buds heralding the spring. A few others were always green enduring the cold. For some days, a pair of doves flew past my compound, carrying twigs in their beaks and to disappear into a tree on the grounds of the next house. Perhaps they were busy making the nest. The lawn had begun to sprout along with many weeds. A few seasonal species of birds had come to the compound, one of which, interestingly, was the mynah, the common one, with brown body, black head, yellow bill and legs, and white patches on the wing linings: common to my hamlet throughout the year. But I rarely saw it in Pretoria.

Time dragged by. With the passage of each day, week and month, the memory of Mandakini grew with even greater intensity, more painfully. Time, its healing capacity on which I had much faith, because of which I had dared to leave the dainty girl I loved so much, was not working as I had expected. She was in mind all the time; I would love to remember her and would love to live with romantic feelings, and I was eagerly looking forward to seeing her again as soon as possible. But along with her would also come the moments of the rejection. I would call her now and again to hear her melodious voice, but as soon as she received the phone call, I would not find proper words to express my feelings.

To deviate from her, I tried to engage myself in the outer world. I began to roam outside and would go to the restaurants and bars until late night. I did things unusual for me. I tried hard, adopted a series of methods, but not to avail. She was always there. Painfully.

I tried to engage myself in housework: cooking and cleaning, polishing the old shoes, removing the cobwebs from the corners of the house, clearing the film of dust from the unused furniture. My daughter Sarita had once said, "Daddy, when you clean your things, you clean your mind as well."

Following the advice of an anthropologist, a professor at a university in Johannesburg – whom I had met in my restaurant and who had said that the men, our early ancestors, *Homo sapiens*, were meant to walk, to move ahead in an upright position in the wide African savannahs either in search of food or shelter, and the atavistic attitude of our ancestors, the genes, was still in our body, so even now, when we, the carrier of the same gene, would move ahead, whether it be by air or vehicle or on foot, we would become happy and I had asked him whether it would help to overcome sorrow and to be happy in response of which he had replied *maybe* – I began to have long walks, cautiously in an upright position, almost strutting like Dorje in Lhasa, which sometimes looked odd and funny. That unique style of walking of a man – non-white, non-black – invited loud barks and furious looks from the dog inside the houses on both sides of the streets.

Mandakini did not go away.

Following Vinod's lifestyle, a club-goer lifestyle, twice or thrice I went to the club somewhere in Kempton Park. He tried his best to amuse me offering drinks and pulling me to the dance floor. I drank and danced with awkward steps mimicking a tall, lanky man, but I soon realised the club was not a place for me. The glitz and glamour of nightlife and the environment there – the plumes of smokes (and in some corners the smell of drugs), the crowds, the loutish words and the blare of music – offered me no amusement at all: I promised myself: *I won't come in the club.*

Mandakini was still there.

Once, in Hatfield, I drank heavily, so heavily that on my way back, I drove the wrong way down a one-way street, and on Duncan Street (later, the name was changed), I took the opposite direction, the north, instead of the south. Afterwards, at the foot of the hill in East Wood, I became almost senseless and my car ended up on the pavement wedged in as if it had flown or had been picked up and kept in that position. Somehow it was not involved in a collision. The police came. The bribe cost thousands. I came back to the house and slept drunk.

The next morning the first thing I remembered was Mandakini.

In further attempts of searching distraction, I visited the parks and game reserves and travelled to the cities with Hemanta who loved travelling. It was in one of those travels, air travel to Durban, he asked me in a serious tone, not very usual to him, "Ashok, since you came back, you look a bit sad. What's the reason?"

After being briefed by Doodh – our driver, a South African of Indian descent with a glossy dark face – about the dune vegetation and the unpredictable Durban weather in his typical Durban accent, we had just entered our room at a hotel at North Beach, which gave on to a wide prospect of the beach and the ocean, he posed me the question.

"Not really, Hemanta. I'm just thinking about how to wrap up the business and go back. That's all I'm worried about," I said and, trying to hide my face, looked at the wakes left by bobbing boats in the ocean. As Doodh had said about the unpredictability of the weather, the rain had ended, opening the afternoon life on the beach. The seabirds circled around over the beach; their brown and white feathers gleamed against the sky. They swooped down into the water and then flew again high up in the air. Surfers rode the crest of the wave and disappeared for a moment to reappear. I could see a few ships, two or three, sailing into the harbour – a little south from the place where our hotel was located – maybe to be docked or to have got loaded and offloaded. Far away, the sea hazed and receded merging with the sky.

"No, Ashok. I can see you and can read you. You have changed a lot. It can't be without a reason. Nobody changes in such a way for nothing," he said, pulling at his cigarette.

"Let's walk on the beach," I proposed, segueing the matter.

"OK, let's go," he agreed.

After the walk, we sat on a rustic bench looking at the sea. There, he said again, "Look Ashok, we're such close friends, tell me what has happened to you. Have you realised how thin you have become?"

For a moment, he set his eyes on me and then, staring into the distant sea, continued, "Do you know everything about my life? Do you know how I'm living?"

"You're an open book to me. There's nothing left to know about you."

"Still, I'm hiding so much of myself. I'm living with great pains within me, yet I'm always laughing with you and all other friends."

"What are you hiding?"

"I'm taking medicines – the antiretroviral drugs."

"What's that?"

"Medicines for HIV-AIDS. I'm HIV positive. Don't tell anybody. I haven't said anything even to Vinod."

"Are you serious?" I looked at him. The revelation was almost unbelievable. More unbelievable was the way he revealed the truth he had been keeping within him for such a long time and the setting he chose to reveal it. Such serious news on a sunny afternoon on a lively Durban beach. We were sitting on a bench beside the coastal path. He revealed it calmly. There was not even a shaft of worry on his face. Was he speaking true? If so, how was he managing to live so happily? Always laughing? His enduring capacity, his humorous style of presenting himself exposed during braai and the gatherings, and his love for and confidence in life was strong, much stronger than mine.

"Are you serious?" I repeated.

"Jo! This man? How can I make you believe? Do you want me to show the medical report and the medicine I'm using," he said as he extinguished his cigarette on the grass and binned the stompie in a nearby bin.

"Where did you get it?"

"I suspect it was in last days in Korea when I would roam a lot of nightclubs to find girls. I came to know about this last year. Anyway, let's go to a bar and have some drinks. Away from the business, I'm feeling relaxed. But you know, this doctor says not to drink a lot." He got up and started walking.

A flock of birds, the seabirds retreating to their homes, flew over us flapping their wide wings the sound of which was muffled by the roars of the waves. As we trod along, the colour of the western sky turned pinkish then purplish. The evening increasingly swept the beach while the waves roared with greater strength and sloshed on the sand.

I followed him, not knowing whether to continue to talk about the same issue or not. He was walking with the same confidence and lightness as if he had long back beaten the incurable disease with his desire to live. He took life as it came. Then why was I so weak? Why was I ruining life after a woman who did not love me?

We returned to Pretoria. The memories of Durban: the walk on the beach, the feel of swash under and around our bare feet, the dune vegetation and Doodh, the birds, the rustic bench, and the revelation from Hemanta about his life became fainter within a few days, but Mandakini remained afresh.

Six

We were on a drive along an asphalt road, which ran along the base of a high mountain. The upper half of the mountain was forested with tall pines, dotted with hanging rocks. The downhill stretch of the mountain, where the fern and wormwood bushes had taken over the pines, sloped smoothly developing into bent spurs, and further down turned into a flat land, a flat land running parallel with a river, almost as large as the Kali River and having a similar type of shingle bank with big round boulders in places.

It was a late afternoon. The sun was about to drop down over the brow of the mountain across the river, creating the shadows on the river and the riverbanks. The absence of settlements and of any other human creations formed a solitary environment on the slope. The view presented by the mountains, the pines, the slope, the flat land and the river somehow resembled the views I had come across many times in my earlier life, although the resemblance was vague, difficult to fit in any particular view or views in my memory, and although the privacy and the seclusion offered by the view, to some extent, spoke of strangeness negating the very idea of resemblance. I was in the driver's seat. Mandakini was reclining on the side seat with her usual curiosity about the outside views. At times, she would come to her normal sitting position to adjust the CD player in the car either to repeat her favourite songs or to skip the songs that did not match her taste. We did not talk, just drove, enjoying the music. The old songs.

After almost half an hour along the curvy road with a number of deep bends, we reached the end of that mountain, from where the asphalt road snaked down and ran amidst the wheat fields. Shortly we were in a small valley, or a wide gorge, surrounded by three mountains. There, the river, joined by another river coming from the opposite side, branched off to the left. The valley was green. Part of it was still gleaming in the late afternoon sunshine. There, on the side of the river before it branched off, we saw a place with tents and stalls, a crowd of people, a gathering – similar to a spring country fair or a Saturday fair. We were bewildered to see the fair in that solitary place. I pulled in the car on the roadside under a bent pine. Then both of us went to the crowded place out of our curiosity.

The farmers under the tents; the bulls and cows chewing at the hay and grain silage in old-fashioned rustic troughs inside the fenced enclosure; all sizes of rabbits hopping and sniffing in the cages; and poultry, which included chickens, geese, and pigeons of varied sizes, from small to big, which I had never seen earlier, were so amusing that we walked around from tent to tent, from stall to stall, from one place to another. Towards one side, there was a rich collection of farm tools, locally produced honey, ghee, cheese, butter, fresh juice, ginger beer, and other country products, the handicrafts, the carved wood and stones.

In one small stall, I saw beautiful stones, the pebbles in different colours and in different sizes. I selected four of them, each with different colour – bluish, pinkish, yellowish, and greenish – and turned to Mandakini to ask about her preference. I wanted to give those stones to her. But what? Mandakini was not there! We were together just now. Where did she go? I looked at the nearby stalls. She was not there either. Worrying, I went to all the stalls, walked around the whole place, yet I could not find her. I shouted, "Mandakiniiii!" No response. The shouting just muffled in the crowd. I tried to call her on the mobile, which I found to have been switched off. It was almost twilight. The crowd was becoming thinner. With the passing of each minute, my anxiety grew rapidly. Where did she go? Where did she disappear? All of a sudden.

Out of desperateness, I went to the place where I had parked the car – under the bent pine and tried to call her again, but to no avail. The stalls were taken down. The animals were carried away in big trucks. The fair disappeared just like in a fairy tale. The evening grew darker engulfing the surroundings: the mountains, the valley, the river and the oddly standing pine. Mandakini was nowhere. A growing sense of alarm and sadness grew in me with the solemnity of the environment and even more with a mournful, echoing sound of a dove. I could not see it, but I could take it that it was perching somewhere in the lower branches of the pine. Perhaps the dove was mourning the loss of a loved one.

I woke up to a melancholic cooing of a dove. The cooing, coming from the back garden, sounded precisely like the mourning of the dove in my dream. The dream was so vivid I remembered almost everything: the mountains, the rivers, the drive through the asphalt road, the valley, the fair, the unexpected disappearance of Mandakini, and the mournful sound of the dove. So the sound of a dove coming from the back of my house came out to me as a continuation of the sad dream. I woke up, walked to the kitchen, drank water, and, with a cup of tea, sat in the children's room where I would spend most of the time nowadays. After the children went back, this house with so many rooms and such a huge compound had become like a big maw. With the memories associated with Mandakini and these dreams with unsolicited endings, the house felt even lonelier.

As I pulled back the yellowish curtain, the light streamed in. The medium-sized room was full with the haphazard collection of teenager's choice. The posters and pictures pasted on the walls varied from Goddess Durga to Mount Everest to a scene of the rising sun viewed from a mountain and to yet another scene of a mountain shadow on a lake. They varied from the picture of Shrek to Madagascar Penguins to a picture of giraffe leaning on a baobab tree, the pink sky as the background view, then to abstract arts by Monir, an artist from Bangladesh about whom I had not heard much until I saw those pieces of art pasted on the walls by my daughter, Sarita. Out of Monir's seven abstract pieces pasted there, there was one, pasted aslant, entitled as *love* sketched in 1975. In that abstract art, I could see, from afar, a figurative picture of a woman sitting on a mattress on the floor with a baby in her lap. But when I observed the picture from near, I saw many human sketches in it: another woman just behind the main woman, two more babies lying on the floor, a man or a woman sleeping on a cot and two women dancing near the wall, all in their abstractness or semi abstractness. The abstract art was not my passion, yet at present with the situation of my life entangled with such deep feelings about Mandakini, I felt my own life had become like an abstract creation of a creator, like an enigma, like Monir's art.

Outside the window, the morning was maturing over the overgrown lawn. The yellowed and rotten leaves of the elephant's-ear plants were not cut away. The expanded twigs of the bladder-nut and the white milkwood, now entangled with the electric fence, were not properly trimmed. The leaves, piled around the trunk of the leopard tree and in the corners of the compound, were not removed. Papers, different-sized balls, and plastic bottles thrown by the schoolchildren during their play had not been cleared away. Even messier was the swimming pool as if it was turned into a crocodile dam and as if crocodiles would come out any time with their jaws wide open. The creepy crawly was detached and floating on the water. The status of the garden spoke of the total carelessness and negligence. It was difficult to decide who was to be blamed: I myself or Joseph? Or both of us?

I had not talked to him much about gardening. After my return from Kathmandu, with my mind always occupied by Mandakini, I had almost detached myself from many things, and the detachment had affected gardening as well. Joseph had taken advantage of my feebleness. He was not sincere like John, the previous gardener, who was professional, sincere, and aware about gardening. The garden always thrived during his period. The pool never turned green. The clear blue water always sparkled. I had learnt many things from him about the gardening, about the care of the pool, about the trees in the compound and also about the local and seasonal birds, which came to the lawn. Joseph did not possess that quality.

Anyway, beyond the compound, the streets were filled with jacarandas, at present perfectly blossoming in the purplish colour. Had Mandakini been here, how happy she would have been to see the purplish trees dominating the whole city!

The leopard tree was yet to see the effect of the spring. It would blossom in full towards the second week of November, and when it would blossom with golden flowers, it would turn into a golden tree, and the underneath earth would be blanketed with the fallen golden flowers. Such a fine-looking view!

Now it had just begun to put out new leaves. A large number of seed pods were still in the tree. Almost the same number scattered on the ground, all with dormant capacity in them to become as tall the tree as the tree in the compound. Most of these pods would be carried away by the gardener and would be composted or would be thrown; many would be swept by the rain. And the rest would sprout themselves in late summer or early autumn – in their hundreds or even in the thousands. Seeing the sprouts, it was not difficult to assume if the tree grew in a wilderness, the whole swath of land would certainly turn into a jungle of leopard trees within a few years. John had told me that it, too, like jacaranda, was not native to this country. It was brought from Brazil almost at the same time when the jacaranda was brought.

After staying a few minutes there, there in that room, I went to the backyard and stood under the oak tree, old and gnarled but bedecked with green leaves. Life had returned to this tree. The same had been the case with regard to the mulberry stump. The white pear, the aloe, the false olive: all had become green. On the other side, the western side of the compound, the tendrils of the climber, the name of which I did not know, and the morning glory had, after the winter break, started off flowering in red and blue. The spring blossoming, the fresh greenness of the trees, the flowers joined with the ripened mulberries had invited varieties of birds in the garden. Chirping, they were hopping about on the ground and the roof. The true weavers' elaborately intertwined nests of grass hung in the trees. The doves and hadedas, the all-year-round birds, were always there in the garden. Lizards had come out of hibernation to bask in the sunshine.

The backyard grass was not watered the whole winter. The weeds were not cleared up. Yet, with the approaching of the spring and perhaps with the previous week's heavy rainfall, the grassed-over part of the backyard had been slowly regaining its greenness, surprisingly, with fewer weeds. Perhaps the Zimbabwean grass planted four years back had found its strength in South African soil as John had foretold.

Yet, despite the spring's beauty, the garden at the backyard did not look less untidy. It spoke of the same carelessness and negligence. Only a swath of land was covered with grass. The corner and side against the wall in the east, where my daughters would do a little vegetable farming in their leisure, had turned into a wilderness, claimed by weeds, tall and dried, many of them exactly the same which were found in Narrow Flatland, perhaps due to the similitude between the part of the Mahabharata Hills where my hamlet was located and Pretoria in terms of altitude and latitude, despite the opposite hemisphere. Of them, there was one typical type overwhelming the wilderness. I did not know its name in English and was not sure if it belonged to the same botanical genus, but similar type of weed was found around my hamlet in plenty.

We called it *kuro* in our language. My mother and wife would always spend hours taking its prickly seeds out of their blouses and saris after they came back from the woods or the fields. John had told me that the weed found its way to South Africa from Argentina mixed with fodder for horses used by the British Army during the second Anglo-Boer War and soon became rampant over the areas where they stayed. The British Army then wore Khaki clothes, and the Boer named the weed as *Khakibos*. I was not sure whether this story was supported by facts, or it was just a rumour, exaggerated or twisted. But it was what I had heard from John, a man with a vast range of knowledge about trees, flowers, grasses, and weeds. This weed during his time was under control. But now it had spread rampantly. The other familiar one in that wilderness was the pigweed, which would grow all over in the hamlet, including in Big Plot during each summer and would be used as the vegetable often mixed with pumpkin sprouts and potato.

The side against the wall to the east had not been taken care of since John left. Joseph cared only about the pavement and the lawn. He did not care about the rest of the compound. Part of the back garden, the part filled up with pebbles, which once had been without any soils and other materials – other than the pebbles – and the walking on it would give a crunchy sensation, was now mixed with soil and other litter. It had not been washed. Weeds had grown on the pavement and under the asbestos shed. The waste, the paper, the plastic and bottles, had been scattered in every part of the backyard while two black garbage bins with the number of my house scribbled on them were lying on the ground, empty. There had been a total negligence.

I stood under the old gnarled oak tree, doing nothing, just scrunching little oak acorns, now separated from the cup-shaped bases. The dove in the aloe tree – the African mourning dove – ruffled its feathers and echoed the melancholic sound reminding me of my dream. With a clear intention to make it afraid and fly from there, I moved towards the aloe tree. The dove flew from there and perched on a wild banana in the neighbouring compound, then continued to mourn. And it was right then, in its short flight from the aloe to the wild banana, I saw that the dove had not its tail feathers. It had lost them and looked pitiable. Was it attacked by the black cat in the neighbouring house? Or maybe, it had moulted its feathers, a natural process of losing the old feathers and getting the new ones. With all those feathers gone, the dove looked pitiable. Its flight looked awkward.

It was Sunday. I spent the whole day inside the house and compound.

It had been three months since I came back to Pretoria after staying in Kathmandu, after the sentimental attachment with a girl half my age, the memories of which were still fresh, disturbing, deeply affecting my life. My belief was that, one day, time would cure my mental situation. However, it was not working as I had thought. When would that time come? How long would it take to overcome the passion? Months? Or years? Here the passage of each hour was becoming difficult.

The frequency of my calls to Devaki had become less. I had lost interest in almost all previous hobbies and had lost interest in the business. Money, the prosperity in business, had ceased to be my dream. When I did not have it, I always ran after it, but once I had a little of it, it could not give me any satisfaction. I could not save my wife. The memories of Mandakini were paining me awfully. Money had no power to heal it.

I had lost patience to stay in Pretoria. Almost a month or so back, I had asked Ahmed to find someone interested to buy the restaurant. Slanting his eyes, he had said, "Sir, what are you talking about? It's making so much money, and you want to sell it! No, sir, don't make that mistake."

I had replied, "I don't wish to stay in Pretoria any longer."

Where to go? Kathmandu was too expensive for me. My interest in that city soon diminished. The nine-month stay there had taken away my interest in the capital city. More honestly, I was afraid of facing Mandakini again. Where to go then?

Towards the late afternoon, the weather, so fine until now, broke. Thick, dark clouds gathered in the sky. Strong winds blew through the compound, showering more leaves. Lightning flashed across and thunder boomed in the sky. It began to rain hard. Within an hour, the sunny day turned into an unusually dark day. I sat in the room, the children's room, looking at the torrential rain spattering against the window and pondering the same question: where to go and what to do?

Devaki had suggested I could settle down in Pokhara after I told her that I did not want to stay in Kathmandu. She had asked me to buy a house in Pokhara and to invest a little bit in the financial market or to do a small business. But now business and making money seemed to come a long way down the list of my interests. Furthermore, I had never thought of Pokhara as an option for a permanent settling.

Yogendra Jha, my friend in Johannesburg, who had made a substantial saving from his almost five-year stay in South Africa, had gone back to Nepal and opened a business, a dairy business in his own village. He was satisfied; he had emailed me.

Chiranjibi, yet another friend working in a security company, who had been cheated by many agents and lawyers and had lost half of his saving in his efforts of obtaining a business visa with which he never succeeded, finally had given up his dream of buying forklifts and hiring them out to a cargo company. One day, he told me that, frustrated with foreign stay, he was now planning to take up farming in his own village.

The Lees in Lhasa, their little farming, and their pride for their daughter after sending her to Chengdu to study, were always in my mind. Then why not to go back to the hamlet and grow something in Big Plot?

As I thought about myself working in Big Plot where my wife had spent the whole of her married life and where I had sprinkled her ashes after her death, and as I imagined myself talking with Gopal, my childhood friend, a shaft of hope ran through my mind. Why not to do that? Doing that, I would be doing justice to my wife as well, after her death though. Over and above, I would be living closer to nature, which could heal me.

The rain continued, spattering on the roof and against the window when the wind blew. The gutters were spouting thick columns of water and leaves gathered on the roof. The outside gradually darkened. And I, as always, set out for drinking, lonely. I had taken to drinking. The drinks had become like a medicine to blunt the melancholy. Drunk, I could sleep. I could take it that Mandakini did not reject me; she needed my trust; perhaps she loved me. Every morning the hangovers were unbearable. I knew it was deteriorating my health, the whole body system. (Sometimes my upper stomach and chest would pain intolerably, and the acid would form quite frequently.) However, I was finding myself unable to get rid of the daily use of alcohol. As soon as the evening would begin, I would sit, drinking with the recollections of Mandakini and would drink until late night. It had become a habit. So, that day too, I drank until late night, recalling Mandakini, Sushmita, and the hamlet.

The rain was continuing.

After a few days, I told Ahmed that I was serious about selling the restaurant. At first, he did not believe. But later, once I said I actually meant it, he showed an interest in owning it in partnership with someone from his country. I talked to Vinod, Hemanta, and the small circle of friends about my final decision to settle in the hamlet. The idea was appreciated by some and openly criticised by many others. In sharp contrast to his previous views, Hemanta supported the idea.

One day, on the side of a dam in Pomona, where we had gone upon Vinod's request, he said, "You know, Ashok, though I said I didn't like your idea of going back, deep inside, I myself always wished to go back. Who doesn't love one's own birthplace? I wish I could go. But this damn disease! How can I tell my family and friends that I have got HIV? Jo, this damn disease!" He took a sip of some sort of juice. He had hugely cut down on his drinking and smoking. Once again, he had come over as a strong man, a man of fortified determination.

"Why can't you go back? There're so many others infected. It's just a disease like any other disease. There's no need to hide," I said, looking at the swans floating towards the tall reeds at the left corner of the dam.

"How can I show my face to my old father and mother? It's far better if I send them some money every month."

"Money isn't everything."

"Still, it's so many things."

"You can't buy happiness with money."

"And how can you be happy without it?"

"Hey, guys, look! It seems a big fish's hooked." It was Vinod, standing on the side of the dam and jerking the rod back. Fishing, like braaing, was his hobby. He had been waiting there for hours. Immediately after we reached there, he had undid his bag and fixed the fishing tackle and, with a bottle of beer, sat there in a camp chair, saying, "Guys, I want to catch a big fish today." He waited patiently for the tug on the fishing line, and finally, a fish was hooked, which was not small.

His bald head and tanned face glistened shiny. The narrow eyes lit with a sense of pride as he unhooked the fish.

The wakes left by the swans rippled and gleamed in the sunrays.

That day, after I came back to Pretoria and sat for drinking, once again, I discussed with Devaki about returning to the hamlet at length. And once again, she tried to persuade me to settle in Pokhara. Right from the beginning, as soon as I floated the idea to her, she was not happy. She told me that the village I had left was not the same, that after living abroad for years, it would be difficult to adjust myself and that there would be no one to take care of me. But, at the same time, she had also informed me that Gopal had returned to permanently settle in the hamlet after his foreign stay tired him: a further encouraging piece of information to me.

I was more determined to go to the hamlet. It was the best option for me.

Ahmed prepared the papers for the legal deal. He had found a good partner. The price had been settled. There was no bargaining. No discussion about the price. He knew the restaurant was running well and was aware of my desperateness to sell it. Yet he did not take advantage of that. He gave me the price enough for the restaurant. He was a true friend. Vinod had said he would buy the car, the Toyota Corolla. For the furniture, he had assured he would find someone. The remaining things, I could give to Amanda.

Thus, I was all set to return.

But I became sick.

Seven

Health-related problems were gradually brought on me by mental stress and continuous drinking down through the months. The sources of illness were accumulated over the years. I was not unaware of that. I knew my health was breaking down every day, with each glass of whisky, but finally it gave in. I became terribly sick.

It was before dawn. Ward No. DG3, Kloof Hospital, Pretoria East. I was lying on a bed waiting for my turn for medical procedures – X-ray, endoscopy, colonoscopy, and many others – according to the symptoms I had complained about to the doctor.

After hours of pain in the chest and upper part of the stomach, sometimes dull and at times sharp, but persistent all the time, I had called Ahmed, who, right away after my call, had come to see me in the middle of the night and had driven me to the hospital. After completing paper formalities and ensuring my admission, he had gone back for the *Fajr* prayer. It had been more than eight years since I met him first at the O R Tambo International Airport welcoming me almost indifferently and driving at breakneck speed using his loutish words. Down through the years, despite his long beard, despite different cultures, sometimes with philosophies contrary to mine, he had been the one whom I felt comfortable to call than anyone else.

Outside, the faint lights from the eastern horizon were increasingly becoming stronger, revealing the outside scene. Gradually, the houses in front of the hospital became visible. A little away, a small hillock became obvious with shrubs and scattered trees, difficult to identify. Amidst those shrubs and trees, a narrow path (or trail) went up to the crest of the hill, reminding me of my birthplace – somewhere in the secluded part of the earth, far from modern artificiality – and of so many paths and trails carved there linking one village to another, one mountain to the other and one valley to another. Walking on those trails through bushes and meadows, through dark woods, going uphill and downhill, and running alongside the rivers was always amusing to me. Those never-ending paths and trails! It used to wonder me who the first humans would have been to put their first steps on the virgin earth and to start the process of carving those endless paths and trails! Those early anonymous humans, lost solely to the history never written! Why would they have done so? For what purposes would they have carved them? In search of food? Or in search of water? In search of wood or grass for their cattle? Or were they pursuing their walks to migrate for a better life? A long and continuous process of development! What lovely days were those days: walking along the never-ending paths and wondering about! The existence of the narrow trail on the hill led me to my childhood memories.

"Good morning, Mr Pandey." A female voice brought me back to the present. A young nurse was addressing me, telling me that it was my turn. She took me to the theatre. A series of tests and procedures continued the whole day and the next day. Each time before a certain procedure, I would be administered anaesthetic drugs, and when I would come around, I would find myself being fed from a saline drip. Then after certain hours, she would take me again to the theatre and, after the test, would bring me back to the same ward.

Ahmed came in the afternoon.

It was on the third day, I was given the detailed information about my health by the doctor, the one who had greeted me the first time in the theatre. He was young and white, maybe an Afrikaner; the English he spoke sounded like that.

He came to my bed and, turning a brown file he was carrying, asked me, "Do you drink, Mr Pandey?"

"Yes, Doctor. I do. Daily. Once a while heavily, almost half a bottle of whisky."

"Do you smoke?"

"Occasionally."

"Do you exercise?"

"I used to but not now."

"What about the food habit?"

"My staples are rice and dal and vegetables. Often spicy. I love hot and spicy food."

"Mr Pandey, it's time to change yourself. I mean your food habit and your lifestyle. Drastically."

"What's that change, Doctor?"

"From today on, no alcohol, no smoking. Light and regular exercise and a healthy diet with fewer calories."

"Oh my god, that's not easy at all. But if a doctor says, I must do," I tried to smile as I responded.

"That's for your own life," he said, scribbling on the prescription slip.

I had developed numerous problems at the same time: high blood pressure, high levels of cholesterol, sugar, uric acid in the blood, and irritation in the stomach, the cause of which was to be analysed after the biopsy test. Abnormalities in my body system must have been developed long back. They should have been treated months back. Now so many problems were found together. I was advised to stay two or three more days in the hospital, then to have a complete rest at home for three weeks.

Before leaving the hospital on the fifth day with those tablets and pills, I looked at the path on the hill once more. It was stretching in the same way through the shrubs and trees and climbing up to the brow. There were a couple of human beings walking on it. A few feet away from the path, a few zebras were grazing under the sunny sky.

The doctor had suggested I needed at least three weeks of complete rest at home. Back in Waterkloof, the lone house, I was puzzling over if it would offer the homely feeling the doctor was talking about. By then, I had not told him that I was living a lonely life. Of course, as per his advice, I wanted to have a complete rest at home. But where was that home? Where was I supposed to have a complete rest? In that big house in Waterkloof? Definitely not. I could not take the house as my home. The big house and its loneliness in later days, once I returned from Kathmandu, felt like always gnawing at me. Home to me always meant the place where I grew up, Narrow Flatland, the little foothills, which was so far. The idea of home made me more desperate to return. Whatever length of life was left to be lived, I wanted to live in Narrow Flatland.

Later, during one of regular visits to him when I shared with him about the feelings and the loneliness I was going through, the doctor said, "Mr Pandey, I think you better contact a psychiatrist. He may help you to overcome your emotional stress."

So I went to see a psychiatrist. The reception itself was depressing to me. The small room; the quiet receptionist, reading a book; the two cats sitting on the chairs, one of them brown and rather furry; the tables, chairs in brownish dark colour; and the scattered cushions, some of them looking like made of the fur of the brown cat itself: everything in that room looked gloomy to my gloomy mind. Inside, the psychiatrist – with his wide bearded face that bore a resemblance to Mark's face (in Lhasa before he was married), his eyes narrow and glistening, sitting on a chair almost covered by the books piled on the table in front of him – said, in a tone sounding grave, "Mr Pandey, I think you're *clinically depressed*. You need to resort to medication."

I returned with yet another list of medicines.

I was desperate to return to the hamlet. I had sold the restaurant. The deal was already signed. I had informed the landlord that I was leaving soon, so I had not signed the lease agreement which was to expire soon, two months later. I had informed Joseph and Amanda. Joseph did not care much (at least I thought so). He just asked me what I was going to do in *Nepaad*, mispronouncing the name of my country once more. In response to my mentioning about my wish to do farming, he uttered *really* with his eyes a bit widened. Perhaps he thought the farming I was mentioning to him was as big as in South Africa, on an industrial scale. Obviously, he was not aware of the little farming in Nepal, in the rural mountains especially; he did not know that the *farming* I was thinking of being involved was small farming: growing a few vegetables or a few grains (just for killing time) in Big Plot, smaller than the compound of the house in which he was gardening now. It must have been the reason of his surprise. After the brief expression of surprise, he engaged in blowing the leaves off the pavement with his gardening blower.

But poor Amanda, who had recently lost her youngest son, responded to my mentioning of going back in her true sentiments. With tearful eyes, she said she would pray to her ancestors for my well-being and long life. She wanted me to come back with the children and wanted me to visit her home either for lunch or for dinner before leaving.

Soon after her request, I went there, somewhere in Soweto, the largest black township in the country. I went there with Vinod. Her home was not big. It was merely a shack, similar to other shacks spreading all around. The yard was full of rubble as if a structure was destroyed and the rubble was yet to be removed. At the far end of the yard was a toilet with a tin door, the old-style lock of which was broken and on the walls of which there were lizards with their half-closed or half-opened eyes. The broken lock was tied with a jute rope. At the other end lay an old gnarled tree, uprooted, but in its entirety; the tree, twisted and stripped of its bark, looked solid.

In the right shack, adjacent to hers, I noticed an iron workshop where a middle-aged bearded man was hammering relentlessly a hot iron reminding me of the father of one of my schoolmates, who was professionally a blacksmith and whom I would always see blowing charcoal with a leather bellows, putting it on an anvil and then heating it hard and shaping it into a shape: a sickle or a knife or a spade or whatever he wanted. So laborious a job! Such an important art! Yet so much neglected in the then stratified society!

The middle-aged bearded man with beads of sweat on his face and his heating the iron at once reminded me of the schooldays when I would halt by the house of a friend on my way back and would see his father sitting in a leaf-roofed hut, on the dusty floor where charcoal, wood and iron oddments scattered dustily. There, sitting beside the forge, he would blow the charcoal, move the bellows up and down and heat the iron to glow bright red, then would hammer it to create different shapes. A real creator, Bishwakarma! He would often say, "The charcoal made of young *chilaune* wood is the best one." But the local authorities did not allow him to cut the young *chilaune*.

As I saw the man in his workshop the memories of those past years, now blurred with the passage of time, at once came to me very vividly.

The middle-aged bearded man later joined us to have drinks: Amanda had invited him. His name was Tsifitso or something sounding like that. It was, indeed, enjoyable to sit with him, having lunch: pap, lamb stew, *mogudu*, pumpkin, and a few other vegetables (made especially for us) and of course *umqombothi*, which we drank one by one without putting the jug on the floor until we finished it as demanded by their tradition. Drinking *umqombothi*, sitting on the hand-knitted mat in the dusty backyard – just like drinking *chhang*, sitting on the straw mat in the yard or in the bare field in Gurunggaun in my birthplace during ceremonies – was like a ceremony. Sitting in the yard, as I further talked with Tsifitso about the cultures and traditions – superstitions rooted deep in society, things of good and bad auguries; the ominous sense after the road being crossed by a black cat or the inevitability of something bad if sweeping the floor after the sunset; the practice of exorcism or the witchcraft and the occult – or about the belief in the traditional way of healing, the use of cow dung while smearing the yard and veranda, the use of grinding and threshing tools and suchlike, how amused I felt! How puzzling it was to note that two faraway societies, between which any kinds of communication were seemingly not possible until a few hundred years back, shared similar sets of beliefs and traditions! Were those traditions carried along with the first migration of humans from Africa to Asia or Europe as suggested by the anthropologists, or did those beliefs travel back from Asia to Africa? If so, how? Or did human societies carry a typical character of imagining similar things in similar ways despite their being geographically so distant? Anyway, it was amusing to be with Tsifitso and to have drinks sitting in the yard somewhere in Soweto, Johannesburg.

Despite my desperate desire to leave, I had to stay a few more months, almost another five months or so after I saw the doctor. He wanted to be assured that the medicines, the different coloured tablets and pills I was administered, had the desired effect and the damaged systems in my body would begin to work again. So, in spite of my efforts to persuade him that the treatments I would receive in Nepal would match his and that the tablets and pills I was taking could be found in Nepal, he did not advise me to leave until he was satisfied, which took nearly five months. Time, each day and night, during those five months, felt weary. With nothing to do, relieved from the business, I mostly strolled inside the compound with occasional drives on the freeways, looking at the maturing leaves on the trees and the browning savannah grass.

Sometimes, I went to see my friends working and doing business with a perpetual feeling of frustration of not knowing when their papers would be ready, and they could go back, or when they would be able to save money to work off the heavy loans, and very often, with a shaft of anger for the agents who had cheated them and who, in most instances, were their own relatives or acquaintances. I could hear their loutish words for the agents. I could see them counting the years, if saving at the current level, how long it would take to pay the loan, which in most cases would not be less than five years to almost a decade. They were worried about what would happen to their family in that one decade. How would they spend such a long time parted from them?

Now with the restriction in our drinking, the Friday braai had become rare. We would rather go to the dam side in Pomona.

Mandakini had not gone away. The only improvement in my feelings about her was that the flame of anger and jealousy, while imagining her with any other man, had subsided a little bit. Was that the effect of time? Or of the pills I was taking?

It was in late July, in my routine check-up, the doctor, after observing the latest reports, said, "Mr Pandey, I can see some improvements in your health. Blood pressure is in control. The level of cholesterol and uric acid has slightly gone down. The sugar level also has become constant. You can go back to your beloved country."

"Thank you, Doctor. I wanted to hear these words for so long. Thank you so much," I said, excitedly.

"But make no mistake. You must continue with all medications every day throughout your life. No interruption. And no alcohol and smoking at all," he said, writing a prescription for me. "I have given you the medicines for two months. I have written the most popular generics of these medicines which are available around the world. If you have difficulty in getting these, you can mail me."

"I *will*, Doctor. Certainly. Thank you so much," I said, shaking his hand.

"Take care and best wishes." These were his last words as I walked out. Outside, a few patients were waiting for their turn, some of them looking at the path across the narrow valley and grazing zebras.

Soon after, the following week, on a fine morning, I left the house in Waterkloof. The departure was not enjoyable. It was true that I was desperate to go back. It was also true that the big house in later days had lost the original attraction that I had for it; it had ceased to offer the feeling of peace that I had felt earlier. But the leaving, the departure from the place where I had stayed for so many years, was sad. The house felt abandoned. The grazing hadedas turned their heads towards me as I got in the car. The twittering birds, the lawn, the trees, and the *chautari-like* creation gave me a sense of melancholic farewell. The street leading to Koningin Wilhelmina Avenue was canopied by the bare branches of jacarandas, through which the young sunlight slanted, making the street striped.

The sky was bright and blue. On both sides of the highway, the savannahs, now in browns, stretched into the distance.

I left Pretoria.

On my way to the airport, I was thinking about the initial days in Africa, those struggles and the successful business, the time spent with Hemanta, Vinod, Amanda, Joseph, and, most importantly, Ahmed, who was driving me for the last time to the airport. Unlike his usual habit, he was driving unhurriedly. He had opened half an inch of the front window on his side through which the wind came in roaring and blowing his hair and the beard, almost a handful long. Hemanta and Vinod were at the airport to see me off. The farewell was simple yet emotional; none of us spoke much. We were choking to utter the few words which we uttered.

As the plane took off, I bade my last farewell to Johannesburg. The buildings and houses, the roads and cars, the wide expanse of South African lands, the veld gradually fell away as the plane took more height and headed north.

And in Kathmandu, as I saw miniature houses from the sky, I tried to locate the house where I had met Mandakini. How would she look like? Had she planted the flowers in the alley way this year too? It became so difficult to resist the temptation to see her, that dainty girl, with frequently changing colours and looks.

I went to the bus station directly from the airport and took a bus to Pokhara. That night, I was to stay with Devaki and the children. The bus ran on the road which itself ran along the gurgling rivers between the lush mountains. The hilly countryside and green rice paddies bespoke a good monsoon. The August sun was strong. Out of my window seat, up in the sky, thin and patchy monsoon clouds were scudding across. And down, in places on the riverbanks, there were fishermen throwing and hauling in their nets. On the riverbanks, there were also the sporadic views of the men and women hammering down the pebble stones, calling up the faint memories of similar views long back in Lhasa, on the riverbank where I would often go with Thakur to watch similar men beating pebbles, and among them an old man holding a hammer in his shaking hand and beating out those round stones in a rhythmic beating sound. The faint memories came and went throughout the travel. But what came to me more acutely and more frequently, or almost continuously, was the memory associated with that dainty girl, Mandakini.

I closed my eyes, squeezed the bridge of my nose with my thumb and middle finger, putting the index one on the forehead and whispered, "Mandakini."

Back to the Hamlet

One

Most of the fodder trees around the hamlet looked bare; obviously, they were pruned to feed the cattle. The poinsettias, which had dominated the untrimmed hedgerows along the narrow path leading to the little foothill with crimson-coloured flowers and green broad leaves until December or even mid-January, became straggly with sticky stems, bare and curvy at the tops. The bougainvillea plants in Gurunggaun flowered in variegated colours. Up the mountain, the rhododendrons had just begun to blossom. The terraced fields across the stream were vacant except for a few terraces cropped with wheat and mustard, on which lean figures of scarecrow (with funny clothes and hats) were put to scare the birds away, but interestingly, birds often dared to perch on those hats. Mulberries were ready to come out. So were raspberry and barberry bushes. Chestnut and *chilaune* trees still remained with old leaves. Though the westerly breeze blew mildly cold through the field, the sun was warm. The season gave a mixed impression of waning winter and approaching spring. It was a fine sunny day of mid-February.

Ashok perched on the berm, looking at Big Plot, now ablaze with new colours. Green wheat plants swayed in the afternoon breeze in the northern allotment. In another allotment, just beside the wheat allotment, mustard plants had flowered yellow, inviting bees to dart and hum around. Plump red tomatoes hung on the bamboo stakes and nylon tendrils in cascades, cauliflowers bloomed white, and wide potato leaves grew green. There were other vegetables, flowers, and annuals growing up in the field, more than half of which was cultivated while another half was left vacant to be used as the playground for the children. He was satisfied with what he had achieved in last six months. A little happiness and peace was finally coming within his reach.

But it had taken weeks to succeed at his idea.

He had come back to the hamlet to spend the rest of life in country solitude and devote the remaining energy to the soil in Big Plot, where he had scattered the ashes of his wife's dead body. He had returned with a hope that all wounds would be healed by the proximity of pure nature where he spent the early years, and the pain would be taken away with the passage of time. And though it had taken time, it was this place, his birthplace, which, at the last, gave him the sense of peace.

The very first day, almost six months back, in August, as soon as he stepped into the yard, plonking the bag on the veranda, he went, through the narrow alley between the house and the shed, to see Big Plot. The thick clumps of rice plants were swaying in the August breeze, the rustling of which sounded as if whispering in his welcome and encouraging him to enjoy life. The memories of Sushmita were evoked nostalgically. He felt that her soul was there. After standing for a while there with old memories, when he went back to the yard, he found Gopal chatting with Devaki.

"Dai, you came back? I was sure you would come back. I'm so happy to see you and to hear that you'll stay here. After Bikram migrated to the bazaar, I was afraid I'm the odd man out in our generation to live in this village. Finally, you're here," Gopal said, touching his feet.

"Gopal, how're you, my brother? Don't touch the feet," Ashok said, giving him a tight hug.

Ashok's eyes met Gopal's. Running around the hamlet, walking in the woods and through the bushes, grazing the cattle, playing in the foothills and on the stream bank: those early years came to his mind.

Perhaps in Gopal's mind too. The sudden meeting after so many years felt emotional. They gazed at each other for long.

"Dai, have a cup of tea. You must be hungry. I'll prepare the meal. Gopal, why don't you take your evening meal with Dai?" Devaki appeared with tea in two cups.

"Why not? But ask your Bhauju not to prepare for me."

"What about your children? How's Pooja," Ashok asked him, though he already knew it from Devaki, who had become more talkative and had informed him of almost everything about Gopal's family and the villagers in the surrounding villages on their way from Pokhara to the hamlet.

"Prakash is in Dubai. You know, Dai, he's a father now?" Gopal responded.

"So you're a grandfather! At such a young age! Is it a boy or girl?"

"A girl. She looks pretty. She's already two years old. Maybe you know he was a Maoist supporter from his childhood, the whys and wherefores I never knew. He was ready to join the combatants. Pooja was worried about him. So we got him married. At first, he declined, but when he saw the bride he couldn't say no. See, this boy!"

Both of them laughed.

That evening, they took their meal – rice, vegetable curry (sponge gourd), and pickled bitter gourd – together, sitting cross-legged on the wooden *pirkas* around the hearth. Ashok found the old round *pirka*, the same on which he used to perch on throughout the years until he left the hamlet, still in the same form, solid and shiny, as if waiting these many years for him to perch on it again.

The conversation continued.

"Dai, what's your plan? Are you going to stay in the hamlet?" Gopal asked. "I heard you made a lot of money. Enough to stay in the cities and do some business."

"Money? You know, Gopal, whatever you earn, it doesn't fulfil your temptation. You're always tempted to earn more and more up until your death. And when you die, you can't take with you even a penny. I'm tired of the city life. I have missed my hamlet a lot. I'm here to spend the rest of life."

"You're right. I ruined quite enough of my energy in foreign soil. But what did I get? Just grey hairs and wrinkles around the eyes," Gopal said, putting a chestnut log into the hearth. "But the people nowadays want to go abroad at any cost. It's difficult to find the young in the villages these days. You see, I asked my son to stay here with me, but he didn't listen to me and went to Dubai after paying almost two lakh. It's already two years, and he hasn't earned even half of that. Thanks to god, I had saved some to bear his cost. If I had to take a loan, it would have already become three lakh with the interest."

"We Nepalese, anyhow, want to fly in a jet and touch foreign soil," Ashok said.

"But what they can do by staying here? If you don't go abroad at least once, you can't even find a wife," Devaki chimed in, snapping more twigs and feeding the fire. The damp twigs were stubbornly resisting the fire. The narrow kitchen filled with smoke, and tears pricked their eyes. "Oh, this firewood! If I cook food with this wood, it's going to kill me. It doesn't burn, just smokes. I already finished almost half a gallon of paraffin, but they don't burn. Dai, the first thing you need to do is to buy a gas stove and cylinder," she added, dousing the hearth with the remaining paraffin. The fire blazed.

"Devaki, you should have told me earlier. I could have already arranged one. Anyway, I'm going to the bazaar the day after tomorrow. I'll take Dai with me. We'll buy whatever he needs."

"I don't know how Dai can stay alone in this house," Devaki fussed.

"Why do you worry, Devaki? I'm here. After all, it's our hamlet. We'll enjoy ourselves here," Gopal said. "Dai, it's becoming late. Let me go now. I'll take you around the hamlet tomorrow. You'll see how it has changed."

"OK, Gopal. See you tomorrow," he said goodbye to Gopal without showing the physical and emotional wreck he was struggling with.

That very first evening of arrival, before going to bed, he stood in the yard, looking into the sky. The post-monsoon sky was clear. Perhaps it was a new moon. He could see the brightly glowing stars and an arc of faded light spraying in the sky – the light from the Milky Way, the *Mandakini*. Then, after taking the pills and tablets, he went to bed with a heavy heart as usual.

From the next day, he began to walk around, sometimes with Gopal and sometimes alone. Devaki busied herself cleaning the house, removing the spider webs from the corners, sweeping the dust away, or layering the walls and floor with mud and dung. When Ashok would come back after his walking, he would find her smudged with dust and smoke and often complaining why he chose to stay in the hamlet.

As was told by Gopal, the hamlet had gone through a lot of changes. The landscape in total, as seen from the yard, had not altered much. Yet the properties therein had gone through vast changes. These were the same woods and fields, the same rural setting with picturesque view in which he had spent so many years, but now there remained only a few properties to offer the feeling of old intimacy he was anticipating. In some cases, the changes had occurred so extensively that the very notion about the hamlet which he had carried throughout his foreign stay seemed to be obsolete. The picture of the hamlet which was pictured in his mind before he left for abroad and was cultivated down through all these years did not match the hamlet he found after fifteen years. On previous occasions, when he had visited the hamlet, he did not notice the changes much or did not care much about them. Now, when he came back with the idea of staying for the rest of life there, the changes were massive. He had to almost struggle to fit his a priori conjecture about the hamlet – the conjecture based on the childhood experience of that solitary Arcadian life – into the present realities.

The sun, as always, rose in the eastern sky and travelled across and dipped down the mountains in the far west as it would when he was a child; at night, the moon cast the silvery light all over as it would cast before; the brilliant canopy of stars was there in the sky as it would exist years back; and the mountains stood calm in all directions, but there was no one to take them in deep. There were no grandmothers to tell the stories of sixty thousand Valikhilyas who pulled the golden chariot of the sun god and of the *Apsaras* who danced in front of him. Nor was there anyone to tell *the Tale of Tota and Maina* or *the Tale of Sisir and Basanta* or the stories of prince and princess with formulaic expressions – *once upon a time . . .* or *there was a beautiful princess with golden hairs . . . .* There was no one keen to spend hours under the moonlit sky, looking at the Pole Star and Orion.

Was it possible for him to stay here for the rest of life, he often asked himself without showing any such feelings to Devaki.

Time and again, Devaki said to him, "Dai, you see the village isn't the same as you left. You can't find any of our generation. I don't think you can stay here. You should have better stayed in Kathmandu or Pokhara."

He would respond, "I prefer to stay here in this hamlet rather than in the cities. The children are grown up. I'm sure they're happy with you. I'm not far from them. It's just a matter of four hours' drive. I'll frequently come to see you and the children. But I want to stay here."

A great deal of change had occurred in the woods, in the little foothills, and in the daily life of the villagers.

He could not see the ones he had left fifteen years back. The whole generation was absent: many had died, many had migrated, and many were still abroad. The elders he had left had died. Even if there were some, they were living solitary lives, obsolete, almost discarded. The young had become adults, and the children had become young. So even though the hamlet and surroundings consisted of not many people, he had to ask Devaki to know who was who when he came back in the post-monsoon evening.

And these new people! They had a new style of living, both culturally and materially. They were trying to adopt or were just pretending to have adopted the modern lifestyle, sometimes feeling ultra-modern. The elders no more got respect from the youths; the idiomatic notion of *your elders and betters* was as though forgotten. Festivals had gone through a great deal of cultural and traditional decadence. They were now more of a mere ritual or an occasion to exhibit possessions and wealth. Teej festival, which fell just two weeks after his arrival and for which he had gone to the primary school to see, felt no more interesting with those recorded pop-style music and songs; they had lost the soothing originality. *Lakhe Naach* was replaced by modern dances. Kali Temple up in the mountain was defiled and the bells therein despoiled, Yam Bahadur said. Dashain mantras were almost forgotten, Gopal informed.

There were very few cattle so they did not have to wander around the fields and woods for the grass. They no longer went to the spring below the hamlet to fetch drinking water, for the water pipe was laid from the little stream to the hamlet. The clay hearths were replaced by the gas stoves, and the paraffin oil lamp were discarded by the electric bulbs. The radio had become obsolete. They had the television sets. The vegetables, creepers and annuals in the vegetable plots in front of the houses and around the manure heaps, were rare. Swaths of fields were left barren.

Devaki once said, "Nowadays, there's no one to work in the fields. It's much easier to buy in the bazaar."

Padam's house was totally pulled down to the sloped level of the mountain. A few other round houses were also absent. New oblong constructions were added to, with corrugated tin roofs.

The old tradition and culture were increasingly disappearing or becoming less cultural and more like fashion.

"After Gurung Sainla Dai and Paudel Dai died, nobody sings *malsiri* in Dashain. We can watch and listen to the *rodhi song* only on the television. They no longer exist in the villages," Gopal sighed.

What a surprising change!

Children did not play at being the prince and princess, rather played at being Spider Man or Ninja. *Kabaddi* and *dandi biyo* were long back replaced by football and cricket, although in the absence of the real cricket bats, they had to use the tree branches.

What an enormous change! Was it the same hamlet, Ashok wondered?

Together with the banyan and *peepal* tree in the *chautari*, all tall trees he was familiar with were gone. The old chestnut that blossomed and bore fruit every autumn had disappeared from the wood to the east of the hamlet. The tallest *chilaune* at the foot of which there used to be the shrine for Ban Jhankri and Banaki was just a stump, decaying fast. The bamboo bush just below *the chautari*, where a pair of squirrels used to play before going to their drey, was also absent.

And with the absence of the tall trees, the flocks of crows and mynah birds had migrated somewhere. They did not perch on the newly grown trees. A few ones had chosen high-voltage electric wires, which hung loose in the sky supported by the pylons posted at the intervals of a long distance, to perch on. The majority had literally disappeared. There were no hawks to pause in the sky and swoop down. He did not see the swallow's nest under the eaves of his house. The green parrots had ceased to come to the millet fields. The *karyangkurungs* had stopped to pass over Narrow Flatland in their long voyage to the south. And those vultures and *kakakuls*? They did not plane high up in the sky. Had they died out? The thought of vultures led him years back, to the vultures, the *dakinis*, around the sky burial place in Lhasa. The angels of heaven, carrying the human souls to the heavens! Was it possible that they too had died out? He hoped not.

In the little foothills, the wormwood clumps were being replaced fast by an alien variety of plant which was rampantly claiming every part of the hills.

"This weed is just spreading everywhere, taking over every other species," Gopal said as they stood atop the eastern foothill.

The weed had grown up to knee-high height in some places. The dusty and dungy trails, made by the cattle hooves, had vanished and been reclaimed by the pasturage. In fact, due to the construction of the motor roads, the narrow country paths used for hundreds of years had lost their relevance. A few had already returned to the pre-construction phase. Some others were increasingly being occupied by nature. People preferred to use the motor roads for their walks and for driving cattle rather than the ancient paths or trails. These new tracks were unplanned, haphazardly running up and down with sharp blinds, dips, and ruts. The jeeps moving on them would get stuck often, demanding pushes by passengers from behind.

Although the changes were enormous, beyond his imagination and affecting every aspect of life, it was his hamlet for which he had always longed. It was the last phase of his life. If he was to survive, if he was to continue for a few more years, he required a peaceful state of mind which was not possible to find anywhere on earth other than here. So he began life in the hamlet.

But it took time. It took time to mingle with the new people, to familiarise himself with the new cattle, to get rid of their dismissive look, to acquaint himself with the new trees, and to carve out the trails in the woods.

He cleaned the spring below the hamlet, which had been discarded by the new people and brought it back to its earlier shape. The other well in the wood had vanished. Gopal and he tried hard, almost the whole day, but could not dig out the source of the well. "It seems the well went dry along with the cutting down of that tall *chilaune* tree," Gopal had said, pointing to a place, a little up, where the tree used to stand.

Ashok sighed, wiping his sweat with a chestnut leaf.

Within a month or so of his arrival, he brought young saplings of the banyan and *peepal* tree and planted them in the *chautari*. He walked in the woods, trying to carve his own paths. He planted a few annuals in the plots in front of the yard and in front of the shed, which was rock-hard to dig for it had not been dug for years.

He chatted with the new people and tried to laugh with the children, which surprisingly began with his speechless communication with Gopal's granddaughter at the very second morning of his arrival. He had gone to Gopal's house to have tea. There he saw her, scurrying behind a pigeon with her odd steps. Maybe all other members of the family were busy in the cowshed or in the kitchen or at the water tap. She was left alone. When she saw him, she got a slight fright and looked a bit nervous.

Sweeping her up into his arms, he asked, "What's your name?"

Touching the collar and the top button of his shirt with her little hands and looking down, she mumbled something, from which he could not make out anything.

A young woman appeared from the cowshed, her hand still dungy. Understandably, she was Gopal's daughter-in-law, the mother of the baby.

Bowing in front of him, she said to the little girl, "Prakriti, don't spoil Grandfather's shirt. Look how dirty your hands are."

"So your name is Prakriti! What a lovely child you are!" he patted her on the back, then, turning to the woman, asked, "How old is she?"

"Last month, she completed two years. Please have a seat. Father is milking the buffalo," she said, bringing a wooden chair into the yard.

Ashok sat, Prakriti still in his arms, burrowing her head into his left shoulder.

Gopal appeared with a bucket of milk and sat on the veranda, saying, "Did you sleep well, Dai? Ishwari, take this milk in and make tea for Dai. Put plenty of milk in."

They drank tea, chatting. The little child followed her mother to the kitchen.

The same day, in the afternoon, he was talking to Devaki about the things required to be done for his settling in. Prakriti walked to his house with her unsteady steps (she had just learnt to walk) and sat beside him. Her coming in her unsteady steps and sitting placidly beside him was so charming that he felt swept along by enormous affection for her.

Such had been the first encounter with Prakriti, Gopal's granddaughter, in a way his too. Along with the passage of time, he knew other children too in the hamlet and the nearby villages, but she became the special one though it had taken long for him to bring her out of herself.

Taking the motor road, he would often walk her all the way up to Magargaun to the west or to Khadkagaun to the east. He would show her the mountain contours being silhouetted against the pink sky, would teach her to catch dragonflies, and show her the birds flying back to their nests. And when a jeep would appear, he would pick her up and would stand a little up on the slope to avoid mud spatters; she was not comfortable with the old jeep, with its loud noise and the honking. She would burrow her head into his chest until the jeep vanished around another bend, blowing out thick smoke. *What an odd addition to the solitude*, he would often think when he would see the smoke-layered and mud-spattered grass verges on the edge of the track. The newly built motor roads had desecrated the pure country nature.

With these walks, Prakriti increasingly became comfortable with him, more comfortable than with her own grandpa.

Ashok adapted gradually. Gradually, it appeared to him that his decision to return to the hamlet was right. The natural surroundings and the simple pleasures of the rural life helped him to heal mentally. Despite the awareness of his sick life and dependency on pills, he grew to feel to have survived. Despite the fact that the memories of Mandakini came occasionally and at times hung long, he grew to enjoy life. The memories were now sweet and soft, pleasant – like the petals of flowers in his garden or the stars in the sky or the light of the moon. He could imagine her with any other man, yet without feelings of anger or jealousy.

In due course of time, the rice plants in Big Plot pollinated, offering sweet fragrances and bore rice. They yellowed. Eventually, in early November, they were cut down and piled in the dome-shaped ricks.

With great support from Gopal, he ploughed the field, divided it into allotments – allowing half of it to remain vacant for the play area for the children – and seeded the annuals, vegetables, flowers, and grains. Much of his time began to be occupied in the plot: watering the plants, packing the manure and soil down around them, staking them, and helping the tendrils go up.

Sometimes, he would visit to Gopal's farm – the poultry farm – to watch the fast growing healthy chickens, their little swivelling colourful heads; he listened to their squeaks; and smelt the sting of guano which was not uncomfortable to him anymore. Gopal's passion for farming had been known to him ever since they had been young, but now, when he saw Gopal involved in his passion, with dawn to dusk devotion,

Ashok realised how satisfactory life would become when someone would become engaged in his real interest.

Now, after half a year of his arrival, as he perched on the berm and looked at his field, flourishing with plants, even in winter, he thought his life at last came to a satisfactory stretch. A few drops of sweats, the little produces, the small pleasures, and the feeling of being near with Sushmita were what he was aspiring for throughout life. Why did he leave the hamlet? Why did he always run after a mirage? Why did he go beyond his Narrow Flatland, despite the request of his wife? He asked himself perching on the field berm.

The sky grew twilit. The children left the play area, the other part of the field. Prakriti appeared in the orchard with a beanie on her head.

"*Glandfathel!*" she mumbled. Along with her age, her mumbling and staggering were steadily progressing. Often, she would come to his field, mimic working with him, try to catch dragonflies and butterflies, speak to him with her mumbles, difficult to decipher, and would then walk staggeringly to the other part of the field.

"*Glandpa* is calling you."

"Come here, my little granddaughter. But *whele* is your *glandpa?*" he mimicked her *l* for *r* and hugged her, squeezing.

"Ouch, it hurts, *Glandfathel*. He's *thele*."

Before she finished, Gopal came and, sitting beside him, said, "Dai, your field looks tempting. You put in lots of efforts into it."

"It'll look nicer once the roses flower. Devaki had sent me at least three or four different varieties of roses. I planted them the day before yesterday in that patch. It may be a little early for the rose, yet I hope it'll work," Ashok said, pointing towards the patch with rose plants, still bare. "It's more than a week I haven't seen your birds. How're they? Are they growing well?"

"They're ready to sell. These boilers grow fast. It was just five weeks ago I brought them. Now the vet says I need to sell them within ten days. I have put aside a few for us. That's why I came here to call you for the celebration. You must be tired."

"What a fantastic idea! But I'm afraid of your vegetarian wife. I don't like to offend her so often."

"We'll prepare in your kitchen and eat in your room, as always. This isn't the first time we're celebrating in your room. Why are you afraid of her?"

"Just give me a few minutes. I'll have a quick shower," Ashok said.

"By then I'll slaughter the chicken and clean it," Gopal said.

"But do it here, in the orchard, not in the yard," Ashok cautioned.

"I'll bring it here. Just wait for me. Prakriti, let's go home. Mummy is looking for you," Gopal said as he left, holding her hand.

After the shower, Ashok came back in the orchard to see Gopal preparing a stone fire pit. A big sickle, two large bowls, brushwood, and tinder were already there. The chicken with soft white downs was lying on the ground: trussed with a jute rope, its wings spread. With its half-closed eyes and its mouth agape, it looked terrorised and nervous at being separated from the group and tied up in the open after the sunset. It was a pity to see the downy chicken in that condition.

Without worrying much about the poor situation of the chicken, Gopal put the firewood and tinder in the pit and lit the fire. A plume of smoke rose and spread into the maturing evening. Putting the sickle under his right foot, the blade turned up, he held the chicken with his two hands – one on the head and the other on the body part – and slaughtered it at once. The poor bird, before being slaughtered, made an odd sound and opened its mouth wider.

"You know, Dai? In Dubai, I worked in a butcher's for a couple of months. The salary was good, but it was a cruel job. It constantly reminds you of human cruelty to innocent animals. I didn't enjoy the job. But what to do? You're not in a position to say no," Gopal said, putting the meat in a bowl.

"In a foreign country you're ready to do any kinds of work. And you feel below your dignity to do that particular work in your own soil. Isn't it? Look at our narrow thoughts!" Ashok said.

Gopal laughed, continuing his work.

"All my chickens grew strongly. Not a single one died of disease. I was afraid. I'm hoping to make more money from this lot than I saved in Dubai in a year. I don't know why I spent so many years in the Gulf?" Gopal said while Ashok poured the millet wine into the steel glasses later that evening.

"You're sweating your blood. You'll obviously enjoy the fruits of that," Ashok said, taking a deep sip.

Despite the doctor's advice, either to quit or not to exceed a glass, Ashok had taken to drinking, every day, often exceeding the limit. The doctor's limit was too little for him. Whenever he poured a drink – the locally produced millet wine – in his glass, the amount always surpassed the amount prescribed by the doctor in millilitres that virtually disappeared at the bottom of the tall steel glass which he used. The steel glass was perfect to hide the drink from other people, particularly from Gopal's wife who might sneak into the room to find Gopal drinking.

"You know, Dai? Prakash has eventually realised. He called me and said he wants to come back forever. Poor boy!" Gopal said. "By coming Dashain, he'll be here. I'm going to slaughter a goat at Kali Temple up in the mountain. Once he's here, I'll begin farming on a larger scale. After this lot, I'll buy two different varieties of chicken. I'll plant ginger in the millet fields and orange trees on the north-facing slope, which I think is good for the orange. Once he's here, both of us will be dedicated to farming."

He was in a jubilant mood.

"You're drinking again? I know you're determined to spoil Dai. Just like you," Pooja shouted from the yard, Prakriti on her lap.

"Don't you see I'm talking to Dai? Go home, I'll come soon. This woman doesn't even allow me to talk to Dai. Prakriti come here," Gopal said with a slight irritation.

"But don't be late. Tomorrow you need to go to the bazaar to bring the chicken feed," she said. Her voice trailed away as she disappeared in the dark.

Prakriti came in and sat on Ashok's lap.

"What's this, *Glandfathel?*"

"My little granddaughter, this is my medicine."

"Do you have a *fevel, Glandfathel?* I had a *fevel* and my *glandma* gave me this much. But it was *bittel,*" she said. Her face grimaced.

"Dai, she feels comfortable with you more than with me."

"Why not? I love her so much," Ashok said, hugging her. "Is she also a vegetarian, Gopal?"

"Everyone in the house except me. It's becoming late. I have to go. Do you need anything from the bazaar?"

"Maybe two packets of cigarettes."

Gopal left with Prakriti.

Outside, the starlit night was cold. After Gopal left, Ashok stood, walked, stood, and walked again across the yard. Blowing a long puff, he looked into the sky, the constellations, *the Mandakini.*

A hacking cough came from deep inside. The chest pained. He went to the room, swallowed the pills, and burrowed inside the blanket, coughing.

Two

The monsoon became relentless. The rain was continuing for not less than a week – sometimes in drizzles, otherwise in torrents. The heavy clouds reigned in the sky throughout. Both the streams around the hamlet swelled and flooded the fields on the sides. The fields, even the ones away from the streams, were filled up to the level of the berm with the rainwater. The baby plants of rice looked like they were struggling to retain their grip on the earth.

Small landslides occurred everywhere: in the fields, on the bare slope, and in the woods. Parts of the motor road linking his hamlet to Khadkagaun were washed away. An electric pylon up in the mountain had fallen down, damaging a cowshed. The underground water pipes were exposed here and there. The same monsoon, which had brought joy to the peasants a month back, was now worrying them. The blessing of *Indra,* the rain god, had turned into a curse. With a *sekhu* on the back and spade in the hand, the peasants came out to their fields to tame the water and to redirect the flow. They became busy staking the dilapidated and slanted walls of their sheds. Looking into the cloudy sky, they babbled to themselves. Pets were stranded inside the sheds. Caked with their own dung and fed solely on hay and dry maize stalks, they bellowed and bleated quite often. Frogs croaked before the evening grew dark. Fireflies studded the nights. With electricity disrupted, Gopal had to hang lanterns to warm up the pullets. The peasants who had prayed for the rain a few weeks back were now impatient for its halt.

"What a rainy monsoon!" saying to himself, Ashok sat in the armchair he had somehow fitted into the narrow room in which he used to sleep: a new arrangement he had made before the rain came. He had shifted the bed to the opposite room and had put a low table and the armchair in that room. He had thought of pulling down the whole structure and making a new house: oblong shaped with wider doors, more windows, balconies, and a bigger veranda. But later, he gave up the idea and continued with the old structure, with the smoke-stained rafters and beams, which retained the strength and solidity even after decades. He preferred to continue with the narrowness inside the thick mud wall. So he gave up the idea of a new house and made just a few changes. He put a cement coat on the lower walls, the veranda, the yard-ridge, and the *tulasi math* and put the corrugated tin on the roof on the veranda and the *mandir*. The woodwork got acrylic paints in blues and greens. The biggest change occurred was with regard to the shed; it suffered a drastic change. It was completely taken down; an outdoor toilet and a goat pen were constructed in that place.

The whole day, he was busy in Big Plot. The continuous rain worried him that the berm could not hold back the rainwater any longer and would crumble down any moment. The whole day, he busied himself: digging small cuts, the outlets, in different parts of the berm to let the excess water out, ensuring that the ditches are not blocked, putting stones and sod in those places where the berm was too soft or was overflowing.

And now he came back, furled the umbrella, hung it on the wall under the eaves, and, after drying the wet hands and legs, sat in the armchair, saying, "What a rainy monsoon." On the radio, the news about rain-wrought havoc throughout the country, landslides in the mountains and floods in Terai, was being broadcast. *What would have happened in Thakur's village, which was not away from the bank of the Bagmati?* He wondered.

The spatters against the roof and on the maize plants with changing rhythms continued to fill his ears. A gust of wind entered the room and flapped the pages of the books on the shelves. He saw Prakriti in the midway walking towards his yard, covered with a plastic sheet, which flapped in that sudden gust of the wind. She stood for a while, as if confused whether to pursue her walking or to go back and play with the tabby cat, which Gopal had brought from Gurunggaun. At first, the tabby, a new animal to her, and its miaowing and sometimes long yowls had made her afraid of it, but during the course of time, she was befriended by it. Its swaying tail, the content purr while sitting beside the hearth, and its licking buffalo milk in a pewter bowl gave her fun. She dared to touch it and then to play with its ears and at the last catch the swaying tail. The cat in turn miaowed, curling its tail around her legs. Later, a kind of special bond grew between them. Nowadays, she mostly stayed inside the house playing with the tabby. The frequency of her coming to his house was reduced only to the moments when the rain came in a drizzle. And each time she came, covered with a white plastic sheet, she slipped on the mossy yard and fell, muddying herself. But courageously, each time, she managed to stand up again before anyone noticed. She was blessed with a remarkable level of tolerance. She never cried. But this time, the gust made her panic. The plastic sheet flew away. She ran to Ashok's house and slipped on the yard. She cried.

Her right knee was cut; the blood was oozing out.

"Oh, Prakriti, my child. Does it hurt you? I'll hit this yard, which hurt my Prakriti. I'll stop this rain and wind, which made you fall," he said.

"Can you close the holes in the sky, *Glandfathel*? My mummy says *thele ale* holes in the sky. The *watel* comes *flom thele*," she said, pointing her right hand up. She stopped crying, but her little plump cheeks still wet with tears.

"Yes. Why not? I can close all those holes."

"*Glandfathel*, can you take me on a plane?"

"Of course. Once you're grown up, we'll fly together."

"Let's take the tabby too."

She then played on her own.

After a little while, when they were having tea, Gopal came running. "Dai, please come," he said with a marked panic in his voice and ran back at the same speed as he had come.

And what he saw there from Gopal's yard was scary. A wide patch of land to the east of the house – a few chestnut and *chilaune* trees and a thick bamboo grove in it – had slid deeply, threatening the very existence of the cowshed. The gap between the landslide and the shed was not more than a few feet and the mud was still sliding. The house itself was at stake. Pooja and Ishwari were looking at the slide with a panicky face, and in that state of panic, Pooja was uttering words of prayer to Indra, the rain god, "Hey Prabhu, hey Indra Bhagawan, please save us."

However, Indra was deaf that day. The rain became torrent again, the landslide spread, and, before they had time to turn the cattle loose and drive them to a safer place, gobbled up the whole shed along with the poor animals. Their doleful bellows and bleats echoed through. They could not do anything to save them. Nor could Ashok stop the rain as he had said to Prakriti a few moments back, who, now from her mother's lap, was looking at him as if she realised he was lying.

After a sleepless night, it was only on the next morning, a clear morning with the blue sky with a few thin streaks of cloud in the western part, they found the cattle buried underneath the mud with some parts – horns and ears, tails and legs, in some cases even the belly – poked out. None of them had survived. Flies were already buzzing around, but no vultures circled overhead in the sky. They had disappeared long back. Disappeared from the surroundings were also jackals and foxes, which otherwise would come at night to scavenge on carrion, Gopal had said while excavating the earth for the proper burial of the dead animals.

Gopal lost almost three lakh on that single night, a large amount for a peasant. He, however, did not allow the despairing feeling to shadow his face. He continued his farming, even more laboriously and enthusiastically. He made a new temporary shed, of bamboo posts and chestnut and *chilaune* branches. He bought a milking buffalo and a suckling calf, some goats, and a few young kids, one of which was for the arrival of his son. Showing a brown kid, he said, "I hope it'll be big enough for the sacrifice in Dashain."

He bought some more pullets, different species. Above all, in the slipped land near his house, he planted hundreds of bamboo plants and cuttings of fodder's grafts of the fast grower types. He did not allow his hopes to fade. He set out with renewed vigour.

The rain came to an end towards the first week of September. The season became balmy as the cool breeze blew through the hamlet and the nearby woods, swaying the rice plants and rustling the tree branches, the fragrances of which permeated the air.

One day, after he returned after a routine medical check-up in Kathmandu, Ashok was sitting in the *mandir* with the doctor's cautionary words still fresh in his ears. "Ashok Ji, your organs have deteriorated to an alarming stage. You have to quit drinking and smoking completely," the doctor had cautioned him after checking the reports.

Now sitting in the *mandir*, near the *tulasi math*, he was pondering over those words. It was not for the first time that the doctor had advised him, but this time the tone had sounded more serious, more suggestive. It was not that he did not consider quitting alcohol and smoking. He had repeatedly mentioned it to Gopal. However, the day never came; the alcohol came to him every day after sunset, sometimes to celebrate, sometimes to accompany Gopal, and sometimes to chase away the loneliness. And whenever it came, it came with smoking.

He plucked a few *tulasi* leaves and put them in his mouth. A little away, on the narrow path striped with hedge plants, Prakriti was blowing bubbles from the sap of *sajiwan* through a straw which she had learnt from him and in which she had found a joy, as much as in running with a propeller made of a dried bamboo sheath which he had made for her. Now running in her fourth year, she had begun to fully exhibit her childhood. The scurrying steps, the child tone, the curious questions, and the innocent laughs: her childhood properties made everyone who saw her enjoy.

In the yard, Gopal was trying hard to chop at a stubborn knotted chestnut log with an axe. A short deep noise came from his mouth with each strike. The brown kid was cropping the bamboo leaves. Every day, the kid was fed with special forage so that it would fully grow before Prakash came. Pooja and Ishwari were preparing plots for the winter vegetables.

Ashok's mobile rang. It was Devaki.

"What Devaki? Is everything fine?" he asked.

She did not speak. She was sobbing.

"What happened, Devaki?" he asked in a louder tone.

"Dai, Prakash isn't alive."

"What?"

"Yes, Dai. Just now, his friend called me from Dubai and told me that he died while working in the company. He came under a fallen wall. I couldn't give this bad news to Gopal." She was still sobbing.

"Are you sure?"

"Yes, Dai. Immediately after hearing this, I called Yam Bahadur's son. I myself talked to him. He confirmed it."

"I'll talk to you later," he said, putting the phone on the floor. His heart pumped. *How to tell this news to Gopal? What to tell his mother and wife? And that little Prakriti, who did not even recognise her father?*

His heart pumped faster. He went inside, took the pills, and came out again.

Little Prakriti was still bubbling the sap. Gopal was still chopping the wood with all determination. The two women were still laughing and working in the field, unaware of this traumatic news.

He walked across the yard, pacing back and forth. *How to give this news to them?*

He walked to and fro: from this end to that end of the yard, from the yard to Big Plot and back to the yard again, trying to find appropriate words to speak to them about the unfortunate incident. *How to tell?* Deaths were not new to him and to Gopal too. But this death was a different one. Here, a young son was lost, a young husband was gone, and a child without a clear image of her father had lost him. It was different and was difficult to reveal the information to a father and a mother, who were more than excited with the thoughts of their son arriving in the upcoming Dashain and offering sacrifice at Kali Temple; to tell a wife, whose eyes were glistening and face was smiling with the hope of the arrival of her husband; and to little daughter, who was told that her father would come with a lot of new clothes and chocolates for her. *How to tell?*

To get more information, he got on to Devaki again. Confirmed, he walked with his heavy steps to Gurunggaun. The news of death had already spread. All those, who came across on his way, expressed the mourning words.

"*Bichara* Prakash!" Yam Bahadur's wife said before he stepped into their yard. "He was such a close friend of my son and would treat me just like his mother. *Daiva* is so cruel."

"It's hard to believe. But what's there to do? Death is always cruel," Yam Bahadur said, putting a straw mat on the veranda. "Does Gopal know this? No father should have to hear the news about the death of a young son." Yam Bahadur had recently retired from the Indian Army.

"No, Yam Bahadur Ji. Devaki called me, but I didn't have enough courage to tell him," he said. "Is it possible to talk to your son?"

"Why not? He had called me, just before you came. He's still at the hospital with the dead body."

He came across with more information that Prakash was working the night shift on the construction site. A wall collapsed, badly injuring him and some other workers. They all died on their way to the hospital.

"Yam Bahadur Ji, can you come along? I don't know how to share this bad news with Gopal."

"Why not? After all, he's the father. He needs to be informed this way or that way."

He put his camouflage cap and jacket on.

Ashok did not know how they walked down to the hamlet and what they talked about on their way, if they had talked at all. He was following Yam Bahadur's quick short steps through the narrow, steep path – overgrown with grass on the edge and these days travelled little. His mind was crowded with so many questions: how to bring the dead body home, how much it would cost, who would pay for that, how long it would take, what would be Gopal's reaction, how Prakriti, whose brain was still unaware of death, would respond, and how Ishwari would spend her long widowed life.

They found Gopal watering the patches of the land his wife and daughter-in-law had prepared. The women were not there, possibly had gone to the wood or the field. Prakriti was now running after dragonflies.

As soon as Gopal saw Yam Bahadur, he put the hose pipe on the ground and came, saying, "Yam Bahadur Dai, you? Are you receiving calls from your son? How's he? It's quite a while since Prakash called me last time."

Yam Bahadur did not say anything. Perhaps he was not ready to hear about Prakash at the very beginning. After a moment of silence, he talked around some other topics: the monsoon, the crops, the struggle of the peasants, and the shortness of life. After several digressions, he paused for a while and finally said, putting as much naturalness in his voice as he thought necessary on such occasions. "You know, Gopal, *hunu hunami daiva le tardaina.* Whatever is going to happen will happen. Nobody can stop it. There're ups and downs in human life, and all we can do is just move ahead . . . . Bhai, there's bad news," Yam Bahadur said in his sombre voice.

"About what?"

"About Prakash . . . I feel unlucky to share this news with you," Yam Bahadur said, letting out a deep sigh.

"What about Prakash?" Gopal became impatient.

"How to say, Bhai, he was working on the construction site. Then . . .," Yam Bahadur paused a while, swallowed hard, and said, "the wall suddenly crumbled down . . . . I mean Prakash was in an accident and . . . ."

"And what?"

"He was taken to the hospital, but he couldn't survive."

The sun disappeared behind the mountains. The cicadas grew to utter long resonant sounds at once. Gopal fainted. It was simply too much to tolerate the news about the death of a young son on whom he had put all his hopes and dreams. So, despite Yam Bahadur's practical and consoling way of telling, he went faint. His life came apart at once.

They put Gopal on the mat in the *mandir.* He came around after about ten minutes, but to faint again. The two women too, when they heard the news, went faint repeatedly. Little Prakriti sat on Ashok's lap. Terrified.

Their fainting and coming around and then again fainting repeated throughout the night and the next day continued. Thank god there was Yam Bahadur, who stayed there all night, trying to console them.

The news spread around, inviting family and relatives with wet eyes and sad faces. Though it was still hard to believe, death had taken Prakash, changing his family's lives forever, with the impossibility of turning back.

The absence of the dead body created additional complications in terms of rituals of the funeral ceremony, such an important aspect of culture and human life in society. They were not sure when the dead body would come. Pundits had different ideas: to allow to cremate in Dubai and to create an effigy, a figurative body of *kush* and do the rituals, or to wait until the body came. Gopal wanted to see his son at least once. Ishwari said she would not let her *siundo* be wiped, and bangles on her wrist are broken.

Ashok and Yam Bahadur put in their entire time and efforts in getting the deceased body back as soon as possible. Almost, once every fifteen days, they visited different offices – from the office of the chief district officer to the minister's office, mostly closed, and with an empty chair, towel, or coat draped over the back of the chair. Even if anyone was there, he was barred by guards and secretaries who often behaved with blithe indifference and presented themselves more powerful than the real person, and when, after the great favour of those secretaries, they got the inside access, the gentleman in the chair pretended to listen to them with his official *uh-huh*, but from inside turning a deaf ear and desperately waiting for when *the unwanted guests* would go out, obvious to notice from his facial expression. Finally, yawning, he would call his secretary or secretaries inside and ask them to deal with the problem. It took more than six months. And when the body came in a coffin, damaged and decaying, the air of gloom became even more intense. Then began the torturous and humiliating visits to the offices for the little money, the blood money, which Gopal at one time had rejected, saying, "What I would do with this money without my son?" Almost three quarters of the money was spent in travelling and in feeding the officials and politicians who claimed to have done a *great social service.*

The tiny hamlet turned gloomy. With Gopal's family struck by grief, the hamlet – of solely two houses – lost its colour. Gopal was broken. His life became just like a machine, living for the sake of living. The enthusiasm and the determination he possessed disappeared. Pooja always wore a depressed look. She grew older within months. Ishwari lost the glow on her face forever. Though she was allowed (in fact, Gopal had asked her) to start another life, she chose to live as a widow. Prakriti somehow came to know that her father, whom she saw beyond her recollection and whose figure and face were based on her own imagination, would not come back and would not bring her clothes and chocolates. He had gone to the sky amidst those twinkling stars, her mother had told her.

The festive season – Dashain and Tihar – could not remove the gloom. The *sayapatri* and *makhamali* flowered, matured, and came off without being plucked. The harvesting became just a ritual. The winter went unnoticed, so did the poinsettia and mountain ebony flowers. The spring did not bring the spring feeling in the hamlet. Without offering the colours and fragrances, it was taken over by the monsoon clouds which too felt dark and gloomy to Gopal and his family.

Yet life was to be lived, to be continued. Time moved on. Ashok hoped time would cure the wound and would blur the memories. Although it might take a long as it had taken in his case with Mandakini, time would heal Gopal inasmuch as it possessed the healing capacity, Ashok was convinced.

Three

His life settled to a considerable extent. At least, he took it that way. It settled with his small farming, settled with the pills and tablets, with the memories of Sushmita, and with his company with Gopal and little Prakriti.

He still remembered Mandakini; the memories now were painless: no carnal feeling and no any feeling of bodily attraction and of the anger and the jealousy. She was comfortably sitting in the deepest part of his heart with peace.

So it appeared to him that his life settled. His working in Big Plot continued. With Lees in Lhasa in his mind, he continued to grow vegetables and flowers, which grew so well that, in seasons, he even managed to give out them to the villagers. The elderly were interested in his farming. But the younger generation did not show any interests. They lacked enough passion for soil and preferred to dream solely of going abroad. Even his own children, when they came to see him, grimaced at his old clothes and rapidly wrinkling face smudged with soil. To them, perhaps, their father was living in an archaic way. But he was satisfied to live in that obsolete way. He had realised that each older generation would seem to have become obsolete and discarded in the eyes of a younger generation. But soon this poor new generation would find itself being worn out and obsolete in the eyes of another newer generation. They would be dominated by their progenies. A social or natural process. He took it in that way and did not mind the grimaced faces and did not take it otherwise. What was most important to him was that he had found contentment with this little farming, with this being spattered with soil and manure, and with this nearness to nature, which he never got during his foreign stay in those big cities.

But physically, he had grown more fragile.

Frequently, he had to travel to Kathmandu for the check-ups, and after each check-up, the doctors would ask him to avoid drinking and smoking, something he was not ready for. If he met Thakur in Kathmandu, the drinking would become even more romantic.

Towards the end of August, the season once again changed. The monsoon clouds disappeared from the sky. The rain receded. The croaks of the frogs in the fields and the songs of the cicadas in the trees became weaker and infrequent. Once again, the rice plants were swaying, giving off the fresh and familiar fragrances. The sky became bluer and clearer. Once again the *sayapatri* and *makhamali* grew in the hamlet and budded.

Time had grown to heal Gopal's family. They had begun to show interest in the daily chores. Tears had become less frequent in Pooja's eyes. Ishwari had begun to smile at her daughter's childlike behaviour. Things were slowly changing. And one day, it became clear to Ashok that time was showing its effect, the healing capacity.

That day, sitting in the *mandir*, he was watching the fledglings under the eaves. (Surprising and amusing him, a pair of swallows had come to his house a couple of weeks back.) Fledged, yet without much experience of flying, they were following their parents over the yard – from the round hole of the mud-pelleted nest under the eaves to the clothes line, then to the hedgerows and the roof of Gopal's house. Quite amusing a view.

He heard Ishwari's laugh followed by Pooja's voice, "Prakriti! What are you doing?" The voice was mixed with laughter. It was the first time that he had heard such distinct laughs from Gopal's yard after the death of Prakash. Why were those two women laughing, so unusual for the last one year? Amazed and curious, he went there. With her frock, face, hands, and a few streaks of hair smudged with a yellow substance, Prakriti was in the middle of the yard, frustrated. Beside her, in the yard, was a recently born kid, not older than a week, moving its little tail, and under the tail the same yellow substance. With that scene, Ashok could take it what might have come about. The little girl must have taken the kid in her arms and tried to play with it, and the kid must have dropped the yellow poo on her body and frock. That must be the reason for the yellowish substance on her body and face, her grimaced face, and the laughs in the yard.

Gopal came from the shed with a bucket of foamy milk and said, "What did you do, Prakriti?" He at once understood what might have gone wrong. More frustrated and more disgusted by the pungent smell (or even maybe by the taste because the yellow substance was smudged on her lips as well), she tried to wipe it from her face, but, in that process, it further spread. "Prakritiiii . . .," Ishwari took her to the tap and washed her. After a chat with Gopal, he came back to his house.

The parent swallows were still training the little swallows to dart.

The incident itself was not uncommon. Such occurrence could have occurred anywhere, in any house with anyone in the countryside, yet this helped a lot to bring smiles to their faces: visibly and noticeably, after a year of the death of Prakash. Time slowly healed the family, and Prakriti became the source of this healing with her amusing deeds, feeling naughty and funny and childlike, which she possessed at her age by nature. The smile on one face, in one person of the family, helped to remove the grief on other faces as well.

The laughs in Gopal's yard offered its positive effect to him as well.

Despite his deteriorating health, he was living a satisfied life. He would spend almost the whole day in the field with small tools, weeding and digging around the plants. In the evening, he would spend his time walking with Prakriti or playing with her or would talk to Gopal and to those who would come to his hamlet to converse about the farming and the seasons. On such occasions, they would sit in the *mandir-like* platform in the orchard – a cemented platform with pillars at the four corners, three of them joined with planks so that anyone could sit reclining on the bar stretching out their legs, designed by he himself to stay in the dry evenings, watching the star-studded sky or the moonlit night – with them and would chat, smoking. Otherwise, he would surf the Internet, which he had procured recently and which was slow and frequently disconnected, to see the news or to see the mails from a limited circle of friends, mainly from Hemanta, Vinod, and Ahmed. Thakur would not use email, if he wanted to talk, he would have to call. The friends in Lhasa were lost to the years. He never contacted them after he left Lhasa. The emails in those days, in the last years of the twentieth century, had not been so frequent or accessible in Lhasa. Nor in Nepal. Telephones were expensive. The contact was not easy. At solitary moments, those memories: those long drives, the fleet of ruddy shelducks, the monasteries, the Lees' farm, Pasang and Pema, those *linka*, those little *chipis*, those cairns would be brought back. *Was Pala still alive? What about the others?* He would often wonder.

One more year passed by. The festive season was just over. Devaki and the children had gone back. The ripe petals of *sayapatri* flowers had begun to come off. The peasants were busy harvesting the rice and millet, which they could not have done in time due to the festival and the election which occurred immediately after the festival. The birds and rats had already done considerable damage.

Ashok perched on the field berm, looking at the winding little walks amidst the rice stubbles in Big Plot, which led to the holes just below the berm where the rats had stored rice panicles. Outside the holes, mounds of soil were formed. These rats! He could never control them. They always came during the rice harvest, worked out their little walks, created holes, and did as much damage as they could do. The patch, where the rice was planted, was still damp and spongy when walked on. The mature fountain grasses on the berm waved in the late autumnal breeze. In some patches, the all-weather flowers had come out in different colours, but of all the flowers, it was the bonsai poinsettia that had dominated the view. Prakriti would love to see these little poinsettias. She was curious to know why they were so short, whereas the poinsettias along the hedgerows were so tall. It was just a day before, she had asked him, blowing a dandelion clock and pointing towards the hedgerows, "Grandfather, are these poinsettias their grandchildren?" Prakriti had become five and could speak without *l* for *r*.

"Where has she gone today?" he mumbled, looking at the poinsettias.

A jeep stopped near the *chautari*. A man got off with a bag. Looking around for a while, he walked towards the hamlet. Who was this man? He was not Gopal's relative. Otherwise, he would have told Ashok days back. Nor was he a candidate or supporter of a political party, who would frequently visit the hamlet before the election. He was certain that those men, those political figures, would not appear in this remote part among these apolitical peasants before the next election. Then who was he? Hanging his bag on the right shoulder, the man approached almost to the other end of Big Plot. Thakur? Ashok gazed at the man. Yes, it was Thakur. But so suddenly! Thakur had told him that he wished to see the hamlet but had not given the exact time.

Surprised with this uninformed arrival, he almost ran towards Thakur.

"Thakur Ji? What am I seeing? It's hard to believe. At least, you should have informed me."

"I wanted to surprise you, Ashok Ji. I was travelling to Kathmandu. I thought why not to take this long route? To see this part of the country," Thakur said. "What a lovely farm! These many things in such a small area! Is it yours?"

"I have to do something to kill time."

"It's such a marvellous planning. You still remember the Lees' farm in Lhasa?"

"Aha, those days! I never forget them and their farm. Come, let's go home. You must be tired."

"No, I stayed for two nights on my way."

"Was it difficult to find this place?"

"No, not at all. I found some men from the next village. They had hired a jeep for their groceries and gave me a lift."

"Where's your grandpa, Prakriti?" Ashok asked Prakriti, who was plucking the ripe *sajiwan* nuts.

"In the wood," she said and scurried to look at this new arrival with dark face and thick moustache.

"So, little child, you're Prakriti? Look, what I have brought for you!" Thakur, sitting in the *mandir*, took out some sweets – *thekuwa, rasia,* and *kasar,* the specialities of Chhat – and a packet from his bag and opened it.

It was a doll, a Barbie doll, wearing a red gown, with her nails and lips painted in deep red. Ashok had told him, during one of his visits to Kathmandu that Prakash had left a daughter behind.

Giving those sweets and the doll to her, he added, "Here you go! She's your friend! Do you go to school, little baby?"

"Not yet. Gopal is planning to send her to Pokhara with my sister, Devaki," Ashok replied before she mumbled.

Prakriti took the doll and stood still, surprised by the precious gifts from a man unknown to her and undecided how to respond to the lavish gifts. She stood shyly. Her eyes moved to the gifts in her hand and to

Thakur. But Thakur was amazing. He possessed the quality of being befriended by the children. Ashok was aware of this quality from quite early on, from when they had visited the Lees' farm or Pala's hamlet in Lhasa. All the children would become his friends within a few hours. He had retained this quality up until now. He won her friendship within two or three hours. She behaved with him as though she knew him for months. Later that evening, after the meal, when they sat in the *mandir-like* platform, Prakriti stayed with them, looking at Thakur and listening to their talks too deep for her to understand, until she fell asleep.

Such was Thakur's capacity in dealing with children! Marvellous! And marvellous he was in talking in his dispassionate tone on any issues. Despite the fact that he did not have a college degree and despite the fact that his profession did not require any great deal of theoretical knowledge, he was brilliantly equipped with a vast range of knowledge and always loved to talk about contemporary issues.

He began, "You know, Ashok Ji? People are wise when it comes to politics. They know how to deal with the parties and the politicians. Throughout my travel from my village to this village, on the bus, in the hotels where I stayed and in the shops, what I heard was about the elections."

He continued, "They know whom to choose and whom not to. In each election, they make wise and appropriate decisions. Last time, when was it? A few years back. They favoured one force and this time they chose the other. Each time, with a hope that something would come out, something better would be resulted in, they give new forces a fair chance. But these new forces after being elected, forgetting all their promises, they behave like Napoleon and his team in George Orwell's allegorical novel *Animal Farm*, trying to establish themselves as *the more equal than others*. Or they behave like the tiger who wishes to eat the saintly person who made the tiger out of a mouse with his magic spell."

"The people, in turn, in the next election, like the saintly person, using their magic spells – *punar musiko bhawa*, may you again become a mouse – dwarf these tigers and Napoleons again into mice and piglets. And these mice, finding themselves in a frustrating situation, behave and speak bizarrely. It has happened in each election. Each time, the leaders who try to be the Napoleons or the tigers are dwarfed by the people's magic spell. They're reminded of their exact position. The people are wise. But what to do? There are very limited choices. The people are compelled to make the best choice from among the worst ones. The country lacks a leadership. It seriously lacks the leaders with wider and deeper vision," Thakur said.

Prakriti, unable to understand what Thakur was saying, had fallen asleep on Ashok's lap with her face towards Thakur.

Thakur added, "Keeping themselves away from the people, away from the real issues, they debate on those matters which, I doubt, are the matters that people in this country want."

"Honestly speaking, when I was working away from my country, I worked with different people, I ate with different people, and I shared a room with different people. Different in terms of language, caste, ethnicity, or even nationalities, but to me, all they were human beings, the workers. I never cared about these man-made differences. What mattered for me basically was whether the person was innately of good nature or not? Now, here, why are we being taught to differentiate between each other?" Thakur said.

"Exactly, Thakur Ji. When we step onto the foreign soil, what strikes us first is the question of survival. We become happy to see anybody from our country no matter where he is from, what language he speaks, and which ethnicity he belongs to. We work together. We stay in the same place and eat from the same plate. Here, we're being taught about our identity. Isn't it our identity that all we're Nepalese? What other basis of identification could be stronger than this. Particularly in this age of globalisation when the world itself is narrowing and the idea of nationality itself is shrinking? Which forces are encouraging us to create division among ourselves? Why are we following their advice?" Ashok commented.

Gopal kept quiet, listening to them.

Thakur lit a cigarette and pulled it long.

Looking at the rising moon, he said, "Anyway, this time, I hope we'll get a new constitution once and for all."

"For us, the peasants, does it matter who's in the power in the capital? I don't think they're serious about us. What they want is power," Ashok said.

Pooja came and took Prakriti.

"Thakur Ji, why are we wasting our time talking about these political nonsense? Let's have *tinpane*," Ashok added.

"Oh, why not? It's long since I last tasted it," Thakur agreed.

"I'll make you drunk tonight. This time we have brought the strongest one," Ashok said.

"Sure, I suppose getting drunk in your village with you and Gopal is an occasion. I don't let this chance slip," Thakur laughed.

"Dai, where's the gallon? I'll bring it," Gopal turned to Ashok.

"Under the bed," Ashok responded.

Gopal disappeared and came back with a gallon and three steel glasses.

And they drank and talked until late, until the moon came straight over the hamlet, and until the owl hooted many times.

Ashok took one more drink after Thakur and Gopal left with staggering feet and stammering voice. Ashok did not have extra bed for Thakur so he was to sleep at Gopal's house.

He drank, remembering Thakur's last piece of conversation, "Ashok Ji, you know? The lady whom I met with you for the first time in Kathmandu . . . what was her name? Mandakini? Yes, she often comes to my salon with her little son whenever he needs a haircut. She always asks about you. The little boy is so lovely."

Ashok felt a slight pain somewhere in his heart, deep inside, different than he usually used to have.

The next day and the day after, Ashok took Thakur around, making detours to give him the details of hilly life.

"Aha, what a fascinating view!" Thakur exclaimed as they finally reached the brow of the mountain. He was thrilled by the view from the mountaintop: those green Mahabharata Mountains, spreading to all sides; the narrow gorges and valleys; the rivers and streams flowing through those gorges and valleys, some of them brilliantly snaking and glinting in the sun; the sprinkled villages over the mountain slopes; and tall peaks in the far north, now turning into golden colours with the descending sun.

"Look, how amazing our country is!" Thakur exclaimed.

"You know, Thakur Ji?" Ashok pointed his hand towards a tall mountain range in the farthest south, in the middle of which stood Oxbow Hill. "From that mountain range, the land becomes low hills and descends to the plain land, Inner Terai and Terai."

"You mean Madhesh?"

"Whichever name you prefer."

Both they laughed and sat on the ground from where they could see the miles long extended views just with a swivel of the head.

Throwing a pebble into a bush, Ashok again said, "And it was right there, where Padam's house was."

"Who was he? You never mentioned."

"Uncle's ploughman. He was a nice guy. Laborious but always poor. Later, he moved somewhere else with his family," Ashok said. His own mentioning of Padam brought back the old days.

Until he left for Lhasa, Padam was still in the village. Every time Ashok visited his house he never allowed him to return without having *tinpane* or *chhang*. Sitting on the south-facing narrow veranda and having *tinpane* or *chhang* in a pewter bowl, while looking at the chickens scratching under the orange trees, which bore fruit heavily in the season, and at the pigs wallowing in the mud: how pleasant it would feel!

When he came back from Lhasa for his holidays, Padam had already left the village.

One time, after he returned from Lhasa, he had met him in the bazaar in a tipsy condition, saying, "Ashok Babu, *dharodharam*, I didn't want to leave my village. But I couldn't raise my family with the pittance I got from my hard labour for your uncle. I moved here, hoping for better. But for us, the poor, the situation is alike everywhere."

Drunk, he had said those words in the middle of the bazaar in the middle of the day. After that, Ashok never saw him. Later, he was told that two of his sons had joined the Maoists, and he himself had migrated somewhere in Terai. He was afraid of the security forces.

Where would he have gone? Was he still alive? What about his two sons who had joined the Maoists? Here, his house was deserted. There were just mounds of stones and soils covered with weeds, making it difficult to imagine that, not long back, there used to be a house full of lives. Not only his house, the other houses, his brothers' houses on the other side of the mountain, on the northern face just below the hollowed pass, part of the brow where would stand the tall ash tree – from which hundreds or thousands of bladed tiny seeds would come off and whirl in the air before settling down on the earth during the windy days in the late winter – were also abandoned. The orange trees in the orchards of those houses which bore even more fruits than the trees on the other side, the south-facing side, had died away. Where would they have gone desolating the place and why? For the same reason as Padam had said in the middle of the bazaar in his drunkenness? Poverty?

They sat chatting and looking around. The sun went down in the west. The western sky became yellowish pink. The mountain peaks in the far north became golden red. The gorges, valleys, slope and the mountain contours progressively faded. A few partridges appeared from somewhere and, scurrying through the flinty graveyard (used by the Gurung community), disappeared on the other side of the mountain. So did a pair of rabbits. Or more. Ashok was not sure. They disappeared swiftly; he had just a glimpse of them, scurrying towards the forested slope. He saw at least two.

"Let's go. Gopal must be there by now," Ashok said.

They were invited by Yam Bahadur to have the local chicken and *tinpane* at his house.

Later, when they took the curvy motor road to descend down to the hamlet, Gopal and Thakur were trying to persuade each other – Gopal trying to persuade Thakur to stay at least one more day and Thakur asking permission to leave the next morning – with their repeated *ple . . . a . . . se*. All they had finished half a gallon of *tinpane*. But he was not feeling tipsy.

He followed them, silently. Down in the hamlet, after they bade their goodnights to him and went on with their persuasion to each other, he came to the orchard and sat on the platform facing east.

His pain was getting worse. Despite the regular dose of medicine, the pain had grown worse for some two weeks. At times, thoughts came to his mind that he needed to go to Kathmandu. Then again, he thought the pain, like other times, would wane after some days. But even after so many days, it did not go away; rather it grew, changing the location and turning into different types of pain, unlike the usual ones.

The waning moon, the fourth or fifth day after the full moon, appeared in the east, casting silvery lights all over. The flowers, difficult to distinguish their colours in the mellowed light, smiled, and called up, once again, the memories of Mandakini and her care for the flowers in the alleyway. In fact, she never went far from his heart; she was always there – with different degrees of effects, at first with strong feelings of love, anger, and jealousy and then, with the passage of time, with gradually weakening yet sweet memories. But she was always there. Now, with the information given to him by Thakur that she would often come to his salon in Kathmandu to have a haircut for her son and each time would ask a series of questions about him – where he was, what he was doing, how he looked, with whom he was staying – she had come to his mind again with greater strength, more vividly and sharply. The previous night, she had come in his dream with the same dainty look and changing colours on her face, talking to him, somewhere, difficult to remember.

It had been more than four years since they parted in a gloomy morning. He wondered how she would look now! With whom she got married! If her son had taken after her! All those moments he spent with her once again came to his mind in that solitary night. His first meeting with her at the gate of the house where he was to stay in Kathmandu, her behaviour with such frankness and easiness and his taking to her so fast, her flowers in the alleyway, and their talking on the rooftop. Her staring at the faraway mountains, his increasing passion for her and his hugging and her sharp reaction, his feeling of being rejected and taunted, the incident at the restaurant, the tears in her eyes and the last sentimental mornings. All those moments became fresh.

Hu . . . hu . . . hoooo . . . . An owl hooted somewhere in the wood. It must be very near. The sound was so loud. A few bats darted into the sky. Frequently, some of them came very near to him and ruffled their wings almost touching him. The stream of memories went on.

His difficult days in Pretoria, such painful feelings of missing her, those suffocating days and nights, such gloomy moments, efforts to overcome those painful feelings and, finally, plunging into sickness and despair, and then, his return to Nepal.

He still wondered how much passion he had for her. It was so overwhelming and so difficult to control. How difficult it had become to win his carnal feeling? How difficult, even after he felt the carnal feeling to be somewhat under control, had it become to remember her normally. Why would he imagine her with another man? Why would he get so angry and jealous while imagining her in that way? Thakur had said her son was nearly three years old, which meant that she got married soon after they had parted. Was her marriage a planned one? Did she know her husband before she got married? If so, why did she not tell him anything about that? Even during the phone calls? Or was it all of a sudden she had to get married according to the arrangements made by her parents? She was always difficult to be understood. He wished to see her at least once.

"Mandakini!" he sighed.

The balmy wind blew. With the moon coming high up in the sky, the other properties in purlieus, too, grew to shine. The untilled slope up in the mountain shone brighter. The terraced field became clearer, stratified. The motor road across the hamlet became distinct and the chestnut and *chilaune* trees stood mellowed. The owl once again made *hu . . . hu . . . hu . . . hoooo . . . .*

He did not know how much of his life was left. The doctors did not say plainly that he would die soon, but every time, the doses of medicine were either increased or changed to stronger generic. He was even advised to go to India for a thorough check-up. He knew what it meant. But he did not wish to spend more money for his health. He had lived long. His wishes had been settled.

He tried to remember Sushmita's face. But why was her face being replaced by Mandakini? The more he tried to remember Sushmita, the clearer Mandakini became.

A sharp pain pierced at some point in his chest and spread across the entire chest and belly. He pressed his chest. Was he supposed to wake up Thakur and Gopal? But what would they do in the middle of the night? Waking them up would be just disturbing them. They were happy during the whole evening. Thakur and Gopal had become close friends within these three days. And Prakriti? She was busy all the time with the Barbie doll Thakur had brought for her. All of them must be in their deep sleep.

He looked at Big Plot, his field.

Sharp pain again. Sharper and sharper. He moved his lips. Some liquid had exuded from his mouth, salty.

Who was in the field? Padam? Ploughing? Or Grandmother and Aama striking the maize plants? Or his uncles threshing the rice? Why was the field looking as if it was changing its image: now vacant, now recently cropped with rice plants, now with sturdy maize stalks, and then again the patched one? No, it was not changing. They were surreal images, just illusions. He fluttered his eyelashes. Things became a bit clearer. The pain was getting worse. Again, he saw Sushmita in the middle of the flowered patch of the field, wearing a white sari and looking at him and smiling. No, she was not Sushmita. She was Mandakini. The figure disappeared.

He turned his eyes again to the sky, the moon now fading. Everything began to fade. Fast.   Sushmita walked towards him, smiling. He tried to smile. The moon further faded and darkened.

Ashok died. A transient human life ended.

His life settled permanently into the unknown dark shadow of death. Along with this settling of his life, all his worldly passions – desires, anger, wishes, joys, sorrows, and even memories associated with Mandakini – came to a virtual end. At once, they became irrelevant and meaningless, temporal. No more pains and distress. And perhaps, there was none other to remember Mandakini so passionately.

The owl once more hooted. The quietness deepened. The moon continued to shine bright in the sky.

The next morning, Thakur came and saw him sleeping.

"Ashok Ji, you slept here the whole night?"

He did not speak. His eyes were open. Streaks of blood had come out of his mouth and clotted.

"Ashok Ji, are you all right?" Thakur went nearer and felt his forehead; it was cold. No breath, no heartbeat.

"Gopal Ji, come here," Thakur screamed. It was perhaps because of this loud scream, not only Gopal, but also the entire family came with a premonition of something bad in their mind, and when they saw him dead, loud cries echoed through and reached Gurunggaun, compelling Yam Bahadur and the others, who heard the cries, rush down to the hamlet.

The body was taken to the yard and put near the *tulasi math*.

Thakur put a spoonful of water in Ashok's mouth and closed the eyes, saying, in his sobbing voice, "He had suffered a lot in his life. He deserves peace, a perpetual peace. Let him rest."

"Life is unpredictable. What happens is just a destiny over which we have no control. He was so good," Yam Bahadur sighed.

After Devaki and the children came from Pokhara, the body was taken to the Kali River and was burnt on the same spot where his wife had been burnt. Gopal had not forgotten the spot. Thakur picked up some ashes without the notice of the mourners and later in the night scattered them in Big Plot. The rituals began in the yard of the old house. Thakur shaved Rabindra's head. Narayan, the pundit, aged and shrunken, undid the old yellowed and blackened packet, took out the leather-strapped worm-eaten books with sepia-coloured pages, hung his thick glasses on the bridge of his nose and grew to utter the same mantras which he had uttered so many times. With his ageing, the pundit's words sounded more serious. Crying herself, Devaki was trying to console Madhu and Sarita.

Thakur stayed in the hamlet throughout the rituals with his dark and serious face, recalling a great deal of memories associated with their life – the time spent in Lhasa, in Mumbai, and in Madagascar, and frequent meetings in Kathmandu, one by one. "How am I to tell Mandakini about this sudden end of life?" he often murmured to himself.

After the rituals, Thakur left. He had to leave; the harvesting season was approaching. He had lost his true friend.

Thus, Ashok was lost forever from the mountain slope. With this yet another death, Gopal was broken again. This time, however, he did not allow himself to plunge into grief for long. Life was to be continued. One day, not long after, he along with Rabindra came to Big Plot and watered the flowers and annuals, packed the manure around them, and weeded. He was determined not to let the farming be left alone and be fallen to decay.

Prakriti sat on the field berm with her elbows on her knees and her two little palms on her cheeks, looking at the field. She sat at the same place where Ashok would always perch. There were butterflies hovering from one flower to another, but she did not feel like running after them. The crimson-coloured petals of poinsettia, both in the field and the hedgerows, looked faded.

Her grandfather came to her mind nostalgically.

Glossary

akshata (Nep)	rice grain
amkhora (Nep)	a traditional metal water pot used for drinking or serving water
amkhoras (Nep)	the plural of amkhora
ana (Nep)	a traditional unit for the measurement of land, especially in the city area
anas (Nep)	the plural of ana
annaprashan (Nep)	the first rice-feeding ceremony (to a baby)
Apsaras (Nep)	beautiful and delicate supernatural females, who, according to Hindu religion, are considered as the wives of Gandharvas and can perform beautiful dances
Asar Pandhra (Nep)	an auspicious day for the rice plantation ceremony, which falls towards the end of June
asare geet (Nep)	the song sung during the rice plantation
Ashwin (Nep)	the sixth month of Bikram Sambat, the official calendar of Nepal
assalamualaikum	a word of greeting in Arabic
asuro (Nep)	the malabar nut plant; a kind of shrubby plant used as a hedge plant in rural Nepal.
babalas (South African)	a word for hangover or hungover
babuji (Hin)	a title used for a respected figure or in some cases for a bureaucrat
Bade Bhaiya (Hin)	elder brother

badhiya (Hin)	*especial*
bagh chal (Nep)	*a board game played by two players, in which tigers and goats are symbolically used*
bahadur (Nep)	*brave; it is also used as a middle name by some ethnic communities in Nepal*
Bahini (Nep)	*younger sister*
Baisakh (Nep)	*the first month of Bikram Sambat*
bakkie (South African)	*a kind of motor vehicle without roof at the back*
balep (Tib)	*a kind of bread*
Ban Jhankri (Nep)	*a kind of supernatural wild shaman, the male one*
Banaki (Nep)	*a kind of supernatural wild shaman, the female one*
Bhai (Nep)	*younger brother*
Bhai Tika (Nep)	*the last or fifth day of Tihar festival, in which sisters worship their brothers for longevity*
Bhanger (Nep)	*one of the deities in Hindu religion*
bhanjyang (Nep)	*the pass between the mountains or hills*
Bhauju (Nep)	*sister-in-law; the wife of elder brother*
bhoto (Nep)	*a kind of vest*
bichara (Nep)	*poor; pitiable*
Bikram Sambat (Nep)	*the calendar established by Vikramaditya (it is some fifty-seven years ahead of the Gregorian calendar and now is used as the official calendar of Nepal)*
Bishwakarma (Nep)	*the creator, one of the Hindu gods; a Hindu caste in Nepal*

Brahman putra (Nep)	the son of a Brahman
chautari (Nep)	a raised stone-paved platform constructed for people to sit, rest, and talk beneath the sacred trees, like peepal, banyan, or shami
chemar (Tib)	roasted barley flour
chemar bo (Tib)	a colourful box, which is filled with chemar and roasted barley and wheat seeds during Lhosar festival and put on the Lhosar altars
chhang (Tib)	an alcoholic beverage, normally made of barley, millet or rice
Chhat (Nep)	a Hindu festival dedicated to sun god; it is very popular among the communities in the southern part of Nepal
Chhori (Nep)	daughter
chilaune (Nep)	the needle wood tree, botanically called Schima wallichii
chillim (Nep)	the smoking pipe, traditionally made of clay
chipi (Tib)	a Himalayan mouse-hare; also called pika
chipis (Tib)	the plural of chipi
chogche (Tib)	a kind of low table
choli (Nep)	a kind of blouse
chowkidar (Nep)	a watchman or gatekeeper
chupa (Tib)	a kind of traditional clothes worn in Tibet or in Northern Nepal
Dai (Nep)	elder brother
dain (Nep)	a traditional way of rice harvesting
daiva (Nep)	god

dakinis	*the angels from the heavens; the sky dancer (in Tibet vulture is considered as dakini)*
dal	*a soupy dish made from lentils; dhal*
damlo (Nep)	*twine or rope used to tether an animal*
dandi biyo (Nep)	*a kind of a traditional game, usually played in rural Nepal*
Dashain (Nep)	*a great Hindu festival, popular all over Nepal*
dekchi (Nep)	*a kind of cooking pot, especially made of steel, copper, brass or aluminium*
dekchis (Nep)	*the plural of dekchi*
desi tharra (Nep)	*local wine, usually strong and used by common men*
Dhami (Nep)	*a shaman*
dharodharam (Nep)	*a word for swearing that someone is telling the truth*
dhiki (Nep)	*a traditional wooden beater*
dhindo (Nep)	*a thick porridge-like dish, normally prepared from the flour of m i l l e t , wheat, buckwheat, or maize*
dhungro (Nep)	*a pipe, normally made of bamboo or iron and used to blow fire*
Didi (Nep)	*elder sister*
Diwali (Nep)	*Tihar festival*
Fajr	*the first prayer of the day in Muslim religion*
firebush	*a kind of shrubby plant with red or orange flowers*
gagri (Nep)	*a kind of metal water vessel*

gagris (Nep)	*the plural of gagri*
Gandharvas (Nep)	*singers (according to Hindu religion, they are considered as the husbands of Apsaras*
geru (Nep)	*a kind of red soil*
ghaito (Nep)	*a kind of earthen water vessel*
ghaitos (Nep)	*the plural of ghaito*
gong bao chicken	*a kind of spicy Chinese dish, usually made of chicken, peanuts and other vegetables*
gundruk (Nep)	*a kind of vegetable made by fermenting green leafy vegetables or radish*
Gurung (Nep)	*an ethnic Nepalese community, who lives mostly in the mountainous part of Nepal*
Gurunggaun (Nep)	*a village where predominantly the Gurung community lives*
guthuk (Tib)	*a soupy Tibetan dish*
Han	*the largest ethnic group in China; belonging to this group*
Harishayani Ekadashi (Nep)	*the eleventh lunar day of the bright fortnight in the Nepalese month of Ashadh (June-July), which is celebrated as a fasting and in which basil plant is sown*
havan (Nep)	*a consecrated fireplace, built during religious ceremony*
jamara (Nep)	*sprouts of barley, wheat, rice, or maize, which are sprouted during Dashain festival and are put on the head along with tika*
janto (Nep)	*the traditional millstones*

jarda (Nep)	*a kind of strong tobacco used to make the paan stronger*
jaulo (Nep)	*soft rice porridge*
jeera (Nep)	*cumin seeds*
Ji (Nep)	*a title; Mr*
jindala (Tib)	*a respectful address for traders; boss*
kabaddi (Nep)	*a kind of game*
kachhad (Nep)	*a kind of loincloth, a wrap-on loincloth*
kakakul (Nep)	*serpent eagle*
kakkad (Nep)	*cheap tobacco*
kalimati (Nep)	*a kind of black soil*
kamero	*(Nep) a kind of white soil*
kapali tamsuk (Nep)	*a legal document by which you give the right to own your land or other property if you do not pay the loan in certain time as mentioned in the document*
karahi (Nep)	*a kind of cooking pot*
karuwa (Nep)	*a traditional metal water pot used for drinking or serving water*
karuwas (Nep)	*the plural of karuwa*
karyangkurungs (Nep)	*a kind of migratory cranes*
kasar (Nep)	*a kind of caramelised sweet made of rice flour*
khada (Tib)	*a kind of ceremonial scarf used basically in Tibet and Nepal*
khadas (Tib)	*the plural of khada*
Khadkagaun (Nep)	*a village where predominantly the Khadka community lives*
khaja (Nep)	*rice cooked in ghee*

khanyu (Nep)	*a type of fig tree, which can be used as fodder; botanically called Ficus semicordata*
kimchee	*a type of Korean pickle*
kora (Tib)	*the act of clockwise circling around a holy place; a type of pilgrimage, very popular in Tibet*
kunde (Nep)	*an iron pot used for heating or boiling milk*
kunjo (Tib)	*a word for swearing that someone is telling the truth*
kuro (Nep)	*a weed with prickly seeds*
kurta (Nep)	*a loose shirt worn, basically, by South Asian*
kush (Nep)	*a kind of grass with religious value in Hindu religion*
La (Tib)	*a word used for a mountain pass; a word used after the first name in Tibet that means Mr or sir*
lachchhin (Nep)	*a good omen*
ladsaheb (Hin)	*a word, which normally means an important person (sometimes this word is used satirically or disapprovingly)*
Lakhe Naach (Nep)	*a traditional dance originally belonging to the Newar community of Nepal, but famous all over Nepal*
Lakshmi Puja (Nep)	*a Hindu festival; the third day of Tihar festival*
lalpurja (Nep)	*a legal document ensuring someone's ownership over a house or land property*

Lhosar (Tib)	*the Tibetan New Year*
linka (Tib)	*a kind of picnic or outing*
madal (Nep)	*a drum-like musical instrument*
Madhesh (Nep)	*the lowland area of the mid-east southern Nepal*
Magargaun (Nep)	*a village where predominantly the Magar community lives*
makhamali (Nep)	*the globe amarnath flower*
malati (Nep)	*a kind of flower plant with red flowers*
malsiri (Nep)	*a traditional song, usually sung during Dashain*
mana (Nep)	*a traditional unit of weighing*
Mandakini (Nep)	*the Galaxy, the Milky Way*
mandir (Nep)	*a temple or gazebo-like structure, usually built at the corner of the yard, which is basically used for sitting*
marda (Nep)	*a male*
masala (Nep)	*spice*
masala tree (Nep)	*Eucalyptus*
maseura (Nep)	*a kind of dried vegetable made of the flour of beans, yam, or other vegetables*
math	*a small raised platform; shrine*
mitha (Nep)	*sweet; mild*
mogudu (South African)	*a kind of traditional South African dish prepared from tripe and intestine*
moksha (Nep)	*emancipation from the cycle of birth and death*
momo (Nep)	*a traditional Newari dish in Nepal*
momos (Nep)	*the plural of momo*
mudras (Nep)	*different postures or positions of the body*

muri (Nep)	*the traditional unit of weighing*
muris (Nep)	*the plural of muri*
murkatta (Nep)	*the headless; a kind of ghost*
naan	*a type of South Asian bread*
namaskar (Nep)	*a Nepalese word to greet*
namlo (Nep)	*a kind of twine or rope, which is used to carry things or piles*
nangma (Tib)	*a kind of cultural programme usually performed in the night time*
natikuti (Nep)	*exactly*
paan	*the betel leaf*
pakora	*a spicy fried dish usually made by mixing flour and different spices and vegetables and used as a snack*
Pala (Tib)	*father*
patuki (Nep)	*a kind of girdle fastened around the waist to keep sari in place*
patukis (Nep)	*the plural of patuki*
peepal (Nep)	*a large tree of ficus genus; botanically called ficus religiosa (in Hindu religion, it has a great religious value)*
ping (Nep)	*a swing*
pings (Nep)	*the plural of ping*
pirka (Nep)	*a wooden seat*
pirkas (Nep)	*the plural of pirka*
pirke (Nep)	*having pirka*
Prabhu (Nep)	*god*
Rahu (Nep)	*one of the planets in Hindu religion, which causes eclipses by swallowing the sun and moon*

487

rasia (Nep)	*a sweet dish often prepared during Chhat Puja*
rekhi (Nep)	*white marks or lines made of rice flour on the floor in a place where puja is performed*
rodhi ghar (Nep)	*a place where people gather after the daylong work in the fields to sing, dance and relax (it is a part of culture, mainly, of the Gurung community of Nepal, but also popular among all Nepalese)*
rodhi song (Nep)	*the songs sung during rodhi*
ropain (Nep)	*the rice planting event*
saala haraami (Hin)	*a swear word in Hindi language*
sahuni (Nep)	*a female shopkeeper*
sajiwan (Nep)	*the physic nut plant, botanically called Jatropha curcas (it is used as a hedge plant in rural Nepal)*
sale jo (Nep)	*a type of rodhi song*
samosa	*a spicy fried dish, usually made by mixing flour and different spices and vegetables (basically potato) and used as a snack*
sangoma (South African)	*a kind of shaman; the practitioner of traditional African medicines or supernatural methods of healing*
sapta (Nep)	*cheers or bottoms up in Tibetan language*
saptapadi (Nep)	*seven steps around the holy fire during the marriage ceremony according to Hindu religion*
satya (Nep)	*a word for swearing that someone is telling the truth*

sayapatri (Nep)	the marigold flower
sekhu (Nep)	a kind of traditional rain cover made of tree leaves (it is used by peasants in rural Nepal while working in the fields during rainy days)
Shoton (Tib)	a traditional Tibetan festival, which falls normally in the month of August (it is celebrated by eating yogurt, a speciality offered by the common people to the monks)
simal (Nep)	red cotton silk tree; botanically called Bombax ceiba
sindur (Nep)	a mark, usually vermilion or red, put by a married Hindu woman on her head along the parting line
siundo (Nep)	a parting on the head
soktala (Tib)	a respectful address for traders; boss
Sorha Shraddha (Nep)	a sixteen-day period (in the Hindu lunar month of Bhadra) in which the sons pay homage to their ancestors
stupa	a Buddhist shrine; a hemispherical structure containing Buddhist relics
stupas	the plural of stupa
sutra	a statement written in religious books
sutras	the plural of sutra
tashi delek (Tib)	a word of greeting in Tibetan language
Teej (Nep)	a Hindu festival dedicated to women
Terai (Nep)	the southern lowland area of Nepal
thangka	a type of painting; usually Buddhist art of painting (it is very popular in Tibet and Nepal)

thangkas	*the plural of thangka*
theki (Nep)	*a traditional wooden container used to store milk and churn it*
thekuwa (Nep)	*a dry sweet often prepared during Chhat Puja as an offering to god*
thukpa (Tib)	*a soupy Tibetan dish of noodle*
Tihar (Nep)	*a Hindu festival, which is celebrated for five days; also called Diwali*
tika (Nep)	*a red dot which Hindu women put on their foreheads; a mixture of colour, rice grain, or any other auspicious object which the Hindu people put on their foreheads on religious or auspicious occasion as god's offering*
timur (Nep)	*a plant with prickly stem and branches and tiny seeds; botanically called Xanthoxylum (it is also called Nepalese pepper)*
tinpane (Nep)	*strong local alcohol*
tithi (Nep)	*a lunar date*
tola (Nep)	*a traditional unit of weighing gold, silver, brass, or other masses (a tola is 11.66 grammes)*
tolas (Nep)	*the plural of tola*
torma (Tib)	*a decorative Tibetan dish made of barley flour and butter, which is used in shrines and as an offering in ceremonies*
tsampa (Tib)	*barley flour*
tulasi (Nep)	*the basil plant*

umqombothi (South African)	*traditional South African wine usually made from maize*
Valikhilyas (Nep)	*saintly persons, each the size of a thumb (in Hindu religion), who sits in front of the sun god and pray to him during his travel, circling the earth (there are sixty thousand of them)*
yarchagumba (Nep)	*a kind of herb found in the Himalayas and Tibetan plateau, botanically called Cordyceps sinensis, believed to be good for immunity and sex drive*
yojana (Nep)	*the vedic measure of distance used in ancient time (Nep: Nepalese; Hin: Hindi; Tib: Tibetan)*

Printed in the United States
By Bookmasters